D0090009

Officially Sam Fisher
doesn't exist—

until his own country
wants him dead.

continued . . .

THE CARDINAL OF THE KREMLIN
*The superpowers race for the ultimate Star Wars
missile defense system . . .*

"*CARDINAL* EXCITES, ILLUMINATES . . . A REAL
PAGE-TURNER." —*Los Angeles Daily News*

CLEAR AND PRESENT DANGER
*The killing of three U.S. officials in Colombia ignites the
American government's explosive, and top secret, response . . .*

"A CRACKLING GOOD YARN." —*The Washington Post*

THE SUM OF ALL FEARS
*The disappearance of an Israeli nuclear weapon threatens the
balance of power in the Middle East—and around the world . . .*

"CLANCY AT HIS BEST . . . NOT TO BE MISSED."
—*The Dallas Morning News*

WITHOUT REMORSE
*His code name is Mr. Clark. And his work for the CIA
is brilliant, cold-blooded, and efficient . . . but who is he really?*

"HIGHLY ENTERTAINING." —*The Wall Street Journal*

Novels by Tom Clancy

THE HUNT FOR RED OCTOBER

RED STORM RISING

PATRIOT GAMES

THE CARDINAL OF THE KREMLIN

CLEAR AND PRESENT DANGER

THE SUM OF ALL FEARS

WITHOUT REMORSE

DEBT OF HONOR

EXECUTIVE ORDERS

RAINBOW SIX

THE BEAR AND THE DRAGON

RED RABBIT

THE TEETH OF THE TIGER

SSN: STRATEGIES OF SUBMARINE WARFARE

Nonfiction

SUBMARINE: A GUIDED TOUR INSIDE A NUCLEAR WARSHIP

ARMORED CAV: A GUIDED TOUR OF AN ARMORED CAVALRY REGIMENT

FIGHTER WING: A GUIDED TOUR OF AN AIR FORCE COMBAT WING

MARINE: A GUIDED TOUR OF A MARINE EXPEDITIONARY UNIT

AIRBORNE: A GUIDED TOUR OF AN AIRBORNE TASK FORCE

CARRIER: A GUIDED TOUR OF AN AIRCRAFT CARRIER

SPECIAL FORCES: A GUIDED TOUR OF U.S. ARMY SPECIAL FORCES

INTO THE STORM: A STUDY IN COMMAND
(written with General Fred Franks, Jr., Ret., and Tony Koltz)

EVERY MAN A TIGER
(written with General Charles Horner, Ret., and Tony Koltz)

SHADOW WARRIORS: INSIDE THE SPECIAL FORCES
(written with General Carl Stiner, Ret., and Tony Koltz)

BATTLE READY
(written with General Tony Zinni, Ret., and Tony Koltz)

TOM CLANCY'S GHOST RECON

TOM CLANCY'S ENDWAR

TOM CLANCY'S SPLINTER CELL
SPLINTER CELL
OPERATION BARRACUDA
CHECKMATE
FALLOUT
CONVICTION
ENDGAME

Created by Tom Clancy and Steve Pieczenik

TOM CLANCY'S OP-CENTER	TOM CLANCY'S NET FORCE
OP-CENTER	NET FORCE
MIRROR IMAGE	HIDDEN AGENDAS
GAMES OF STATE	NIGHT MOVES
ACTS OF WAR	BREAKING POINT
BALANCE OF POWER	POINT OF IMPACT
STATE OF SIEGE	CYBERNATION
DIVIDE AND CONQUER	STATE OF WAR
LINE OF CONTROL	CHANGING OF THE GUARD
MISSION OF HONOR	SPRINGBOARD
SEA OF FIRE	THE ARCHIMEDES EFFECT
CALL TO TREASON	
WAR OF EAGLES	

Created by Tom Clancy and Martin Greenberg
TOM CLANCY'S POWER PLAYS
POLITIKA
RUTHLESS.COM
SHADOW WATCH
BIO-STRIKE
COLD WAR
CUTTING EDGE
ZERO HOUR
WILD CARD

Tom Clancy's

SPLINTER CELL®

ENDGAME

WRITTEN BY

DAVID MICHAELS

BERKLEY BOOKS, NEW YORK

THE BERKLEY PUBLISHING GROUP
Published by the Penguin Group
Penguin Group (USA) Inc.
375 Hudson Street, New York, New York 10014, USA
Penguin Group (Canada), 90 Eglinton Avenue East, Suite 700, Toronto, Ontario M4P 2Y3, Canada
(a division of Pearson Penguin Canada Inc.)
Penguin Books Ltd., 80 Strand, London WC2R 0RL, England
Penguin Group Ireland, 25 St. Stephen's Green, Dublin 2, Ireland (a division of Penguin Books Ltd.)
Penguin Group (Australia), 250 Camberwell Road, Camberwell, Victoria 3124, Australia
(a division of Pearson Australia Group Pty. Ltd.)
Penguin Books India Pvt. Ltd., 11 Community Centre, Panchsheel Park, New Delhi—110 017, India
Penguin Group (NZ), 67 Apollo Drive, Rosedale, North Shore 0632, New Zealand
(a division of Pearson New Zealand Ltd.)
Penguin Books (South Africa) (Pty.) Ltd., 24 Sturdee Avenue, Rosebank, Johannesburg 2196,
South Africa

Penguin Books Ltd., Registered Offices: 80 Strand, London WC2R 0RL, England

This is a work of fiction. Names, characters, places, and incidents either are the product of the author's imagination or are used fictitiously, and any resemblance to actual persons, living or dead, business establishments, events, or locales is entirely coincidental. The publisher does not have any control over and does not assume any responsibility for author or third-party websites or their content.

TOM CLANCY'S SPLINTER CELL®: ENDGAME

A Berkley Book / published by arrangement with Ubisoft, Ltd.

PRINTING HISTORY
Berkley premium edition / December 2009

ISBN: 978-0-425-23144-9

BERKLEY®
Berkley Books are published by The Berkley Publishing Group,
a division of Penguin Group (USA) Inc.,
375 Hudson Street, New York, New York 10014.
BERKLEY® is a registered trademark of Penguin Group (USA) Inc.
The "B" design is a trademark of Penguin Group (USA) Inc.

PRINTED IN THE UNITED STATES OF AMERICA

10 9 8 7 6 5 4 3 2 1

ACKNOWLEDGMENTS

The author gratefully acknowledges the support and cooperation of the following individuals:

Grant Blackwood, for his collaboration, creativity, and great sense of humor.

Vietnam veteran and retired chief warrant officer James Ide, for his considerable technical experience, research assistance, and unceasing passion.

Jackie Fiest, for her proofreading, enthusiasm, and technical knowledge of the Splinter Cell universe.

Tom Colgan, for his continued support and encouragement as editor of these books.

Sam Strachman, for his trust and belief in the Splinter Cell book franchise and caretaking of its ideas.

Tom Clancy, for creating a body of work that continues to inspire readers and writers everywhere.

PROLOGUE

THE first blow loosened one of Ben Hansen's molars and sent his head wrenching to one side.

Captured . . . killed . . .

He never saw the second blow, only felt Rugar's pointed knuckles drive into his left eye.

Captured . . . killed . . .

Hansen's head whipped back, then lolled forward as warm blood spilled down his chin.

Now Rugar's screams grew incomprehensible, like panes of glass shattering across the hangar's concrete floor.

Make no mistake. If you're captured, you will be killed.

Hansen tugged at the plastic flex-cuffs cutting into his wrists and binding him to the chair. He finally mustered the energy to face Rugar, who loomed there, a neckless, four-hundred-pound, vodka-soaked beast crowned by an old Soviet Army *ushanka* two sizes too small for his broad head. He was about fifty, twice Hansen's age, and hardly agile, but at the moment that hardly mattered.

Rugar opened his mouth, exposing a jagged fence of yellowed teeth. He shouted and more glass shattered, accompanied by the rattling of two enormous steel doors that had been rolled shut against the wind.

Hansen shivered. It was below freezing now, and their breaths hung heavy in the air. At least the dizziness from the anesthetic was beginning to wear off. He tried to blink, but his left eye did not respond; it was swelling shut.

And then—a flash from Rugar's hand.

Captured . . . killed . . .

The fat man had confiscated Hansen's knife.

But that wasn't just any knife—it was a Fairbairn Sykes World War II–era commando dagger that had once belonged to the elusive Sam Fisher, a Splinter Cell few people knew but whose exploits were legendary among them.

Rugar leaned over and held the blade before Hansen's face. He spoke more slowly, and the words, though still Russian, finally made sense: "We know why you've come. Now, if you tell me what I need to know, you will live."

Hansen took a deep breath. "You won't break me."

For a moment Rugar just stood there, his cheeks swelling like melons as he labored for his next breath. Suddenly he smiled, his rank breath coming hard in Hansen's face. "It's going to be a long night for both of us."

Rugar's left ear was pierced, and the gold hoop hanging there caught the overhead lights at such an angle that for a moment all Hansen noticed were those flashes of gold. He realized only after the blood spattered onto his face that Rugar had been shot in the head, the round coming from a suppressed weapon somewhere behind them.

All four hundred pounds of the fat man collapsed onto Hansen, snapping off the chair's back legs as the knife went skittering across the floor. Hansen now bore the Russian's full weight across his chest, and he wasn't sure which would kill him first: suffocation or the sickly sweet stench emanating from Rugar's armpits.

With a groan, he shoved himself against the fat man's body and began worming his way out, gasping, grimacing, and a heartbeat away from retching.

He rolled onto his side and squinted across the hangar, toward the pair of helicopters and the shadows along the perimeter wall and mechanics' stations.

And then he appeared, Sergei Luchenko, Hansen's runner. The gaunt-faced man was still wearing his long coat and gripping his pistol with its large suppressor. An unlit cigarette dangled from his thin lips.

Hansen sighed deeply. "What happened? Why didn't you answer my calls?" He groaned over the question. "Strike that. I'm just glad you're here."

Sergei walked up to Hansen, withdrew a lighter from his breast pocket, and lit his cigarette.

"How about some help?" Hansen struggled against the flex-cuffs.

"I'm sorry, my friend. They sent me to kill you."

"Bad joke."

"It's no joke."

Hansen stiffened. "Not you, Sergei."

"I don't have a choice."

Hansen closed his good eye, then spoke through his teeth. "Then why did you save me?"

"I didn't. The kill must be mine. And . . . I didn't want you to suffer."

"This is not who you are."

"I'm sorry." Sergei drew a compact digital video camera from his pocket and hit the RECORD button. He held it close to Hansen. "You see, he is alive. And now . . ." Sergei raised his pistol.

Hansen cursed at the man.

There would be no life story flashing before Hansen's eyes; no images of his youth growing up in Fort Stockton, Texas; no scenes from his days at MIT, which he had attended on a full scholarship; no moments from that bar with the director, Anna "Grim" Grimsdóttir, who had recruited him out of the CIA to join Third Echelon and become one of the world's most effective field operatives—a Splinter Cell. No, there would be nothing as dramatic or cinematic as that—just a hot piece of lead piercing his forehead, fracturing his skull, and burying itself deep in his brain before he had a chance to think about it.

The gun thumped. Hansen flinched.

And then . . . Sergei collapsed sideways onto the concrete, a gaping hole in the back of his head.

Hansen swore again, this time in relief. He squinted into the shadows at the far end of the hangar. "Uh, thank you?"

No reply.

He raised his voice. "Who are you?"

Again, just the wind . . .

He lay there a few seconds more, just breathing, waiting for his savior to show himself.

One last time. "Who are you?"

Hansen's voice trailed off into the howling wind and creaking hangar doors. He lay there for another two minutes.

No one came.

Tensing, he wriggled on his side, drawing closer to his knife, which was lying just a meter away. He reached the blade, turned it over in his hand, and began to slowly, painfully, saw into the flex-cuffs.

When he was free, he stood and collected himself, his face still swelling, the hangar dipping as though floating on rough seas. And then, blinking his good eye to clarity, he lifted his gaze to the rafters, the crossbeams, the pipes, and still . . . nothing. He turned back to the bodies and shook his head in pity at Sergei. Then he glowered at the fat man, who even in death would get the last laugh, since disposing of his body would be like manhandling a dead Russian circus bear.

There was still a lot of work to do, but all the while Hansen couldn't help but feel the heat of someone's gaze on his shoulders.

He shouted again, "Who are you?"

Only his echo answered.

— 1 —————————————

MAYA Valentina saw it in the man's gaze, which flicked down from her low-cut blouse to her well-tanned legs to her feet jammed into a pair of stilettos. She tossed back her hair, which fell in golden waves across her shoulders, then put an index finger to her lips, as though to nervously bite her nail. Oh, yes, he liked the shy schoolgirl routine, and Valentina could pass for a freshman, too, though she was nearly twenty-eight.

"Hi, there. You must be Ms. Haspel," he said, drawing in his sagging gut and probably wishing his thinning hair were two shades darker.

She reached across the desk and accepted his hairy paw. "It's nice to meet you, Mr. Leonard, and thanks for the interview."

"Well, as I said, we only have one position to fill, so the competition is fierce. Please have a seat."

She settled down and leaned toward his desk, keeping her blue eyes locked on his. "Can I ask a question before we start?"

"By all means."

"Does the company have a sexual-harassment policy?"

His lip twitched. "Of course."

"Well, I've had some problems in the past."

"I'm sorry to hear that."

"Yeah, the one guy was married and claimed I was a stalker, which was totally not the case. The other guy kept saying I was making lewd remarks. He even said I flashed my panties, and there's no way I did that."

He hesitated. "Are you serious?"

"Yes. I like to get dressed up for work. It doesn't mean I want to have sex with everyone I see."

He cleared his throat. "Of course not. But you should know that we have a dress code. Business casual."

Valentina nodded and gazed salaciously at him. "Is what I'm wearing okay?"

He swallowed before answering.

* * *

HANSEN was sitting in an SUV parked outside the four-story office building. The complex was comprised of ten equally nondescript buildings: the headquarters for a lengthy list of companies that were, according to an intel report, "assembling stacked layers of silver and nonconducting magnesium fluoride and cutting out nanoscale-sized fishnet patterns to form metamaterials."

Grim had explained that metamaterials held the key to developing cloaking devices to render objects invisible to humans. Leonard's company in particular was developing paint for military vehicles and fabric for military uniforms. This was all quite serious business, which was why Hansen could only shake his head as he listened to Maya and Leonard. What the hell was she doing? All she had to do was get hired.

Admittedly, she'd hated the tired old plan of playing dress up to ensure Leonard took the bait, so overplaying the role was her way of protesting. She wouldn't just be the attractive new hire; she was now the quirky sex addict who'd called way too much attention to herself. Hansen was a breath away from reporting her misconduct to Grim, but then he thought better of it and just sat there as Maya told Leonard she was always available for overtime and "after-hours" work. Hansen grimaced.

* * *

AT 10:05 A.M. Nathan Noboru parked his utility van at the curb outside William Leonard's seven-thousand-square-foot home. Sprawling front lawns, well-manicured grounds, and tree-lined brick-paved driveways unfurled to a grand entrance shadowed by twenty-foot columns painted in a glossy antique white. This part of southwest Houston was called Sugar Land, and it was sweet indeed: Multimillion-dollar homes were nestled among well-tended golf course greens and tranquil lakes. The senior citizen manning the neighborhood guardhouse had taken a perfunctory glance at Noboru's forged work orders and immediately waved him through.

With a sigh, Noboru grabbed his utility belt and started up the driveway. But then he slowed, furtively glanced around, and scratched his crew cut. He gazed out past the lawn toward the neighboring home, another mansion where an old man in a pink shirt and oversized sunglasses stood near his Mercedes, preparing to load a golf bag into his trunk.

Off to Noboru's left lay another spectacular three-story château with a tremendous brick facade and five-car garage. Noboru studied the windows, trying to spot the lens of a telescopic camera or other such observation device. Nothing. He continued on, but something wasn't right.

Or was that just his paranoia? Again. They weren't after him anymore. He had a new life now. He needed to believe that.

Noboru shifted up to the front door, made a call, heard the phone ring inside the house, and then he tapped a series of numbers into his phone and heard the rapid ringtone of the alarm being disarmed. He took out his double-sided lock-pick set and got to work. Three, two, one: The door opened—

And if the explosions hadn't started at the back of the mansion, he would've already been dead.

Twin thunderclaps resounded, and the ground literally shook beneath his feet as the door slammed back toward him, knocking him to the ground.

He rolled over, shot to his feet, and sprinted down the driveway. He might as well have been back in Kao-hsiung, chased through the crowded streets by Horatio and Gothwhiler, the night air humid, the sweat pouring down his face. Several more explosions ripped through the house, and he stole a look over his shoulder as huge windows burst outward, sending showers of glass to the driveway while flames shot through the holes and wagged like dragons' tongues.

He reached the van and whirled around. Clouds of black smoke backlit by more roaring flames now devoured the entire mansion, while fiery debris floated down like confetti and got trapped in the thick canopy of leaves and limbs.

The old man who'd been loading his golf clubs was now backing out of his driveway. He stopped, climbed out of his car, and hurried over while dialing a number on his phone.

Noboru's mouth fell open. This was supposed to be a pathetically simple entry to place electronic eyes and ears. In fact, he'd balked over how rudimentary the whole operation was (he was entering through the front door!) and had loathed the fact that Director Grimsdóttir was wasting his talents on such a menial task. He had only been employed by Third Echelon for less than a year, but didn't his four years with Japan's Special Operations Group, its own Delta Force, count for anything?

Apparently not . . . but what was going on now?

Were Horatio and Gothwhiler tailing him? Did they known he'd be here? Were they trying to finish the job? If the others learned about them, about Noboru's *real* past, he would never be trusted. Grimsdóttir had promised him a new identity, a new life, and utter secrecy.

A voice crackled in the nickel-sized subdermal embedded in the skin behind his ear; it was the Grim Reaper herself. "Nathan, I'm looking at the satellite feed—"

"I know! I know!" Noboru ran back to the van and yanked open the door. "Ma'am, you'd better call Hansen!"

* * *

VALENTINA was about to stand and thank Leonard for the interview when the man's BlackBerry rang.

"Please, let me take this, but wait," he said. "I want to introduce you to the rest of my staff."

"All right."

He shifted away from the desk and headed toward the window.

Suddenly, Hansen's voice came through her subdermal. "Maya, get out of there. Now!"

Even as she gasped, Leonard cried, "What? Oh, my God!" into his phone.

"I'm sorry, Mr. Leonard, I need to go."

With that she started for the door, which suddenly took a bullet, the wood splintering as she ducked and craned her neck to see two more rounds punch through the office window, the first striking Leonard in the chest, the second in the shoulder. Blood sprayed across the back wall as Valentina dropped to her hands and knees, drew her SC pistol from her purse, and crawled toward the door.

She chanced a look back at Leonard, lying there, bleeding, reaching out to her, his mouth working, a word barely forming: "Please . . ."

ALLEN Ames was on the building's roof when

the shooting began. He'd been up there only as an observer, gathering intel on the comings and goings of visitors to the building and hoping to get some up-close-and-personal pics of at least two of Mr. Leonard's "special" friends from Beijing.

Ames felt at home on rooftops. He'd grown up in Brooklyn and had spent years atop apartment buildings, hanging out with his friends, getting drunk, and dreaming of a better life that would help him forget about the fire . . . about the screams from Mom and Dad, about Katy's face at the window, looking at him, coughing . . . until she fell backward into the flames.

Now, twenty years after that fateful night, Ames was staring down through the telescopic sight of his sniper rifle. The shooter had set up on the roof of a building across the street from Leonard's and had only revealed himself to take the shots. He'd been in Ames's sight for all of two heartbeats before he'd vanished behind the air-conditioning units. Ames had been on the roof since sunrise, and he'd neither seen nor heard the shooter's approach, so the man might have been there even longer and had obviously cloaked his heat signature.

Ames cursed, slung the rifle over his shoulder, and muttered, "I'm going after the shooter."

The SVT, or subvocal transceiver, a butterfly-shaped adhesive patch on Ames's throat, just north of his Adam's apple, picked up his voice so it could be broadcast over the channel for all, including Grim, to hear.

Ames took off, running for the stairwell door, wrenched it open, and began storming down the steps. At just five feet eight and 140 pounds, he was the fastest runner on the team; still, that didn't stop the others from quipping about his size. Oh, they never ridiculed him to his face, but he overheard their remarks. He didn't care. He knew he was ten feet tall when standing on his skills and charisma. Moreover, with a little gel worked into his unruly blond hair, he easily added three inches.

How many staircases had he mounted during his tenure as a New York City cop, back at the old 4-8 precinct? Too many to count. And just when he'd grown so cynical that he thought he'd abandon public service forever, he'd joined the National Security Agency (NSA) and become a police officer in Fort Meade, Maryland. They'd given him a nice milestone recruitment incentive, and the money and new mission had lifted his spirits. While there, he'd been tapped for Third Echelon—despite his lack of a special-forces background—and so here he was, back to racing down stairs, trying to help out his fellow Splinter Cells who, of course, had no idea what he really was.

"You don't have the temperament for this job," Sam Fisher once told Ames during a particularly brutal training session.

Fisher was a very good judge of character.

* * *

A motley crew of overweight soccer moms hopping around like sea lions in spandex, and fifty-year-old cougars who'd left their rich husbands to lust after group fitness instructors half their age had crowded into the Gold's Gym fitness room for the morning's body-combat class.

Under the harsh glow of overhead lights that beamed off the waxed wooden floor, the class was in full swing, with the instructor, Greg, booming into a headset while techno music blared from speakers taller than Gillespie.

Kimberly Gillespie had donned her workout gear and stood within a meter of Mrs. Cynthia Leonard, the fabulously wealthy wife of the team's target. The first break in the music finally came, and they stole a moment to towel off and gulp down their water.

"You're really good at this," she told Cynthia.

The woman smoothed back her bleach-blond hair, then blotted sweat off her chest—her impossibly perky boobs threatening to explode from her tight top. "Thanks. I've been doing it for a while. Takes time to learn all the punches and kicks. But you look like you've had some training."

Gillespie smiled. "A little bit."

"I like you're accent. You're not from Houston."

"North Georgia."

"And I love all that red hair and your freckles. You know, I once dated a man who said he stopped for blondes and brunettes, but he took two steps back for redheads."

Gillespie chuckled under her breath. "I tend to scare away most men. They don't step back. They run."

"All right, ladies, break time is over," cried Greg.

"My Lord, he's a real drill sergeant," said Gillespie.

"Yeah," Cynthia agreed. "But look at that ass."

The remark reminded Gillespie of army boot camp, of her old friend Lissette, who helped her get through the misery by making jokes and lusting after all the sergeants. The army had allowed Gillespie to escape from Creekwood Trailer Park and her father's grocery list of emotional problems and addictions. She'd finally been able to make a name for herself as an intelligence analyst who advised special-forces teams and operations.

Four years in the army, then another four years at University of Central Florida to earn a degree in civil engineering, had prepared her well for a career with the NSA. When she was handpicked by Grim herself to join Third Echelon was one of the proudest moments of Gillespie's life. Someone had finally noticed her, recognized her skill set, and appreciated her sarcasm and take-no-prisoners attitude.

As they were about to move forward and prepare

for the next phase of punishment, Cynthia glanced down at the BlackBerry sitting atop her purse and shifted back to take a call.

Gillespie assumed the fighting stance, then turned as Cynthia suddenly rushed from the room.

2

ALLEN Ames slammed open the stairwell door and squinted in the brighter light. He charged across the parking lot, threading between parked cars as his senses reached outward for the shooter.

Thankfully, most people were inside and not stopping to watch a semicrazed, darkly clad man running with a rifle slung over his back. But did that even matter now? The operation had already gone so far south that they'd need an icebreaker to get home.

He rounded a row of bushes, mounted the sidewalk, and, at the far corner of the building, he spotted a man emerging from a delivery entrance near a UPS truck.

The guy was no more than five feet five, with a black crew cut, and clearly of Asian descent. He took one look at Ames and sprinted off, a rifle slung over his back.

LEONARD'S receptionist was hiding under her desk as Valentina rushed by and broke her heel. She wrenched open the office door, kicked off her shoes, and ran barefoot down the corridor. She found the nearest entry to the stairwell and nearly ran head-on into Hansen, whose glossy eyes and pained expression must have matched her own.

They stomped together down the stairs, with Valentina crying out, "The receptionist can identify me!"

"I know. How the hell did they get to him first?"

"They must've been tipped off."

"Yeah, because some of us were sloppy."

THE shooter sprinted all the way to the back of the parking lot, and Ames quickened his pace to keep him in sight. This guy was, in fact, the fastest runner Ames had ever seen, probably faster than himself, and they were both pounding the pavement at full tilt. But the shooter stole a glance over his shoulder, missed a step, tripped, staggered forward, then exploited the moment to stop and draw a pistol.

Ames ducked behind the nearest car as the round punched into the side mirror not six inches from his head. He cursed, tugged free his own sidearm, then lifted his head ever so slightly to see the shooter running off.

Taking a deep breath, Ames rose, steeled himself, then took a shot, the round suppressed and thumping quietly into the shooter's right arm. The guy jerked to one side, clutched his wound, but kept on.

Still . . . he was wounded prey. *Time to close in.*

Baring his teeth, Ames propelled himself forward as though ready to leap the hurdles. He closed in on the shooter and finally saw his opportunity.

With a groan of exertion, he launched himself into the air and landed on the trunk of a black Corvette, the fiberglass crackling and crunching beneath his feet as he ran up to the roof.

The shooter turned, saw Ames.

Ames, about to lose his balance, fired anyway. Though he missed, the round drove the shooter onto the grassy median between lots.

That was when Ames leapt off the car and tackled him. The thick scent of mud and wet grass wafted into his face as they rolled over and Ames drove his elbow into the man's nose, immediately breaking it. Then he found the correct pressure point on the man's wrist, forcing him to release the pistol, which he tossed aside.

Now bleeding from his gunshot wound and broken nose, the shooter was too disoriented to struggle. Ames quickly cuffed him and rolled him onto his back.

The guy was no older than Ames, his eyes burning with hatred—the only fight he had left in him. It was at moments like this—post-adrenaline-rush moments—that the compulsion clutched Ames and he could not stop it. Not yet.

Trembling, he reached into his pocket and produced a Zippo lighter of the kind he'd been carrying since he was sixteen. Unconsciously, he rolled the lighter through his fingers and opened it before the shooter's eyes with remarkable precision and dexterity, the flame appearing as though from a magician's hand. Pale yellow light flickered over the shooter's face, and the hatred in the man's eyes began to melt into something else as Ames brought the lighter even closer.

For just a few seconds, they remained there, locked firmly in the grasp of that hypnotizing flame, and all Ames wanted to do was see the man burn.

But he was stronger than that. No government or police shrink had ever been able to crack him. He snapped shut the lighter, took a deep breath, then grabbed the shooter by the shirt collar and hauled him to his feet—just as a pickup truck with darkly tinted windows rolled by.

Ames glanced in the truck's direction. The driver's-side window lowered, and another Asian man holding a pistol with a long suppressor appeared.

With a gasp, Ames shoved the shooter between himself and the truck, even as the driver fired two rounds that punched hard into the shooter's back. Ames released the man and picked up his own pistol in time to fire into the truck's tailgate, but the vehicle was already screeching away before Ames could read the tag. Now their only witness lay dead at Ames's feet.

"Hansen, it's Ames," he began over the channel. "I got the shooter. He was alive but now—"

"What happened?"

"Uh, no time now."

"Rally back at the hotel."

"What about the body?"

Hansen cursed. "We're coming down."

TWENTY minutes later they all gathered in Hansen's hotel room, and as team leader, he insisted on debriefing them before they spoke to Grim.

Gillespie had been the last one to show up and now cursed and said, "This can't be our fault, can it? It's all bad intel. They were on to him before we even moved in. That's all it is. Bad intel."

"Maybe, maybe not," said Hansen.

"Maybe the Chinese didn't off him. Maybe some one else did," said Ames. "Maybe they want us to believe the Chinese did it."

"This is all ridiculous," cried Valentina. "My part of the recon was flawless. I can't speak for any of you . . ."

"Why don't you just say it, honey?" snapped Ames. "Tell us how much you love us."

She glowered at him.

"Whoa! Please don't burn me." Ames threw up his hands in mock surrender.

Hansen balled his own hand into a fist. "Listen up. This is why Grim won't cut us loose yet. We need to earn her trust, and we start by trusting each other—not placing blame."

"Don't call me a Splinter Cell if I'm not working alone," said Valentina. "I don't need any of you."

"The feeling's mutual," said Gillespie.

Noboru picked up the TV's remote and turned on the news. There it was: a three-ring circus of police and TV news crews outside the office complex. The report shifted to Leonard's estate, still smoldering behind a young field reporter who gaped at the blackened skeleton. "I think the bombs in the house were meant for his wife."

"Genius over here," said Ames. "Make this guy a general. How do you say 'general' in Japanese?"

"Shut up," spat Noboru.

"Look, as far as we know everything went according to plan," said Hansen. "The shooter and the bombs were already in place. No one saw anything else, right? No sloppy work on our part, right? No footprints."

Noboru shrugged. Ames did likewise. Gillespie and Valentina just sighed in disgust.

Then Valentina spun around and said, "What're you worried about, Ben? When you say Grim won't cut us loose, you mean *us*, not yourself. You're the only one who's worked as a real Splinter Cell, on his own, without any . . . *baggage*." Valentina looked daggers at the others.

Ames puckered up for a kiss.

"Yeah, I went out once. More than a year ago."

"And you came back from Russia a hero, so they put you in charge of the rest of us of noobs," said Gillespie. "So what now? Have we just screwed ourselves out of the NSA?"

"I don't think so," said Ames. "I wouldn't ask for a raise right now, but the government's always looking for suicidal maniacs who can fit into tight corners."

"Speak for yourself," said Valentina.

"I will, because you look like you're putting on a few pounds there, Maya."

"Ames, enough," snapped Hansen. "Get back to

your hotels. Pack up. We're out of here. I'll call Grim, and we'll work out what to do with this body."

ON the flight back home, Hansen dozed off, and in the shadows between consciousness and dreaming he strained to see a face. . . .

Then he heard Gillespie's voice echo: *"You came back from Russia a hero."*

A hero.

Nothing could be further from the truth.

Hansen took himself back to that fateful day when he'd marveled over the NSA office complex and gone in to receive his very first mission. . . .

3

WALLS of obsidian-colored glass rose from the Maryland countryside and reflected swaths of deep blue and green across their mottled surfaces. A series of barbed wire and electrical fences cordoned off the grounds, and gatehouses were placed at designated intervals to allow entrance into parking lots that could accommodate more than eighteen thousand cars. The length and breadth of the NSA complex repeatedly amazed Hansen, and he sometimes felt like pinching himself as a reminder that, yes, even though he was still so young—*painfully* young, as Grim had once put it—this was his life now.

The agency was, according to the rest of the world, not in the business of covert field operations. They were the technology geeks, the code makers and code breakers who built supercomputers and called those seventy-two-hour workweeks "good times." They were the analysts who could gain access to, and examine, every piece of information available, no matter the media—from highly encrypted satellite phone calls between heads of state to extremely low-frequency transmissions from naval vessels to the e-mails and text messages passed between average citizens. They were rarely in direct competition with the military services, although most military folks wished for a one-handed intelligence representative—not because they wanted to hire the handicapped but because pronouncements like "On the one hand they could attack, and on the other hand they could retreat," never helped in military decision making.

That these geeks would ever be involved in the covert and/or human angle of intelligence would surprise some individuals within the agency. Moreover, if Third Echelon's existence were ever made public, accidentally or otherwise, liberal-minded bureaucrats across the United States might very well clutch their chests and drop to the waxed wooden floors of their offices. Obviously, the often morally ambiguous business of protecting the nation could not be left to the faint of heart.

Enter Third Echelon's Splinter Cells.

Splinter Cell operatives aggressively collected intelligence vital to U.S. security. They protected critical U.S. information systems and kept all operations invisible to the public eye. They worked outside the boundaries of international treaties, knowing full well that if captured the United States would neither acknowledge nor support their operations. They bridged the gap between gathering intel and acting upon it, and Hansen could not be more honored or more proud to dedicate his life to something as important as protecting the country he so dearly loved. Perhaps that sounded cheesy or naive; he didn't care and assumed that in ten years he'd be just as cynical as any other government employee. But right now he believed in the ideals and in the fact that freedom was, of course, never free.

To that end, Hansen now stood deep within the subterranean confines of the NSA, in a sector that did not exist. With some trepidation, he swiped his ID badge through the reader, listened for the muted beep, and the LED turned green.

He found Grim seated alone at the diamond-shaped conference table inside the situation room. All around her, intelligence seemed to course through the room's veins, the unseen servers reverberating like a thousand heartbeats per second. Big-screen LCD status boards hung from the walls, and three-dimensional maps, streaming security-camera videos, and electronic dossiers of known terrorists flashed and scrolled and rotated like the collected imagery extracted from some colossal brain. In fact, the entire power grid was in a constant state of upgrade in order to accommodate the agency's ever-increasing demand for electricity. As Grim liked to muse, "The beast must be fed."

Hansen shuddered as he made eye contact with her. All right, she was his boss. She had hired him. But damn if he didn't feel a connection. Act on it? That would take some serious courage. Nevertheless, there was something deliciously reckless about lusting after a woman ten years his senior, especially one as strong-willed and incredibly intelligent as Anna. Hansen imagined some serious fire lurking beneath her conservative exterior. Her short, medium brown hair barely touched her shoulders, and she frequently wore shirt/jacket combinations in earth tones or pastels, along with matching skirts and those glasses that Hansen longed to see removed. Her eyes were a blue-green flecked with gold, and as she stood, he forced himself not to probe anywhere near her ample chest, unsuccessfully hidden beneath her jacket. She moved silently around the table in her flats, rubbed a sore spot on her lower back, then gestured to their left.

"So this is it, Ben. I'm sending you to Russia. This will be your first real field operation. Think you can handle it?"

A chill worked its way across Hansen's shoulders. Finally, a chance to prove himself in the field after six months of hard training. He took a deep breath, but before he could answer, Grim added, "That's a rhetorical question. I wouldn't have picked you if I didn't think you could do this."

"Yes, ma'am."

"I've never seen anyone challenge our trainers the way you have. . . . Well, maybe one other. But the point is that we've been very impressed with your skills. Who knew that a country boy from Fort Stockton would end up here?" She grinned broadly and gestured to the web of technology spanning the room.

Hansen shrugged. "I wasn't much of a cowboy."

"Lucky for us. And, you know, when I met you at the bar that night, I knew you were Splinter Cell material. And I knew you were wasting your talent at the CIA. So this moment is, in fact, unsurprising. You belong with us. And you belong out there, in the field."

He wanted to say, *I belong with you*, but instead said, "I'm ready, ma'am."

"All right, then." She crossed to a computer terminal, where she called up several photographs of a balding, bearded man in his late forties. He wore a dark brown parka and stood beside a snow-covered sedan, lighting up a cigarette. Hansen focused on the two most significant aspects of the man's appearance: his large hoop earring and the ponytail that writhed down his coat like a snake. Hansen also recognized the area behind the man as Lubyanka Square, in downtown Moscow, not because he'd visited but because he'd learned that Russia's old KGB had once been head-quartered there.

Grim sipped her coffee. "This is Mikhail Bratus, a longtime agent with the GRU."

The GRU (Glavnoje Razvedyvatel'noje Uprav-lenije) is the Main Intelligence Directorate of the Rus-sian Armed Forces' General Staff. It gathers human intelligence through military attachés and agents and relies upon a vast network of SIGINT (signals intel-ligence) satellites.

A recent defector from the GRU warned that all of the United States had been penetrated by agents who had orchestrated the delivery of secret arms caches—including suitcase nukes—that were hidden and waiting for Russian special forces poised to invade the country. Government leaders in every state were being watched and targeted by assassination squads that were ready to strike once war got under way.

It was quite a story, and not a word of it had ever been verified, but Hansen was fascinated by the account and had read the interviews several times.

"Bratus is a very clever and well-respected agent. He has dangerous ties to several drug cartels, both in the Russian Federation and Afghanistan. He employs many of the drug runners to serve as his eyes and ears while they move their drugs on the trains and highways out of Vladivostok."

As Grim spoke, Hansen had a hard time concentrating. Her perfume was intoxicating.

"Ben? Are you listening? Why are you looking at me like that?"

"I'm sorry, I was just, uh, thinking about Bratus. Is there information I need to get from him?"

Grim took a deep breath, then removed her glasses and rubbed the corners of her eyes. "I wish it were that easy." She called up another photograph. A lean Chinese man with gray hair at his temples was getting out of an economy car. Other than the hair, he was quite nondescript, one Chinese man among 1.4 billion. Typical. Forgettable. And that was exactly how they wanted him.

"This is Yuan Zhao. We've identified him as a field agent with the Guoanbu. Works out of their technology bureau."

China's Ministry of State Security, or Guoanbu, was the government's largest and most active foreign intelligence agency. Headquartered in Beijing, the agency's operations encompassed a broad geographical scope and included the stealing of secrets and technology from other nations as well as thwarting operations against the government. It was a well-known fact that Guoanbu agents had penetrated and been living and working in the United States for decades. Hansen had read and studied reports by a few of the agency's defectors, and those documents were as enlightening as they were disturbing.

The Guoanbu also engaged in domestic operations, including the monitoring of political dissidents and the repression of internal dissent. These actions caused Chinese citizens to refer to the agency as a secret police. Other internal efforts included acts against nonofficial churches and the censoring of the Internet to prevent China's population from knowing what was going on outside the country. No surprise there.

Grim went on: "Now, we've picked up some intel that indicates Zhao and Bratus have had several meetings in the past month at a small town about ninety minutes north of Vladivostok, right near the Chinese border."

"Maybe Bratus is selling drugs to the Chinese military, and Zhao's their point man. Wouldn't be the first time agents turned to drug running, especially those guys. It's not like they're making a fortune as spies."

"That's an interesting premise, but this is where it gets even more interesting . . . and more troubling."

"What do you mean?"

She hesitated, then finally said, "We think Kovac is somehow involved."

Hansen blinked. Hard. Then he shook his head, as if to clear the noise. "Can you say that again?"

"We think the deputy director of the NSA is nego-
tiating something with Zhao and Bratus, but there's
nothing conclusive at this point, and we need to know
what's going on."

Nicholas Andrew Kovac was the NSA's chief
operating officer, who guided strategies and policy
and served as chief advisor to the director. He had
a résumé so long and detailed, so perfect, that Hansen assumed the man was a cyborg and did not sleep.
Kovac had graduated from the U.S. Air Force Acad-
emy, received multiple graduate degrees in computer
science and engineering, served as an officer and pilot,
and had been a visiting professor at West Point. He
had joined the NSA and, through assignments with
the Directorate of Operations, had worked his way up
the ranks to become the deputy director for analysis
and production. After a three-year stint as a special
U.S. liaison officer in London, he'd been promoted to
deputy director. Reading his résumé left you bored or
green with envy, perhaps a little of both.

Hansen would not have known so much about him
except that Grim had sometimes implied that Kovac
did not exactly trust Third Echelon. Hansen thought
something in the man's character or past experiences
might've had something to do with that, so he'd done
a little research, as was his wont, but had come up
empty.

Still, the obvious fact remained that while Third

Echelon and its Splinter Cells had pulled off some remarkable operations, they had also had some monumental failures, including the deaths of not one, but three veteran field operatives in the last two years on an operation that Grim would not disclose, even to Hansen. That tragedy had prompted the organization to more aggressively recruit replacements.

Then there was, of course, Sam Fisher . . . and what his actions had done to tarnish Third Echelon's reputation. . . .

Hansen thought for a moment, then said, "How do you know it's Kovac?"

"Because we have an agent working closely with him."

"You mean Third Echelon is spying on its own bosses?"

Grim wriggled her brows. "Why not?"

Hansen snorted. "Well, I'm sure they're returning the favor."

"I'm sure they are."

"Has it occurred to you that I could be a mole, working for them?"

"No."

Hansen furrowed his brows. "Why not?"

"Because they hate you. Because I had to fight to bring you here. And because you keep staring at my chest."

That last part caught him completely off guard. He

opened his mouth. Nothing came out. Then . . . "Uh, I'm sorry. Uh, why didn't you tell me—"

"Forget that." She worked the touch screen. "This is Michael Murdoch." A well-groomed businessman in his fifties, with closely cropped gray hair, glowed on the screen. In another picture Murdoch was having lunch at an expensive restaurant with a man about the same age. A third pic showed Murdoch playing golf with Kovac himself, and in a small video frame Murdoch was being interviewed on one of the cable business channels. He had a commanding baritone voice and perfect teeth.

"Murdoch has a half dozen different companies, some importing and exporting out of Vladivostok, but he also has two technology companies in Houston, both with military contracts."

"So what's the deal? You think Kovac is helping Murdoch sell secrets to the Chinese and the Russians?"

"I'm not sure. He could be using Murdoch to sell them chicken feed. At any rate, Zhao, Bratus, and Murdoch are scheduled to meet soon. I need you there. I need to know what they're talking about."

"How much time do we have?"

"You'll be on a plane tonight, because we want a very deliberate and slow insertion. No HAHOs from a 130, if that's what you're thinking."

"Would've been fun. Do I get a runner?"

Grim took a deep breath, as though bracing herself before she spoke. "Sergei Luchenko will meet you in Vladivostok."

Hansen winced. "Sergei? Really? I haven't seen him in a few months. You think he's gotten over it?"

"I think he has. He wanted to be in the field. He got his wish. He's just not a Splinter Cell, and that proves that my intuition isn't always correct."

Luchenko had, for all intents and purposes, flunked Third Echelon's training program and been forced to either become a runner or wind up behind a desk. Hansen felt badly for the man, since they'd both been recruited out of the CIA and known each other for a few years. Still, it would be nice to see a familiar face in a sea of red-nosed strangers.

"Ma'am, I won't let you down."

"I know you won't." She lifted her chin to a table across the room. "There's a folder with your credentials and cover."

Hansen started for them.

"And one more thing."

He hoisted his brows.

"When you get your gear, you'll find a knife. Take good care of it. It was given to me by an old friend, and now I'm passing it on to you. Despite everything, I think it'll bring you luck."

"It was Fisher's. Wasn't it?"

She nodded.

"Kind of an odd gift."

"From an odd man. Now, one last thing. Make no mistake. If you're captured, you will be killed."

"Tortured first. But, yes, I understand. Thank you." Hansen scooped up the folder, headed for the door, but before he left, he turned back to Grim. "Ma'am, I'm sorry about the—" He gestured to his eyes, trying to apologize for ogling her.

"Just get out of here . . . *kid*."

Ouch! That hurt.

Once in the hallway, Hansen dug out his passport, which had been heavily stamped and dog-eared by one of Third Echelon's document engineers, a man known only as Perez. He was a Mexican national sent to prison for making fake credentials to help illegal immigrants cross the border. He'd been serving the last few years of his sentence when he'd been offered an early release if he came to work for Third Echelon. Perez was an artist—the best forger the agency had ever employed.

And, at the moment, Hansen wished Perez had chosen the cover name instead of Grim, because the woman had a cruel sense of humor.

Hansen was now Vyacheslav Zamolodchikova.

Say that three times fast.

4

HANSEN had flown from Baltimore to Tokyo; then he had traveled by taxi for six hours to the port city of Fushiki, walled in by majestic mountains whose summits were now veiled in fog.

Dressed like an ordinary businessman in suit and overcoat, and clutching a duffel bag with toiletries and a garment bag with a few changes of clothing, Hansen walked along the dock, where ahead lay the *MV Rus*, a thirteen-thousand-ton ferry whose dark blue hull glinted in the neon floodlights strung along the walkway. Although it was just 4:00 P.M., the shadows had already grown long as vehicles rumbled up the gangways and into the hold.

The ferry was primarily an auto transporter, with new and used cars from Japan being exported to Vladivostok by individuals and Russian businessmen. There were 114 cabins to service four hundred passengers and crew, and, surprisingly, the ferry was equipped with phones and air conditioners in every cabin, though at the moment Hansen could use a good blast of heat, as his breath came thick in the frigid February air. He had learned from the taxi driver, who spoke a little Russian (Hansen's cover language), that the restaurants were good and that he should definitely visit the veranda casino.

Hansen mounted the aluminum gangway and ascended upward with a throng of other passengers, mostly middle-aged Russian men, with a small number of Japanese and one family with small children that might've been from the Netherlands or Belgium, as they scolded their kids in Dutch.

At the top of the steps Hansen was ushered into a waiting area, where he was asked to produce his passport, and his nearly unpronounceable name, Vyacheslav Zamolodchikova, was checked against a list. He was then permitted into the reception area, where a friendly if not cherubic Russian woman handed him a card with his cabin number and some brief instructions on how to find it. Before he left, he gave a furtive glance around, quickly studying the other passengers, trying to pick out a tail, if he had one, but the others paid him no attention.

For the next few minutes he ventured through the halls, grinning at the dark veneer paneling and orange carpets, wondering if he'd just been transported to the 1970s. There were yellowing pictures of other ferries on the walls and lots of faded warning signs in Cyrillic.

Third Echelon had booked him cabin 4456 on the starboard bow—a very nice room, really—and had paid handsomely to ensure that he did not have to share that room with any other passengers, as that was not uncommon.

He found his cabin, opened the door, and collapsed onto the small bed, finding the blankets cold and slightly damp. He activated the OPSAT on his wrist and sent off a highly encrypted signal to Grim, notifying her that he was on board the ferry. Now all he had to do was sit back and relax for the forty-hour ride to Vladivostok.

If his father could only see him now, on a ferry, heading toward Russia to eavesdrop on a conversation between Chinese and Russian intelligence agents. That sort of drama rarely occurred back home, where his town's population barely hit eight thousand and Dad

was still a high school science teacher. The only remarkable thing that had ever happened to Harold "Buck"
Hansen was back in 1974. During his first year as a
teacher, he had witnessed a boomerang-shaped UFO
hovering over the school. Hansen had heard the story
a thousand times, and his mother had dismissed the
tale as many had. Dad had waited more than twenty
years before he'd shared the story with "authorities"
and expert "UFO hunters," for fear of being labeled a
crackpot and losing his teaching job. Since then Dad
had become a UFO nut, and Mom was the sane wife
of the UFO nut, who tried to keep him in line while
she kept the books for the Comanche Springs Truck
Terminal. They were pretty comical and were planning
a big trip to Nevada, to the famed Area 51, next year,
when Dad finally retired after, as he put it, "more than
a hundred years of service with the school district."
Hansen was glad his colleagues would never get a
chance to meet his parents. He wasn't sure they could
handle that much weirdness in one sitting.

Hansen had no siblings, but he did have a cousin
who had once stolen a bass boat and served time for
it. Other than that, the rest of his family tree was
painfully boring, and he was the only apple that had
rolled away, as it were. But as far as they all knew,
he worked a desk job at the NSA, analyzing pieces of
computer code, which was "watching the grass grow,"

according to Dad. Hansen drove a Corolla, lived in a two-bedroom condo with a strict homeowner's association that prevented him from planting flowers other than those found on the approved-colors list, and he rented so many movies from Blockbuster that his late fees had become legendary among the college kids working at his local store.

These bogus facts, or similar ones, he detailed every year in his Christmas newsletter, which was as painful to read as any of the others that slipped into mailboxes crowded with overpriced holiday cards and junk-mail flyers.

He wished he could buy a postcard in Vladivostok and mail it to his parents—just to blow their minds—but he knew better. He was doing the business of his country, and nothing would ever compromise that.

With a sigh, he rose from the bed, worked the little thermostat, and finally got the heat to come on. He heard some talking outside his door, so he opened it. Far down the hallway stood two Japanese coast-guardsmen, one holding a German shepherd. Well, no surprise. There were drug dealers on board, probably returning to Russia from a run into Japan. In fact, Hansen watched as a Russian emerged from the room, his hands held high, and one of the coastguardsmen immediately cuffed him. Hansen grinned to himself. If those coastguardsmen really wanted to clean up the ferry, they'd have to arrest more than half of the Russian businessmen, who were undoubtedly connected to the mob. He waited until the group left, then decided to go to the restaurant to complete a more immediate mission: filling his grumbling stomach.

— *5* ———————————

APPROXIMATELY forty hours after leaving Fushiki, Japan, the *MV Rus* reached Vladivostok, at 8:17 A.M., and Hansen congratulated himself for two small accomplishments: He had not become seasick nor had he contracted food poisoning, even though the ferry had crossed into some rough seas and the sanitary conditions in the kitchen were undoubtedly questionable.

Given the circumstances, Hansen had kept to himself for the entire voyage, bowing out of conversations at meals and spending the majority of his time in his cabin, brushing up on his Russian. He had checked out the casino and spent some time observing people, ferreting out their histories based on the details of their appearances. As far as he was concerned, he had no one tailing him. Now he stood on the upper deck, waiting as the ferry made final preparations to dock.

A thick mantle of clouds hung over the craggy hills of Vladivostok, the name meant "Lord of the East" in Russian. The city did, indeed, seem to lord over not only Golden Horn Bay, but most of Russia's weather-worn hinterlands. All around him, high-rise buildings jutted up from patches of snow-covered forests, and the windows on the closest buildings were fogged and framed by icicles.

Nikita Khrushchev, leader of the old Soviet Union, had once referred to the city as the "Russian San Francisco," which was a fairly accurate comparison. Both cities were located on hills that offered spectacular views, and Vladivostok had been home to the Soviet Navy's Pacific Ocean Fleet. Since being opened up to foreigners in 1992, the place was simultaneously clutched by the cold hand of lawlessness and warmed by the promise of new wealth and commercialism after years of being a closed region dedicated to the support of the military. In short, Vladivostok was a city seven time zones away from Moscow and truly a world unto its own, heavily influenced by the peoples of China, North Korea, and Japan. Though his visit would be brief, Hansen looked forward to breathing in what he could.

Within twenty minutes, he was off the ferry and walking along the icy pavement toward the bustling train station, where he would meet Sergei Luchenko. Unsurprisingly, a knot had already formed in his stomach. Part of him wanted to apologize for being selected as a Splinter Cell; the other part wanted to tell Sergei, *"Too bad, buddy, but you didn't cut it, and I did."* Hansen didn't want to feel sorry for his own success.

But hell, Hansen did. Sergei's reflexes and mental agility had been good enough for the CIA, but substandard for Third Echelon. He could've returned to his old three-letter agency (or another, like UPS, they liked to joke), but Hansen figured Sergei might be too embarrassed to return. Besides, his fellow operatives would wonder exactly why he hadn't lasted in his new position with the NSA (which was all they'd been told).

Hansen reached the train station, a pale yellow and alabaster-white affair with ornate glass-block windows and thick columns and spires suggesting that its architects had once worked for Disney. The word "Vladivostok," in bright red Cyrillic letters, hung high above the main entrance, and out front lay a bus terminal and a parking lot jammed with private cars and taxis whose drivers stood by and chain-smoked, waiting for their next fares. A pair of footbridges over the tracks gained passengers access to the buses and lots, and Hansen already noted how someone could lie low behind the railings and observe the comings and goings of those passengers. It was there that he spotted Sergei.

Before Hansen veered off the sidewalk, he chanced a quick glance over his shoulder. Then he hustled forward and slipped down behind the railings, where Sergei came to greet him.

Hansen was taken aback by the weight his old friend had lost—at least twenty, perhaps thirty pounds, his face thin and unshaven. Sergei took a long drag on his cigarette, dropped it, stamped it out, then proffered his hand. "I see you found me, Ben. I thought I was being more discreet. Guess that's why they flunked me, huh?" Sergei spoke in perfect Russian, but that was one of the many languages he had learned—or relearned as he liked to say. He'd been born and raised in Sacramento, California, the son of Russian immigrants.

Tensing, Hansen took the man's hand, shook firmly, and answered in Russian: "Sergei, thanks for being here."

"Just doing my job. Equipment transporter. Taxicab driver. All in a day's work."

"Look, I wish things had worked out differently."

"You? Hell . . . me, too!" He shuddered against the cold and pulled the collar of his woolen coat tighter to his neck. "Come on, I have the car parked over there."

"No tails?"

"None that I can tell. But are you trusting me, the flunky?"

"Come on, enough of that."

"I'm just busting your chops. I knew this would be awkward for you, and you know what a wiseass I am."

Hansen sighed and curled his lips in a weak grin.

They started across the street, toward the parking lot, and Sergei led him to a late-model Toyota Mark X sedan with right-hand drive. The lock chirped, and Hansen crossed to the left side, stored his bags in the backseat, then climbed in.

"Murdoch still hasn't checked in to the hotel, so I'm getting a little worried," Sergei reported, switching to English.

"We headed there now?"

"Yeah, I've been there for a couple of days."

"And the meeting is still on for tonight, 8:00 P.M., in Korfovka."

Sergei shrugged. "No one's told me otherwise."

"How far is it from the hotel?"

"About ninety minutes, give or take."

"Give or take what?"

"Give or take a snowstorm, an ice storm, a nuclear event."

Hansen looked at him. "Always the wiseass."

"Always."

Despite his not being accepted into Third Echelon's Splinter Cell program, Sergei, like Hansen, had received some of the best training in the world, compliments of the CIA. The average citizen had no idea of the length, the breadth, the sheer scope and magnitude of such schooling and the areas it encompassed. Both men had been given courses on advanced military technology; military strategy and tactics; computer security; countersurveillance; the art of disguise; etiquette and arts in foreign cultures; languages; explosives; fake IDs and secret banking; field medicine; forensics; guerrilla warfare; hand-to-hand knife combat; incendiary devices; international and local law; lock-bypassing techniques; photography and videography; poisons; psychology; drugs; sniper techniques; and, finally, surveillance.

Third Echelon's training had taken those areas to the next level by incorporating more unconventional warfare techniques borrowed from American special forces as well as hand-to-hand combat techniques like *krav maga*, borrowed from the Israelis. The French-born art of *parkour* was also studied as a technique for deftly navigating around obstacles while fleeing. And then, of course, was the newer, more controversial training conducted by a pair of world-famous Chinese acrobats seeking political asylum in the United States. Those lithe men taught Hansen to hook his arms and legs around pipes and other objects in ways he had never considered. That they were contortionists helped, if not frustrated, the rest of the recruits.

"I still think about Somalia, even after all this time," Sergei said out of nowhere.

Hansen took a deep breath, wishing he could forget about his short time in that country. "All we did was light their fires. And now look: We have even more pirates."

"You didn't believe me."

"I know. But it's the hits that count, not the misses, and I still love this. I still think it's important."

"Still a rush, huh?"

"I won't lie. But listen to us. We sound like a couple of vets when we haven't put the time in, not really."

"I don't know, buddy. Took me a long time to wind up here. And I just turned thirty. You never trust anyone over thirty."

Hansen chuckled. "My old man used to say that. Some mantra from the 1960s."

"I thought it was a quote from the *Planet of the Apes* movie," Sergei said with a frown.

Hansen shrugged and leaned back on his seat to take in the sights for just another two minutes before they reached the Gavan Hotel at 3 Krygina Street. According to a travel brochure Hansen found on the seat beside him, there were fifty-seven guest rooms "where customers can find a maximum comfort. Following the home-away-from-home style, the Gavan hotel shows a unique combination of homelike atmosphere and modern comfort."

They parked, and Sergei led him up to a room on the seventh floor. When they entered, a young woman was standing near the bed, wearing only a bra and panties.

Hansen's jaw fell open as Sergei rushed into the room, grabbed the woman by the wrist, and back-handed her across the face. Then he screamed at her in Russian, "What the hell are you still doing here! I told you to leave! Get your clothes and get out!"

"I was talking to my sister." The woman groaned, clutching her face.

"Get out!"

The woman quickly wriggled into a cheap dress, grabbed her purse, and rushed past Hansen, who remained in the doorway, dumbfounded. "Sergei, what the hell are you doing here?"

Hansen's old friend dismissed him with a wave and turned to the desk, where he wrenched open a laptop, took a seat, and began typing furiously. "I've hacked into the hotel's registration system. We'll see if our boy has checked in yet."

"She was a hooker, wasn't she?"

"Whatever. Just shut up."

"Did she see you do this? You left her alone with your computer? She could compromise this entire mission! How the hell do you know her? How long has she been here? Maybe she works for them. Maybe we're being set up."

"Jesus Christ, dude, sit down before you have a heart attack. She's just a whore I picked up."

"You can't do that!"

"I'm here to give you your gear and get you to the location. Where the hell does it say I can't screw a hooker?"

Hansen threw his duffel and garment bags onto the bed and began to activate his OPSAT. "This is ridiculous. Insane. Beyond unprofessional."

"What're you doing now? Calling Mommy to tell on me?"

Two empty bottles of vodka sat on the desk beside Sergei's computer, along with two glasses and several packs of cigarettes. Sergei lifted one of the bottles, sipped the remaining few drops, then shook his head in disgust, while Hansen stood there, deciding what to do.

Hansen took a deep breath. "You're not all right, are you?"

"I'm perfect. And you know why? Because I'm

helping you, my old friend. It could be a lot worse, right? Look, I'm sorry about the . . . Just forget about it. She's not working for them." He rapped a knuckle on his computer screen. "And right here . . . this shows our boy just checked in, about fifteen minutes ago."

"What room is he in?"

"Eighty-four. Eighty-three is empty."

"Then let's get to work—if you're still a part of this operation."

"I never left."

Hansen took a deep breath. "Sergei, you've put me in a terrible position. When this is over, I *will* have to say something."

"I understand where you're coming from, but you forget that you still owe me."

Hansen's brows knitted. "Owe you what?"

"When they were getting ready to send us over to the 'Stan, who got you through Dari? Or should I say, who helped you cheat your way through Dari? And if they really sent us there, you wouldn't be talking jack to anyone because you couldn't hack the language. But it was okay to cheat then, huh?"

"That wasn't a live operation. And I passed the oral. That was just a multiple-choice exam."

"And you wanted to go so bad that you'd do anything to get there, even cheat, and so you did—and you still didn't get to go. Now here we are."

"So you want to trade a hooker for a multiple-choice test?"

Sergei grabbed a cigarette, stuffed it between his lips. "Now you're talking." He reached below the desk and grabbed a backpack. "You ready?"

6

HANSEN and Sergei had drilled small holes in the wall and set up a pair of flexicams with views of Murdoch's room from the empty one next door, where they sat in darkness. The angles from the flexicams were low, the light dim, but between those snakelike spy cameras and a pair of tiny microphones they had introduced through the electrical outlets, they had established a rudimentary but effective surveillance of the man's room. They had gained access to the other suite via a sophisticated key card with microprocessor, which not only bypassed the electronic encoding system but also remained hidden from the hotel's staff. Pretty standard equipment as Third Echelon toys went.

For most of the day, Murdoch remained there, sleeping off his jet lag. Hansen and Sergei spent long hours just listening to the man snore and taking turns napping themselves. At one point, around two in the afternoon, Sergei began whispering to himself, and Hansen interrupted him. "Who are you talking to?"

"Anna 'the bitch' Grimsdóttir."

"Sergei—"

"I'm telling her what I should've told her."

"If you hate it that much—"

"I'll be all right. I just thought it would be easier. But seeing you here, knowing you got it . . . and I . . ."

Hansen reached out and put a consoling hand on the man's shoulder. "I'm your friend."

AROUND five, Murdoch rose and took a shower. On the other side of the wall, Hansen and Sergei continued watching their four-inch monitors. Meanwhile, Sergei had been running a program to keep tabs on the hotel's registration system. The program would alert him should the suite they were occupying be booked.

Mr. Michael Murdoch was in good shape for a man who'd spent half a lifetime dining in only the finest restaurants. He obviously made time for the gym, the tennis court, or long weekends of golf, and Hansen immediately hated him, not only for being rich, but for having the abs of a college athlete. Murdoch dressed, picked up his cell phone, and dialed a number. He spoke quickly in Russian: "I'm here. Going to have dinner. I'll be on time this evening. See you then."

Now it was Hansen's turn to verify some data. He'd already pressed his thumb to his OPSAT's touch screen, activated the device, and established an encrypted link with Third Echelon. After a pause, the screen displayed data on Murdoch's outgoing call number and location: KORFOVKA—LATITUDE 43.8833 / LONGITUDE 131.3000 / ALTITUDE (FEET) 728. The phone, however, was registered to Beijing High Mountain Exports. No discernable owner, just the company name, a company Hansen suspected would turn out to be a shell. So Murdoch had just spoken in Russian to a man using a Chinese company's phone.

"Bratus and Zhao are already up there," Hansen told Sergei.

"But we don't know exactly where, because they don't meet in the same place twice. Same town, yes, but different locations every time. That, we've already confirmed," Sergei explained.

"Well, it's not a very big town. What's Murdoch using to get up there?"

"If he hasn't changed his routine, it'll be a rental car with a driver."

"We'll tag it," said Hansen.

"That's your job."

"So we're done here. Why don't you get cleaned up yourself? I'll keep an eye on our buddy from Texas."

"Whatever you say, Boss."

Hansen rose quietly to his feet.

ALLEN Ames sat in the Gavan Hotel's main lobby. He had not shaved in a week and was wearing thick nonprescription glasses and a latex stomach apparatus that added fifty pounds to his girth. He had also donned a woolen cap and heavy coat, and to any observer was simply another fat tourist or business traveler engrossed in his smart phone. Were you standing over his shoulder, though, you'd frown at the images displayed on his phone's screen, images from the hotel restaurant, hallways, and main lobby, courtesy of Ames's expertly planted microcameras.

He saw that Murdoch had just entered the restaurant, and then he perked up even more when he spotted Hansen doing likewise. But where was Luchenko? Still upstairs? He thumbed back to the image from the hallway outside Murdoch's room and spotted Luchenko walking forward.

Ames had a question to answer . . . and that question was *when*. When should he make his move? He could not allow Hansen to follow Murdoch out to Korfovka. The meeting must take place without Third Echelon's prying eyes and ears. Moreover, any hint of mistrust on the Americans' part would ruin the entire deal. Those orders had come down to Ames directly from his true superior, NSA Deputy Director Nicholas Andrew Kovac. Ames was a Splinter Cell, all right, but in the end he did not answer to Grim, and his true mission was to provide constant surveillance of Third Echelon's operations for the deputy director himself. That Kovac did not trust one of his own subagencies was unremarkable; that he had gone to the extent of planting a mole within Third Echelon itself was a bold move, one that Ames fully appreciated, especially since he had the honor of being that man.

Grim thought Ames was on a weeklong vacation, and Kovac had even borrowed a low-level analyst to pose as Ames and take that very vacation down on the island of St. Barts in the French West Indies. So while some computer schmuck got to frolic on the topless beaches, Ames got the glory job of going to the miserably cold and depressing Russian Federation.

But this was how you made a name for yourself. When Ames was a cop, he'd nearly been recruited for internal affairs. He'd seen so much corruption that he was losing track of right and wrong, but he couldn't bring himself to become "one of the rats," even though he'd wanted to take down the men who tarnished the badge. Now he was getting his chance to help keep Third Echelon on the straight and narrow, especially after what had happened with Fisher.

Who could blame the deputy director? Grim's more aggressive management style, coupled with a group of eager new recruits, was, in the deputy director's words, "a serious threat to the stability and credibility of this institution."

Now, the trick was to ruin Hansen's operation without ever revealing that Ames had been there. That was the key. Hansen could never know that Ames was behind his failure. The cocky young punk thought he was on his first mission alone, thought he was going to really prove himself to the Grim Reaper. Not on Ames's watch. No, sir.

But when to strike? Ames had an anesthetic dart pistol in his hip pocket, ready for use. He didn't want to kill Hansen, only incapacitate him, but Kovac had made it clear: Ben Hansen was expendable, as was Sergei Luchenko. The meeting's security took precedence over all other concerns.

Ames waited another thirty minutes in the lobby. Hansen sat alone in the restaurant, eating a meal. Murdoch, too, sat alone, finishing up dinner. Murdoch paid his bill and stood. Hansen summoned his own waiter. Ames took a deep breath.

"Excuse me, sir?" said a voice at his shoulder.

With a start, Ames shoved his smart phone into his pocket and whirled back to face a skinny man, about forty, with a birdlike face and narrow eyes. "Yes?" Ames answered in Russian.

"I don't mean to be rude, but I've been watching you now for a while. Are you a guest here at the hotel?"

"As a matter of fact, I am. Who are you?"

"I am Boris Svetlanoff, hotel security." The man offered his hand, and Ames tentatively took it. "Would you mind coming with me?"

Ames hustled to his feet and spotted Murdoch coming into the lobby. Ames's attention was now riveted on the man.

"Sir, I said: Would you mind coming with me?"

"What?"

The security man shifted in front of Ames, blocking his view of Murdoch—just as Hansen came shifting up behind the businessman.

"Sir, I must insist," grunted Svetlanoff.

Ames snorted. "I'm not going with you."

"We just want to ask a few questions. Can you show me your key card?"

Ames tried to step aside and head after Hansen and Murdoch, but once more the security man cut him off. "Sir, you will not leave without talking to us first."

"Oh, really?"

"I'm sorry, sir, but you *will* come with me." The man slid open his coat to reveal a pistol tucked into a shoulder harness. "I don't want to embarrass you."

At that moment Luchenko appeared in the lobby, and for a few seconds Ames locked gazes with him.

Do as you've been told, Sergei, and you will be rewarded. . . .

Then, when Ames turned back, a second man was standing beside Svetlanoff. This guy was six feet five, three hundred pounds, and he could have auditioned for a part in one of the old *Rocky* movies. He smiled at Ames, then turned to his partner. "What do we have here, Boris? Another pedophile? A voyeur? What do we have?"

Ames began swearing to himself. He was going to lose them . . . for now.

WHILE Murdoch waited outside the hotel lobby for his car and driver to arrive, Hansen strolled down the sidewalk; then he leapt over a low-lying concrete wall, of sorts, that ran parallel to Krygina Street. The wall was just a meter tall, and covered in ice, but it would do. There had once been a wrought-iron fence attached to the top, but the fence had long since been torn down, and its rusting metal supports rose like humps along the spine of stone. Hansen lay behind the wall, drawing his SC pistol and loading up a very particular shell.

His OPSAT read 6:28 P.M. local time. His pulse drummed. He shivered. And then a voice buzzed in his subdermal: "He's getting in now. Black Mercedes. Very nice. Coming your way." Sergei had come through.

Hansen waited, and then there it was, the black Mercedes in question, rolling down the street. In the steadily growing darkness, Hansen rolled up onto the wall, bracing himself with his elbows. He held his breath, thought of the wind speed, adjusted his aim . . . and fired at the car.

His round struck the lower right bumper, and he doubted the occupants had noticed anything more than what seemed like a tire dropping into a little pothole—and the streets were full of them.

The round contained one of the world's smallest and most effective GPS tracking devices. The average citizen who wanted to spy on his cheating wife could buy a shoe-box-sized unit and secretly install it in the trunk of his wife's car. That was fine if you had prior access to the vehicle and could find some extra room in one of the wells.

However, Hansen's tracker was infinitely more advanced and resembled a tarry gray lump that might be easily dismissed as bird droppings stuck to the car. The device's flexible GPS chip was just $7 \times 6 \times 1.28$ millimeters and disguised by the goo. A similar model had been incorporated into the Sticky Cam system used by prior operatives, but this newer unit had better stealth capabilities and extended range because it was designed solely as a beacon. He immediately rolled over and checked his OPSAT for a good signal.

Nothing. He cursed, took a deep breath, and then . . .

V-TRAC > GPS ENABLED > ONLINE >
SIGNAL: 98.563

As the signal-strength numbers continued to fluctuate but remained well within the green, he pushed up, hurried back onto the sidewalk, and jogged up to the hotel, where Sergei waited.

They headed to the parking garage and reached their car, where Hansen pulled his gear box from the trunk and threw it on the backseat. He took a seat beside the box. Sergei got in on the driver's side and pulled out, giving Murdoch's Mercedes an appreciable lead and putting several cars between them.

Hansen immediately began slipping into his black bodysuit. The now-standard DARPA Mark V tactical operations suit was, in his humble opinion, overkill for this short-duration op, so he'd packed one of the older models equipped with interwoven Kevlar, a thermoregulation system to maintain its temperature, photosensitive threads to detect a sniper's laser, and water bladders to keep him hydrated. The suit's weight, simplicity, and reliability made it a perfect choice. Hansen also tugged on a pair of Blackhawk light assault boots and buckled on his weapons belt. He'd wait to shoulder the backpack, a narrow satchel only 2.5 inches thick. Before leaving the car, he would put on a heavy woolen coat and cap, so that on first glance he could pass for one Korfovka's fifteen hundred residents, his gear fully hidden from view. He placed the butterfly-shaped SVT on his throat, then activated his OPSAT, notifying Grim that he was online. A few seconds later, her voice sounded through his subdermal:

"Excellent work so far, Ben. We see you've tagged Murdoch's car, and we're also monitoring the signal. The road out to Korfovka is, in a word, rural, so keep your distance, lights off."

"No problem, ma'am."

"Grim will do. Or Grim Reaper—as I've heard some of you call me behind my back."

"No, ma'am. I mean Grim. I mean—"

"Ben, listen carefully. I've had my eyes on the satellite feeds. Two cars arrived in Korfovka earlier today. We ID'd Bratus and Zhao, and they've just driven from a small restaurant to a pub on the east end of town. Take a look."

The OPSAT screen switched from the V-TRAC indicator's multicolored map of the territory to a satellite image, zooming in on a row of single-story buildings, outside of which were parked two late-model sedans. The level of detail was, as always, remarkable.

"Bratus and Zhao are inside, waiting for Murdoch," Grim added.

"I need more pictures of the place—the roof, the rear entrance."

"Working on it."

"Anything else I should know?"

"There's a storm front moving in. Should be blizzard conditions in three, four hours, which leads me to believe that this meeting will be short, so you'll need to get in there as quickly as possible."

"Roger that."

"All right, more pictures of the pub coming through now. Saving to your OPSAT. I'll be here if you need me."

"Thanks, Grim."

Hansen tapped Sergei's shoulder and handed him the trifocal goggles that had become synonymous with Splinter Cell operations.

Sergei shook his head. "Don't torture me, Ben. I'm not good enough to wear them. They made that very clear."

"Put 'em on. Lights out." Hansen's tone left zero room for argument.

After groaning in disgust, Sergei accepted the goggles, slipped them over his head, then switched off the car's headlights. Hansen returned to studying the new images glowing on his OPSAT screen.

—— 7

HANSEN and Sergei took highway M-60 out of Vladivostok, passing into the city of Ussuriysk, situated on the Rasdolnaya River, about ninety-eight kilometers north of the hotel. Then they turned onto A-184 out of Ussuriysk and made a left turn onto A-186, heading west toward Korfovka. There wasn't much to see beyond the windows, especially with the lights out—just stretches of a barren valley blanketed in ice and snow. Only a few other cars passed them on the road, and the driver of a small truck flashed his lights to warn them theirs were off. "It's okay, buddy," Sergei had muttered. "I can see you just fine."

They were on A-186 for just a few minutes when Grim called to say there were two cars traveling about a half kilometer behind them.

Hansen told Sergei, "Grim thinks we might have a tail."

"What do you think?"

"Two cars. Hard to say."

"Better safe than sorry, right? I'll take care of them after I drop you off."

"But do me a favor. Don't wind up in Khabarovsk."

"Have you seen the ladies up there?"

Hansen snickered. "What's your plan? To come home with a Russian wife?"

"Worse things could happen."

"As a matter of fact they could."

AMES had finished answering the hotel security man's questions and had explained that he'd been sitting there, observing the lobby, because he thought his wife was having an affair and he wanted to catch her in the act. Svetlanoff and his muscle-head partner chuckled and made a comment about Ames's diminutive size in multiple areas and suggested that his wife wouldn't be cheating on him if he were man enough to satisfy her. Ames knew they were just trying to provoke him so they could detain him even longer, maybe even slap him around a little, so he quickly agreed with them, apologized, and was summarily released.

Instead of punishing himself for the rookie mistake of drawing the security man's attention, he got back to work. There'd be plenty of time later to bang his head against a wall. He hired a taxi to follow him to Korfovka, though the driver had a difficult time understanding why he should do so when Ames had his own car. "Are we picking up a large number of people? Are we hauling cargo? Because I do not haul cargo, only suitcases and bags." Ames paid him double, in advance, and the questions ceased.

Now, as they headed up the bumpy road, he imagined Grim sitting there in the situation room, wired on caffeine and watching the stream from her satellites. He even felt her electronic gaze on his shoulders. He glanced up and thought, *Don't worry, my dear Reaper. It's only me, come to fog up your lenses. You really should switch to contacts. . . .*

He grinned. What a witty bastard he was. *Ah . . .* He took a breath, reached into his pocket, and found his Zippo. He began rolling it between his fingers, growing more relaxed as he imagined a warm yellow light engulfing him.

Lying on the passenger's seat was a digital video camera and a suitcase containing $250,000 in small, unmarked bills—part of plan B, in case Hansen made it to Korfovka.

"WE'RE almost there," said Sergei. "There's a little petrol station up ahead. About two blocks from the pub. I can drop you off out back. I'll let the other cars go by and follow them for a while. I'll be in touch."

Hansen took in a long breath. "Sounds good."

"You all right?"

"Yeah."

"You sound nervous. I would be, too. First real mission as a Splinter Cell."

Hansen took another long breath and nodded.

"All right, Murdoch has just pulled up to the pub," Grim said. "You'd better move!"

Hansen gave the order to Sergei, who tugged off his goggles and returned them to Hansen. They pulled behind the petrol station, a very modest-sized building with a long red awning and two ancient-looking pumps. The place was closed. Hansen gave himself the once-over, slid on his goggles, then said, "Here goes nothing."

Sergei smiled weakly. "Good luck."

In one quick motion, Hansen was out of the car and running down the long alley between the first row of buildings. If Korfovka had a downtown district, this was it: perhaps fifteen structures in all, with a small water tower to the northeast. A private airport lay out in that direction as well, with several Quonset hangars and a helipad lying adjacent to the single airstrip.

With the night vision switched on, Hansen kept to the deep shadows, working his way north toward the pub. To his west lay small clusters of old houses, with every third or so looking boarded up and abandoned. Most of the roofs sagged under the weight of heavy snow. Only then did he realize how cold it was getting, but the suit began to compensate. An electric current ran through his senses as he remembered who he was, what he was doing, and what this moment meant to him. All he had to do was get the information and get out. No footprints.

He reached the corner of the next building, and, on his haunches, peered around the side to the main street. In the distance came the sound of car engines, and he hoped Sergei was still hiding behind the petrol station and watching those cars go by. Hansen darted off, running now with some impunity, the alley still clear. One more side street to cross before he reached the pub. He had to guard his steps, though, as his boot hit a patch of ice and he nearly went down. To fall and break his leg en route to the location would not only ruin the mission, it would make him the laughingstock of Third Echelon. The others would spend long nights inventing nicknames for him. There would be no living it down.

Another car engine resounded, this one from in front of the pub. Hansen hazarded a peek around the next corner and spotted a dilapidated old pickup truck parked across the street. Two old Russians got out, both wearing parkas and caps, their faces doughy, cheeks red. The older one waved to his partner, and they lit cigarettes and walked across the street toward the pub.

Hansen hadn't just run out of time; the clock was now running positive, and the meeting had quite obviously started. He cursed and took off, gritting his teeth as he reached the pub's back door. For the sake of argument he tried the lock. He lost the argument.

Ignoring the tremor in his hands, he gave himself five seconds with his picking tool, counting each one until on exactly five he had the door open and, keeping low, gingerly stepped inside.

The air smelled of something delicious, fresh-baked bread perhaps, but that heavenly scent was tinged by cigarette smoke and beer. Hansen came into a small storage room, its shelves stocked high with boxes of spirits. Light from a small fixture shone overhead. A pair of folding shutter doors about half the length of a normal-sized door separated the storage room from the front. Abruptly, those doors pushed open and a heavyset woman in her sixties pushed into the room. She had a badly stained apron folded over her considerable girth, and a thick scarf held back her shock of silver hair.

Hansen hunkered down, drawing his SC pistol with an anesthetic dart already loaded.

As she lumbered toward the back, toward him, he slowly stood. She took one look at him—a dark alien with three eyes—and opened her mouth.

Even as he imagined her scream, Hansen fired the dart into her neck and dashed forward to catch her. Indeed, she'd had time to scream, but he realized that she hadn't because she'd fainted even before the anesthetic took hold.

Welcome to Real-Life Spy Work 101, he told himself, *where you're not hanging inverted from the rafters, completely obscured and cleverly firing Sticky Cams to eavesdrop on the bad guys while you remain fully undetected.*

No, this was a lot less glamorous, clutching a fat Russian woman and lowering her to the ground as he considered how long it would take before someone else came into the back room, looking for her—and how long after that Murdoch and the rest would become aware that something was wrong.

He was not ten seconds into the mission and it had already gone to hell. . . .

But it wasn't over yet. Hansen stood, withdrew the laser microphone from his breast pocket, and, keeping tight behind the doors, stole a quick glance over the tops of them. The decor seemed borrowed from an old Bavarian inn, with paneling and beams spanning the rafters. Candles at the half dozen tables, and more positioned along the broad wooden counter, created a warm and hypnotic atmosphere, perfect for drinking on a cold night. An old chandelier hung from the ceiling, but three of its four bulbs had burned out.

Off to Hansen's left was the bartender: a slightly hunched-back man with a wiry white beard, serving a drink to one of the two men who had just entered. They were the only ones at the bar. Behind them, seated at a table near the wall, were Murdoch, Zhao, and Bratus, all nursing drinks.

Hansen tucked himself back a little farther behind the doors and aimed the laser microphone (officially the LM7: laser microphone, seventh generation) at one of the glasses near Bratus. Any object that could resonate or vibrate, like a glass or a picture on the wall, would do so because of pressure waves created by noises. The invisible NIR, or near-infrared, laser was able to detect the tiny difference in the distance traveled by the light to pick up resonance and reproduce the sound causing it. Sure, any Joe could go to YouTube and learn to build a rudimentary laser microphone, but to build one the size of a ballpoint pen with NIR technology and a range in excess of a thousand meters was better left to Third Echelon and its subcontractors. The LM7 operated according to Snell's law, which required sharp alignment and correct aiming of both the transmitted and received laser beams, so Hansen needed to aim the beam and remain perfectly still while the conversation was picked up and automatically transferred to his OPSAT, where it would be heard through his subdermal, recorded, and later sent to Grim.

All of which was to verify that he did, indeed, have his ear on the conversation, as all three men spoke in Russian:

"I don't understand what the problem is," said Murdoch.

"The problem is money," answered Zhao. "Kovac promised me twice what he's now offering."

"But you can't stop now," Bratus said. "Because if you do, I don't know what to tell my people. We will all die."

"Look, I'll go back to Kovac. I'll tell him what you said. I'll tell him that if he wants the rest of the names on that list, he's got to pay the full amount."

"Just like I did," said Bratus. "See the difference between the Russians and the Americans, my friend? The Russians know how to keep a promise."

"That's not fair," snapped Murdoch. "The initial data was corrupt. We don't pay for something we don't get."

Hansen was trembling. He was getting it all. They had implicated Kovac. They'd even mentioned him by name! This was the real deal, his first mission, and he was kicking ass and taking names . . . or, rather, getting names, *the* name. Grim would not only thank him, she would rip off her glasses and—

He shuddered, forced calm back into his thoughts as Zhao went on: "I have a little surprise for you, but we'll have to go to the airport." Zhao checked his watch. "He should be arriving soon."

All three men stood. Hansen rolled back behind the doors, glanced down at the old lady, then heard the bartender cry, "Nadia! What's taking you so long?"

Hansen held his breath. If he could just stall the old man until Murdoch and his buddies left . . .

Footfalls drew closer.

Bratus called out, "Thank you, and have a good night!" The bartender responded in kind.

The front door opened.

And the back doors swung inward. The old bartender entered the storage room, glancing around.

Hansen took him from behind, drawing one of the old man's arms behind his back and wrapping a gloved hand over the man's mouth. Hansen muttered, "Don't struggle, and you'll be okay. Nadia is sleeping. Just wait for another minute. Don't move."

Outside, the car engines fired up. Hansen listened

a moment longer, then suddenly released the man and charged out the back door and into the alley.

"Sergei? They're going to the airport. Come on! I'll meet you behind the petrol station."

Hansen raced as fast as he could along the walls, waiting for his runner to reply. "Sergei?"

8

WHILE Hansen was off on his glory mission, Sergei had driven around the front of the petrol station, as Allen Ames had instructed him to do. Sergei waited there for Ames and his taxicab tail to show up. When he arrived, the short man remained in his car and motioned for the cabdriver to turn around and head back to Vladivostok; then Ames parked under the awning, hidden from the satellite's prying eyes. He left his car, carrying a video camera and suitcase. He climbed into Sergei's Toyota and took a deep breath. "Hello, Luchenko."

"It's too late. He's already implicated Kovac. Grim knows. I did what I could to delay him."

Ames raised a finger and speed-dialed a number on his satellite phone. He waited. "It's me. Yes, sir. I'm afraid that's already happened. Yes, sir. I know what to do now, sir. I was already prepared." He hung up.

"What now?" asked Sergei.

"You didn't delay Hansen. You second-guessed yourself. I told you what we had planned for you in the NSA, and you threw it all away on drinking and whores and feeling guilty about your buddy, who is *not* your friend, trust me. You don't have what it takes, and that's why you're not a Splinter Cell. I told them we were wasting our time on you. They didn't believe me. We gave you a second chance, and you blew it."

"Doesn't matter now. Nothing matters."

"Oh, you're wrong. I have new orders. Hansen's not just expendable. The boss wants him dead. I've brought money and a camera. You bring me the proof, and you get paid $250K." Ames opened the suitcase and showed Sergei the stacks of bills.

Sergei stiffened. "You guys were planning this all along. I wasn't just a mole. I'm an assassin."

Ames slapped shut the suitcase. "You wanted to be a field operative. Welcome to the big leagues. And you don't have a choice."

"As a matter of fact, I do." With that, Sergei had a

pistol with a long suppressor jammed against Ames's head.

The little weasel didn't flinch. "What's the point? If you kill me, you're only delaying the inevitable. They'll find you."

Sergei began to lose his breath. "Why do we have to kill Hansen? He's just a rookie operative. A nobody."

"Kovac wants him dead. That's enough for me."

"Why?"

"Maybe to punish Grim. Maybe he thinks Hansen is Grim's pet. He's got it in for her. I don't know. I once heard him say that Grim was grooming Hansen to become the next Sam Fisher. Maybe that's why."

"If your boss wants him dead, you do it."

"I can't get close. If he saw me and I failed, it would ruin everything. They've got a lot invested in me."

"So I do your dirty work? What makes you think I won't talk?"

Ames chuckled under his breath. "Come on, Sergei. You're dealing with the most powerful intelligence operation on the planet. Even a man like you has one thing you love more than anything in this world: one . . . woman. And if that woman's life were threatened, you would do anything to protect her. Did you think we would bring you into our fold without knowing everything? When you're little people like us, you do what the big people say. And if they throw you a bone, you take it and run as fast you can."

Sergei began to choke up. His life had come to this. He was just a hired killer. A thug. And he'd been wrong. He had no choice. It didn't matter that Victoria said she no longer loved him. He would love her forever, and as Ames had said, he would never allow anything to happen to her. He could smell her now, her perfume, and he felt her long, blond hair brushing against his cheek and the smooth curves of her back as her lips opened slightly, warm and wet, to touch his.

If he did what they asked, the woman he loved would be saved. He would collect a quarter of a million dollars. And a man that made him green with envy would be dead.

Sergei lowered the pistol.

Ames nodded. "Here's the camera. The money comes back with me. Bring me the video. You tell them Hansen never came back. They'll find his body, it'll be another mess for Third Echelon, and we'll laugh our way to the bank."

"Hansen called. He's on foot. He was coming here, but he decided to double back to the airport."

Ames's smile evaporated. "What?"

"Hansen's been calling me. He's running over to the airport right now. The group's meeting there. Zhao says he has a surprise for them."

"This is . . . unexpected. We'll leave my car here. Drive!"

Sergei nodded and threw the car in gear. They

roared away from the petrol station, and for a moment he glanced over at Ames and, with a shudder, imagined himself putting a bullet in the mole's head.

Maybe he would.

HANSEN had been running for about ten minutes, heading past groups of old houses whose icy roofs glistened in the night. He followed a rickety old fence that cordoned off an open field, and he suspected that the occupants of the two cars, well ahead on the road about a quarter kilometer to his right, couldn't see him. The airport lay farther northeast, not far from the water tower and another collection of buildings, the tallest of which was an old Eastern Orthodox church, the three-bar cross casting a deep silhouette against the gray clouds.

"Ben, Sergei's car has left the gas station and is headed toward the airport," reported Grim.

"And the other car?"

"Still parked there."

"Any idea who it is?"

"Trying to check now, but we didn't get a tag. He's got it under the awning, and we can't get a good shot."

"Why isn't Sergei answering me?"

"Not sure, and, quite frankly, I wouldn't trust him at this point."

"Don't write him off yet. Maybe we were being tailed, and he took out the guy. Maybe he's just got a problem with his OPSAT."

"From our end his OPSAT looks fine. Anyway, just get to the airport. We need to see Zhao's surprise. . . ."

"Roger that. I'm on it."

"And one more thing. Don't forget to breathe."

Hansen grinned to himself and jogged on across the snow. As he turned toward the church, the wind and swirling snow began buffeting him head-on.

He spotted another fence about a hundred meters ahead, charged toward it, crouched over, and ran along to the corner. There he climbed over and found himself in a small cemetery behind the church. Gnarled and seemingly ancient trees ringed the perimeter, theirs limbs bowing and creaking against gusts reaching at least thirty miles an hour. About two dozen grave markers sprouted up from mounds of snow, with pieces of wind-whipped ice tumbling from their granite tops. The scent of burning wood wafted everywhere now, as the flames in fireplaces farther north were stoked against the oncoming cold.

Hansen reached the church's back door and found it spanned by yellow warning tape and signs: The place had been closed because of a roof collapse. He shifted around the side of the building, saw the airport and Quonset huts ahead; then he stopped and glanced up at the steeple. An oval-shaped window was positioned just below an ornate clock with a diameter of at least two meters. Hansen glanced once more down to the airport, then up at the steeple. The angle looked good, so he raced around the back, got to work on the lock, and gained entrance.

The west side of the church appeared untouched, with pews lined up before an ornate altar whose walls had stained-glass windows and holy icons of the saints and large wrought-iron sconces. Giant murals spanned the domed ceiling, and the smell of incense was still pungent.

Off to the right, lying in sharp contrast, was a disaster of fallen cross members and drywall and shingles, along with pieces of the ceiling's amazing artwork scattered in sad piles all over the pews. It seemed the parishioners and others had just started on the cleanup work, and above it all was a gaping maw in the ceiling. Pieces of insulation and loosened shingles still attached to the ragged edges flapped in the wind, and the snow was already piling up inside.

Hansen picked his way around the debris and found a side door that led into a stairwell barely wide enough for one person. He rose straight up the steep staircase, crinkling his nose at the scent of sweet-smelling incense that was even stronger here.

At the top he found a small door, which was open,

and he moved into a room with a creaking wooden floor that allowed access up and into the back of the clock, whose steady ticking was at once comforting and annoying. The window he'd seen from outside was there, but heavy wooden shutters sealed it from the inside. He unlatched and tugged open one of the shutters, and the entire piece of wood came off in his hands. He swore, set it down, then removed his backpack and got out his glass-cutting kit with suction-cup handle and blade. He etched a rectangle about twelve inches square in the single pane of glass, then affixed the suction cup, gave a tap, and eureka! The cold rushed inside. He set down the glass, then peered out across the courtyard to the airport and huts, which lay 221.6 meters away, according to the map on his OPSAT's screen.

He brought himself closer to the opening in the window, zoomed in with the goggles, and saw now that Murdoch, Bratus, and Zhao were standing in front of two cars, arms folded, talking. Zhao turned and pointed out to the west, and Hansen looked in that direction, but he couldn't see anything yet. And then he noted something else: The driver's-side window was down on Bratus's car, and there was man seated at the wheel, but Hansen couldn't quite distinguish his face.

"Grim, you seeing this?"

"Yes."

"Any idea who he is? Or is he just a driver."

"Need a better image of him."

"It's damned windy out there, but I think I'll deploy the COM-BAT."

"Standing by. And it looks like now you've got a helicopter moving toward you."

Hansen glanced down at his OPSAT. The map of his position zoomed out to show the oncoming helicopter's position as a red point moving toward his green triangle. Then the image zoomed further in on the red dot and dissolved into a file photo of the helicopter, an MD600N light, single-turbine bird with NOTAR (no tail rotor) technology. The chopper could carry up to seven passengers and was fast.

With the clock drumming in his ears—both literally and figuratively—Hansen removed from his pack the nylon sleeve containing the COM-BAT, a six-inch, steel-winged robotic spy plane. While the device seemingly took its name from the Batman universe, COM-BAT actually stood for the Center for Objective Microelectronics and Biomimetic Advanced Technology, part of the University of Michigan's College of Engineering, which had been tapped by the military, through a five-year grant, to develop the sensors, communications tools, and batteries for "the bat."

In addition to the usual array of cameras, minimicrophones, and small detectors for nuclear radiation and poisonous gases, the bat also featured quantum dot solar cells that were twice as effective as current photovoltaics and an autonomous navigation system that was a thousand times smaller than current systems. The bat's body was shaped like a bullet, with a clear domed nose within which you could see its sensor array and solar panel. Its wings extended out at forty-five-degree angles in a V pattern and were slightly hooked at their ends, like a bat's.

Exercising extreme care, Hansen unfolded those wings, tested to be sure they were locked in place, then activated the bat via its smart-phone-sized remote with touch screen. He carefully slipped it through the hole he'd cut in the window, then gave the bat a slight shove, and it immediately took to the wind. With a barely perceptible buzz from its tiny motor, the bat headed toward the airport as Hansen worked the touch-screen controls and adjusted the main camera to point down at the airport. Meanwhile, Zhao's chopper drew closer. The gusts were increasing in strength and frequency, and it was all Hansen could do to maintain control of the little plane.

Then, without warning, the signal from the bat turned to static. Hansen checked his OPSAT. Same thing.

Someone was jamming him.

9

SERGEI left the keys in the ignition and quietly stepped out of the car. He eased the door shut. The snow and wind immediately cut across his face, forcing him to turn up his collar. He squinted as he turned back to Ames, who crossed to the driver's side.

They had taken a dirt road through a forest adjoining the airport and had pulled off into the brush so Sergei could move in from the west, hopefully undetected.

"If you leave me here," Sergei began in a warning tone.

"Why would I do that? You need to finish the job, and I need to collect the video."

Sergei gave a little snort. "Right. But after I hand you the video, you won't give me the money. You'll kill me."

"That's a chance you have to take. You walk away now, and we push that special button."

Hissing, Sergei slipped the camera into his deep front pocket. "I'm not sure I can find him."

"I'm jamming his OPSAT, his SVT, and his little spy plane. He's deaf and blind. He'll get in closer. He has to."

"Whatever you say."

Sergei took a deep breath and started away from the car, the snow already collecting on his shoulders. He saw a fuel truck parked beside the easternmost hangar. He'd have cover from the group and a good view of the west side of the airport, Hansen's most likely route of advance because of the drainage ditches and better cover.

Sergei glanced back one last time at Ames, who was inside the car and on his satellite phone, then stopped and thought for a moment.

He could go back now and kill the little bastard. Just be done with it. Then he would find and warn Hansen. He could do the right thing, and maybe Grim and the rest of Third Echelon would deem him a hero for exposing their mole, even though he'd been one himself. Maybe they'd reconsider their decision to drop him from the Splinter Cell program. He could save Hansen now. He still had that chance.

But Victoria . . . They would kill her. And then, yes, they would come for him. The consequences were that simple . . . and that deadly.

Sergei pushed on through the trees, ducking below low-hanging boughs as the whomping of the helicopter resounded like a racing heart.

HANSEN had darted out of the church and dropped down into a long embankment running parallel to a service road near the main airstrip. He'd seen how several culverts could provide fast and temporary cover before choosing his course, and he dropped into one drainage pipe just as the chopper thundered overhead and descended toward the helipad. He waited there for another few seconds, then slipped back out, dropped to his hands and knees, and crawled forward for a better view of the pad—about two hundred yards away.

He wasn't sure if the people on board the chopper or Sergei or someone else was jamming him, but he still had no contact with Grim and no electronic surveillance of the area via the COM-BAT plane, which now was circling the airport in an endless loop, waiting for its next set of instructions. Sergei's silence raised questions about him; but, then again, maybe he, too, was being jammed, and his signal had been cut off before Hansen's. He wanted so badly to give

the man the benefit of the doubt, but a more powerful sense told him, *No, you can't trust him anymore.
He's turned*.

The chopper pitched up, but the pilot was skilled
enough to lower the bird into a hard but efficient
landing despite the crosswinds.

Bratus, Zhao, and Murdoch had moved back
toward the hangars and were shielding their faces from
the rotor wash as the engine began to wind down.
Hansen also noted that while the window was down
on Bratus's car, the driver was no longer there. He
scanned the area. No sign of him. *Hmm*.

It took several moments before the door on the
chopper finally popped. *Here we go*, Hansen thought.
This was either going to get very enlightening or very
frustrating, depending upon what he could capture with
the laser microphone in this weather and with all that
rotor wash.

AFTER making his phone call, Ames got out of the
car, donned a black balaclava to conceal his face, and
followed Sergei's boot prints until he reached a stand
of trees on the edge of the airport grounds. He sat on
his haunches beside a thick oak, shivering. From this
vantage point, he could survey most of the airport
with his pair of 18 × 50 all-weather binoculars.

Within ten seconds, he spotted Sergei crouched

down near the fuel truck. The fool was partially exposed and easily identifiable from this angle. Not so from where the agents and helicopter were positioned, but Ames would not have chosen that spot. *Rookie.*

Then, almost losing his breath, Ames spotted Hansen tucked in tightly along the embankment, surveying the scene with his trifocals and trying to listen in with his laser mic. He'd done an admirable, if imperfect, job of concealing himself from the group near the helicopter, but from the rear he was vulnerable, and that was when Ames noticed the monster of a man in a long coat and Soviet Army *ushanka* crouched over and drawing up behind Hansen. Unbelievable. Perhaps it was the wind or the continuing rotor wash from the chopper, but Hansen did not react to the guy's approach. It was Bratus's driver, and he was about to make contact.

No no no. This was not acceptable. Ames began to hyperventilate. If this fat ape reported trouble back to Bratus, then the meeting could go to hell. Ames looked to Sergei, still sitting there like a little bird in a nest, waiting for his mother. *The fool!* Ames flicked his gaze back to the helicopter, then back to the fat man, who was already on his phone. Ames's mouth fell open.

TWO men exited the chopper and moved toward the group, ducking slightly against the wash. Hansen zoomed in even more, and the floodlights from the hangar revealed both men as Asian, assumedly Chinese. They shook hands with Murdoch, Bratus, and Zhao, who steered them toward the chopper, where another pair of men was unloading a black Anvil case about the size of a coffin, with a pair of heavy locks. Hansen couldn't get a good beam with his laser mic so he pocketed it and just observed.

Abruptly, Bratus raised a phone to his ear, then suddenly backed away from the group and drew a pistol.

"Oh, my God," Hansen muttered aloud.

Even as the words came from his mouth, Bratus shot Zhao in the head; then he fired at Murdoch, striking him in the chest. Both men dropped to the icy tarmac.

But Bratus wasn't finished. He shot the two men unloading the large case, then pushed into the open chopper and shot the pilot and copilot.

He killed everyone except Murdoch's driver, who attempted to squeal away in his car, but not before Bratus put four bullets into the driver's-side window and the car simply came to a slow halt on the tarmac.

Just then a baritone voice rose from behind Hansen:

"Hello!" The cry was in Russian. "I am Rugar! What is your name?"

Hansen whirled back, tore off his trifocals, and found the business end of a suppressed pistol in his face. The man holding the gun, Rugar, was of inhuman proportions, and besides offering a promise of death, he flashed a carnivorous grin that left Hansen as shocked as he was breathless over his grave error. He'd been so engrossed in the images coming to him via his goggles that he'd failed to check his six o'clock, and the snowstorm had done an excellent job of helping to conceal the big Russian's approach.

"You didn't answer my question," added the fat man. "What's your name?"

Hansen just stared.

Rugar chuckled lowly, clearly enjoying himself. "What's the matter? You don't speak Russian?"

Before Hansen could reply, Rugar's phone rang, and in the instant he flicked his gaze down, Hansen lifted onto his left leg and delivered a roundhouse kick to Rugar's hand, knocking the gun from the fat man's grip. The pistol flew through the air several meters and landed in a pile of snow beside the service road.

Hansen then rolled around, reaching for his own pistol, but Rugar dropped on him like an avalanche, the snow blasting into Hansen's face and blinding him.

As he groaned and struggled against Rugar's immense weight, he realized the man had already seized his hand, the one going for his gun. He blinked, tried to move it, but then an elbow came down into his cheek, striking like a lead hammer.

In point of fact, Hansen had never been hit so hard in his life, even during all his training exercises, where they "trained as they fought." Pinpricks of light winked among the snowflakes, and for a moment, he thought he might pass out. The blow now seemed to reverberate through his entire head, the pain growing roots that wrapped around his brain.

Nearly blind now, Hansen reached out, all his martial-arts training escaping from his memory, as though squeezed away by the man's sheer weight, but he still had sheer instincts and muscle memory. He found Rugar's cold ear, just beneath his hat, and seized it between his fingers.

Hansen tugged so hard that the fat man screamed and broke his grip, and as he moved slightly up, Hansen, in one massive expenditure of energy, rolled from beneath him. He came around onto his knees, drew his SC pistol, but Rugar was already there, delivering a solid jab to Hansen's jaw that sent his head back even as once more the Russian seized his gun hand and began to pin him back onto the snow.

The knife. Where was the knife Grim had given him? *In its hip sheath,* Hansen remembered. He tried to reach across with his left hand, but he couldn't get the angle, and Rugar was repeatedly hammering at his fingers to get him to release the gun.

Hansen grabbed a handful of snow and shoved it in the man's eyes, but Rugar didn't need to see a damned thing in order to keep holding down Hansen's wrist and pummeling the hell out of his hand. After three more blows, Rugar groaned and opened his mouth, a rabid dog ready to take his bite.

Suddenly Hansen's fingers gave out, and the weapon fell free. Rugar grabbed the pistol and fell back on his ass, the snow falling on him, the wind cutting across them as Hansen sat up to face him. His hands throbbed as he lifted them and, in a voice that cracked, said, "I do speak Russian. My name is Dmitry Anatolyevich Medvedev."

Rugar did not appreciate the quip. Hansen was certainly not the president of the Russian Federation. Rugar cursed at him and, still holding him at gunpoint, finally answered his ringing phone: "Yes, I have him. What? You did what? Oh, no. Okay? You want me to kill him?"

Rugar lowered his phone.

"You can't kill me," Hansen told the man in a jovial tone.

"Oh, really?"

Hansen began to laugh. "Yes. My gun is empty, you fool."

In the moment it took for Rugar to look down at the weapon, Hansen was rushing away, up toward the service road, where Rugar's weapon had landed.

Rugar screamed for Hansen to halt, and Hansen

wasn't sure why he did, but he stole a look back just as Rugar fired.

The anesthetic dart struck on the neck, just below Hansen's left earlobe.

The fat Russian recoiled in surprise. "Tranquilizer?"

"See you when I wake up." Hansen grinned and collapsed to the snow. A warm wave broke over his head and traveled down into his feet. The throbbing from Rugar's beating withered away, and every other ache and pain was replaced by the strange sensation of being weightless in a dark pool, in which he saw Grim shaking her head at him.

She opened her mouth, but when she spoke, a fat Russian man's voice came out: "He's unconscious but alive. I'm going to bring him back, and I will question him."

10

SERGEI had remained behind the fuel truck and watched in shock as Bratus gunned down his colleagues, the two loading men from the chopper, and the pilots. The Russian operative was a one-man killing machine, his silenced weapon thumping, his shots expertly placed. He'd taken out Murdoch's driver, and then, almost matter-of-factly, he'd made a phone call.

Following that, he'd begun trying in vain to open the big Anvil case that now lay on the snow-swept tarmac. The locks must have had digital combinations, because he didn't bother to check the bodies for keys. At one point he rose, stepped back, and fired a round into one lock to no avail.

And then a most amazing sight: A lumberjack of a man came forward from the service road with a body slung over his shoulder. Not until he came much closer did Sergei realize that the giant was carrying Hansen.

With his pulse beginning to race, Sergei thought of heading back to the car, but he had to be sure that Hansen was dead. At least the job had been completed, if not by Sergei's hand. He wouldn't collect the money, but perhaps they'd leave Victoria alone. Who was he kidding? Nothing was certain now.

For just a moment Sergei allowed himself to feel the pain of his friend's loss. He heard Hansen assure him, "I'm your friend." He remembered their time together at the CIA, their training on "The Farm," the practical jokes and the camaraderie, the pain they'd shared in Somalia, and that time Hansen had taken him out for drinks on his birthday and treated him like a brother. . . .

With eyes beginning to burn, he shifted around the truck to get a better view. The giant in the funny little hat set Hansen's body down near one of the cars; then, as Bratus shouted, the gaint hurried over to the Anvil case. They carried the case to Bratus's car and were able to open the pass-through so they could load it between the trunk and backseat, along with Murdoch and Zhao. They transferred all the Chinese bodies from the helicopter into Murdoch's car, since Zhao had left his car at the pub and had ridden along with Bratus.

After that, the big guy picked up Hansen and headed toward one of the hangars. Meanwhile, Bratus stood by his car and made another phone call, waiting impatiently for an answer.

Sergei frowned. The fat man was taking Hansen inside the hangar. Why? To question him? That meant Hansen might still be alive. They'd knocked him out? How? And why would they remain here, at the scene of multiple murders, to question a spy they'd captured? Why not take him someplace else? Maybe they didn't feel rushed. Maybe this was all planned from the beginning.

Sergei waited a moment more; then he darted away from the fuel truck toward the back of the hangar. He found the rear service door locked, of course, but he always carried his picking tools, and within a few breaths the knob turned freely.

Wincing, he carefully opened the door and slipped, save for a slight gust of wind, soundlessly inside. He now crouched behind a pair of helicopters, small ones reserved mostly for business travel. Nearby was a wall of mechanics' stations with power and air tools cluttering the benches. A pair of rolling carts with stacks of drawers sat beside one bird, and Sergei took up a position behind the taller cart while the fat man switched on a light near another station on the opposite side of the hangar. Once more he set down Hansen's body. Then he went into a small adjoining office and returned with a wooden chair. He propped Hansen on the chair and proceeded to flex-cuff him to it. That the fat man walked around with flex-cuffs in his pocket said a lot about his line of work.

He grabbed Hansen by the hair, stared into his face, then grumbled something and let Hansen's head drop. He began searching Hansen's pockets and weapons belt, along with the pack, which he'd removed before setting him down. After the fat man moved the gear to a nearby table, he grabbed Hansen's wrist, studied the OPSAT, whose touch screen remained dark, then decided to remove the device and toss it down with the other stuff.

Just then Hansen began to stir, his head lolling from right to left, and suddenly the fat man smacked him across the face. "Wake up! Wake up!"

Slowly Hansen lifted his head, glancing vaguely, and that was when the fat man reared back and delivered a solid blow to the jaw. Sergei flinched and glanced away for a moment, even as the Russian let loose another fist.

Then the bastard went over to the table, took something, and returned.

A blade sprang to life in his hand.

Sergei wasn't sure he could watch any more of

this. In his mind's eye, he saw Hansen's severed fingers dropping to the floor . . . then an ear . . . another ear . . . and shrieks of agony from his old friend.

"We know why you've come," growled the fat man. "Now, if you tell me what I need to know, you will live."

Like Sergei, Hansen had been trained on how to steel himself against torture, but you never really knew how you'd react until it was real. Would Hansen really hold it?

And then Sergei wondered why he was crouched there, just watching. Why hadn't he already reacted? Would he let the fat man kill Hansen? Why not? Wasn't it easier that way? But then, what about Victoria? He needed to ensure that she would not be harmed, and all he had left was the mission.

"You won't break me." Hansen gasped.

The fat man grinned and leaned over to stare directly into Hansen's eyes. "It's going to be a long night for both of us."

I don't think so, thought Sergei.

AMES was at a precipice between sheer panic and utter violence. The bile was already gathering at the back of his throat, and he clutched his binoculars with a white-knuckled grip.

Then—as if watching Bratus kill everyone wasn't

enough, as if the universe had a personal vendetta against him, one Allen Ames, Third Echelon operative and NSA mole—someone from somewhere took a shot at the Russian operative, who'd been standing by his car, on the phone.

Bratus's head snapped back like a PEZ dispenser, and he dropped out of sight behind his car.

Trembling and swearing aloud, Ames scanned the area. He searched the low-lying forest, the ditches, the hangar areas, and all along the service road.

It was as though the bullet had been fired by an apparition that had dematerialized into the night.

Now everyone—save Bratus's fat driver, Hansen, and Sergei—was dead. Ames thought of that Anvil case inside Bratus's car. If he could recover it . . . But there was a shooter out there.

As much as he hated the decision, Ames knew what he had to do. Nothing. Except watch.

SERGEI slid from behind the tool cart, took aim at the fat man, and fired a single suppressed round into the back of the man's head.

As the Russian fell forward, Sergei sighed and shrank behind the cart, just breathing and wondering if he could go through with the rest.

And then, for just a few seconds, his hackles rose and he sensed that someone else was inside the hangar.

He craned his neck, shot glances toward the big doors, the office, and all along the workstations. The shadows seemed to come alive as his paranoia grew, and he imagined a man dressed all in black and wearing tri-focal goggles. He leapt down from an impossibly high rafter, stood before Sergei, and tore off his goggles.

It was Hansen, who took a deep breath and said, *"Don't kill me."*

Sergei ground his teeth, shuddered off the image, then reached into his breast pocket and dug out a cigarette. He placed it between his lips, stood, and moved around the cart.

Hansen had dug himself out from beneath the fat Russian and was lying there, asking questions.

Sergei barely heard the man. He grabbed his lighter, lit his cigarette, and took a long drag.

They talked, and it was a like dream, the words floating on currents of blood that wound their way through a dark forest at the end of which lay Victoria, on a stone altar, her hands folded over her chest, her skin alabaster white to match her diaphanous dress, which fell in great waves across the mossy earth.

Sergei took a deep breath and stared through the image and finally saw Hansen. There was so much he wanted to tell the man, but he feared that if he turned his apology into a speech, by the time he finished, his pistol would be back on his belt and he'd be helping Hansen off the floor.

All Sergei really wanted to do was thank Hansen for what he'd done in the past, for his unconditional friendship, for his belief that Sergei, despite his failures, could still make something of his life. Even Sergei's own father did not believe in him the way Hansen had.

Hansen deserved the truth. At the very least. Sergei apologized and added, "They sent me to kill you."

That was all he wanted to say.

But Hansen demanded the details, so without hesitation he supplied them. And again, he wanted to say so much more, to somehow justify what he was doing, but there were no words that could ever do that. All he could say was, "I didn't want to see you suffer."

When he showed Hansen the camera, his old friend cursed at him, and that was all right. That was natural. And that helped, didn't it? It was better if the man hated him.

Sergei had been thinking about how they'd been trained to deal with torture, and now he would use the same methods to steel himself against the killing of a friend.

He was now a being of cold flesh and function.

Action. Reaction.

There was the camera, the tiny screen with its crystal-clear image of Hansen lying on the floor, glowering at him, but there were no emotions now, just the camera in one hand, the gun in the other, the cigarette dangling from his lips.

"You see, he is alive," Sergei began for his audience of NSA thugs. "And now—"

A sharp pain woke deep inside his head, and for a heartbeat he thought he was falling forward, the world tipping on its side and framed in darkness.

He didn't feel the concrete, but he sensed he was on it and realized with a curious resignation that he'd been shot, that he wouldn't have to worry about forgiveness or about them killing Victoria or about a career or about anything else except what lay out there, waiting for him. . . .

11

HANSEN had braced himself for death. He'd always imagined that if he were captured, he would use his last breath to curse his enemy and never, ever be broken. It was one of those grand dramatic moments in his mind's eye, brought fully to life by his inflated ego and his arrogance.

And, yes, at that second when he knew Sergei would not change his mind, that his buddy from the CIA would not only kill him but record the act for his bosses, Hansen had fulfilled that promise and taken the starring role in the climax of his life. He had cursed at Sergei, yes, but his thoughts had not focused with rage on what was happening. He could only ask two questions: Was it going to hurt? And was there something more beyond this life?

The questions hung before him even as he faced the ugly truth that his own runner had been blackmailed into turning against him, and that his death wasn't going to be glorious or noble or memorable . . . just pathetic.

Then came another improbable turn of events as Sergei himself was taken out by a shooter so stealthy that Hansen had wondered if the shot had come from some higher power. His father would attribute the miracle to the "visitors" who'd always been here among us. No, a little green man or a "gray" had not saved Hansen. The bullet and the blood had been real, and while the shooter was seemingly incorporeal and godlike, those facts remained.

Hansen did a quick search of the hangar but came up empty. His savior must've had a very good reason for concealing his identity, and that was already driving him mad with curiosity. As he frantically gathered up his gear, his neck felt warm, and he swung around and screamed again, "Who are you?"

His voice echoed off the metal walls.

It occurred to him only then—and he would later attribute the oversight to the pummeling he'd received from Rugar—that he hadn't checked outside to be fully aware of his current situation. He rushed to the front door, eased it open, and peered out.

He saw the cars, and then . . . there was Bratus's body lying supine and draped in snow.

Hansen ducked back inside and glanced at Sergei, whose head was turned to one side, his eyes as vacant as a mannequin's. Swallowing back the bile creeping up his throat, Hansen rifled through his old friend's pockets and found Sergei's satellite phone, but, of course, it was password protected. He pocketed it anyway. He removed Sergei's OPSAT, pressed the dead man's thumb to the screen, and saw that it was still being jammed like his own. He then went to Rugar and took the fat man's wallet and smart phone. Curiously, when he opened the Russian's phone and tried to pull up numbers, the address book and call logs had been erased.

Outside, a car engine sputtered, and Hansen darted to the door, cracked it open, and watched as Bratus's sedan took off, the tires spinning out and kicking up rooster tails of snow.

Hansen thought of his SC pistol, but he knew by the time he loaded another V-TRAC round, the driver would already be gone. He whirled back toward the bodies, to Sergei. *Time to go.*

AMES was still crouched along the tree line, shuddering with indecision as he stared through his binoculars. From his angle, he'd been unable to see who'd climbed behind the wheel of Bratus's car. With a start, he burst from his position and ran through the snow, back toward Sergei's car. He jumped in, turned the key, and nothing. Not a sound.

He popped the hood, climbed out, and saw that the battery cables, the spark plug wires, and a half dozen other hoses had been cut. He'd been careful to lock all the car doors. The saboteur was a chillingly efficient professional. Ames wasn't going anywhere . . . but the man in Bratus's car sure as hell was on his way.

Ames rushed back through the woods. Other than the fuel truck, there was one car left at the airport: Murdoch's. Never mind that it was loaded with murdered Chinese pilots and crewmen, a dead Russian chauffeur, and that its driver's-side window had been shot out; it was still the best ride in town.

Still wearing his balaclava, he was about to sprint toward the airport when he spotted a side door on the hangar swinging open. He dropped down, lifted his binoculars, and zoomed in to full power. It was Hansen, who ran to Murdoch's car, stuck his head inside through the shattered window, then returned to the hangar.

HANSEN had thrown Sergei's body over his shoulder and was ready to get going in Murdoch's car. That the keys were still in the ignition was the night's second miracle—if anyone was keeping score. Still, he'd glanced longingly at the chopper, which could whisk him out of there in mere seconds.

While Hansen had his fixed-wing pilot's license, he'd not yet added the helicopter category and class to his certificate—which at the moment was just Murphy's Law kneeing him in the groin.

He set down Sergei near the car and, wearing his gloves, began dragging the bodies of the Chinese guys out onto the tarmac. Next was Murdoch's driver, who'd bled all over the front seat.

Hansen gritted his teeth as he slid the man out; then he opened the back door, lifted Sergei, and set him down on the seat. He'd wrapped Sergei's head in an oily rag so he wouldn't have to see the gaping wound.

He was about to hop into the front seat when something thudded on one of the hangar's tall main doors. He saw it there, in the snow . . . his spy plane. It had been forced down, either by the wind or by Grim, who might've somehow regained control of it. At any rate, the little COM-BAT was there and Hansen ran over and fetched it, then returned to the car. The only other loose end was the dart that Rugar must have pulled from his neck, and Hansen had not seen it inside the hangar.

Leaving piles of bodies in his wake—the antithesis

of what a Splinter Cell ought to be doing—he took off.

In the final analysis, the mission was a colossal failure. Sure, he had confirmed that Kovac was linked to Murdoch, Bratus, and Zhao, but now with all of them dead and a massacre at the airport, the people tied to them would sever those gossamers and shrink back into hiding. Whatever they'd been doing, whatever their deal was, might never be known . . . unless whoever had stolen Bratus's car was working for the NSA or another intelligence organization that would tip off Grim. But why would that operative's identity and operation be kept secret from Hansen? Had he been tailed and watched? Was all of this part of some elaborate test?

All he could do was shake his head and try to control his breathing. He caught a glance of himself in the rearview mirror and wished he hadn't. His eye had become a plum, and he kept tonguing his loosened molar. Oh, sure, he'd be keeping a low profile now— the guy who looked as if he'd just come from a barroom brawl. He needed to get in touch with Grim. He needed an escape plan. With his OPSAT still jammed, he couldn't even transmit the code word "Skyfall" to tell her he was in escape-and-evasion mode. So here he was, driving through a blinding snowstorm with the body of his friend in the backseat. This was what he had wanted, what he had studied so hard for; here it all was, the glory and the excitement and the unending challenge of becoming one of the world's most elite field operatives.

His good eye welled with tears. And just as he was about to rage aloud, his OPSAT beeped.

< < SIGNAL REESTABLISHED > >

A slight crackle came through his subdermal, and then . . . "Ben, it's me. Are you there?"

"Here, Grim."

"You must be out of range of the jammer now."

"I guess so."

"Are you all right?"

"Sergei's dead. . . . Everyone's dead. Something happened. Bratus shot everyone. Then someone got to him."

"We know. Just glad you're all right. You did well, Ben. You got us what we need."

"If you say so. I need to get the hell out of here."

"Just hang in there. We'll help get you and Sergei's body out of the country. All we need right now is for you to stay on the road and get back to Vladivostok. I'll set up a rendezvous point for you."

"Roger that. Someone took off in Bratus's car."

"We know. We're tracking him now."

"There's an Anvil case in that car. I don't know what's inside. Zhao and Murdoch are in there, too."

"All right. You just concentrate on the road. That weather looks horrible."

"You saw the car leave?"

"We did."

"Even with this weather?"

"Ben, our birds in the sky are a lot more powerful than you know. Trust me."

But he didn't. She knew a hell of a lot more than she was telling him, but he was too intimidated to call her on it. He wanted to tell her about the phantom shooter, but he doubted she'd be surprised. Maybe she'd assigned someone to babysit him, someone who had driven off in that car, which was why all she cared about was getting him home with Sergei's body, tying up one final loose end. Maybe she'd known Sergei was a traitor all along.

Well, Anna Grimsdóttir wasn't so sexy anymore. She was cool and cunning and made him feel insignificant, a pawn in her much larger game. But what had he expected? And now he knew firsthand why most operatives guard their emotions. To do otherwise would get you killed. There was only the immediacy of the mission, the task at hand, and your loyalty to your country. To think you were any more important than that was kidding yourself. He glanced back at Sergei and sighed in grief.

With the wipers thumping fast across the windshield, Hansen now leaned toward the wheel and squinted through the chutes of falling snow. He'd slipped on his trifocals, but even with night vision his visibility was down to just a few meters, and the snow kept on coming.

As he neared the petrol station, he slowed to get the tag number from a car parked under the awning; then he drove on.

AMES figured he'd pick his way into the fuel truck and drive it back to the petrol station, where he'd switch to his rental car. As he got to work on the truck's door, he began to craft the elaborate lie he would feed to Kovac like a T-bone with all the trimmings. But once news of the massacre reached Kovac's desk, Ames had better be well into a mission for Third Echelon or far away from the man. He could already hear himself saying, "But it's not my fault. Either Third Echelon was on to us or someone else was. Maybe Zhao. Maybe Bratus. Maybe even that arrogant bastard Murdoch."

Wincing over these thoughts, Ames finally got the door open, but it took him nearly ten more minutes before he got the truck started. Oh, he was a hell of a lot better with a sniper's rifle, that was for sure, and the delay was pretty damned embarrassing, but only he would know about it. He threw the old heap in gear and lumbered through nearly a foot of snow that had fallen since they'd arrived.

With one broken wiper blade, he headed out to the petrol station, where he found that the locks on his rental car had also been picked, the wires cut. He raged aloud and got back in the truck.

He drove for about fifteen minutes before he realized that the fuel truck he was driving was about to run out of fuel. The truck sputtered to a halt halfway back to Vladivostok. Ames sat there and finally, reluctantly, got on his satellite phone and called the NSA for help.

— *12* —————————————

HANSEN was met at the rental car agency by a scholarly looking, leather-faced man who introduced himself as Fedosky. He took possession of the car and Sergei's body; then another man half Fedosky's age pulled up in a black Mercedes.

"Get in."

"Where am I going?" Hansen asked in Russian.

The young punker with a pierced nose raked his fingers through his spiked hair and answered, "The airport. Now shut up. No more questions."

Hansen climbed into the front seat, and the punk floored it. The international airport was about an hour's drive from the city, and the punk navigated through the snowstorm, scowling in silence. While Hansen sat there, knowing he'd probably have to wait till morning to fly out, the mission returned in vivid detail. He even flinched as Rugar's fist came down. The Blu-ray player in his head was caught in a loop, and shutting his eyes only made things worse.

Grim would want to know what happened after Hansen was taken inside the hangar. She would want to know how he'd escaped. He would either reveal the presence of the phantom shooter or not. If Grim already knew about the shooter and he failed to say anything, she'd know he was holding out.

But if she was ignorant in that regard, he could construct the story of his escape. Omitting details to further his career was not a morally sound choice, but maybe there was a way to avoid lying. He realized he would have to feel out Grim, learn exactly how much she knew, before he shared the details of his interrogation by Rugar. Perhaps he could get Grim to admit that another field operative had been assigned to the mission, that she hadn't really taken a chance on him, and then he could be honest with her.

Or . . . he could be entirely wrong about all of it. The shooter could be someone completely unexpected, a wildcard from another agency, who'd done Hansen a favor while still accomplishing his own mission to secure whatever was inside that Anvil case. If that was what had really happened, then Hansen was staring at the same fork in the road: Tell Grim he'd been saved . . . or tell her he'd saved himself.

NSA HEADQUARTERS
FORT MEADE, MARYLAND

THREE days later Hansen was sitting inside the situation room with Grim. He'd told her he was ready to talk the moment he'd stepped off the plane in Baltimore, but she'd insisted that he receive a complete physical exam and get a day's worth of bed rest. The X-rays revealed no permanent damage, and his eye, though still purple, was far less swollen.

"Before we begin, I assure you, Ben, that we're very happy with the work you did. No plan survives the first enemy contact, right? You were able to improvise. Now we know Kovac is watching us. We know he got to Sergei. And we know he had some kind of relationship with Bratus and Zhao and that there's a list of names."

"Who drove off in Bratus's car? You said you were tracking it."

"We were, but we lost it. And we don't know."

He stared at her. "You lost it?"

She returned his gaze. "That's right. The weather finally cut us off."

"Any leads? Speculation?"

"A few, but I can't comment at this time."

Hansen thought for a moment. "Can I ask you a question?"

She frowned. "Sure."

"Was I really working alone? I mean, just Sergei and me out there? No one else?"

Without hesitation she said, "I sent you out there myself. One agent, one runner. Why do you ask?"

He averted his gaze. She had not flinched, and her voice had not wavered. They could hook her up to a polygraph and the needle wouldn't budge. She was either the most proficient liar he'd ever met or she really didn't know.

He blurted out, "I was in the hangar. Rugar was going to torture me. I wouldn't have broken. I know that. But Sergei was there, and he shot Rugar. And then . . . he was going to shoot me."

She set down her cup of coffee. "But you took him out."

"I was lying on the floor with my hands cuffed behind my back."

"What're you saying?"

He closed his eyes and he was back there, squinting toward the shadows, the cold rafters, the long seams in the metal ceiling. "Someone shot Sergei and left me there. I think that same person took off in Bratus's car."

The tension in Hansen's chest began to loosen, and he finally opened his eyes and looked at her.

She'd removed her glasses, and her gaze had gone distant. "Oh, my God . . ." she muttered.

"What?"

"Nothing."

"And I'm going to sit here and let you tell me nothing?"

She sighed. "I can't say much more."

"You know who it was."

"I can't confirm that."

Hansen leaned toward her. "But you have an idea. Did you send someone to babysit me? Yes or no?"

"I told you no. And you'd best watch that tone."

He huffed. "Sorry. And if I can still ask . . . Did we get anything from the phones or that tag number?"

"They've wiped clean any traces. You shouldn't expect anything less."

"I guess not."

She took a long breath, then said, "I'm putting together a squad."

"Squad?" He'd uttered the word as though he'd never heard it before.

"Five field operatives, all new recruits, and you've earned your place as the team lead."

"Are you trying to change the subject?"

"I'm not trying, Ben. This is my meeting."

He nodded. "Okay, but one more thing. About Sergei. His body got back here okay? He'll get a proper funeral? Family notified?"

"It's all been taken care of. Kovac used him, Ben. He knew Sergei was vulnerable, and he used him. I feel terrible about that, and even more concerned about our current operations."

"So . . . you've decided to build a team? Wouldn't a group pose a greater security risk?"

"Or would a team be even more proficient than a single operator?"

"Depends on the situation."

"Exactly. And, you know, you never work alone. You always have a runner, you have us, you have eyes in the sky, watching."

"It's a test, isn't it? A test to see if the new guys have what it takes. I just told you that someone bailed me out of my mission, and now you're giving me team lead."

"Someone helped you evacuate. That's all. You got the information. You earned the spot."

"I'm not sure I want it."

Her frown deepened. "Are you kidding me?"

"Who are these people? I don't even know them. We've been training alone. And now I'm supposed to trust my life to them?"

"You'll start training together."

"I've been out there alone. I'm ready."

"You are. But I still want you to play nice with others."

"Do we at least get a cool code name?"

"It was randomly generated."

Hansen rolled his eyes. "What is it? Lard Barrel? Cow Dung?"

She almost smiled. "Delta Sly."

Hansen repeated the name. "Not too bad. And there's no significance?"

She shook her head.

The door behind them suddenly opened and a rather short, clean-cut man with dark eyes and a deep tan that looked more manufactured than natural strode into the room.

"Hi, Grim. Sorry I'm late."

Hansen rose from the table and turned to their visitor.

"Ben, let me introduce you to one of your new teammates," Grim began. "This is Allen Ames."

Ames beamed at Hansen. "Hi, Ben. Nice to meet you."

— *13* —————————

AFTER returning from the mission in Houston, Hansen was accosted at the Baltimore-Washington International Airport by a pear-shaped man in his fifties wearing shorts, Birkenstocks, and a Hawaiian shirt emblazoned with purple parrots and palm trees. The guy had a camera case strung around his neck and a thick beard encrusted with pieces of his lunch (a thick sandwich, probably). He squinted through a pair of Harry Potter glasses and asked, "Are you Matthew Pine?"

Hansen froze. That was his alias for the work in Texas. "Who's asking?"

"If you'll come with me, Mr. Pine?"

"You have to talk sexier than that."

The fat man sighed, then spoke in an agitated sing-song. "I don't have time for this. I was told to pick you up. If you won't come, I'll have to call my boss."

"Let me call mine." Hansen tried to hail Grim on his OPSAT. No response. He whirled back to the man, who was speaking rapidly on a cell phone. "Who are you?"

The big guy flashed an ID: NSA. Then he ended his call.

"Great," Hansen said through a sigh. "Am I under arrest or something?"

"Not technically."

"But technically I have to go with you."

"Technically, yes."

"Do you think you can outrun me?"

"Dude, come on. I'm a fat bastard. Don't make my life miserable. Just come along and play nice."

"Where are we going? Back to Hawaii?"

"Someplace out in the 'burbs. That's all I know."

"How long's the drive?"

"Not long."

"Not much of a detail-oriented guy, are you?"

He snorted. "You sound like my wife."

"You got an iPod?"

"Yeah."

"You got any AC/DC?"

The fat man grinned.

THEY arrived at a small, one-story house on a narrow street lined by old oak trees and warped telephone poles. A late-model SUV was parked in the driveway. This was typical middle-class America, about as non-descript as you could get. The front lawns were beginning to turn green from their long winter brown, and the ticking of a sprinkler sounded in the distance. Two black boys, about seven or eight, were standing on the driveway and shooting each other with water rifles that resembled antitank guided missile launchers.

"This is it," said Hansen's well-dressed NSA taxi driver.

Hansen shook his head. "What am I doing here?"

The man rapped a knuckle on the GPS unit mounted on his windshield. "Look, bro. This is where they told me to bring you. You mind getting out? I'm sure they got some pizzas they want me to pick up."

Hansen sighed, grabbed his small carry-on bag, and climbed out of the car. As soon as he slammed the door, the driver floored it, leaving a trail of sarcasm and echoing AC/DC in his wake.

With a deepening frown, Hansen started up the driveway, breathing in the sweet scent of hamburgers grilling on a barbecue from the house next door. One of the boys looked at him, wriggled his brows, then shot Hansen in the face with his water rifle.

"Hey!" Hansen cried, blinking through the incoming fire.

"Tyler! James! I told you to stay in the backyard," came a voice from the front door.

Hansen met the gaze of a young black woman, about thirty-five, wearing expensive business attire and alternating her gaze between him and the smart phone in her hand.

He was about to open his mouth when she added, "Come on. They're waiting for you in the basement."

"Okay . . ." Hansen started forward and asked, "Am I supposed to introduce myself?"

She made a face. "No one else did." She led him through the modestly decorated living room and toward a door adjacent to the kitchen. Hansen descended the narrow wooden staircase, reached the bottom, and turned to face the rest of his team, who were sitting in metal folding chairs arranged in a semicircle.

Standing before the group was a bald black man with a gray goatee. His muscular chest tented up a black silk shirt unbuttoned to reveal the requisite bling around his neck. His expensive pants looked cut by a tailor, and his matching shoes were shined to a rich gloss. He also sported a large gold class ring on his left pinky. He could easily be mistaken for a retired NBA star, and when he looked at Hansen, it was with an eerie fire in his eyes, the way you'd look at someone you planned to kill.

He spoke loudly, aggressively, establishing within the first sentence who was in charge: "Well, it's nice of you to join us, cowboy. There's a cooler over there with sodas. Grab yourself one and take a seat."

Hansen glanced incredulously at the others, who simply shrugged and returned his frown. They each had a soda and a seat, but Hansen wasn't quite ready for either. "Uh, excuse me, but who are you?"

"My name is Louis Moreau. Most people around 3E call me Marty. You'll call me Mr. Moreau. I'm your new technical operations manager, basically taking Grim's old job and kicking it up a notch."

"Where's Grim?"

"Couldn't make it."

"You got ID?"

Moreau began to chuckle. "Get your soda and sit down."

"I'm not thirsty."

Moreau crossed the room. Hansen hadn't quite realized that the man was a full head taller than him, and he seemed to grow wider as he drew near. "The only tough guy in the room is me. Mad Dog Moreau. Get over it. Get a chair."

Hansen rolled his eyes and complied. He flicked his glance to the pipes spanning the ceiling, the cinder-block walls, the laundry piled on the washer and dryer. "Nice basement. You got, like, a secret panel where you keep all the high-tech crap?"

"It's just a basement. And you can thank my sister for opening up her house to us. Now, I know you have a lot of questions. But most of them I won't answer, so just forget about those."

Valentina threw back her blond hair and snickered.

Ames raised his hand. "Uh, sir, I don't have a question, just a comment. You're an asshole."

Moreau widened his eyes in disbelief, narrowed them into a glower, then broke into a broad grin. "I like you, Brooklyn. I like that large attitude. Helps compensate, you know?"

"So that's how we get on your good side?" asked Gillespie, sipping her Coke. "We insult you?"

"You get on my good side, Ms. Longstocking, by doing your job."

"What did you call me?"

"Oh, I forgot—you guys aren't even thirty. When you're bored or drunk sometime, look up Pippi Longstocking. You'll have fun. Now I want to talk about Houston."

Everyone groaned.

"Sir?" began Noboru.

"You *don't* have a question, do you, Bruce?"

"Uh, no, sir. Uh, my name is Nathan."

"No, you're Bruce Lee. Deal with it. Now, what do you want to say?"

"Um, nothing, sir."

Moreau moved over to Noboru and leaned down. "Speak."

"Sir, I just wanted to say that—"

"What, that you're honored to be here? That the United States of America has become your new home? That what happened in Houston wasn't your fault?"

Noboru thought for a moment. "That's right, sir."

"Good. Very good, Bruce. Now we can move on."

Valentina rose from her chair. "This is ridiculous. Are you going to conduct a meeting or entertain yourself by giving us nicknames? And God help you, if you give me one . . ."

Ames leaned forward and grinned at Hansen.

"Take a seat, Ms. Valentina, before I assign you a nickname you'll regret." Moreau faced the group. "So . . . excellent job in Houston."

Ames nearly spit out his soda. "Excuse me, sir, but this morning I went online to see how I'm supposed to file for unemployment—and you're telling me good job?"

"Leonard's dead. His data was destroyed in the house fire. We've confirmed that. In trying to kill him, the Chinese destroyed their prize."

"Who tipped them off?" asked Valentina.

"We're working on that."

Valentina shook her head in disgust. "I don't like leaks that I can't control."

"Me neither," said Ames. "I scanned the perimeter for heat signatures at least ten times. And suddenly I've got a shooter. What's up with that?"

Moreau took a deep breath. "If every operation went according to plan, none of us would be here. Third Echelon wouldn't exist. So 'what's up with that' is the unexpected. And we like that. It keeps us in business."

"We were hoping to retrieve the data and arrest Leonard for selling secrets to the Chinese," said Hansen. "We failed on both accounts. You call that a good job? Hell, I'd like to see what you call a screwup."

"The data didn't fall into the hands of the Chinese. That's all that matters right now. And Leonard's ties to Russia have also been severed. It began with Murdoch, Bratus, and Zhao, Mr. Hansen, and it may have ended with Leonard. Be proud of the work you've done so far."

"If you say so."

"I know so." Moreau took a deep breath. "Boys

and girls, I've been with the NSA longer than you've been alive, so you'll have to accept my apologies in advance."

"Why is that, sir?" asked Hansen.

"Because I have no patience and even less tolerance for inefficiency. God, young man, is in the details. And that's where I come in. I will speak. You will listen. You will learn. You will act on my information. You will not fail. Now, excuse me for a moment." Moreau crossed to another chair, picked up his laptop, and took a seat, balancing the computer on his knees.

Meanwhile, Valentina leaned over to Hansen and lowered her voice. "Grim had to do major damage control in Houston, and we're getting pats on the back?"

"Maybe they're sweetening us up to feed us to the wolves," said Gillespie.

Ames leveled an index finger at her. "Now, that's the first intelligent thing I've heard you say, Ms. Longstocking."

"All right, people," said Moreau. "We're not just here to discuss Houston."

Hansen raised his hand. "Mr. Moreau, I know you're not answering questions, but before we go any further, could you tell us why we're in your sister's basement instead of the situation room?"

"We have reason to believe the situation room has been compromised."

"What?" cried Hansen.

"You heard me."

"So you think your sister's basement is safer? Why don't we go to Taco Bell?"

"We're clear here, cowboy. Now, purge all that white noise from your head and listen up."

Moreau turned his computer around so they could see the screen, and there, with a deep scowl lining his face, was a shaggy-haired, unshaven, all-too-familiar man.

"I was supposed to debrief you folks and get you set up for another operation in Pakistan, but it seems Mr. Sam Fisher has changed those plans. He's just surfaced in Reims. If I'd received this information sooner, we'd be at the airport already."

"Fisher's in Reims. So what? Alert Interpol," said Valentina.

"That's already happened, but we like to take care of our own problems, thank you," snapped Moreau.

"So Fisher's where?" asked Ames.

"He's in Reims. It's in France, idiot," said Gillespie.

"What the hell's he doing there?" Ames continued, ignoring Gillespie's barb.

Moreau shrugged. "You're flying out today. And let me remind you: Fisher is *not* a Splinter Cell. He's a traitor and a murderer. He killed Irving Lambert, a good friend of mine and your former boss."

"No," cried Gillespie. "I know Sam. There's more to it than that."

"I agree," said Ames. "I've never doubted for one minute that Sam was anything but loyal to us. If he killed Lambert, then maybe Lambert was the traitor!"

Moreau raised his own voice. "Sam Fisher tried to bring down Third Echelon. As a consequence, you people are going over there, and he's coming back in cuffs or a body bag."

"Sir, to be clear, we have orders to shoot to kill if necessary?" Hansen asked.

"What did I just say, cowboy? Cuffs or body bag."

Noboru raised his hand. "Uh, excuse me, sir? Why are you sending us?"

Hansen snorted and answered before Moreau could. "Because we're the best."

"Some of us," corrected Ames.

"I was not privy to the selection process," said Moreau. "And to be fair, no, I wouldn't have selected you rookies to go after somebody like Sam Fisher. I told Grim it's like sending hamsters after a rattlesnake."

"Oh, my God, did you just say that?" asked Gillespie as the others swore and hissed.

"You don't like that comparison, Pippi? Prove me wrong. Now, we'll finish this up on the way to the airport." Moreau consulted his watch. "The van should be here any minute."

"Didn't we just get off a plane?" asked Valentina, sighing in disgust.

"Look on the bright side, sweetheart. You're going to France," said Ames. "You can go shopping and get your nails done."

"And when my nails are done, I can use them to reach into your chest and rip out your still-beating heart."

"I was going to say you could scratch my back while we—"

"In your pathetic dreams."

Ames wore a mock-wounded expression. "Why are you so mean to me?"

Valentina raised a perfectly tweezed brow. "Because when I was a kid, you were that boy who pulled my ponytail all through school."

"I think you like me. I think you're struggling with that. You're afraid to admit it. Don't be afraid, Maya. Don't be afraid."

"Ben, can you shut him up?"

Hansen waved them off and started up the stairs. In his mind's eye he saw himself putting a gun to Sam Fisher's head.

"Why did you kill Lambert?"

"It's complicated."

"I see. They want me to bring you in."

"I can't let that happen."

"Then I'm sorry." Hansen pulled the trigger.

Fisher crashed to the ground, lying faceup, and began bleeding all over the pavement.

With the hot sun on the back of his neck, Hansen shifted over Fisher's body, his shadow passing over Fisher's face, the eyes glowing, a third equally bright eye appearing on Fisher's forehead as his mouth moved and he gasped out, *"Ben, I need to tell you something. . . ."*

14

THE Cessna Citation X, the fastest civilian aircraft in the sky, swept over the Atlantic Ocean at six hundred plus miles per hour, climbing to a cruising altitude of some forty-five thousand feet.

Maya Valentina leaned back in her well-padded chair and sipped once more from her glass of champagne. Some bubbly was the least they could do. Since joining Third Echelon, she'd logged as many hours aboard aircraft as the average commercial airline pilot. Well, that was probably an exaggeration, but she was beginning to feel a constant state of lag taking hold beneath her eyes.

She glanced over at the black ash burl panels beside her seat and ran her fingers across the smooth, polished surface. She knew a lot about wood because of her father. He was a framer, trim carpenter, cabinet maker, and amateur knife maker in their hometown of Geneva, Florida. Her dad's grandfather had been a wood carver in Sicily and had come to the United States in the early 1900s to find work in New York City as a piano maker. The family had eventually moved down to Florida, and her father continued practicing the family trade of woodcraft.

Valentina had been raised in a farmhouse built in the 1860s and nestled on ten acres that bordered state-owned lands. With all that room to roam, she and her four brothers spent their summers exploring the woods and creeks. She had been on a path to becoming a typical tomboy and could hunt, fish, and shoot with the best of them, but she was still attracted to fashion and makeup and all those things that made her feel like a girl. The colorful dresses she wore to Sunday-morning mass were some of her favorite clothes, and her mother had made sure that she had access to all of those feminine things and told her that, no, she was not just one of the boys, despite being outnumbered. Once she entered high school, she shed the last of her tomboy roots, and her mother taught her how to apply makeup and add highlights to her hair. Much to her father's chagrin, the boys noticed . . . in droves. Her dad liked to show her dates his gun and knife collections, not because he was trying to threaten them, but because he was always trying to sell a piece or two. She had to yell at him for trying to solicit her friends.

What troubled her most, though, was the stereotypical dismissal given to her by her peers when she'd attended Rollins College to get a degree in political science with an aim toward doing something in the government. Her colleagues couldn't wrap their heads around the fact that a woman with her looks wanted to do something with her brains instead of her boobs. Her own roommate told her, "You're either a beauty or a geek. Don't try to be both. You could get a job as a stripper and make more in a few months than you'll make in a year as a lawyer."

There were darker days when she'd stand in front of the mirror, put a knife to her cheek, and wonder what the scar would look like, how it might change their perception of her. She'd trace a line down from the corner of her eye, across her cheek, then wind it down beneath her chin. Yet the scar would just draw pity, and they still wouldn't see her as smart. The dumb-blond jokes would keep coming. What do you call a dead blonde in a closet? The 1986 hide-and-seek world champion. Hilarious. The injustice of that stereotype annoyed her so much that she'd developed a rant she'd often unleash on her dates.

All of which underscored the fact that when Hansen told her to go into Leonard's office and seduce him, she'd died a little more inside. The degree from Rollins meant nothing. The three years she'd spent at the NSA as an intelligence analyst—demonstrating her understanding of world history, geography, and the social, economic, and political events that affected global change—were a waste of time. That she had been recruited from her desk job by Irving Lambert himself and somehow survived the Third Echelon training program didn't mean a goddamned thing.

She was a pair of boobs and legs.

Why couldn't she get past that? Just use her looks to her advantage, allow men to let down their guards as they dreamed of doing likewise with their flies. Why would they take her seriously only when she had a pistol jammed into their temples? Oh, yes, they were shocked that the dumb blonde, the piece of ass, was a whole lot smarter than they'd thought, so smart, in fact, that they would now lose their lives to her, and she wouldn't give them a second thought because, like all the rest, they couldn't see past the flesh. *Damn it,* she had to stop letting that bother her. She needed to empower herself. But how was she supposed to do that when it was all about the team now? You couldn't just throw an "I" in front of "team" and get some trendy word that meant she was suddenly more important than the rest and should take credit and be recognized as a highly intelligent woman. . . .

Was she bitter? Oh, God, don't get her started.

Valentina looked down and realized she was clutching her armrest. She took a deep breath, then finished the rest of her champagne in one gulp.

To accommodate onboard meetings, the seats were arranged in pairs and facing one another. She sat beside Hansen, and they faced Ames and Noboru, both of whom were scanning maps on their laptops. Gillespie had opted to take a seat behind them but had turned around and pushed up on her knees like a curious kid in coach staring over the top of her seat at the people behind her.

On the way to the airport, Moreau had gone over the particulars: The Police municipale had received an anonymous tip that a man named François Dayreis was responsible for a brutal assault in a warehouse on the outskirts of Reims the night before. Five men had been severely beaten by a lone perpetrator, their IDs stolen. The story had made the local news and the Police nationale was now working with Interpol and the Central Directorate of Interior Intelligence, France's FBI, to apprehend the criminal. The six victims were Romain Doucet, Georges Blandin, Avent Quenten,

Pierre Allard, André Canivet, and Louis Royer. Doucet, it turned out, was a local thug and head of a gang that had intimidated his neighborhood, subsequently keeping him well stocked with alibis. However, he had nearly been implicated in the rape of a fifteen-year-old girl, and that, Moreau had said, took him to an even deeper level of hell. That Dayreis had pounded the crap out of these thugs was vigilante justice, no doubt.

That François Dayreis was a known alias of Sam Fisher's had everyone at Third Echelon on the edges of their seats. Consequently, Delta Sly had some things to do and people to see.

Since IDs had been stolen, Moreau had consulted a list of high-end forgers known to Third Echelon, and the name Abelard Boutin was not only at the top of that list but his apartment was located not far from the incident.

"I have a few ideas on how to set up overwatch outside Boutin's place," said Ames, glancing up from his computer.

"Can I stop you right there?" said Gillespie from her perch behind the seat. "If Sam went to see the forger, then he did so deliberately. He doesn't make mistakes like that."

"Oh, and you're the Sam Fisher expert because he spent, what, about two weeks of his life training you?" asked Ames. "The guy's getting old . . . and he's old school. He's stressed out. He'll make mistakes."

"Sam Fisher, stressed out? Are we talking about the same Sam Fisher, the guy who also trained you?"

"The world's changed. Sam knows that. And maybe he can't deal with it anymore."

"Wow, that's all heady and philosophical and—"

"Kim, what're you trying to say?" asked Valentina.

"I'm saying I don't like this. I'm saying that maybe Nathan was on to something when he asked Moreau why we were picked for this job. Maybe they didn't want operators with more experience because we're not supposed to capture Sam."

"Oh, don't give me that BS," said Ames. "We're new. We're unconventional. We're unpredictable. That's why we got picked."

"I have to agree with that," said Hansen. "But it does worry me that Fisher confided in Boutin and the man turned on him so quickly."

"Maybe they trusted each other, but Fisher screwed him over somehow, and he turned," said Valentina.

Hansen sighed. "That's a possibility."

"Sam went to the forger because he knew the guy would talk. He wants us to come to France," said Gillespie.

"Oh, yeah?" asked Ames. "Why? So you can sleep with him again?"

Everyone fell silent. Valentina blinked. A mental switch was thrown. And suddenly she burst from her seat and threw herself on the little bastard, wrapping her fingers around his throat. "Haven't you had enough with that mouth? Haven't you had enough!"

Hands dropped onto her shoulders and wrenched her away from Ames, who panted and cried, "I'm just getting started, baby!" He cocked a thumb over his shoulder at Gillespie. "You don't see her getting all upset. Why? Because it's a fact! Maybe we ought to get that out in the open right here!"

Gillespie lowered her gaze and shook her head. "You bastard."

Ames pushed himself up and turned to Gillespie. "They need to know—because you could compromise this mission."

"I don't want to go there," snapped Hansen. But then he glanced up at Gillespie. "But did *you* go there?"

"Tell him, Kim. We don't have a choice," said Ames. "She slept with him. She's got feelings for him."

"I don't have feelings," cried Gillespie.

"Kim, you really slept with him?" asked Valentina.

Gillespie moaned through a sigh. "I'm an idiot, okay? It was months after he trained me. He was in a bad place, and I took advantage of that. He didn't want to . . . but I . . . I just . . . I don't know what happened."

Hansen pursed his lips, thought for a moment, then swore under his breath. "When we get to Paris, Kim, you stay on the plane. You'll fly back. I'll tell Grim. We can't have you here."

"Don't do that, Ben. I'm telling you, this whole thing is bigger than we think. They put me here for a reason. . . . They put all of us here. And I'll promise you, right here and right now, that if it comes down to it, that if I have to kill him, I will. I'll do it."

"I'm unconvinced," said Ames. "Me, on the other hand, I'd whack him in a heartbeat. I never liked the bastard. He was a crappy teacher, and he's got the weirdest sense of humor."

"A team of rookies, and a woman personally involved with the target," Hansen began through a groan. "Like sending hamsters after a rattlesnake."

"I am a special-forces operator," said Noboru, his tone steely. "I am nothing else."

"We're happy for you, Bruce," said Ames. "Now, shut the hell up and let us figure out what to do with the slut back here."

This time it was Gillespie who was ready to strangle Ames, but he slipped back into his seat and said, "I'm just kidding! I'm kidding!"

Gillespie swore at him and looked to Hansen for help.

"Who's got the terrible sense of humor?" Valentina

asked Ames. "And you know something? I've been dealing with guys like you all my life. You wind up miserable and alone."

"Not really. I wind up on a private jet, with a hot blonde, drinking champagne." He winked.

Hansen hardened his voice. "Ames, I've had enough of you, too."

"I'm just here for your entertainment pleasure— since you're not here for mine."

Hansen snorted. "Show's over. Back to work. Now, we're going to go see this guy Boutin. Maybe Fisher's paid him a visit."

"Ben, if Fisher is as good as everyone says he is, he may be long gone," said Noboru. "Maybe all we can do is follow his trail. Maybe he's not even in France anymore."

"Good point. Why would he stick around?"

Valentina thought about that. "Maybe there's something he needs to do. Someone he's waiting for?"

"Like us," said Hansen. "Why do I get the feeling that we're being baited?"

"Still no word from Grim?" asked Valentina.

Hansen shook his head.

"Look, guys, stop worrying," said Ames. "Like I said before, I've got some ideas for overwatch on Boutin's place. Let's talk about those, catch a few z's, then wake up and have breakfast in Paris."

Valentina took a deep breath and folded her arms over her chest. "What makes you so confident?"

"I'm more excited than anything else," answered Ames. "We take down Fisher and we've really done something. We'll be the guys who brought in the traitor. Then his legend becomes ours. . . ."

— 15

GRAND HÔTEL TEMPLIERS
REIMS, FRANCE

THE flight to Paris took about six hours, and Reims was exactly six hours ahead of Baltimore, so while the team seemingly arrived at Paris–Charles de Gaulle International Airport at midnight their time, it was 6:21 A.M. by the local clock. Between yawns and the rubbing of red eyes, they rented a blue Opel and a green Renault and drove to the east side of Reims, to the Grand Hôtel Templiers, where the agency had already booked two rooms. The five-story hotel was on rue des Templiers, a narrow street lined on both sides by subcompact cars. The place was about a ten-minute drive from Boutin's apartment, affording them enough distance for security yet reasonable proximity to the target.

Much to Hansen's chagrin, Ames decided he was bunking with Valentina, who drove her heel into the short operative's foot, and that was the end of that. Ladies in one room, men in the other, thank you. When would that guy ever let up?

Hansen stared through the window at a courtyard whose landscape swept outward like a chessboard, its walkways cutting at right angles through perfect squares of sod and trees. The image was fitting, as the game was, indeed, afoot.

He wrung his hands and checked his watch. He and Ames decided that after breakfast they would reconnoiter Boutin's place to be sure there wasn't anything surprising they hadn't seen on the maps. They would do a hasty drive-by, as Hansen felt certain that Fisher, if he was still in Reims, would be keeping a close eye on the forger. Hansen decided, though, that they wouldn't make their move on Boutin until 11:00 P.M. at the earliest, when they could be more certain that the streets would be deserted and the forger himself had settled down for the evening.

Behind Hansen, Gillespie was munching on French toast, which she said tasted better in the States, and working her laptop's touch pad, scanning data from

Moreau—*Mr.* Moreau. They'd searched the registrations of every hotel in France for a François Dayreis, along with every other alias Fisher had ever used during his tenure at Third Echelon, and they'd come up empty. They'd also searched for the names of the victims of the warehouse assault, but it seemed Fisher hadn't used those IDs yet. If Boutin didn't know anything about Fisher's whereabouts, Hansen wasn't sure what their next move would be.

There were, however, two other leads to follow: Doucet and the warehouse.

Noboru and Valentina were already out to meet the team's runner in Reims, from whom they would pick up the gear and be outfitted for their visit to see Doucet, who'd been admitted to the Centre Hospitalier Universitaire at 45 rue Cognacq-Jay, about four kilometers southwest of the team's hotel.

Ames entered the room, car keys in hand. "You ready, chief?"

Hansen turned from the window. "Hold down the fort, Kim, all right?"

She nodded.

"And, you know, if you want, take a nap. Just leave the channel on in case I need to get you through the subdermal, all right?"

"You got it."

Hansen walked over to Ames and ripped the car keys out of the man's hand. "I drive."

* * *

NOBORU took the Opel to the parking garage of the Hôtel Azur, located just five minutes west. He and Valentina drove to the far end of the garage as instructed. Noboru let the car idle. He glanced over at Valentina, who draped an arm across her eyes and rested her head on the seat. He felt compelled to say something but simply sat there.

"How come you're so serious, Nathan?" she blurted out.

"What do you mean?"

"I don't think I've ever seen you smile."

"I smiled once. Back in 2007."

She opened her eyes and smiled. "I like you. You're one of the first guys I've met who doesn't want to have sex with me."

"What makes you assume that?"

"Because you don't look at me that way."

"It's impolite."

"Yes, it is. Your parents raised you right."

He took a deep breath. "I would still like to have sex with you."

And then he shocked her . . . by smiling. "Does that make you feel better?"

She punched him in the arm. Hard. "The smile part does. So . . . I'm going to try to take just a little nap, just rest my eyes, okay?"

"Okay."

Within a minute she was out. They were all exhausted, and Noboru repeatedly checked the rearview mirror while blinking his vision back to clarity and stifling a yawn.

He didn't want to close his eyes, because if he did, he knew he'd begin to hear the car horns and smell the herbs and roasting meat from the restaurants.

The back window of his second-floor apartment in Kao-hsiung was open, and below lay piles of trash surrounding a pair of Dumpsters. Noboru was lying in bed, reading a newspaper, when they kicked in his door.

Horatio moved in first, lifting his pistol with an attached silencer. He was forty, broad shouldered like a linebacker but narrow waisted and light on his feet. He'd been severely burned on his neck and lost part of his right ear. He'd never talked about how or why. He kept his bald pate shaved and glistening, and his right arm was entirely tattooed, probably to disguise more scars.

Behind him came Gothwhiler, the scrawny extraterrestrial, pale as a ghost with hair dyed jet-black. He was older than Horatio, wore diamond earrings, and seemed to own only khaki cargo pants. Noboru had never seen him wear anything else in the ten months he worked for the man. Horatio and Gothwhiler were both Brits, former military men (they would not reveal more about that), and had founded a private military company, or PMC, called Gothos and headquartered in the United Kingdom.

Noboru rolled off the bed, started for the window, but Horatio was already crying out, "Don't do it, mate."

He hesitated, glanced back at the hard-eyed Brit.

"Just return the money," said Gothwhiler, lifting his own pistol.

"I took back what was mine. Nothing more."

"We don't care," snapped Horatio. "You're a very naive young man. And trust me. I know what it's like to play with fire. . . ."

Noboru had completed a two-part assassination job for the company, killing the CEO of a competing PMC headquartered in Hong Kong. Once he'd killed the old man, he'd been instructed to kill the man's wife and seventeen-year-old daughter, in order to make a "lasting impression" on the firm's remaining employees, whom Gothos wanted out of the mercenary business.

After assassinating the CEO, Noboru had spent a week studying his targets and realized that he couldn't bring himself to complete the job. He returned and asked for half of his two-hundred-thousand-dollar payment.

Because he had not "completed" the mission, Gothwhiler had refused to pay him anything.

With the help of an old friend in the special forces, Noboru hacked the company's account and withdrew half his fee—only the half he believed they owed him.

Consequently, Horatio and Gothwhiler had made it their mission in life to find him, get back their money, and then, of course, make Noboru suffer a long and painful death.

Noboru had no intention of ever returning the money. He had already sent it to his parents in Yokohama, and they had already used it to save their house and get ahead on the bills. And if these two Brits were going to kill him, he'd force them to do it quickly, which was why, without a second's hesitation, he threw himself out the window. Horatio fired and Gothwhiler screamed for him not to, since only Noboru knew where the money was and could return it.

But Horatio was no amateur marksman, and his round had managed to catch Noboru in the right arm just as he'd been passing through the window.

He landed in the garbage below and immediately rolled down the bags and came up, as the first stinging from the gunshot wound took hold. He rose, raced to the brick wall, and glanced down at his bleeding arm.

Then he raced to the main entrance of the building, where he knew Horatio and Gothwhiler would emerge.

They had surprised him in his apartment. He only wanted to return the favor.

Gothwhiler came out first, and Noboru, in one fluid movement, took him from behind, wrapping an arm around his neck and seizing the man's wrist so he could direct his pistol toward . . .

Horatio, forcing both men to hold their fire, if only for a few seconds. Noboru drove his knee into Goth-whiler's spine, and as the man groaned, he shoved him forward, into Horatio, who lost his footing and dropped back onto his rump.

Two old men on the opposite side of the street began shouting, and, in that instant, Noboru made a decision.

Run.

He bolted around a row of parked cars, and, using them as a shield, crouched over and reached the next cross street.

Now he was into a full sprint, weaving his way through the throng of pedestrians, stealing glimpses over his shoulder, feeling the blood dripping from his arm.

His heart was drumming in his ears, rapping hard, sounding strangely like a knuckle rapping on glass.

"What the hell is this, Bruce? Open up!"

Noboru shook awake, his arm throbbing as it had back then, and found himself staring directly into

Mr. Louis Moreau's ugly mug and grateful there was a piece of glass between them.

Moreau stepped back from the car and waved him out.

"Maya, wake up. Our runner is here. I don't think you'll be happy."

HANSEN and Ames were about halfway to Boutin's apartment when Grim called, and he spoke to her via his SVT and subdermal. "Ben, I need to make this brief. There's been a slight change in how this operation will be coordinated. When your runner arrives, he'll explain everything. I'll be out of touch for a little while."

"Grim, wait. I have questions."

"I wish I could answer them. I really do. Suffice it to say that you need to focus on the job. Good luck, Ben."

"Wait."

She ended the call.

"She says there's been a change in plans, in how we'll coordinate."

"What does that mean?" asked Ames.

"The runner's supposed to tell us."

"WHAT is this?" asked Valentina, standing outside their car. She was furious that Moreau et al had lied to them about his whereabouts and probably more. "You were just talking to Kim on the computer, and she said you were back at Fort Meade."

"First, let's slow down, Nurse Ratched—and speaking of which, I've got your uniforms and IDs in the trunk."

"Nurse who?"

"I don't believe it. Are you going to stand there and tell me you have not seen *One Flew Over the Cuckoo's Nest?*"

Valentina frowned. "It's a movie?"

"Of course it is, sunshine!"

"I am not familiar with that movie, either," said Noboru.

"Aw, you boys and girls got to be kidding me. When you're drunk or bored sometime, Google it. For now, listen up."

Valentina snickered. "For the second time, why are you here?"

"I'm getting to that. You'll be coordinating directly with me right here in Reims, but we want them to think I'm at 3E headquarters."

"We want who to think?"

"Kovac."

"What're you talking about?"

"He's got his eyes and ears all over us. Grim and I decided that it was more important for me to work hands on this time around. So I brought you the gear and my shining personality, and I'll be staying right here while you track Fisher. You'll have a secure, encrypted link directly to me, and I'll update Grim. Bottom line: Tech operations has just gone mobile. Hallelujah!"

Moreau stood there a moment as Valentina and Noboru faced him, resigned to their fate.

"What's the matter, Nurse Ratched? You're not happy to see me?"

"Thrilled."

"Sir, I am glad to see you. I have been thinking about a nickname for you, and I wanted to share it."

"You're not going to use foul language, Bruce, are you?"

"No, sir. Have you seen the movie *Pulp Fiction*?"

"Of course I have."

"You are Jules Winnfield, sir. You are a black hit man, but you don't have the Jheri curls. When you retire, you will walk the earth like Caine in *Kung Fu*."

"You bet your ass I will." Moreau threw his arm over Noboru's shoulder. "Just don't call me Grasshopper. Now, come with me. I got all kinds of heavy gear bags for you to load while I supervise. Then we're going to dress you up nice and pretty like a nurse."

As they went to Moreau's car, a silver four-door Mercedes (leave it to him to rent a Mercedes), Valentina activated her OPSAT and opened the channel to Hansen. "Ben?"

"You make contact with the runner?"

"Unfortunately, we did."

"What's wrong?"

Valentina took a deep breath and told him.

— 16 ————————

ROMAIN Doucet was sitting up in bed, his leg
wrapped in a heavy cast and elevated by a sling. His
face was a mottled mess of purple and yellow bruises,
and somewhere amid those venous flowers was a pair
of dark, narrow eyes. Valentina could only imagine
how much swelling there had been, but some of it had
subsided. Admittedly, it was unnerving to see a man
this imposing as battered as he was; it suggested that
his attacker was either bigger and stronger or a whole
lot smarter. Valentina suspected the latter to be true.
Indeed, Doucet was a giant of a Frenchman, over six
feet, to be sure, with a chest like the front bumper of

a pickup truck. You wouldn't call the things at the ends of his arms hands, but paws, and his pitch-black hair was matted as though he'd been rolling around on a thick carpet.

Behind Valentina, at a nurses' station walled in by glass, Noboru was presenting the four duty nurses with a stack of bogus paperwork he'd brought in from central administration. Noboru's English was very good, but his French was poor, which only added to the mayhem. The nurses were gaping at the reports, which included new work schedules for each of them, new sets of duties, and enough other incendiary material to keep them diverted for a week, let alone five minutes. The geeks back home must have had a good time composing those documents—geeks enjoy wielding their intellectual power to piss people off. Valentina ought to know—she was in their club and just needed to make other people realize that.

For now, though, she was back to the same old pathetic ploy: using sex as a weapon to get what the team needed. She undid one more button on her uniform, opened the glass door, and sashayed into Doucet's room.

Playing on the TV was a rerun of *Magnum, P.I.* with Tom Selleck. Magnum's lips were moving, his mustache fluttering, but French was coming out of his mouth in a rapid fire that made him at once appear feminine and ridiculous. Doucet glanced away from the screen and abruptly beamed at her. The pig liked what he saw. "You're a new one."

"That's right, Mr. Doucet. My name's Nurse Ratched."

In fact, that was the name Moreau had placed on her ID badge; he'd planned that from the beginning. Valentina reached around and drew the curtain around his bed . . . so they'd have privacy.

Doucet raised his brows. "What do we have to do now?"

"That's up to you, sweetheart." Valentina did her finger-to-the-lips thing that all the dogs loved.

The look in his eyes made her want to put a shotgun to his crotch and pull the trigger.

But she had work to do.

"You're not a real nurse."

"And I thought you were a stupid man."

"Who hired you?"

"They did. They want me to make you feel better."

He started to chuckle. "They're good friends." He stopped and winced through the pain.

"Oh, my poor baby. What happened to you?" She crossed around the bed and stared at his leg.

"Skiing accident."

"That's not what they told me." Valentina undid another button, leaned back, and showed him more of her cleavage.

He gasped and said, "What did they tell you?"

"Something about a very bad man who came to see you." She moved toward the bed, leaned down, undid the clip and let her long hair fall into his face.

He breathed in the scent and said, "I'm going to find him. And I'm going to kill him."

She pulled back. "You're not afraid?"

"No."

"You're a strong man. I wish we weren't here. I wish we were someplace else."

"Me, too."

"This man who did this to you . . . he must be so strong."

"No, he's just a smart bastard. Very smart."

"How're you going to find him?"

"I'm not sure."

"In my business, I know a lot of people on the street. Maybe I can help you. Is there a reward?"

"There could be. But are you going to keep talking or take off your clothes?"

Valentina smiled and undid the rest of the buttons on her uniform. She moved back toward the bed and pressed her cleavage into his face. Doucet groaned softly. She rolled her eyes. She pulled back once more and said, "What does this guy look like?"

"White guy. About six feet. Longish hair. Unshaven for a week. His French was excellent, but something tells me he's an American."

"That could be anyone. You'll never find him. Maybe a police artist could draw a picture for me."

"We're not using the police. I do this my way."

"Okay. I'm sorry to talk about this. I'm here to make you feel better."

"Then climb up on top of me, and take my pulse."

She grinned, and just as he reached out to grab her wrist, the curtain wrenched open, and in walked a gray-haired, potbellied nurse who took one look at Valentina's exposed black bra and screamed, "Who are you? Not another stripper on my floor! Get out! We've banned you people, you should know!"

Noboru was standing behind the woman, giving Valentina the high sign with his eyes.

She quickly folded her blouse closed and slipped past the nurse, dropping in behind Noboru. They raced to the end of the hall, turned right, and hit the stairwell.

"I'm sorry, Maya," Noboru said as they charged down. "One of the nurses saw you close the curtain. I tried to distract her."

"It's all right. I got what we need. It was definitely Fisher."

"He didn't touch you, did he?"

She gritted her teeth. "Don't worry about me."

They reached the ground floor, and Valentina took a few seconds to finish closing her blouse.

"I am worried about you," Noboru insisted.

"Why?"

"Because my life depends on you."

"All right, I guess that's a pretty good reason. Maybe . . ." She winked.

"That was kind of fun." Noboru looked at her, then smiled weakly.

"Keep working on that smile. It's still rusty."

They pushed through the heavy exit door and started across the parking lot. "Ben?" Valentina called after activating her OPSAT. "No surprise: Doucet got his ass kicked by Fisher. I just wish Fisher had finished the job. That guy is scum."

AS Hansen cruised down another impossibly narrow street, he told Valentina to meet them back at the hotel. He and Ames wanted to make one more pass by Boutin's apartment.

They had a couple of surveillance images of the man taken several years ago. Abelard Boutin was pushing sixty, and if you described him as being taller than five feet four, you were being generous. He squinted like a rodent through dark-rimmed glasses and attempted to cover his freckled and pockmarked skull with all of sixteen long, gray hairs in the classic comb-over style that fooled no one but has remained inexplicably popular for centuries. He was a gnome, a savant whose singular talent lay in the perfect artistry of his work.

And after all these years and all that work, the best he'd been able to afford was a basement apartment in Reims. Was he hoarding all the money? Helping to support someone? Or did he have certain . . . *weaknesses* . . . that siphoned off his income? These were interesting questions, but all Hansen needed to know was, first, had Fisher gone to see Boutin (as it seemed he had), and, second, did Boutin know where Fisher was headed.

Boutin's apartment was located just west of the center of Reims, on the corner of rue de Vesles and Marx Dormoy, behind a clothing store and several other storefronts. Hansen was glad they'd made a dry run, since there was no parking at all on rue de Vesles because of some road construction and repair. There were signs posted up and down the street, with red railings fencing off the torn-up cobblestones. The maps had not revealed that.

A tunnel-like alley called the passage Saint-Jacques lay between a small pharmacy and several ATM machines. A wrought-iron gate with a security touch pad secured the entrance to the tunnel, and that gate stood in sharp, contemporary relief against the passage's ornate stone arch, which made you feel as if you were walking through someplace very ancient and somehow sacred. Hansen and Ames had already decided that at least one, possibly two, of them would gain entrance to the courtyard beyond, either by hopping the gate or picking the lock. A second inspection revealed motion detectors, so those and the lock would have to be neutralized.

Hansen took them around the block one last time. Within the courtyard near Boutin's apartment was an old church, and behind it an ornate carousel ride with bright lights and gleaming horses. Once again more fences lay between them and the courtyard where Boutin's apartment was located, so entrance from the north would also require some climbing or lock picking. No big challenge. Just a nuisance.

Ames finished taking his pictures and lowered the camera. "You see the ass on the girl back there?"

"No, I was too busy reconnoitering the target and considering our plans for tonight."

Ames shrugged. "You missed quite an ass."

"Where in the training manual for covert field operatives does it say that you need to be loud, the class clown, and the center of attention?"

"Dude, it's in the footnotes. You don't read the footnotes?"

Hansen snorted. "If you don't take this operation seriously—"

"Benjamin? Are you trying to seduce me?"

"Shut up! Listen to me. The quips are just irritating and they need to stop."

"Whatever you say."

"And leave the women alone. Maya will kick your ass, and I won't stop her."

"I'm just trying to have some fun. You people are so uptight. We could die out here because, yeah, maybe this whole thing's a setup. Maybe Grim's a traitor. Maybe we're being used, so we might as well have a little fun along the way—because you know what, Mr. Hansen? Life's too goddamned short. All it takes is one little spark, one little flame, and it's all burned away. . . ."

"You don't think I know about that?" Hansen asked, wishing he could fix Ames with a hard look but keeping his eyes on the road. "We're all spies here. You found out Gillespie slept with Fisher the same way I found out about your family dying in a fire, about that Zippo you carry around, about your little problem with anger management. I even read Fisher's report about you and your bad temperament."

Ames began shaking his head and laughing. "You really think you know me, huh? You really do!"

"You're about as uncomplicated as they come."

"All right. I'll accept that. Just a blue-collar kind of guy . . ."

Hansen stole a glance at the man and just sighed.

THIRD ECHELON SITUATION ROOM
FORT MEADE, MARYLAND

ANNA Grimsdóttir stiffened as the door opened and in strode Nicholas Andrew Kovac, deputy director.

Kovac had an expression on his face that he assumed would intimidate her—but he should have thought again.

She nodded curtly at the regal-looking man, his hair the color of sea salt and perfectly coiffed, his eyes stunningly blue and suggesting he'd had no trouble with the ladies in his youth. His suits were tailor made, his shoes professionally shined, his ties picked out by his personal assistant. His watch cost more than the average commuter car, and, speaking of cars, he drove several different exotics to work, taking turns between the Lotus, the Porsche, and the "Lambo." It was all remarkably egocentric, and far too flaunting for Grim's taste, and Kovac had already inspired a legion of haters among the low-level analysts. But the deputy director didn't care. He was and would forever be terse, demanding, and unflinching, and he had on more than one occasion lectured his subordinates about how hard he'd worked to reach his goals.

He was an ass. No two ways about it.

In fact, while he knew most people referred to her as Grim, he never once called her that, relying only upon Ms. Grimsdóttir, spoken in the tone of a private schoolteacher addressing his unfortunate pupil.

"Hello, Ms. Grimsdóttir."

She winced and fired back, "How you doing, Nick," in her best New York accent, as though addressing one of the boys.

He took a long breath. "I've come for an update on Fisher."

"I would've been happy to call or e-mail you. . . ."

"You still think Fisher is in Reims?"

"We do. The team's already begun its investigation."

"But Fisher could be long gone."

"He's not."

"You're certain? Why?"

"Because I know Sam. If he made a mistake, he'll wait around, shake the tree, see what falls out."

"Well, I expect daily, even hourly, updates."

"Of course."

"Where's Mr. Moreau?"

"We had a problem with one of the servers and he's down there supervising."

"Well, tell him I want to see him in my office before the end of the day."

"I will." *Oh, this is going to get interesting,* she thought.

He started for the door, hesitated, turned back. "Ms. Grimsdóttir? We don't have to like or trust each other to do the good work of our country."

"But it would make things easier."

"What position would you have me take at a time like this"

"A supportive one, sir."

"You have my support."

She took a long breath. "But not your trust."

"When Fisher is taken out of the equation, we'll all be able to breathe easier."

"If only it hadn't come to this."

"But it has. And I would hope that you've instructed your team to neutralize the problem with extreme prejudice."

"Is there any other way?"

He winked. "Good girl."

She glowered at him as he turned and strode arrogantly toward the door.

17

KIMBERLY Gillespie had just finished an encrypted text chat with Mr. Moreau when the man himself walked into the hotel room, holding his own key card and smiling like a bull shark.

Gillespie looked at the LCD screen, then at him, and had a WTF moment before finally opening her mouth.

But he beat her to the punch. "What's up, Pippi? You done chatting with me?"

"What the hell?"

"Relax. You've been working with one of my young

apprentices. He's just a wannabe. That's why it's just text and no video."

"Okay, that's supposed to enlighten me . . . how?"

"You're thinking too hard. You just keep working with the electronic me, and the NSA will be happy. Meantime, I'll also be here, and we'll set up some encryption of our own."

"I wish I knew what the hell you're talking about."

"Put away that big brain and just close your eyes and ride the wave. . . ."

The door opened and in walked Hansen and Ames. Neither of them was surprised to see the operations manager, further confusing Gillespie.

"Are you working out of a room here or somewhere else?" Hansen asked Moreau.

"I've got a room here."

"Wait a minute. You knew about this?" asked Gillespie.

Hansen shrugged. "I should've called you. Relax."

Gillespie folded her hands over her chest. "Okay, I'm listening."

Hansen spelled it all out for her, and then Moreau added, "Are you comfortable with this arrangement, or would you like to call Grim and suggest an alternate plan?"

Gillespie thought for a moment. Capturing Sam

Fisher was hard enough. Now they were expected to put on a front, so that Kovac and his cronies didn't know exactly what they were doing, because the deputy director, it seemed, was bent on dismantling Third Echelon—at least according to Moreau.

"The plan sounds fine, sir," said Gillespie.

Moreau widened his eyes. "Glad we have your approval."

Valentina and Noboru entered, and Noboru wheeled in a hotel luggage cart piled high with black duffel bags.

For the next five minutes they took an inventory of all the gear—suits, rifles, pistols, and a host of other toys—until Hansen looked up at Moreau and asked, "No trifocals? They're on the list."

"Are you kidding me?" cried Moreau. "They didn't pack them?"

Hansen shook his head. "We got the NV binoculars but no goggles."

"The geeks back in shipping must've screwed up again," Moreau said with a heavy sigh. "We'll do without them for now. I have a feeling we'll be doing more hiding in plain sight than anything else. Try walking down the boulevard wearing trifocals and *not* getting noticed."

"All right," said Hansen. "But see if they can overnight them to us."

Moreau nodded. "Leave that to me."

Gillespie detected a slight tremor in Moreau's voice . . . very odd. The ops manager then added that they were maintaining surveillance of Boutin's apartment via satellite to ensure that the old man was home when they came knocking. Boutin had left only once to do some grocery shopping; otherwise, they were certain he was home.

LATER in the day, Ames volunteered to call room service and order lunch. The others were unaware that his call was received by a field operative working for Deputy Director Kovac. This operative, a man known only by the code name Stingray, was Ames's cutout so that he could safely pass information back to the deputy director. Ames placed the order, saying, "Yes, there are five of us. . . . Oh, wait a minute, I forgot Moreau's here. Make that six drinks."

Stingray got the message, and within five minutes Kovac would know that Mr. Louis Moreau was in Reims, and that he and Grim were attempting to thwart the director's information-gathering efforts. That Grim and Moreau still had no idea that Ames was a mole on the Splinter Cell team was a testament to Ames's first-class tradecraft. They could pick on him all they wanted. They could hate him as much as they wanted.

Because when it was all over, Fisher would be dead,

and Moreau, Grim, and the rest of them would be locked up. Ames would be the only man standing, and he and the deputy director would rebuild Third Echelon. Eventually, Ames would ascend to his rightful place as director of all operations.

DRESSED in civilian clothes, including mock turtleneck shirts to conceal their SVTs, Hansen and the others left the hotel, bound for Boutin's apartment. Moreau remained at the hotel to monitor the open channel and the satellite feeds. It was 10:46 P.M. on Hansen's OPSAT as they left the hotel's parking garage.

They drove both rental cars to rue de Thillois, a street a few hundred yards southeast of Boutin's apartment. A slight chill hung in the air as they parked, waited a few moments, then exited the vehicles, moving swiftly onto the empty street.

While Noboru and Gillespie approached from the north, gaining access past the fences to take up positions in the trees, Hansen, Valentina, and Ames would enter from the south, through the passage Saint-Jacques.

They reached the gate, and Valentina got to work on the lock while Ames patched into the security network and turned off the motion sensors.

Keeping to the long shadows near the wall, they slipped into the passage, and Ames did a wholly impressive job of silently climbing his way into the old tree just to its north so he could cover the north side of the courtyard and the gate entrance.

Hansen motioned for Valentina to halt. He took several long breaths to calm his nerves, then whispered in his SVT, "Nathan? Kim?"

NOBORU was covering the north–south entrance to the courtyard directly opposite Boutin's apartment. He had already found a particularly large branch on which to set up and was scanning the area with his NV binoculars when Hansen called. He checked in and listened to Kim do likewise. She was in much closer, having glided up like a wraith to the left side of the apartment building's main entrance and found good purchase in a tree right there. In Noboru's humble opinion, no one could approach the operational area without being detected.

And while they didn't have the luxury of thermal scans, Moreau's satellite feeds could detect anyone approaching from outside their bubble.

Noboru glanced over at the old church, just visible through all the leaf cover, and for a moment, he thought he saw a shadow creeping across the ancient stone wall. In fact, he had. Hansen and Valentina were approaching Boutin's place and had donned their balaclavas.

HANSEN checked his OPSAT once more: 11:14. He put Valentina to work on the main door, and then, on the periphery, he spotted something—a perfectly straight silhouette, unnatural against nature's curves. He shifted over, leaned down, and there it was: a cell phone, the prepaid type, leaning against the wall, its antenna sprouting up between some weeds. He glanced back at Valentina as she finished with the lock. He motioned for her to step back; then he lifted the doormat and found a tremble sensor, the kind from a vehicle's antitheft GPS tracker. A tiny, almost invisible wire snaked from the sensor back to the cell phone.

Hansen cursed and stage-whispered, "Let's move. He already knows we're out here!"

The old forger was a clever bastard, having jury-rigged his own personal alarm system to back up the building's standard security. He must've assumed someone would be coming to visit, someone who knew how to bypass the gate and door, and that deeply troubled Hansen. He withdrew his SC pistol loaded with anesthetic darts, and Valentina did likewise as he announced to the others that they were moving in.

The sensor at the door had tripped a mental alarm, and Hansen immediately decided to abandon stealth in favor of shock and awe. He gave Valentina the high sign, and they stormed through a short hall illuminated by a lone bulb, hit a stairwell, and thundered down it to reach Boutin's door.

Hansen's single kick sent the door smashing inward, and he dropped to his haunches as Valentina came in over him.

MOREAU sat at the desk in his hotel room and faced his computer while wearing the Trinity System's virtual-reality headset and gloves. The gloves were fixed with dozens of wireless sensors, and the headset resembled a narrow pair of sunglasses with attached microphone that could be mistaken for an integrated Bluetooth device. The headset was both comfortable and discreet, so wearing it in public was not entirely out of the question. The gloves were another story. Images were produced by a low-intensity laser projecting them through Moreau's pupil and onto his retina. The laser scanned vertically and horizontally at high speed using a coherent beam of light, and all data was refreshed every second to continually update him.

The system was the result of a joint venture between the Defense Advanced Research Projects Agency,

DARPA, the army's Natick Soldier Center, and Third Echelon (whose involvement was kept classified from Kovac and the rest of the NSA through Grim's careful maneuvering). Trinity allowed Moreau and Grim not only to meet in a virtual environment, but to interact directly with that environment in order to more expeditiously and visually share data with each other. Trinity was protected by a hybrid version of QKD, or quantum key distribution, that enabled participants to produce a shared random-bit string known only to their computers. That string became a key to encrypt and decrypt messages. Should anyone attempt to hack their link, they would be notified immediately while the system attempted to trace the hack to its source.

At the moment they stood improbably in midair, about five hundred feet above Boutin's apartment and its environs, the backdrop shimmering with a phosphorescent glow. Gravity meant nothing in this place. Moreover, these weren't wire-frame images but a near-real-time streaming satellite feed enhanced by night vision, so that even the light from traffic well in the distance, gliding down the boulevards and autoroutes, was represented with only a slight delay.

Moreau could look down past his avatar's boots to see the apartment entrance, the positions of each member of the team denoted by green triangles, and the team's cars parked on the street. He glanced over at Grim, her avatar remarkably lifelike, right down to the hair color and brand of glasses. Some of the best producers, programmers, and artists from the video game industry had obviously been tapped for this project, and the results were no less than stunning.

Ahead of them, superimposed against a backdrop of stars and narrow rafts of clouds, were stacks of slightly translucent data boards similar to the home pages of websites. The boards floated like tabbed windows and were organized into groups created by Grim. She reached out with her finger, lifted one board from the stack, and drew a small circle with her finger that caused the board to hover before her. This one contained classified information regarding an NSA employee code-named Stingray. She widened the board by extending her thumb and index finger, then lifted her hand to a navigation bar and began to tap deeper into the information, flicking documents aside with her finger, the illuminated pages arcing high and away from the board and vanishing into the night. She wasn't just surfing information; she was bulleting through it with a vengeance.

"I think our subroutine on Kovac's network finally picked up something," said Grim. "This code name was attached to an agent who died three years ago. Why is it that agents who die always come back to life?"

"That's the zombie factor," quipped Moreau.

Grim stood back from the data board to reveal the

face of an old man, probably in his sixties, with closely cropped white hair and beard. He had penetrating blue eyes and an earring in his left ear.

"So that's our tail," Moreau sang darkly. "I know him. William Harvey Deacon. Special Forces. Black ops. Deacon the Beacon. I'll kill his ass and be done with it."

"No, let's see if we can put him on a diet of junk food."

"I like your style, Grim."

"The feeling's mutual—except for the part about, ahem, killing his ass. We'll just keep him misinformed."

"All right. But big and noisy is more fun."

"One other thing troubles me. I told Kovac you went home sick. No one ever followed up on that. I had someone take your car home. No tails, nothing."

"Maybe he bought it."

"Or maybe he already knows you're in Reims."

"How?"

Grim faced him, the avatar's eyes narrowing. "I don't know. But I'm going to find out."

HANSEN and Valentina confronted Abelard Boutin in his sitting/TV/work room. The little forger was seated on his couch and just reaching over to his metal TV stand, where a pistol sat next to a large bag of potato chips. On the TV was a rerun of *Miami Vice*, in French. Hansen had hoped that Boutin would be sleeping when they broke down the door, but it seemed the gnome was a fan of pastel-colored suits and white Ferrari Testarossas. Nearby was a maple workbench with attached magnifying lamps, clamps, spools of multicolored thread, and the sheets of hooks of a fly-fishing-lure maker. This, of course, was part of Boutin's cover, and those same tools could also be used as part of his forgery business.

The old man stopped in midreach as Valentina hollered in French, "No no no, monsieur. I'll take it."

Boutin blinked hard, hesitated, then sighed and collapsed back into the sofa as Valentina took his pistol and shoved it into her waistband.

Hansen shifted up beside her and asked, "Did François Dayreis come to see you?"

Boutin removed his thick glasses, rubbed the bridge of his nose, then said wheezily, "Who's going to pay for my broken door?"

Hansen took a deep breath. "I'm going to blow your brains out if you don't talk." He glanced over at Valentina, whose eyes were emphatic: *What're you doing?*

Boutin returned the glasses to his nose. "I think you have the wrong apartment."

"Someone gave the police an anonymous tip about the warehouse assault. Was that you?" asked Valentina.

The old man sighed. "I don't know anything."

Hansen leaned in closer. Held up his free hand. And in the blink of an eye came a blade jutting from his fist. "You're an artist. Your hands and eyes are your most important assets."

"You don't sound like a torturer."

With that, Hansen grabbed the old man by the wrist, dragged him from the sofa and over to the workbench, where he pinned the man's hand to a broad plank of maple, the stubby fingers with long gray hairs nice and flat, like sausages ready to be sliced. "Which one first? And then maybe a hook in each eye? It happens. Fishing is more dangerous than you think."

Boutin began to lose his breath.

Hansen spoke more slowly for effect. "So, I ask, is Dayreis worth it?"

The old man's face flushed, and his cratered pate was growing slick with sweat. "So you're looking for Dayreis? Okay, I'll tell you what I know. Let go."

Hansen complied but held his blade to the man's throat. Boutin rubbed his hand, took a deep breath, and said, "He came to me with five driver's licenses, and then hours later the names on those licenses were on the news. Five men assaulted. I knew Dayreis was more trouble than he was worth, and I had to suspend my business because of him."

"Marty, you hearing this?" Hansen whispered into his SVT.

Moreau's voice came through the subdermal. "I'm hearing you calling me Marty."

Hansen repressed a snicker and widened his gaze on Boutin. "Do you know where Dayreis is now?"

"He said he had a friend in Tuscany."

"He's not in Tuscany," said Valentina.

Hansen looked at her. "How do you know?"

"Because he had to go see another forger since our friend here ruined his plans. So, monsieur, if you were Dayreis, who would you go see?"

"I don't know."

Valentina sighed loudly for effect. "Give us the name, and you can get back to your TV show."

Boutin closed his eyes. "I would go see Emmanuel Chenevier. He is very good."

"Spell the last name," Valentina ordered.

Boutin did.

"Run that name," Hansen whispered to Moreau.

"On it," snapped Moreau. "Give the old man some money for his door."

Hansen reached into his pocket and produced two hundred euros (about $270). Boutin took the bills and counted. "That door was an antique. I'll need twice as much."

With a snort, Hansen looked to Valentina, who managed to produce another hundred euros. "That's all we have," she said.

"It will have to do," said Boutin. "And you, lady,

you are a smart one to ask me about another forger. I think you will find Mr. Dayreis. And when you do, tell him I said hello and that I hope he dies."

"I'm sure he'll be pleased," said Valentina.

Hansen tipped his head toward the door, and they hustled out of the apartment, notifying the others that they were on their way.

MOREAU and Grim were still connected through the Trinity System and watching as Hansen and his team went though a series of maneuvers to discreetly collapse back in on their vehicles. The team was at its most alert now, and Moreau was impressed by how deftly they came together, if not by the fact that Hansen had chosen to park both rental cars in one spot.

"Look at that," said Grim suddenly. "There's someone on the park bench, right there."

"You're not thinking what I'm thinking . . ." Moreau began.

Grim reached out toward a compasslike control and used it to zoom in on the satellite feed, where they glimpsed a bum with a newspaper folded over his head but lying on his side so that he could peer out from beneath it.

"I don't believe it," said Grim. "Look at Kim. She's walking right by him. Thirty feet! I told Sam to keep them close. But not that close!"

As the cars drove away, the bum rose and began photographing them, and, yes, Moreau and Grim made a positive identification of Mr. Sam Fisher, Splinter Cell—the man who was going to bring down Kovac and stop an even bigger threat in one fell swoop.

Grim felt a pang of guilt that she couldn't tell Hansen and the others everything; however, she was even more thankful now that she hadn't. Kovac's man Stingray was close. Too close.

18

HANSEN and Moreau had agreed that questioning Emmanuel Chenevier would need to happen in the morning, lest they catch the man in a very foul mood at 1:00 A.M. The team was now driving straight out to Doucet's warehouse to confirm that Fisher had been there and see if there was anything that might indicate his next move. It was a long shot, to be sure, but failing to at least inspect the warehouse would be foolish . . . and Hansen had already made one such mistake.

Taking a tip from Moreau, Hansen made sure that the team parked its rental cars about a quarter mile apart. He should've had them do likewise back at Boutin's apartment, but he was so pumped full of adrenaline that his better judgment had been clouded. Parking the cars together was a tactical error he would not make again. Paying attention to the minutiae kept you alive. Period.

Doucet and his thugs had been living out of a twenty-five-hundred-square-foot Quonset-style warehouse within a mostly deserted industrial park on Reims's west side. Brown and green quilts of tilled fields unfurled to the south and west, dropping off into darkness, with the only significant light coming from the streetlamps dotting the road.

After a quick radio check, the team fanned out. Noboru and Gillespie would descend from the north and set up overwatch. Valentina would advance from the south and cover the loading dock entrance. Hansen and Ames were threading between the buildings just east of the warehouse and would cross to the dock itself and enter through that rear door.

Within two minutes, the calls came in:

"Nathan here. I'm in position. All clear."

"Kim here. Same deal on my side."

"Ben, I'm just behind the white truck near the dock," said Valentina. "There are a few cars parked across the street, but they look empty. I can see a Range Rover and a couple of others. You're clear to go."

"Roger that. Hold positions. Here we come."

Hansen and Ames darted along the building directly east of the warehouse, the sheet-metal walls already growing damp with dew. On three they sprinted across the parking lot, bounded up the stairs to the loading dock, ducked under the blue police tape, and reached the front door.

Hansen covered Ames, who was about to pick the lock when he simply tried the handle: open.

"Nice police work here," Ames said softly. "They didn't even lock up on their way out."

"Works for me," Hansen replied.

Drawing their pistols, they eased into the warehouse and switched on their penlights, illuminating the open spaces in dim shades of red. Off to their right was a living room of sorts, with torn-up couches and recliners positioned around a big flat-screen TV, fifty inches or larger. Nearby sat a DVD player with literally hundreds of movies stacked beside it. Most of the titles were either kung fu flicks or porn. A trash can near one sofa was overflowing with garbage, and a rat scurried off as Hansen caught it with his light.

Directly ahead stood a flight of metal stairs leading up to a loft along which ran a metal railing. "I'm going up. Find me something down here."

"I'm sure I will," said Ames. "Fisher's getting sloppy. I'm telling you. . . ."

Hansen sighed and quickly mounted the staircase. At the top, he moved along the railing, then crossed into the kitchen. Farther back were a breakfast nook and laundry area partially obscured by a makeshift bedsheet divider.

Oddly, the door to the base cabinet under the kitchen sink hung wide-open. Hansen thought about that as his light played over the floor, looking for any signs of blood. Nothing. He moved out of the kitchen and found a bathroom with a simple toilet and sink. Again, his light swept along the floor, where he spotted a tiny sliver of black plastic. He reached down, picked it up, turned it over.

Plastic from what?

Hansen lifted the toilet seat, saw that someone had urinated but not flushed. Urine stains were on the seat and the floor. He thought about that. Then he turned to a door, swung it open, and found that he was in a closet with wall-mounted ladder leading up to a skylight. The warehouse had obviously been a conversion project; thus the closet had been constructed to preserve that roof access, probably for maintenance purposes or even escape in case of a fire.

"Ames, anything?" Hansen called into his SVT.

"Not yet."

"Get up here."

"You got something?"

"Maybe. Move it."

Ames's footfalls came soft but swiftly, and within a few seconds he stood beside Hansen.

"How much you want to bet that skylight was opened from the outside?"

"Nothing, because it was." Ames mounted the ladder and climbed up twelve feet to the top. He pushed open the skylight, which folded soundlessly out of the way.

Soundlessly.

Hansen followed, and they both emerged onto the roof. Hansen leaned over and ran his finger along one of the skylight's hinges. His finger came up slick. "Fisher sprayed the hinges with silicone so they wouldn't squeak. This is definitely his entrance point."

"How'd he get up here?" Ames crossed the roof and spotted the air-conditioning unit. "Oh, here we go. I think he climbed up on the AC; then he could reach the ladder there." Ames climbed down the ladder and jumped onto the AC unit affixed to the wall. Again, Hansen followed, and in a few moments they both stood on the ground, staring up at the building.

"So if he came in from up top . . ." Hansen began aloud. "Wait a minute." He jogged around the front of the warehouse to the door, his gaze probing . . . and then he saw it—a long two-by-four lying near the wall about twenty feet away. He went over, picked up the wood, and inspected the ends. As he suspected, the wood was indented on one side. He brought the piece up to the door handle, and the indentation matched.

"If we go back to the loading dock, we'll find another two-by-four over there."

"He locked them in," Ames concluded.

"Then he came in from up top. They didn't stand a chance."

Ames snorted. "Yeah, well, they were fools. Fisher's playing with us now. Old man Fisher's going to cry like my sister when I get down with him."

Hansen made a face. "Pride cometh before the fall."

"You quoting Shakespeare?"

Hansen smirked. "No, Oprah. Let's go."

They crossed to the loading dock, where Hansen did, indeed, spot the second two-by-four, the indentation once again matching the door handle.

They went back inside the warehouse and Hansen crossed to the oak coffee table, where at each leg he found a black plastic ring: flex-cuffs. He was painfully familiar with them and felt his wrists ache from that night in Korfovka. Sure enough, the plastic matched the sliver he'd found upstairs in the bathroom.

So there it was: Fisher had probably lured them one by one upstairs, where he'd neutralized and cuffed them. But he'd saved the questioning of Doucet for the main arena. He imagined Doucet bound to the table and Fisher conducting the interrogation in his deadpan voice:

"*We're done with questions. You talk. Otherwise, pain.*"

"*No!*" Doucet cried.

"*All right. You choose pain.*"

Hansen flinched and shuttered as he noticed, on the floor, the scratch marks where Doucet had tried to free himself. All of it jibed with the police report.

Hansen and Ames spent another fifteen minutes searching for anything else of interest. Hansen discovered that the clothing dryer had been pulled back from the wall, and the floor was clear of dust in an area about the size of a briefcase. Something had, no doubt, been stashed there and removed.

Outside, they slipped back to their cars and took off, with Hansen, Ames, Noboru in one car, the women in the other. They would take separate routes back to the hotel, yet another tradecraft detail Hansen employed this time around.

He and the others were about five minutes away from the warehouse when Moreau called: "Ben? Maya and Kim are okay, but it looks like you boys have picked up a tail."

After swearing under his breath, he answered, "Talk to me."

"Black Range Rover. Two occupants. Driver's got the lights out. Can't see their faces. The driver's a pretty big guy, though. They're keeping pretty far back. What're you going to do, cowboy?"

"You testing me?"

"Life's a test, young man. Every day. Every hour. Every minute."

Hansen sighed and looked over at Ames, who was at the wheel. "Just keep driving."

Ames frowned. "You kidding me? I can lose these bastards, but you'll need to hang on."

"No. If they followed us out here, then they saw us leave the hotel. They know where we're going. Let's just head back and see what they do."

"I agree with that plan," said Noboru. "We don't know who they are, and if we react, we will lose the element of surprise."

NOBORU had forced the emotion out of his voice—and that wasn't easy. Two men were following them, one larger. This wasn't his paranoia rearing its ugly head. Horatio and Gothwhiler were back there in that Range Rover. They had tracked Noboru to France. They were coming to finally, inevitably, settle the score.

But how had they found him? Had someone within Third Echelon tipped them off? As far as Noboru knew, only Grim was aware of his past. But perhaps that wasn't true. Perhaps there were others, those who worked for

Kovac . . . those who would like nothing more than to expose another conspiracy within the organization: that one of Third Echelon's Splinter Cells had once been employed by Gothos, a corporation currently identified as an enemy of the United States.

Noboru swallowed. He reached for the door handle, saw himself leaping from the car, rolling down the ditch, then coming around to bring his pistol to bear on the car. He would kill them. The nightmare would end tonight.

But what if he were wrong? What if these men had been hired by Kovac or even Fisher himself? If Noboru were to confront them, he'd be doing the very thing he had just advised Hansen against: tipping his hand to the enemy.

But to remain silent, in place, knowing that they could be back there, would take inhuman reserve. He could barely breathe and the bile was building in his throat.

"Moreau?" Hansen called. "We're not reacting."

They drove on, all the way back to the hotel, with Moreau finally telling them that the Range Rover had pulled into a parking garage about five blocks away.

As they parked in their own garage, Moreau continued to feed them reports. Still no sign of the drivers.

"Ben, I suggest we search our cars," said Noboru.

"Good idea."

And within five minutes they found a pair of GPS

tracking devices, both placed within the back sides of the cars' rear bumpers.

"Those are British made," said Moreau. "Interesting. Excellent encryption. They're not amateurs."

"Let me shadow them," said Noboru. "Let me go alone."

"I'd advise against that," said Moreau.

"Sir, are you telling me how to run my team?" asked Hansen. "Is that within the purview of operations management?"

"Young man, I'd like a word in private. Come on up here, ASAP."

"Tell him you'll wear your sexy bathrobe," said Ames with a wink.

"I heard that," cried Moreau.

Hansen looked at Gillespie and Valentina, who were holding the tracking devices. "Stick them on two other cars. We'll have a little fun with our tails."

The women smiled and got to work.

BACK up in Moreau's hotel room, Hansen stood before the man and lifted his shoulders. "Time for answers."

Moreau turned away from his computer, sat back in the chair, and pillowed his head in his hands. "You're getting ahead of me, cowboy. I haven't asked any questions yet."

"I'm asking the questions. First and most obvious: What the hell are we doing here?"

"I'm about to tear you a new one for your insubordination," answered Moreau. "After that, we can order ice cream."

Hansen spaced his words for effect: "You know what I mean."

"Mr. Hansen, we are in the middle of an operation to bring in a rogue agent. You didn't get the memo?"

"Don't give me that BS. Geeks forgot to pack the goggles? Now we got a tail?"

"What're you suggesting?"

"You don't want us to capture Fisher."

"That's ridiculous."

"He's working with Grim. He's up to something. And we're running defense. We're the screen. And Kovac's beginning to figure that out, and he's got people all over us."

"Your job is not to stand and speculate on what-ifs and maybes and, *Oh, I think I got this all figured out with my MIT education.* Your job is to bring me Sam Fisher's head." Moreau leapt to his feet and raised his voice. "Jesus Christ, cowboy! What part of that equation don't you understand?"

"The part where you lied to us."

Hansen took a step forward and riveted his gaze on Moreau.

Standoff.

19

WHILE Hansen was meeting with Moreau, Noboru was already three blocks down the street and heading toward the garage where the Range Rover was parked. The others thought he'd gone down to a little all-night café on the corner to bring back some fresh-brewed decaf.

With a woolen cap pulled tightly over his head and the collar of his trench coat turned up, Noboru entered the five-level parking garage and kept low behind the first row of cars. The attendant booth was empty, tickets and payment being issued by an automatic system.

Noboru stole his way up to the first level, eyes probing with an almost mechanical precision. He dashed from car to car and ventured up to the second level, squinting once more at every dark vehicle he spotted.

By the time he reached the third level, he was growing frustrated and breathless. There were plenty of open parking spaces within the garage, yet the Range Rover was not there.

Again, no luck on the fourth level. In fact, there were even fewer cars parked this high up.

He took himself all the way to the edge of a wall beside which stood the rooftop parking area. If the Rover had been parked there, Moreau would have picked it up via satellite. Noboru checked the lot anyway. No Range Rover.

He began to panic. Wrong garage? Had the car pulled out while he'd been on his way there?

Sweating profusely now, he sprinted all the way down to the first level and once more took up a position behind a small sedan.

And then he saw it, a bank of garage doors located along the rear wall of the garage. A sign indicated that these were secured garages for rent.

Fool! He'd missed that the first time around.

The bad news: There were six garage doors, and the Range Rover could be behind any one of them.

Noboru had tools but not much time.

He reached the first door, then opened his coat,

removed his lock-picking set, and used one of the handles to open up a small gap in the first door, where the rubber base met the concrete floor. Through that gap he inserted the end of a flexicam, activated the base unit, set it for night vision, and slid the probe up to examine the car. No car. Empty garage.

On to the next one.

A Renault. And the next one. Empty. And as he was about to check the next one, headlights flashed behind him. He dove for cover beside the nearest car and waited there.

What the hell? It was the black Range Rover.

No. He blinked hard. It was a black SUV but not a Range Rover.

Noboru swallowed. Tried to calm himself. The SUV pulled into a spot near the exit, and a young couple exited, giggling. The man grabbed his partner's ass as they ventured across the street, toward a row of small hotels.

Back to work.

And as fate, luck, and a cruel and merciless universe would have it, Noboru had to check all six garages before finding the Range Rover parked inside the last one.

The doors were opened by remote control, with rolling codes, and Noboru waited while his CBT Code-Scan, a Third Echelon–engineered magic box, got to work. It took another five minutes for the CBT to cast its spell, and the door finally cycled open. Noboru entered, then shut the door behind him.

He flicked on his penlight and took a deep breath. Picking the lock on the Range Rover still wouldn't disable the vehicle's alarm system, but if you had a key fob—or a device that could precisely mimic one, like the CBT—then you could simply press a button, resynchronize the forty-bit random codes, and gain access. Noboru understood that the device would reprogram the car to allow him entrance, and then, quite remarkably, return the car to its original codes so its owner would be none the wiser.

After a few seconds, the CBT's LED screen flashed, the car chirped, and the locks opened. Noboru immediately searched the glove box for a rental-car agreement and found it. The name on the papers was an alias breathtakingly familiar to him.

Horatio and Gothwhiler were in France. After him. No doubts.

Noboru activated his OPSAT and opened a channel directly to Grim, who answered after a few moments. "Uh, what is it, Nathan?"

"My old friends are here."

A few seconds of nothing, then, "I understand."

"You made a promise."

"I know."

"How'd they find me?"

"I don't know. We can't talk about it now."

"I need to do something."

"Leave that to me."

He paused. "I'm sorry, but I don't trust you anymore."

"You have to. If you do something, you could compromise your mission."

"I'll plant a V-TRAC and route the signal to you. If you don't take care of this soon, I'll have to do it—even if it costs me my job."

"I understand. But you need to trust me. Okay?"

Noboru shook his head. "Take care of the problem. Good-bye, Grim."

After planting the V-TRAC device well up inside the Range Rover's body, Noboru left the parking garage, hustled back to the coffee shop, and returned to the room with five tall cups of decaf.

"Where the hell were you?" asked Valentina.

"One of the coffee machines broke, and I helped the lady fix it. She gave me the decaf for free." He forced a grin, and he thought his cheeks would crack off.

Hansen accepted his coffee and said, "Was the Range Rover there?"

"Uh, what do you mean?"

Hansen's tone grew harder. "Yes? Or no?"

Noboru opened his mouth, thought better of lying, and then suddenly said, "We'll be tracking it."

"Any idea who they are?"

Noboru braced himself. This time he would have to lie. "Not sure who they are."

"Kovac's people, no doubt. All right." Hansen faced the others. "Moreau's a tough nut to crack, but here's what I got out of him. For all intents and purposes, Kovac wants Fisher dead. And he's pressing Grim hard to make it happen. Grim, of course, would like to talk to Sam before we put a bullet in his head. You don't shoot your best friend for no reason. So if we ever catch up to him, my plan is to capture first. Moreau swears to me that they're not lying about this, but to suggest that Fisher is just on the run in France with no agenda is ridiculous. He's up to something, and we're going to find out what."

Ames snorted. "You're damned right we are. And you all need to listen to me: You don't capture Sam Fisher. And you don't talk to him. You take him out. Those were our orders."

Gillespie shifted over to Ames and deliberately spilled her coffee across his shirt. He cursed as she said, "Oh, I'm so sorry. Did I burn you?"

While the others tried to stifle their laughter, Hansen cleared his throat. "If we can take Fisher alive, that's the way we do it. If it comes down to it, though, then we'll have to kill him."

HANSEN spent most of the night tossing and turning. In fact, he'd barely slept in the past two days, so when the courtesy wake-up call came, Hansen was ready to smash the phone against the wall. He rose, showered, shaved, dressed quickly, then gave up the bathroom to Ames, who was complaining about "pretty boy taking too much time."

Noboru remained dead to the world, and Hansen took a moment just to stare at the man who'd been a little too eager to check out their tail. Hansen mulled that over for a moment before heading down to the restaurant for some coffee.

Moreau had rented them another pair of cars, two Renaults—one burgundy, the other blue—and they loaded the gear and left by 8:00 A.M. for the sixty-mile drive east on A-4 to Emmanuel Chenevier's apartment in Verdun, near the quai de Londres—and its many shops, restaurants, and discotheques—along the Meuse River. They were wary of tails, especially from those men in the black Range Rover, but Moreau reported that the Rover was tailing one of the decoy vehicles within which Valentina had planted the tracker. Moreau warned them that the ploy wouldn't last long, and when they discovered what had happened, they would search their own vehicle for a tracker and/or abandon it. By that time Hansen and the others should be long gone.

They drove though the French countryside, the farmlands reminding Hansen of some of the Sunday drives he'd taken with his parents through Texas, although none of that terrain appeared even remotely as fertile as these grounds. However, the same sense of loneliness and utter quiet was still there.

Thankfully, Ames kept his mouth shut for most of the ride, and Gillespie sat quietly herself. Noboru and Valentina followed closely behind in their car, with Moreau still back at the hotel, monitoring the team's progress. He planned to catch up with them later in the day.

Hansen had already decided that he'd be the one to speak with the forger. He reviewed the intel Moreau had given him.

Emmanuel Chenevier was a thirty-year veteran of the Directorate-General for External Security, a rather important-sounding synonym for France's foreign intelligence agency. While the data did not indicate that Fisher and Chenevier had a prior relationship, Hansen had a strong feeling that they had known each other for years. At the very least, Fisher would be aware of the agent and his impressive record that indicated he was fiercely loyal to his country. That Chenevier would help an American on the run might prove surprising to some—unless of course Hansen's initial premise was correct: The two were old friends. Fisher's record indicated that there had been a time, back in the early 1990s, when he would've had the opportunity to meet and perhaps work with Chenevier; however, that was speculation on Hansen's part.

When they were about ten minutes away from Chenevier's place, Moreau told them he'd tried to call the man's home phone. No answer. Chenevier did not have a cell-phone number that Moreau could find, so there was a chance he had stepped out. The geeks back home studying the satellite feeds had reported that they had not seen Chenevier leave his building, so perhaps he was home but not answering the phone.

Valentina, Gillespie, and Noboru kept close to the river, taking pictures of one another like goofy tourists. Ames established an overwatch position near the courtyard beside the entrance to the first-floor apartment.

Hansen walked by a redwood lounger, on which sat a copy of *The Count of Monte Cristo*. He grinned over the title (written by a Frenchman, of course), then went up and knocked on the old man's door.

He waited. He knocked again, waited some more. "I don't think he's home." He groaned into his SVT.

"And so we set up. And we wait," said Moreau.

"Let me go inside and take a look around."

"Don't do that."

"Why not?"

"If we play a gentleman's game, he'll be far more likely to talk. If you violate his privacy like a rookie, he'll shut down. Trust me."

"How do you know?"

"Because I know men like Chenevier."

"What if you're wrong? What if he's left the country?"

"He hasn't. We'd know about it."

"Then where is he?"

"He's probably watching you right now. Give him some time. He'll come around. He wants to feel you out first, see what he's dealing with. When he realizes that Fisher's got a bunch of young bucks after him, he'll talk to you."

"Why?"

"Because it'll amuse him."

"So you already think this is a dead end?"

"No, I don't. If Fisher was here, and he knows this guy, then what can you do to get him talking?"

Hansen considered the question. His first thought was to shove a gun in the man's head or threaten to chop off his fingers, as he'd done with Boutin.

But if this were a gentleman's game, as Moreau had suggested, then Hansen needed something far more sophisticated and tactful.

"If they're friends," Hansen thought aloud, "then Chenevier wants what's best for Fisher."

"Now, that sounds like a good place to start."

"But, then again, if they're friends, he won't give us anything."

"You never know."

As Hansen stepped away from the man's door, he checked his watch: 9:17 A.M.

How long were they supposed to wait?

20

CHENEVIER'S APARTMENT
VERDUN, FRANCE

HANSEN and the others waited most of the day for the old man to come home. During that time, they shifted positions, rotated in and out of locations, even changed jackets and maintained their surveillance as deftly and discreetly as possible. They might as well get some on-the-job training and practice, Hansen had told them.

They'd gone off in pairs for lunch, while the others kept watch. When Hansen and Valentina had been sharing a sandwich and some tea, Moreau had called to say the two men in the Range Rover had finally grown wise to the team's misdirection and had abandoned the Rover. Trouble was, Moreau lost them since they returned to another parking garage, and with many cars coming in and out, he couldn't be sure which vehicle they might have used or if they'd even left in the first place. He and the geeks back home would attempt to pick them up again.

Hansen was sitting on a bench across the street from Chenevier's apartment when he spotted the man's approach. It was about three fifteen. Imposing at more than six feet tall, and with a thick shock of white hair, Chenevier was the epitome of a distinguished gentleman and as leonine as they came. Of course, he was impeccably groomed and dressed in an expensive suit and overcoat. He carried an ornate cane that he used more for show or for security than to help him walk. His gait seemed true, if not a little slow.

"Monsieur Chenevier?" Hansen called.

Chenevier turned back and paused near the red-wood lounger as Hansen hurried toward him. "May I have a word?"

"You're an American. And my English is pretty good. So let's dispense with that."

"How do you know I'm an American?"

The old man grinned, and a twinkle came into his blue eyes. "You've been waiting around all day for me. I went to see my grandchildren. They're getting so big."

"I just have a few questions."

"Of course, you do. Come inside, and I'll make us some tea."

"Just a few questions. It won't take long."

Chenevier lifted his cane, pointed at the door, and eyed Hansen. You don't turn down an offer for tea.

With a nod, Hansen followed the old man into the apartment and was led into a small living room. The sofa, bookcase, end tables, and even the TV stand were beautiful antiques, nothing short of elegant. The artwork on the walls appeared to be original and notably expensive, not that Hansen knew much about art, but he could tell the difference between a print and real canvas. This was class, hardly small-town Texas.

"Please." Chenevier gestured to the sofa.

Hansen took a seat, and the pillows felt hard, as though they'd barely been used.

While the old man prepared the teapot in the adjoining kitchen, he called out, "I suppose you're wondering why no one saw me leave."

"That had crossed my mind."

"Any man who lives in a place with only one door is a fool."

"There's a basement? Tunnels?"

"Of course. I suspect that on any given day there are a half dozen governments keeping an eye on me. A man needs his privacy once in a while."

"I see."

"Don't be coy. You know who I am. And you've come here looking for him."

"Will you help us?"

Chenevier returned to the living room and sat in a chair opposite Hansen. "Why do you need my help? Haven't they turned you into expert blood-hounds?"

Hansen smiled wanly. "He came to you after Boutin. We thought you might know where he's headed."

"And if I knew, why would I tell you?"

"Because we're all on the same side. He's in trouble. And we're here to help."

Chenevier chuckled under his breath. "Our friend is always in trouble . . . or he's taking a day off."

"Can you give us anything? Any indication of where he might be?"

"There is a mutual understanding between men like us. I would hope that someday you would make such a friend and reach such an understanding."

Hansen took a deep breath and stood. "Thank you for you time, monsieur."

"But I've just put on the water for the tea."

"I'm sorry."

Chenevier stepped up to Hansen. "He's just a man who's tired and wants to go home. And so he shook a tree, and you fell out. So young. Just be careful. He casts no shadow, and you won't see him until it is too late."

* * *

HANSEN was about to tell the team they had wasted an entire day, and then go on to lash out at Moreau, when the operations manager called to say they were getting on a private charter bound for a small town called Errouville, about seventy-five miles northeast of Verdun. Moreau wanted them on that plane immediately, since there wasn't time to lose. "Fisher was at a Sixt car-rental office in Villerupt. He used Louis Royer's driver's license to rent a car. You need to fly to Errouville, and then get up to Villerupt ASAP."

Louis Royer was one of Doucet's thugs, and Hansen was dubious as to why Fisher would take the chance of using that license when he must've known it'd tip off Third Echelon. No, Fisher wouldn't make that mistake. This was part of the game, and the more Hansen played, the more frustrated he became.

It was already late afternoon as they took the highway designated D903 down to the small executive airport southeast of Verdun and boarded a single-prop Cessna 207. The pilot was a terse Frenchman with a sun-weathered face and permanent scowl. He barely said ten words to them as they boarded.

"French hospitality," said Ames. "Can't wait to bring the entire family back here so we can all be treated like dogs."

"Shut up, Ames." Gillespie groaned.

As they took off, Valentina, who was seated beside him, leaned over and said, "Nice vacation."

"Yeah, right."

"I actually found some shoes while we were waiting for Chenevier."

"Are you kidding me? Shopping while on the job?"

"If you call this work. I feel like an actor."

"Something has to give. Something . . ."

They both leaned back and settled in for the short hop. The engine volume rose, so there'd be little talking inside the cabin. Hansen glanced up at Ames, two chairs ahead of him. The team's favorite operative was rolling a Zippo lighter through his fingers, a nervous habit Hansen had seem him indulge on more than one occasion. He was such a control freak that being forced to sit in a plane and not pilot it was already driving him crazy. The more Hansen thought about it, the more he realized that Ames's presence was actually a good thing. Finding new ways to despise him was a pleasant diversion from the half-truths of the mission.

THE airport just outside Errouville was little more than a dirt tract four miles southwest of Villerupt. As they landed, they left a long plume of dust in their wake. Their friendly pilot, who'd been silent, cursed as the plane bounced over ruts like a monster truck in the Arizona desert.

Gillespie announced that she was going to throw up. She didn't, but Valentina told her to aim at you know who. Ames smirked.

The billowing dust from their landing partially clouded the three outbuildings, but Hansen thought he saw the two SUVs that Moreau had mentioned. He'd rented them yet another pair of transports: Renault Koleoses—one black, the other silver. The SUVs were strikingly similar to the Nissan Murano, and Valentina called dibs on the silver one as they taxied up to the end of the strip, turned, and neared the buildings.

In the distance, Hansen spotted a lone car traveling down the narrow road, but it was too far off to see clearly. The pilot helped them unload their gear; then Hansen went inside the door marked BUREAU and caught the attention of a heavyset woman with red hair.

"Vous désirez?" she asked.

Hansen told her in French that he needed the keys to the rental cars that had been left there by the agency. She handed over the keys and said, "You just missed your friend."

"Excuse me?"

"There was a man here who said he was expecting five friends."

Hansen frowned deeply. "Was he a tall black man?"

Moreau had *said* he was still back in Reims, but Hansen was no longer ready to assume anything.

The woman shook her head. "He was a white man. He was clean shaven, crew cut, tall. Dressed like tourist: red polo shirt and green trousers."

And Hansen was already reaching for the photo of Sam Fisher he kept in his breast pocket. "Him?"

"That's him. Are you the police?"

"No . . ."

"But your friend is in trouble."

Hansen raised his chin. "Thanks for your help." He ran outside, shouting, "You're not going to believe this! Fisher was just here!"

MOREAU was talking to Grim via the Trinity System. They floated over the airport in Errouville, watching as Hansen and his team rushed off toward Villerupt.

"The tail I placed on Stingray just reported in," said Moreau. "Guess where Stingray's headed?"

"Villerupt," said Grim. "And since I haven't issued my next report to Kovac yet, we have confirmation."

"Let me say it out loud so we're both clear on this: Stingray is a cutout for someone on our team. Someone on Delta Sly is a mole working for Kovac." Moreau took a deep breath. "That's the only way Kovac would've known I'm in France and the only way Stingray would know where the team is headed. Someone on the team is feeding the information back to him."

"So all our efforts to bypass him—meeting here, everything—have been for nothing."

"Don't pop the Prozac yet," sang Moreau. "This just makes the game more fun. First question: Do we notify the team?"

"No, we don't. That'll heighten the paranoia, interfere with the mission, and tip off Kovac that we're on to him. We've already got Noboru's mercs to deal with. We need to handle the mole problem from our end."

"All right. How about this: If we can identify the mole, then we feed that information to Fisher. He'll need to remove the problem and the team can be left out of it."

"Excellent. I could pass this on to Fisher's cutout, though I'm not sure when they'll be able to link up again. I'll have to risk contacting him to see."

"Any thoughts on who the mole might be?"

"I'd love to rule out Hansen, but there's no ruling out anyone at this point. He could've been working for Kovac before I recruited him. And I confided in him, even picked him for the mission to Russia. That could've been a grave error."

"What about Ames? I hate that little bastard."

"Who doesn't? That's why I like him. He's a thorn in everyone's side—including our enemies. And you've read his fitness report. He's scored higher than anyone else on the team, across the board. Fisher told me he doesn't have the temperament for this line of work, and I agree, but temperament isn't everything. I think he's too loud, too noisy, too obvious to be our mole."

"Or he's overplaying it so he becomes too obvious."

"Maybe."

Moreau squinted into a thought. "What about one of the women?"

"I don't know. I'll do some more probing. Noboru could be our man. Maybe Kovac promised him something we couldn't."

"Maybe I'm the mole," said Moreau.

"Don't even go there, Marty."

"You know if I am the mole, the entire NSA had better watch out, because I'm so wired into the intelligence community that it wouldn't take long to bring the walls tumbling down."

"But instead we got Kovac, who wants to line his pockets and arm our enemies."

"I'm sure he thinks he's saving America. As long as our enemies are armed and dangerous, we're all gainfully employed. No war on terror, no threats, and the NSA downsizes us onto the streets. They'll say, *Let the CIA do the field work. We're here to cut government spending and lower taxes!* So Kovac's boosting the American economy by making sure the bad guys remain very, very bad."

Grim smirked. "Our enemies don't need *his* help."

21

VALENTINA drove while Noboru rode shotgun, and it took the team a good forty minutes to get from the airstrip at Errouville to the Sixt rental-car office on place Jeanne d'Arc in Villerupt. Valentina ran inside and cried out breathlessly to the man at the counter, "My father was here earlier and rented a car." She showed him a picture of Fisher. "He had on a red shirt."

"Yes, that man was here. Is something wrong?"

"He told me he was going to pick me up, but I can't find him. He was telling me what color the car was, but the signal dropped on the phone, and now he's not picking up."

"I think he took one of our Aveos. A yellow one."

"Really? Thank you! I'll go see if he's waiting for me!" She ran back outside, where Hansen confirmed that the car he'd seen leaving the airport was light colored, probably yellow, though it had been pretty far off.

"I don't get it. Why would he rent a car, and then come back to the airport just before we arrived?" asked Valentina.

Hansen's tone darkened. "The target has gone asymmetrical on us, and so have our superiors."

"Now what?"

Hansen flipped on his OPSAT, pulled up the map, and scrolled around. Valentina read the map over his shoulder.

"He could be anywhere now. He could've gone west to Sainte-Claire or south down to Cantebonne. Or maybe he just went straight out to Audun-le-Tiche, right here." Hansen tapped his finger on the screen. "I'll be surprised if he's not heading to Luxembourg."

"So has he stopped dropping bread crumbs?" Valentina asked.

Hansen shrugged. "I'm calling Moreau. We need eyes in the sky to find that car."

Valentina raised her brows. "Why don't you let me talk to him?"

"You?"

"Yeah, I've been dying to give him a piece of my mind."

He grinned. "Be my guest."

She activated her OPSAT and called Moreau on one of the secure tactical channels. He answered after a four-second delay. "What is it, Maya?"

"We're done here."

"Excuse me?"

"You heard me. We're done playing. Fisher shows up at our airport. Now you got us running around. You already know where Fisher is. Maybe you want us to eventually bring him in, but maybe you want us to do that at a certain time or at a certain place, so just tell us; otherwise I'm done."

"Young lady, you're not anything until I say so."

"Adios, Moreau. I just can't do this anymore. I won't let myself be used by you people. This operation is a joke. I thought I was being hired and trained as a professional operative. I'm not an actor."

"The hell you're not."

"You know what I mean."

"You walk away, you'll regret it."

"No, I won't." She smiled at Hansen. "Nice working with you, Ben. Maybe one day you'll wise up, too. They'll probably get you all killed—because of their pathetic little games." She turned, strutted down the sidewalk.

All right, so she was calling Moreau's bluff and was waiting for him to chime in. But the bastard kept silent.

Thank God for Hansen, who came running after

her and said, "Maya, don't be like this. You know we're part of something bigger. If they told us everything, they could compromise whatever else they have planned."

"I guess I'm more of a straight-up fighter. I'm really sick of this."

Hansen suddenly looked away, and Valentina realized he was being contacted through his own subdermal. He turned back, eyes wide.

"What?" she asked.

"Car accident at a McDonald's on rue du Luxembourg in Audun-le-Tiche. Yellow Aveo. It's just a couple of minutes away!" He went storming back toward the SUVs.

Valentina fell in behind him. She really *was* getting tired of all the lies. If there was a certain artifice to their chase, then Grim and Moreau should come clean about it. But maybe they couldn't, and maybe whatever Fisher was up to was so important that, as Hansen has implied, they needed to engage valuable human resources like themselves in order to get the job done. That was an eloquent way of kidding herself and continuing to live in denial about what she really was: a Barbie doll on a fake spy mission.

She could only hope that Fisher didn't see it that way, and if they stayed close to him, she would definitely see some action. The real stuff, no doubt.

He was, after all, a magnet for mayhem.

* * *

THE sun was already on the horizon, the sky fading from light blue to deep saffron as they reached the McDonald's parking lot. There they found several police cars, along with a few gendarmes talking to witnesses in front of the restaurant.

Fisher's yellow Aveo was smashed into the rear bumper of another subcompact. The Aveo's door was still hanging open. The vehicles' positions made it difficult to see who had been at fault. Fisher could have been in some sort of frenzy, perhaps pursued by someone else—and had hit this other car. *Or this could be another bread crumb,* Valentina thought. *He slammed his car into the other to bring the team here.*

She spun around, studied the area, saw a train station in the distance and some kind of commotion up there. The side streets were blocked off by a few barricades. Some kind of party?

Hansen approached after having questioned one of the witnesses. "They say a guy in a red shirt. They weren't sure which way he ran."

"Nathan and I will go up there, toward the train station," Valentina said.

"Good. We'll spread out south toward that greenbelt. Everybody open a channel and put on your SVTs."

Valentina applied the flesh-colored transmitter to her throat and took off running, with Noboru at her side.

They headed up rue du Luxembourg, then turned northwest toward what her map called the Audun-le-Tiche station, where a train had just come in from its run to Esch-sur-Alzette on the other side of the border in Luxembourg. Valentina did a double take because the train was a nineteenth-century locomotive pulling three carriage cars and seemingly transported right out of Disney's Magic Kingdom.

If Fisher's plan was to cross the border, then he had picked an excellent avenue of approach. There was so much traffic moving between France and Luxembourg, so many connections between the inhabitants of each country and the sister cities of Russange and Esch-sur-Alzette, that it was quite routine for a French family to spend as much time in Luxembourg as it did in its own country, crossing the border dozens of times each week. As a result, border standards were loose and fast, and Fisher could very well exploit them.

As they neared the station, Valentina spotted a large billboard that announced the decommissioning celebration and carnival of the Audun-le-Tiche rail line. Ah, there was the explanation for the old train; it was part of the festivities and making hourly runs across the border. She and Noboru were running smack-dab into a crowd of weekend revelers—yet another perfect situation for Fisher to exploit. Hundreds of colorful balloons had been tied to the platform, and rows of equally festive flags billowed above rows of vendors' portable stalls with awnings striped red, blue, and white. Valentina could smell the coffee and the pastries, and her stomach growled as she ran past the stalls. There were, she estimated, at least five hundred people at the station, perhaps more, and she and Noboru began cutting through them, trying their best not to shove people and draw attention.

A cry of "All aboard!" in French lifted above the din of the crowd, and with a clank, groan, and sudden hiss, the train broke forward, and those still standing on the platform raised their arms and waved to their friends seated in the carriages.

As Valentina neared the station doorway, she and Noboru strained to see past all those arms and spot a man with a red shirt on board the train. By the time they reached the edge of the platform, the train had already pulled away.

"He might be on the train," said Valentina. "We're just not sure. Moreau? Do you see it?"

"I'm on it. I'll let you know if I spot anything."

THE automatic streetlights were beginning to switch on as Hansen called back Ames and Gillespie from the greenbelt area. They hadn't spotted anything, and Moreau had done a thorough scan of the area with the help of his satellite feeds. They rallied back at the SUVs, where Valentina and Noboru were already waiting for them.

"We searched the entire station," said Noboru. "Very crowded. But no red shirt."

"Did you know that on *Star Trek* the guys who wear red shirts always die?" asked Ames. "I wonder if Fisher knows that. I wonder if, maybe, he's suicidal. But subconsciously, you know? That's why he picked a red shirt."

Nearly in unison Gillespie and Hansen told Ames to shut up; then Valentina said, "If I were him, I'd be on that train."

"Then let's go up there and have a look."

Hansen cocked his thumb back in the direction of his SUV, and Gillespie and Ames jumped in while Valentina and Noboru rushed back to theirs. They took off, heading up rue Napoléon 1er and veering off along a side street running parallel to a large, triangular-shaped reservoir in the distance.

Suddenly Hansen slowed to stop. Gillespie hopped out the back door.

"What's going on?" asked Valentina.

"I see something down there. Looks like a bike," said Hansen. "Moreau, can you get a fix on it for us?"

"No, I've got a signal issue right now. Give me a minute."

"Great timing," grunted Hansen.

"Take the wheel," Valentina ordered Noboru; then she grabbed her weapon and hopped out. She crossed to the black SUV and joined Gillespie, who'd donned a long trench coat, just like Valentina had. Ames climbed out as well, and all three started down the slope, toward the bike Hansen had spotted. They were shouldering their SC-20K rifles with long-range scopes and under-barrel attachments loaded with Cottonballs, LTL (less-than-lethal) projectiles that resembled shotgun shells but were, in fact, aerosol tranquilizers with stronger, faster-acting agents that began taking effect on impact. The round would strike the target, release its contents, and render the subject unconscious for about twenty minutes, depending upon the size of the dose, the target's body weight, and a host of other factors. Valentina thought it'd be a small miracle if they actually got to fire one of those rounds.

"Keep going. It's right there," came Hansen's voice through their subdermals. "Near the bottom of the slope."

"Wait a minute . . . wait a minute . . ." began Ames. "I got movement. Wait . . . red shirt! There he is! He's running!"

Ames sprinted off ahead of them, and Valentina cried out for him to wait up, but then she saw him, too, climbing up the opposite slope and heading toward the trees—and for a moment it was like a dream, utterly surreal—Sam Fisher dressed like a goofy tourist but Sam Fisher nonetheless, stealing looks over his shoulder as he bolted away from them and spirited into the dark cover of the woods.

Valentina's heels dug deeply into the soft earth, and she and Gillespie fought to catch up with Ames. They reached the top of the slope and once more spotted Fisher darting into the woods, heading east.

"You're about 120 feet from the reservoir, 200 feet across, and there's a dirt road on the other side. Looks like he's headed there," said Moreau.

"We're standing by in the cars," said Hansen. "Noboru and I will be ready to pick you up. Just don't lose him!"

"No chance of that now," said Ames.

Valentina was about to snort when the short man in front of her lost his footing and suddenly dropped to his rump. And in the next second she and Gillespie found themselves stumbling downward as the forest gave way to a forty-five-degree slope. Gillespie fell; then Valentina lost her footing and slammed onto her butt, and now all three of them were careening down, gliding across thick beds of leaves, trying to push off trees and find a path toward the flickering sheet of darkness that was the cool, calm surface of the reservoir.

And then . . . a splash . . . and Ames grunting into his SVT: "He's in the water."

22

**BORDER CROSSING
RUSSANGE, FRANCE**

AMES smacked into the tree so hard that he was wrenched sideways and his rifle flew off his shoulder. He whipped his head as the weapon slid away and landed beside another tree a few meters away.

Before he could get up, Valentina and Gillespie were already back on their feet and running past him. He cursed, rose, and crawled on his hands and knees to scoop up his weapon.

He stood and headed farther down the embankment to where the women had dropped down to their bellies, along a rocky ledge with the water about ten feet below.

"Wait for him to come up," said Valentina. "I have the first shot when he does."

"No, I got it," snapped Ames, hurrying up to the edge himself.

"I have it," Valentina insisted. "Do not test me, little man. . . ."

Ten, twenty, almost thirty seconds passed. . . .

Ames impatiently stared through his scope, searching in vain across the dark waves dimly lit by the moon. The night scope lit up the darkness, but there was still some distortion coming off the water. Mist perhaps.

And then, sans any forewarning, Valentina launched a Cottonball.

Ames jerked his rifle left, toward the sound, and spotted Fisher in the water. The old man had come up to steal a lungful of air, and Valentina's round hit him perfectly in the back of the head.

But that wasn't how Ames would interpret it.

"You missed," he said through his SVT. "Damn it, you missed!"

"No, I didn't! He's hit," barked Valentina.

"No, he's not!" Ames insisted, paving the way for what he'd do next. . . .

He tracked Fisher's intended path, and he assumed that the man, clearly alerted to their presence, wouldn't make the same mistake twice.

Fisher had taught Ames that water was cover, escape, and safety, and he'd also taught him to swim on his back and steal breaths so that only his mouth broke the surface, not his head. This was a basic escape-and-evasion technique often forgotten by operative in the heat of the moment.

Imagining Fisher doing just that, Ames zoomed in with his scope and spotted a faint outline in the water, the slightest disturbance across the waves.

Ames shuddered. He had him.

But now to set it up for the others.

"He's getting away," Ames cried. "But he's submerged. The Cottonball's no good. I have to stop him."

With Kovac's orders to kill Fisher echoing through his head, Ames took in a long breath and steadied his rifle. Fisher was shifting through his sights. Ames would not waste this opportunity. No way.

Was there any guilt? Even the faintest trace? No. It was just business. Time to put the old boy out of his misery. Fisher's ghost would probably thank him for it.

Ames blinked and stared more intently through the scope. He took another deep breath, held it. Then he trained his crosshairs over the disturbance in the water.

Moment of truth. He was ready, with thirty 5.56-mm bullpup rounds at his disposal. The SC-20K's bullpup design meant that the magazine and action were located behind the weapon's trigger, allowing the rifle to have a longer barrel length relative to its size. The design was popular with NATO operators and quite useful for Splinter Cells who needed the capabilities of a longer-range weapon in a compact design for stealth.

Indeed, that longer range would come in handy, since now Ames would use the Splinter Cell's favored rifle to kill the program's most lethal operator. Ironic? Fitting? Oh, it was hardly that dramatic. He just wanted to make sure he got credit for the kill.

He took his first shot, the pop much sharper than the one produced by Valentina's Cottonball.

"Is that live fire?" cried Gillespie through her SVT.

Ames gritted his teeth, spotted even more waves, and realized he'd missed.

He adjusted aim and fired another round.

That one must've hit Fisher.

"Ames, is that you? Hold fire! Hold fire! I already got him with the Cottonball," said Valentina.

"You missed."

"I'm telling you, I didn't!"

"All right, hold up," said Ames.

"Ames, are you firing live rounds?" Hansen demanded over the channel.

"She missed him. I'm not shooting to kill. Just forcing him toward the shoreline."

More BS from the king of BS, Ames thought.

"We're trying to take him alive," insisted Hansen.

"Roger that. He's still in the water. He has to come up soon. We'll get him."

"I'm coming down," said Hansen.

"You sure? We'll need you up there," said Ames. "If he heads farther north, you'll need to circle around. I'll let you know."

"He's right," said Moreau. "Stay with the SUVs."

"All right, but you watch that fire, Ames!" ordered Hansen.

A moment passed, with Ames just listening to the sound of his own breathing.

"I don't see anything now," said Gillespie.

"Me neither," added Valentina.

Below the huge concrete embankment to the northeast lay patches of thick weeds Fisher could use for cover. Ames focused on that area and waited.

No sign of movement. He slowly lifted his rifle to pan farther west, to an unpaved road running beside the opposite shoreline, then back down to the weeds. Fisher might try to rise from the water and break there.

"Moreau, you got anything?" Valentina asked.

"No sign of him yet. I've got a good image of the reservoir right now."

Ames frowned. What was Fisher waiting for? Distance was survival. They both knew that.

And then, out of the corner of his eye, Ames

caught the faintest shift in the shadows that seemed to be gathering along the road. He swung around his rifle, brought it to bear on the movement, and saw the silhouette of a running man.

Ames wanted to take another shot, but he couldn't. He had to exercise some reserve lest he betray himself. Two shots was already pushing it. The kill had to come naturally, organically, not in a hell-bent fury.

Fisher dropped down into a depression in the road and vanished. Ames swore.

"I've got him now," reported Moreau. "He's heading toward the woods just north of the road. Hansen? Noboru? Looks like if you take the SUVs north and west, you might be able to cut him off while the rest of you keep pushing him forward."

"That's the plan, everyone," said Hansen. "Let's go!"

Ames struggled to his feet. The women were already ahead of him, running along the trees, the water rippling down below. His footfalls were heavy, his pulse high, and in the seconds that followed he relived the shots he'd taken at Fisher. What kind of a marksman was he? Certainly this demonstration did not reflect his Third Echelon training or his police background. Was he just succumbing to the pressure? No, he couldn't think that way. He'd nail Fisher. In time. *Patience. No hell-bent fury.* He would neither beat himself up nor get too far ahead of himself. At least now the old man knew they meant business.

Perhaps he'd step up his game and make the kill more interesting.

KIMBERLY Gillespie turned northwest, heading straight for the pine trees near which Moreau reported he had last spotted Fisher. She was moving in directly behind him, from the south, and began to slow as she neared the first cluster of pines, their boughs still. Not a sound. She raised her rifle, made sure the fire selector was set for Cottonball.

She tried to ignore her eyes. The burning. The old aches and pains. The guilt of taking from him what she shouldn't have, and still hoping that somewhere, deep down below all those shields against emotion, there was a man who would, at the very least, remember her.

She once again smelled the chicken they'd roasted that night, tasted the wine—too much wine—and listened to him speak softly in that near whisper that at once captivated and drove her insane with lust. And for just a moment, she was back there, feeling his lips on hers, and then . . .

"This was a mistake," he'd said afterward. "You were my student."

"And now I'm your lover."

He shook his head. "I'm sorry this happened. You can do better. You deserve better."

"Relationships are about people, not numbers on a calendar."

"It's not the numbers I'm worried about. It's me."

Gillespie's foot came down and snapped a branch. Loudly.

She mouthed a curse. Froze.

Then she waited a few breaths more and crossed to open ground, heading west now.

Had she heard something? Breathing? She thought for a moment that he was close, watching her, his gaze warm on her cheek. She wanted to call his name, beg him to turn himself in, to end the game here and now. She could help. She would do anything. She imagined him emerging from behind the trees, hanging his head, reaching out to her.

She heard herself, *"Sam, come home. Just come home."*

Then she shook free the thoughts, willed herself back to the task. She scanned the trees. *That's right, back to work. Get rid of the baggage.* She'd made a promise to Hansen. *All right. If Sam had cut to the north instead of crossing the road . . .* But she couldn't abandon the plan or the others. She had to keep moving. It was all part of small-unit tactics. She could still hear his admonishments as she continued, carefully measuring her steps, wincing at the crunch of twigs.

Her pulse began to slow, and then, reaching out with all her senses, she tried to detect him, taking her mind beyond the flesh to see if maybe, just maybe, the connection they'd had could transcend physical distances.

A cold breath washed over her.

She stopped, looked around, and something told her that Sam Fisher was already long gone.

THEY were getting just a little too close for comfort, thought Moreau. He was alone, using the Trinity System, floating over the reservoir now and watching as Fisher neared the Esch-sur-Alzette's train station. Fisher stepped onto the dirt shoulder just as a motorcyclist came barreling toward him. Moreau winced and through a gasp cried, "Get out of the way, Sam!"

This was hardly planned. Unless Fisher had decided to suddenly check out and wanted to be run down by a motorcycle, he needed to move.

But then the guy on the bike swerved to avoid him and wound up dumping the bike in a ditch, his body tumbling off at shockingly steep angles, as though he were an action figure tossed aside by an angry kid. Fisher ran down after him. Others gathered around; then Fisher took off, northward up the road, moving another fifty yards.

Moreau checked the locations of the team, the pieces on his chessboard, as it were, and so far everything was falling into place.

"I've found some clothes here," called Valentina. "No more red shirt! He's changed!"

Of course he has, thought Moreau.

"Anything, Moreau?" asked Hansen.

"Still looking," he answered. "But we've got a motorcycle accident. That'll back up some traffic."

Fisher was now positioned between the highway to the left and a large soccer stadium to his right, its lights burning brilliantly.

Hansen's SUV was up on the north side of the road, picking up Gillespie, Valentina, and Ames, while Noboru remained behind, and he would be in plain sight to pick up Fisher. A little nudge from Moreau couldn't hurt at this point.

"Hey, Bruce Lee, you still with us? Wake up, Grasshopper."

"I'm here, Mr. Jules Winnfield. Would you like me to get you a Royale with cheese?"

Moreau laughed under his breath. "Fisher might be heading your way, just behind you."

"I'm out for a look."

NOBORU pushed forward in the seat of the SUV, grabbed his binoculars, then hopped out of the SUV and crouched down near the wheel. He trained his binoculars on the road, about a quarter mile back.

"Nathan, we're coming around, back to your position," said Hansen.

"Roger. Nothing yet . . . Wait . . ."

Noboru zoomed in toward a hurricane fence that was twisted and had fallen in all directions. The fence had once secured an ancient-looking building with towers and crumbling bricks and exposed girders and more stone, like an old fortress abandoned a hundred years ago.

Noboru lowered his binoculars, brought up the map on his OPSAT, then tapped on the building to get more data. A box indicated that the place had once been a steel foundry. Noboru raised the binoculars once more. Still nothing, but the place presented a definite point of cover, so they had to check it out. "This is Nathan. Still nothing, but there's an old steel foundry down the road. He might be going there. Let's check it out."

Not thirty seconds later, Hansen arrived, and they pulled a couple of U-turns and headed south toward the old building.

"All right, boys and girls, better get a move on, because Bruce Lee is right," said Moreau. "I've picked him up near the foundry."

"Damn it, the traffic's backed up," said Noboru, slamming on his brakes and looking for a spot where he could rumble onto the embankment and skirt around the other cars.

Just then, the traffic moved, and they rolled closer to the foundry's main driveway and shifted into the turning lane to cut across the road.

The size and decay of the building unnerved Noboru. If Fisher wanted to lure them into a gauntlet of horrors and systematically dispose of them, the abandoned foundry presented the perfect opportunity.

23

HANSEN barked his orders, but Valentina barely listened and deliberately partnered up with Noboru, the one man on the team who regarded her as an equal. She led him toward a vertical slit where it seemed the sheet-metal wall had been pried back enough to permit a person to enter.

She slipped inside and flicked on her light to reveal a cavernous warehouse of sweeping concrete ceilings with shattered skylights, as though bombs had been dropped through them to explode inside and tear apart the brick walls and rusting ladders and catwalks. A latticework of iron girders and concrete lintels was spanned by thick cobwebs, and dust motes trickled through her flashlight's beam.

Valentina wondered if the dust in her light had been created by their entrance or by someone else's movements. She worked the light a moment more and could almost hear the ghosts of steel workers bustling about while fires spat, water hissed, and more men shouted to get the next load ready. It was the early 1900s, and the place thrived.

Noboru suddenly cursed in Japanese behind her, and Valentina heard a splintering of wood.

She whirled and saw that one of his legs had dropped through the floor up to his knee. "Hold on, hold on. . . ."

He began falling onto his side and caught himself, groaning as his leg twisted. She wrenched her arms under his, swore, then hauled him up. . . .

Only to have both her legs plunge through the same rotting floorboards. She released him and broke her fall at midknee with a hard slap of the palms and a gasp. She hung there for a moment, legs kicking in midair, coughing as the dust billowed into her face. Yes, they'd just learned the hard way that the foundry had a basement. Noboru managed to pull his leg free, then crawled around and got behind her.

"Don't put too much weight," she whispered as he lifted, and within a few seconds, she was sitting back on the wood and inspecting her legs for cuts.

They took a quick breather, and she directed her light back toward the floor, as did Noboru. More ash, dust, and something else, silt or loam, maybe, lay across a dark avenue of broad wooden planks, and within that dust were footprints, dozens of them, some larger than others. Kids, adults, all sorts of people had ventured into the foundry to play or explore over the years. She tried to find any that looked fresher than the others. It took a moment before she finally noticed a fresh break in the floor, a place where wood and soil had given way. She crossed to it, directed her light into the hole to reveal intersecting pipes and the reflective sheen of water far below. She shifted the light to pick out a canal far below. And now, from this new angle, she looked up again.

And there they were: a fresher set of footprints leading off to a staircase. She tipped her head to Noboru, and they rose.

Valentina's foot clanged loudly on the steps, and she grimaced. Her light showed footprints clearly evident on the third step but no others. Odd.

Noboru shone his light above the staircase.

"What?" she asked; then she understood.

Fisher had gone vertical.

And now they were easy prey. She imagined him descending, inverted, like a spider, only to sink the fangs of a tranquilizer or something worse into her neck. She held her breath, and for a few seconds thought she would be sick.

* * *

GILLESPIE found herself paired up with the little runt Ames, and as she followed him along the foundry's east-side exterior wall, she twice plotted his murder.

The first scenario involved a knife. The second had her putting a bullet in the back of his head. But then she realized those methods were too merciful and too quick. She considered slower ways that had her getting creative with water and insects and, lest we forget . . . *fire.*

She wondered if the others knew about his past. They were all spies, and you had to assume they had thoroughly investigated one another, both professionally and personally. Gillespie had many friends in military intelligence who could get her whatever she wanted. She'd read the news stories about Ames's family dying in the fire. The world was unfair, and Ames railed against it with much more than words. His entire personality had been shaped by two facts: the loss of his family and his height. He probably asked himself: *Why did my family have to die? Why can't I be taller?* Gillespie thought she had him all figured out, and there were times when she saw through his remarks and found the frightened little boy behind them. She wanted to sympathize with him, feel his pain, tell him he'd be all right, and say that if he'd just drop all the defenses, there were people who could help.

But he was such an ass that he made helping impossible.

"Slow down," she told him. "You're not going in there alone."

"You worried about me, sweetie?"

"Well, if something happens to you, I want to make sure it's permanent."

"Great. I got your back, too."

"And remember, we're taking him alive."

"So you can have your little reunion?"

"Sure. You want to watch?"

He snorted. "Look, there's the door." He yanked open the bent metal, and they entered a stairwell. Her flashlight's beam raced up toward the distant ceiling.

HANSEN had opted for a classic Sam Fisher entrance by coming in from the roof. He felt a bit wistful about that. Here he was emulating a man who should have been his mentor but was his target. The assumption was that you had to think like Fisher to capture him, but, then again, he knew you'd be doing that, so perhaps he'd be engaged in some very un-Fisher-like maneuvers. . . .

Maybe that was thinking too hard and second-guessing himself, Hansen thought—which was, of course, thinking. Again. Mr. MIT Education needed to turn off the big brain.

Hansen startled a group of sleeping pigeons, which nearly knocked him off his feet as he reached the top of an exterior staircase running along the foundry's west side. He waved them off, then slipped quietly toward a roof-top doorway. The door itself was long since gone, lying near the opposite wall, and Hansen eased himself down the metal stairs, one hand clutching the rail. He reached the top floor, the floorboards of which had been torn up here and there, perhaps by looters, and carefully worked his way toward the center of the vast room.

"We think he's gone up to the second floor," said Valentina.

"Roger that," said Hansen. "I'm above." Hansen glanced down through a rectangular opening in the floor, lost his balance, and reached toward the wall, but his hand came up empty. He slipped down onto the floor, land-ing across a piece of broken pipe and breaking off several chunks of concrete that went tumbling down through the hole. He bit back a curse, stood, and then carefully chose his next path, across sturdier-looking boards, and searched for a way down to the second level.

He spotted a wrought-iron spiral staircase off to his left and stepped toward it.

Even as his foot came down, he realized the floor plank would not hold him. Yes, he was a fine judge of sturdy-looking wood, all right. The plank suddenly split. . . .

And down he went, keeping silent in an act of utter

self-discipline. His fall already betrayed his location. No need to betray anything else.

Finally, he allowed himself a breath and strained to push himself up, feeling the burn in his shoulders and triceps. His one leg had folded, so he was propped on the knee, while the other foot and leg had crashed through the floor, wedging his upper thigh deeply between two more planks. He rolled his left foot so he could sit on it and ease the pain now shooting through his thigh. He tugged. Nothing.

Some team leader. The man who'd been to Russia and back. The hero, right? He balled his hands into fists and thought of a string of epithets that would've had nuns fainting where they stood. He closed his eyes and took a deep breath. *Admit the mistake and move on.* There wasn't time for self-loathing.

Resignedly, he whispered into his SVT: "I'm snagged up here."

Hansen jerked his leg again, but now it felt as though he'd caught his leg on something, a power cord perhaps. "Shit!"

Oh, man . . . He'd said that much too loudly.

"Hang on. We're almost to you," said Ames in the subdermal.

Within a few seconds they were there, and Ames offered his hand. "No," Hansen told him. "I'm snagged on something from below." He looked to Gillespie. "Go down there."

She took off toward the staircase while Ames came

over to him and whispered, "What're you doing, Benjamin? Taking the path of least resistance?"

"Oh, you're a funny bastard."

"Hilarious. I'm laughing so hard I'm crying as Fisher gets away."

Hansen told him where to go, and Ames rose and took a few steps back. "No respect."

"Okay, I see what's happened," said Gillespie via the subdermal. "You're ankle is . . . What the hell? There's some kind of cord tied around your foot."

"What? What kind of cord?" he asked.

"Looks like paracord."

Hansen shuddered. *Oh, my God!* Fisher had tied him to the pole. Fisher was that close!

AMES opened his mouth as the arm came around his throat, but before he could react he was being lifted from the floor and dragged backward into the darkness. He gasped, reached up to seize the arm, which was like a piece of steel pressing even harder against his throat.

He tried to breathe. Tried.

And then a moment of panic before . . . darkness.

"Ames? Ames?" Hansen whirled his head around as the paracord suddenly slipped off his foot.

"All right, you're free," said Gillespie from below.

Hansen wriggled a moment more, then finally

turned his hip and his leg broke free of the wood. He rolled to his left and disengaged himself from the floor.

Gillespie rushed up the stairs, looked around, then said, "Where's Ames?"

"I don't know. Ames?"

They waited. He did not respond through his SVT.

"See if he went up top."

She nodded, ran off.

"Oh, man . . ." Hansen checked his OPSAT.

A message had come in, and the OPSAT's ID number told Hansen the note was from Ames:

SVT MALFUNCTION. INOPERABLE. MOVEMENT ON LOWER FLOORS, NORTH SIDE. INVESTIGATING.

Ames had switched the team's comms from VOICE to VOICE AND TEXT TRANSCRIPTION in view of the SVT problem, which in and of itself was suspicious. Why he'd suddenly slipped off alone would be a discussion they'd have later—of that Hansen was certain.

"We're already in the subbasement," reported Valentina. "Nothing yet."

The OPSAT transcribed her report, and Gillespie chipped in her own regarding the third floor north being clear.

"Ames, report," Hansen ordered. "Say position. Ames, respond. . . ."

Nothing.

In the distance came the bend and creak of the floorboards, both from above and below, and then the pattering of boots and a slight groan from a pipe somewhere behind him.

Hansen took a step forward, directing his light toward a hatch he hadn't seen before and a pile of fallen bricks. And just behind the pile a boot was visible. He started over there, holding his breath, and then he turned, looked down, and there he was: Ames, lying on his back, dead or unconscious. His rifle was lying beside him, but the magazine had been ejected, and the holster for his SC pistol was empty. Fisher had taken his weapon.

With a start, Hansen dropped to his knees and checked Ames's neck for a carotid pulse. Strong and steady. *Damn!* Fisher was a goddamned ghost— perfectly silent.

"This is Hansen. I—"

He cut himself off as a loud crash—the crunching of rock and snapping of more floorboards under heavy weight—echoed through the foundry.

"Who was that?" cried Hansen. "Report!"

24

VALENTINA was jogging toward the west side of the foundry when she stopped short and looked back over her shoulder a split second after someone had crashed through the floor.

Not a heartbeat later, as the broken wood continued to crash down, a loud splash echoed up from somewhere below.

"Nathan, did you hear that?"

"Yeah, I'm coming back to you," he said.

She and Noboru met up in the center of the ground floor, and their lights led them to where a man-sized hole had been punched through the floorboards.

Pieces of wood jutted up from the crossbeams, and Valentina knocked a few out of the way and directed her flashlight below, while Noboru appeared beside her, scanning with his rifle.

The slimy black canal lay below, shouldered by smooth concrete walls rising a few feet above the murk. More important, a trail of disturbed algae, oily puddles, and bubbles wound off into the darkness.

"There he is," cried Noboru; then he dropped to one knee and fired his first Cottonball.

Valentina brought her rifle around and launched one herself, as he fired again, then switched to live rounds, firing to Fisher's left and right to bracket him.

"What're you doing?" she hollered.

"He's getting away!"

"Is your name Ames? Hold fire. Jesus, stay here. I'm going out to see if we can cut him off."

She rose and dashed back toward the slit in the metal wall where they had first entered.

NOBORU had already decided that if he could anesthetize Fisher, he would; but if he had to, he'd fire to wound him. There was only so much you could do with Cottonballs, Sticky Shockers, ring airfoil or CS gas grenades, and wall-mine stunners—especially when your prey had intimate knowledge of each and every one of those less-than-lethal weapons.

Admittedly, he hadn't been able to clearly see Fisher in the water, but he'd rather shoot first and apologize later. That was, perhaps, the only thing he and Ames would agree upon. It was readily apparent that taking Fisher alive would be like capturing a tiger with your bare hands—and that wouldn't be fun for you or the tiger.

Fisher wasn't going to double back. Noboru felt certain of that, but he had to remain on overwatch just in case. Valentina had just taken him out of the pursuit. He could ignore her, but, then again, he thought that, maybe, just maybe, there was a spark there. If he gave her a little power over him, she'd probably find that very attractive. He chuckled to himself. That logic was faulty, to be sure, but when you're thinking with your libido, logic, of course, has nothing to do with it.

A sound like a dull clap came from below, followed almost instantly by a louder, closer thump from a piece of wood not twelve inches from his elbow.

Incoming fire!

Noboru jerked backward, tripped, and landed on his rump, heaving a cloud of dust.

Fisher had returned—or maybe he was trying to make them believe he had. . . .

"I'm taking fire over here," he reported into his SVT.

Three more shots ripped into the wood, blasting up splinters and streaking on toward the ceiling, where they ricocheted across the concrete. From the corner of his eye, Noboru saw sparks dance off the stone and steel.

Then . . . silence. He edged back toward the hole, balancing his rifle and light. If Fisher wanted to play with live fire, he'd come to the right place.

Noboru swallowed. He imagined the old spy sitting down there, one with the shadows, watching as Noboru shifted his head just far enough into the hole—and then, bang! The bullet would tear through Noboru's forehead, and his last thought would be that he'd been shot for being stupid.

He set his teeth, took a breath, then winced and stole a peek below.

But down there, the waters of the canal had grown deathly still.

STAY with him! Stay with him!" Hansen ordered as Ames slowly opened his eyes, coughed, tried to swallow, and made a face registering pain.

Hansen just shook his head. "He's got your pistol and your OPSAT—and he disabled the OPSAT's GPS so we can't track it. What the hell happened?"

Ames's voice was low and blurred. "What're you talking about?"

"What do mean, 'What am I talking about'? You're lying here on the floor. It was Fisher. . . ."

"It wasn't him."

"You know what we used to say at MIT? He took you out of the equation like a math professor with one swipe of the eraser. *Whoosh.* Just like that."

Ames sat up and rubbed his throat. "It wasn't him. I'm positive."

"How do you know?"

"Because this guy was much bigger. I mean, he was huge. Arms like my thighs. He would've dropped you like a bad transmission."

"Don't lie to save face."

Ames took a deep breath. "I'm not."

Hansen looked at him.

"All right. The son of a bitch got me . . . and I never heard or saw a thing."

"Fisher. Well, if you're ready, get up. Let's move. Kim, Maya, where are you guys? You got him?"

KIMBERLY Gillespie slammed her shoulder hard against a rusting fire-escape door in an attempt to get outside. A small courtyard lay below, and Valentina had just told her that Fisher might be headed there.

The door finally gave way. The wings of the main

building jogged off to her left and right, lined by dozens of windows. A long hedgerow stood below and rose maybe twelve feet as it wrapped around the corner. Fisher had 101 places to hide, and she had only one pair of eyes.

Somewhere outside, far off, a crowd roared, and she glimpsed the soccer stadium's lights reflected in the clouds. If he saw those lights, he might get the idea to lose himself in the crowd. Yes, that could work, because he'd be surrounded by innocent civilians, making him much harder to apprehend without causing a panic or a riot.

If she were him, she'd head there.

She raced down the stairs, reached the courtyard, but something, she wasn't sure what, made her turn back toward an archway for a second look.

And there he was, crouched near the wall! He was still wearing the red shirt? He'd changed, hadn't he?

Two sets of identical clothes? Well, isn't that clever.

"In the arch! Three o'clock low!" she reported.

As she bolted toward him, Fisher charged back through the arch and sprinted out of sight, back into one of the building's side wings.

Gillespie entered through the same side door and took another stairwell down to a subbasement, finding herself directly below the section where Valentina and Noboru had first entered.

She'd been right behind him . . . but he was already gone? How? That was impossible.

She stopped. Behind her, through a busted-out window, she spied two people running across the courtyard, probably Valentina and Noboru. They entered the building above her.

The basement was much larger than she expected, perhaps larger than a football stadium. Catwalks were suspended over the main canal and a half dozen stone staircases led back up to the first floor.

A chill fanned across her shoulders.

He was close.

Suddenly, three rounds from somewhere just above punched into the water, sending her diving for the ash-covered floor.

"Kim, you all right?" asked Valentina. "Where are you now?"

"I saw the shots," she whispered. "He's above me. Very close! He's shooting to kill!"

"Try to take him alive," Hansen interrupted through her subdermal.

Gillespie pushed back up to her feet and sprinted toward the nearest stairwell. At the top she found herself in a maintenance tunnel barely wide enough for a person and spanned by conduits, pipes, and more wall-mounted ladders.

Her light picked out footprints in the dust. She stopped, examined them. They looked fresh. She followed the prints to the first ladder, whose rungs were rusty and revealed clear signs of his ascent.

She climbed another ten feet, becoming enclosed in a narrow shaft, and then another twenty feet took her toward a door with a rusted knob. She assumed she'd reached the first floor. The knob looked dusty. She kept on, finding another door on the second floor—again no signs of exit—and then yet another door on the third floor: it, too, untouched. But the ladder betrayed his passage, and there was no clever way to conceal that.

"Kim, where are you?" asked Hansen.

"I'm in some kind of shaft. Check me on the map. I think he came up here."

"Hey, it's Maya here. Kim, I think I know where you are. Nathan and I just checked that out, but we didn't climb up."

"Well, I think he came this way."

The ladder terminated at a small hatch. She opened it, set the prop-arm into place, then climbed out, finding herself on an expanse of patchy gravel and peeling tar paper that extended across the wing's E-shaped roof. In some areas the roof had collapsed: Exposed ceiling planks and the remains of the skylights created dangerous voids promising injury or death below. Several brick chimneys stood in various stages of decay, a few resembling teeth in silhouette.

Out to the west, three towerlike structures made her feel as though she were atop a medieval castle, and off to the north and west the courtyard was enclosed by the two wings of the E-shaped building. She was up pretty high; correction, make that *damned* high, probably close to a hundred feet, and while she had no serious fear of heights, standing atop a dilapidated structure, with just the pale beam of her flashlight to help her find a safe path, wasn't exactly comforting.

She thought she heard a shuffling sound to the north, then directed her light to the exposed beams and thought, perhaps, she saw footprints. She followed them slowly, gingerly, toward the north wing.

With her gaze focused on the roof, she failed to see the tree as she came around the side one of the chimneys. Before her was a colossal oak whose heavy boughs and thick branches overhung the roof like the claw of some beast ready to devour the stonework and steel.

She took a few more steps, lifted her flashlight. . . .

And there he was, standing at the ledge, facing away, about to climb into the tree.

Surprised by his sudden appearance, she could barely speak, and when she did, her voice sounded unrecognizable, even to her. "Don't move a muscle."

She wanted to say, "*Sam, please, don't do this. Come with me now. It's all over. This is for the best. . . .*"

But only that order came out, cued by instinct, reaction, her time spent in the military listening to hundreds of people issue thousands and thousands of orders. Commands. Do this. Don't do that.

Don't move a muscle.

And the expectation was compliance.

But if your name was Sam Fisher and you were on the run, orders meant little, even if they were issued by a former lover, by someone who still cared very, very much. . . .

And so Fisher did not turn back. He did not obey her.

He simply jumped.

25

HANSEN was at the exact opposite end of the foundry from where Fisher was escaping, and it might as well have been on the opposite end of the universe. Hansen's competitive nature and jealousy had boiled up to the surface; *he* wanted to be the operative who captured Fisher. Maybe that sounded immature—something Ames would no doubt admit and not apologize for—but the desire was there and Hansen needed to wrestle with it while maintaining control of his team and always putting the mission first. But it was damned hard.

He and Ames were in a full sprint, racing along the

wall toward the next corner as the others issued their breathless reports.

"He jumped through the trees! He just jumped right through," said Gillespie. "I think he caught himself. Wait! He's on the ground now! I need to find a way down."

"We're coming to you," said Noboru. "Almost there."

"Don't lose him," said Valentina. "Do you hear me, Kim? Don't move—just maintain surveillance."

"But now he's already gone," she cried.

"Moreau, you got him?" Hansen asked.

"I had him coming out of the tree," said the operations manager. "Zooming in again. Aw, I've lost him now."

"The side street! The side street!" cried Gillespie. "I think he's heading for the stadium."

"Ames, go!" Hansen hollered, then waved him on.

"Boys and girls, listen to me," began Moreau. "I think he's definitely crossed the side street, but I've got multiple pedestrians down there. I'll see what I can do, but you need to close with this target!"

As Moreau continued his satellite-fed commentary, Hansen slowed to a stop. It was time to act like a team leader and not a glory-seeking operator. It was time to hold back and let his people do their jobs while he kept them organized and on task. He lifted his wrist to view his OPSAT and thumbed to the map. On the other side of the street lay a maze of alleys and intersecting roads, and Hansen estimated that a three-minute run would get Fisher to the stadium—if they didn't cut him off first. "Moreau, I *need* you to pick him up."

"I'm on it, cowboy. What the hell do you think I'm doing over here, sipping Coke and eating French fries?"

BACK at his hotel room in Reims, Moreau was, in fact, patched into the Trinity System while consuming a Coke and fries. He'd already finished off two cheeseburgers that tasted no more *royale* than their American counterparts. . . .

More important, he had a perfect fix on Mr. Sam Fisher, not that he'd disclose that to the team. Fisher needed to put a little more distance between himself and Delta Sly before Moreau would tip off those youngsters.

He munched on another fry. *Mmm.* Salty. Good.

"Moreau, you got anything?"

"Still working on it."

"Are you eating?"

Moreau smacked his lips. "Wait a minute. Hang on. I think I might have him!"

* * *

GILLESPIE should have raced down from the roof after she'd lost Fisher, but for a long moment she was a statue against the weather, against time, against all the BS that separated her from him. Of course he hadn't recognized her voice. Of course he'd never turn back. Of course he was gone before she could say something *meaningful* to him.

There was only the hollow pang in her gut upon which to reflect, only the memories, like a pair of jeans with so many holes in them that you should throw them away, but you just can't, you couldn't, you wouldn't—even if you tucked them in the drawer and never wore them again. Knowing they were still there meant something.

What was left between them? Was there anything at all? Anything?

Seeing him again brought too much back. Far too much.

Would she have taken the shot? He hadn't allowed her the decision. He'd been too quick, and she should thank him for that. Somehow.

Hansen would grill her, want to know if she'd had the opportunity and failed. She would tell the truth and hope they believed her.

After a deep breath, she fled the roof, picking her way down the stairs, the ladders, the tunnel, until she emerged outside to find that she was the last one left at the foundry. Hansen ordered her to get in the remaining SUV. Noboru had already taken off in the other.

VALENTINA had crossed rue Barbourg well ahead of everyone else and had the lead. She'd be the one to nab Fisher now, and as she ran, she thought how excellent that would be and how much that would prove to not only Grim, Moreau, and the others, but to herself. She was not a Barbie with an SC-20K. She was an operator, through and through.

The cheering of fans grew louder, and she spotted the banks of lights outlining the main entrance to the stadium and began racing through the parking lot, her gaze reaching out toward anything red, any shade of red, from pink to deep crimson, but most of the Jeunesse Esch fans leaving early were wearing the home team's black shirt with black and yellow logo.

All right, if Fisher had gone inside the stadium, he would've had to buy a ticket. She could not ask every attendant if he or she had seen a man in a red shirt. There were seven ticket booths and certainly other folks dressed in red. She quickly handed over her credit card to the young man behind the nearest booth, and he told her that the game was almost over. She told him she didn't care and double-timed it inside, resisting the temptation to run so as not to draw too much attention to herself.

"All right, I'm in the stadium," she reported.

Now, what would Fisher do?

What would she do?

She glanced up and down the large hallway below the bleachers. Souvenir shops and food vendors lined the left side. And there it was: the men's room.

"What would I do?" she muttered aloud. "I'd change."

She charged toward the men's room and brushed by a pair of young men in their twenties, who did a double take as she pushed through the door and hurried inside.

The place reeked. Men were pigs with bad aim. Three such swine stood at the urinals, and one, a portly middle-aged man with white sideburns, turned his head and suddenly frowned at her as his neighbor, an equally old man, turned and said, "Hey, sweetheart, are you looking for me?"

She ignored the perv and went straight for the white steel trash bin near the bank of sinks. She knocked it down to the tile floor. The lid crashed off and out came Fisher's clothes, along with piles of crumpled-up towels.

She cursed and reported her findings. She snatched up the clothes and ran out of the room, leaving the old gawkers behind.

Valentina then ventured up to the stadium proper and stood there at the foot of the bleachers, her face panning the sea of faces, some five thousand in all. He'd changed and probably bought himself a hat. Hundreds of identical caps seemed to bob as though floating on waves across the stands.

"Maya, report," ordered Hansen.

"I don't think he planned any of this." She gasped. "I just think he's one lucky guy."

Her shoulders slumped. They would never find him now.

But part of her said don't give up, and she kept probing the faces, probing . . . and then came a thought that she voiced to the others: "He might try to leave on the east side."

HANSEN sent Noboru back to the train station in Esch-sur-Alzette. He ordered Gillespie to take her SUV up rue Jean-Pierre Bausch, north of the stadium, and remain there. He, Ames, and Valentina eventually met up on the east side of the stadium, and Hansen realized that a densely wooded area lay before them.

Fisher could have easily left the stadium via the east exit and vanished into that perfect cover. Beyond the forest to the northeast lay the town of Schifflange with its mushroomlike water tower. Fisher could reach

Highway 31 and simply hitchhike or walk farther east to the towns of Rumelange, Kayl, and Tétange. At any rate, he was pushing farther into Luxembourg, a country slightly smaller than Rhode Island and bordering France, Germany, and Belgium. Was he just running through here? Or did he have a clear purpose in mind?

After five minutes of surveying the tree line with their binoculars, Hansen ordered Gillespie to come back down and pick them up. They would head out to Highway 4.

"I've got all our resources online," said Moreau. "He tries to rent car, we got him. He buys a train ticket, we got him."

"If he's not using cash," said Hansen. "Don't humor me, Moreau. We've already lost him. We're just going through the motions now."

Abruptly, Noboru's breathless voice cut over the channel: "It's Nathan. I'm at the train station. I think I have him."

NOBORU was running along the platform, weaving through the few other people and chasing after the man in the red shirt and white ball cap.

After first spotting the man, Noboru widened his eyes. They made eye contact from afar, the man's face half in shadow—but his shirt said enough. Noboru had started for him, and he charged off.

"What's he wearing?" Valentina demanded.

"Back to the red shirt. White cap."

"No, he's changed," she cried. "And if he hasn't, the team caps are black."

"Or maybe he wants us to think he's changed but hasn't."

"No, he has," she insisted. "You got the wrong guy."

"Then why's this guy running?"

Noboru launched himself into the air and came down from the platform with a heavy thump on the soft earth, as the guy started across the train tracks toward a long row of maintenance buildings on the other side.

That he might be the one to capture Sam Fisher didn't register much with Noboru. He felt badly about what had happened to the man, but he wouldn't think twice about killing him. In truth, Noboru knew exactly what it felt like to be on the run, and in one respect killing Fisher would be ending the man's suffering. It was a difficult thing to live your life always looking over your shoulder; it wore down your spirit even as the nightmares drained you of sleep.

Horatio and Gothwhiler were there. Always there.

Noboru caught up with the man, dropped to the ground, and threw his leg out, in an expert maneuver, to trip his prey.

The guy dropped hard as Noboru rolled upright,

stood, and aimed his SC pistol. He finally saw the man's face.

"It's all right, you got me now. They're in the top right pocket. I don't care. Tell Pierre it's all over. I'm not doing this for him anymore. I quit."

Noboru fought for breath and released a string of curses in Japanese; then he said, in English, "Maya, you were right. Wrong guy."

"Who are you?" asked the man, who was in his twenties, clean shaven but built exactly like Sam Fisher. "What's that tape you got on your neck?"

"What's in your pocket?" asked Noboru.

The guy frowned. "The drugs."

Noboru continued to catch his breath and shook his head. "Don't wear red ever again."

"Why not?"

Noboru leaned down and, still panting, put his gun in the man's face. "Because I'll come back and kill you."

MOREAU agreed with Valentina that the team should focus its search efforts east of the stadium, and Hansen could only assume that the man knew more than he was sharing, as usual. They drove the ten minutes out to the small village of Kayl, where they waited for Noboru to join them. Then Hansen sent him and Valentina down to Rumelange, while Gillespie and Ames would check out Tétange. They, too, were small, rural villages nestled into the countryside. Hansen would remain in Kayl and maintain a constant surveillance of the main road from an embankment cordoned off by clusters of tall pines.

If Moreau didn't pick up Fisher soon, it'd be all over for now. And as Hansen settled down with his binoculars, he couldn't get the image of a Coke and French fries off his mind. He remembered the McDonald's, remembered Moreau's comment, and now the advertising demons were playing product placement with his mind. In point of fact, he'd barely eaten all day, barely slept in the past few days, and if he somehow managed to remain in position and not fall asleep, well, that would be an accomplishment. Some of the others had packed granola and other kinds of energy bars in their packs; he'd opted for a pack of gum, and, boy, wasn't that a mistake.

The air grew still, and the night seemed to wrap more tightly around him, like a warm blanket against the cold. The night-vision binoculars picked up headlights in the distance. He watched as the car approached and realized it was actually a pair of scooters. They raced on by, their small engines issuing a rather irritating buzz.

"Kim, how 'bout a sitrep?"

"Ames here. She's busy right now."

"Doing what?" Hansen said.

"You don't want to know."

"Shut up, fool," said Gillespie. "We're almost in town. No sign of anyone. Place looks dead."

"Same here," said Valentina.

"All right, team, we have a couple of minutes to kill while you're en route," Hansen began. "What's Fisher doing in Luxembourg?"

"Getting drunk," said Ames.

"If you don't shut up," warned Valentina.

"No, I'm serious," Ames snapped. "Luxembourg is in *Guinness World Records* for most alcohol consumption."

"A fact you know how?" asked Gillespie.

"Everyone knows that," he argued. "And besides, I just pulled it up on my phone."

"Using Google while on the job?" asked Gillespie.

"What's wrong with that?"

"Moreau? You still with us, Moreau?"

Hansen frowned. It wasn't like the man to sign off unannounced.

26

MOREAU was so fully immersed in the Trinity System that he failed to notice the man who had bypassed the door lock, entered the hotel room, and now stood behind him, pressing a noise-suppressed pistol to the back of his head.

"Hello, Mr. Moreau."

He tried to read the voice, the pitch, the tenor, and already decided that the man was a smoker. This was not Stingray, the mole's cutout to Kovac. He was someone else; someone probably hired by Kovac to come and take care of the problem—because the team was getting closer to Luxembourg. Without Moreau, the team would be forced to communicate directly with Grim or through cutouts, all of whom Kovac had already tapped.

Moreau snorted. "I love this country. I order room service and they send me an asshole with a gun."

"Funny man . . . and a dead one—unless you tell me what I want to know."

Moreau swiveled his head a fraction of an inch.

"Ah, don't do that," warned the man.

This was not an American. He was doing his best to adopt an American accent, northeastern to be precise, but he was failing miserably. This guy was probably a Frenchman. Or a German. Undoubtedly a fool. You don't threaten a man and then tell him you need information. That tells your victim you'll hesitate because you need something.

"Listen to me," Moreau began; then he used a word that rhymes with "trucker" to describe his assailant. "You got 3.5 seconds to get that goddamned gun off my head."

"Such bravado, Mr. Moreau. Is this where you say what you'll do to me? Break my nose? Throw me out the window?"

"One . . ."

"We know Grim is communicating with Fisher. We want the encryption codes, the name of the cutout. We want them all. Right now."

"Two . . ."

"If you don't talk, I have orders to kill you."

"Three." Moreau took a deep breath, held it.

The man snickered. "What's the half second for?"

"This!"

Moreau tipped his head, then pushed back with all his might, driving his chair directly into the man's abdomen.

Of course the guy didn't fire. He wouldn't. He had orders to get the information. Anything else was BS. Killing Moreau without getting the data would result in his own death. Now that that fact was established, Moreau would begin teaching this fool a lesson.

As soon as his legs cleared the desk, Moreau spun around. The man staggered back.

And, wouldn't you know, the idiot made the impetuous decision to fire.

The shot thumped no more loudly than a hand clap and kicked into Moreau's shoulder. He jerked back across the desk, even as he drew his own sidearm and fired at the man's crotch.

Sensory overload: pain and images and a trace of gunpowder all coming at him.

Who was his attacker? So far, he was a guy dressed in casual business clothes and wearing a long leather jacket. He was no more than thirty and most definitely European, with a simple conservative haircut, no earrings, and nothing to distinguish him save his twisted grin. He leaned forward, groaned, then fell back onto his rump.

With a fire now burning in his shoulder, Moreau charged forward from the desk, and fired again, his suppressed round hitting the man's arm point-blank and causing him to drop his weapon.

Moreau dove for the gun and came up with it just as the man began to sit up, shivering and groaning.

"This would've been the part where I ask you questions. But I'm not doing that."

"You're not?"

Moreau shook his head, took both pistols, and placed them on the floor beside him. Then, remembering Noboru's words and imagining himself as Jules Winnfield, Moreau crawled forward and began choking the man with one hand.

Now, with a grimace of pain, Moreau wound up and punched the guy so hard in the mouth that several teeth loosened. The thug tried to reach up to stop him, but Moreau delivered another blow that sent both of them falling forward onto the rug. Teeth flew from the man's mouth as Moreau loosened his grip.

"I'll tell you what you want to know," the guy lisped through a gurgle of blood.

Moreau straddled him and widened his eyes as blood rolled down his arm. "You want to talk to me?

You don't know jack. All you know is that a man named Stingray hired you. You don't even know who Grim and Fisher are. And I bet when you go to the beach, you wear a little Speedo like all those other European fools trying to show off."

The man shook his head. "I know about Stingray. Let me tell you something about him. Please don't hit me anymore. I'm just doing a job."

Moreau cursed, winced over the pain, then struck the man in the temple so hard that the thug passed out.

Beginning to shudder with the throbbing in his shoulder, Moreau stood, breathing heavily, and rushed to the bathroom to check the wound. He slowly sloughed off his shirt. Damn, off to the hospital he'd go, but the wound didn't look too bad—clean entry and exit. He'd have time to pack up and get down to the hospital.

Moreau got back on the Trinity System and told Grim what had happened. She ordered him to get treatment.

"What happened to our tail on Stingray? He should've let me know about this guy. They must have met," he said, growling more than speaking.

"I know. They either took him out or bought him off. I've had no contact from him."

"Damn it. Fisher needs to flush out that mole."

"He will. Now, Marty, go get help. Let me worry about the mess in your room."

TÉTANGE, LUXEMBOURG

AMES and Gillespie arrived on the outskirts of Tétange and parked near the train station, which, according to the map, was on Line 60 connecting the city of Luxembourg to the Red Lands in the south. Tétange was the second stop on the branch line that split from the main line at Noertzange and led to Rumelange. Of the three cities to the east, Tétange seemed, at least to Ames, the best choice for Fisher. He could catch a train up to the city of Luxembourg, if that was his destination.

Moreau spoke evenly over the team channel and said he'd be off-line for a few hours. Hansen was understandably pissed, more so since Moreau offered no reasonable explanation for his absence. Ames told Gillespie to hold her position at the car while he reconnoitered the train station.

If there were six people at the station, that was a lot, and Ames did his best to keep close to the wall, near a vending machine, while he scrutinized those waiting near the taxicab ramp. His hand went unconsciously into his coat pocket, and he began to roll his Zippo through his fingers.

For just a few seconds, he imagined Sam Fisher strapped to a table while he poured gasoline over his entire body.

Fisher wanted to talk, though he never once let down his tough-guy demeanor. *"We're both going to hell. I'll get there first. And you'll be in second place, as always."*

"Maybe you're right. But first I want to see you cry. I want to see you beg for mercy."

Fisher cursed; he would die before doing that.

Ames's Zippo clicked open and came to life—the thin, perfect flame glowing as he touched it to the table. The whoosh of flames nearly sent him toppling backward.

Fisher screamed and writhed in agony, tearing at his bonds as the flames swallowed him whole.

Shaking off the thought, Ames let go of the Zippo and reached for the satellite phone Stingray had given him. He dialed the number, heard the man's key code, then returned his own code, the tones communicating that they were both free to talk.

"We've split up," Ames said abruptly.

"I know where you are now."

"Moreau's off-line."

"How long ago did you hear from him?"

"A minute."

Stingray swore and said, "All right. I'll let them know."

"You do that."

After he hung up, it occurred to Ames to check the train schedule. He consulted his watch, then said, in French, to the wizened man behind the glass partition, "Did a train just leave?"

The old man frowned. "If you want to speak French, okay. . . ."

Ames had forgotten that he was not in France anymore, and in Luxembourg they spoke Luxembourgish, a high dialect of German, as well as some French and German.

"The train?"

"You missed it. Five minutes ago."

"And that was the last train for the night?"

The old man nodded.

"You see a guy come here and buy a ticket?"

The man made a face. "I see a lot of them."

"Guy in a red shirt? No, wait, uh . . ." Ames reached into his pocket and pulled out a picture of Fisher. "This guy."

The man frowned at the photograph. "I don't really look at people when I sell tickets."

"Why?"

"Because I don't."

"Even the hot women?"

"No."

"So you didn't see this guy?"

"Maybe. I'm not sure."

"Maybe is not an answer." Ames hardened his tone. "Did you see him or not?"

"Are you the police? Where's your ID?"

Ames sighed and turned away. There was a strong chance that Fisher could have run from the stadium or gotten a ride and caught that train. He walked back to the SUV, opened the door, and said, "I'm bored. Let's have sex."

Gillespie spoke through her teeth. "I would rather eat your entrails."

"Oh, Pippi, my dear, Pippi. I guess you would. You want the good news or the bad?"

She rolled her eyes. "What now?"

"Last train already left. We might've missed him."

"I'll call Hansen."

"Don't. Not yet."

"Why?"

He wriggled his brows. "Because I want to talk to you."

She smirked and activated her OPSAT. "Ben, it's Kim. We're at the station here. Last train left already."

"Roger that. Hold position. If he missed it, Fisher might think there's another train."

"All right." She glanced up at Ames. "Get back to the station."

"No." He grinned.

"If you're insubordinate, we can get you removed. Don't put that past me."

He nodded slowly, then narrowed his gaze on her, making sure she could feel its heat. "You let him go, didn't you?"

Her brows tightened. "What're you talking about?"

"You had Fisher, up on that roof. You had him in your sights, but you let him go."

"I don't owe you anything."

"I got your back, but I'm not sure if you got mine—and you owe me that . . . *Pippi*."

"Get back to the station."

"Okay. But if I see Fisher, I won't let him go. I'll shoot him. You hear me?"

She shook her head. "Just get out."

"I don't want to be mean to you. And I want you to think about what I've said."

"I'm about to draw my pistol."

"Me, too." He winked.

Ames exited the SUV and smiled to himself as he started back for the station. Gillespie had some nice color in her cheeks now.

RUMELANGE, LUXEMBOURG

RUMELANGE, population about four thousand, was known for its underground iron mines; otherwise, it was but a blip on Valentina's map, and she and Noboru had established an effective observation post off the main highway near a small petrol station. They began to survey the main road with their night-vision binoculars.

"You see anything?" she asked.

"No."

And then, two minutes later:

"You see anything?" he asked.

"No."

And then another two minutes later:

"You see any—"

He cut her off with a loud sigh. "I don't see anything but a beautiful woman next to me."

Had he said that aloud?

He wasn't sure.

"Nathan, can I ask you something?"

Whew. Her tone said that he hadn't. He'd only said, "I don't see anything," but he'd heard the rest in his head as clearly as if he had.

"Hello, Nathan. Are you with me?"

"Yeah, sorry. Just thinking."

"You were born and raised in the United States, right?"

"Yeah. I lived in San Francisco until I was about sixteen; then my parents moved back to Japan."

"Who taught you how to treat women?"

"That's a weird question. My mom, probably . . . She never let my dad get away with anything. Women have come a long way in Japan, but there are still a lot of old-school attitudes there. My father was pretty open-minded."

She began to say something, stopped, then finally: "I know it's not right for me to be attracted to you."

He glanced over at her, his heart beginning to race. "I'm . . . sorry."

"For what?"

"I don't know. We're going to do a good job here. I've wanted to be a Splinter Cell more than anything."

"Me, too."

"So we have to think about that."

She grinned weakly. "I know. It's not like I'm Kim and sleeping with Fisher."

"Maya, I think you like me because I treat you like an equal, not because you like *me*."

"That's not true."

"Maybe it is. I believe in you. That's all you really need."

"Well, I believe in you." She laughed. "Well, we're a couple of believers, but that doesn't change the fact that Sam Fisher is still on the loose."

He smiled, wishing he could tell her how he really felt. The exquisite agony of her lips there . . . right there . . .

AS Moreau boarded the single-engine prop plane bound for Luxembourg, the pilot, a French woman about his age, looked him over and said, "Nice suit, monsieur."

"Merci."

Moreau took his seat, buckled up, then checked his OPSAT. He scrolled through a police report regarding a body that had turned up in Russange. The body matched the description of the tail they had placed on Stingray. All right, Kovac's boy was a clever bastard, but he was dealing with the king of the bastards, who was not only clever and cunning but one hell of a sharp dresser. Moreau decided that when this was all over, he and Stingray would have a very special "conversation," and Moreau would make sure to dress appropriately for that occasion.

27

BEST WESTERN HOTEL INTERNATIONAL LUXEMBOURG

HANSEN had rallied the team back at Kayl, then received word from Moreau, who was flying into Luxembourg. They linked up with the ops manager at the airport, and Moreau seemed to be favoring his right arm but ignored queries about it.

They all drove to the city of Luxembourg, and Hansen debriefed the team during the ride. They checked into the Best Western near the train station. Moreau said everyone back at the fort was working on picking up Fisher's next location and that he had a few ideas of how they could accomplish it. But first . . .

much-needed rest. Being strung out would result in grave errors. No one on the team argued with that.

Much to Hansen's surprise, he slept a full eight hours and was awoken to the sound of Ames on the toilet.

"Jesus, can you close the door?"

THIRTY minutes later, at about eleven, the team met in Moreau's room. As the ops manager finished pulling up more data on his computer, Hansen drifted over to Gillespie and motioned her toward the window, away from the others. They spied a remarkable clock tower casting its long shadow over the train station below. The tower resembled Big Ben, and the clock's white face shimmered above layers of gray stone. Beyond the station lay rows of train tracks and the requisite maintenance shacks. To the west and east lay more cobblestone roads, and Hansen felt as though he'd been transported back in time. He half expected a horse-drawn buggy to appear around the corner, hooves clacking as the driver worked his quirt to urge the steeds onward. Luxembourg was a country as old as it was beautiful. Hansen's gaze remained on the window as he spoke. "You know what I'm going to ask you."

"And you know what I'll say," she answered quickly.

"What if I don't?"

"Then you don't trust me."

"I need to trust you."

"You can."

He took a long breath. "All right, then." He started away from the window.

"Ben. He jumped before I could shoot."

Hansen nodded.

She pursed her lips. "You don't believe me."

"I do."

They headed back into the suite's living room, where Moreau had turned away from his computer to face them:

"All right, boys and girls, here's what we know—"

Moreau's expression shifted markedly, and, for a moment, Hansen couldn't tell if the man was in pain or if an idea had just struck him like shrapnel.

"Mr. Moreau, are you all right?" asked Noboru.

Moreau took a deep breath. "Aw, I might as well tell you. Some clown broke into my room last night. Thought he'd whack me. Fool got off a shot. I'm all right. Just sore."

"Damn," said Ames.

"Did you go to the hospital?" asked Valentina.

He waved her off. "I'm fine."

"Damn," Ames repeated.

"Yeah, that about sums it up," said Moreau. "All

right. Now, Ames, you got another reason to say damn, since you danced with the devil himself last night."

Hansen watched as Gillespie and Valentina turned their evil eyes on the little man. They were loving the moment.

Ames fired up his best smirk. "Sir, to be honest, Fisher's not much of a dancer."

"Well, I'm glad you can joke about it!" Moreau cried, rolling the dial on his voice up from 2 to 10. "I'm glad you can joke about how Sam Fisher got your goddamned OPSAT and relieved you of your weapon!"

Ames shrugged, ever the haughty bastard. "These are trivial facts we're all familiar with. I thought we were focusing on Fisher's next move."

"Shut up. I've switched all the frequencies and cut off your old OPSAT so Fisher can't use it anymore. He knows how we play. He may or may not still have your weapon. But we suspect he'll try to better arm himself now."

"Why do you expect that?" asked Gillespie.

"Well, he knows about you, for one thing."

"But there's something else," said Hansen.

"Don't get ahead of me. Fisher needs to resupply—"

"The caches," said Hansen.

Moreau pointed at him. "Exactly. We've got three in Luxembourg and another four in Germany, Belgium,

and northern France. Closest one to our location is
in Bavigne."

While the weapons caches were small and had been
in place for years (and assumedly contained outdated
weaponry), they could be life savers for operatives on
the run. Third Echelon had such caches stashed all
over the world. Sam Fisher was either well aware of
their locations, or he knew who was.

"Sir, any idea why Fisher's here and where he's
headed?" asked Ames.

"You think asking politely will get you a straight
answer?"

"I could ask you like this: All right, fool, what's up
with this BS wild-goose chase? Tell us where Fisher
is!"

Moreau chuckled till he winced. "That's more
honest. Well, obviously Fisher's been hiding out in
Europe. He's still got more contacts and resources he
can tap here. It's anyone's guess what his master plan
is, but we've got a lot of work to do today."

"Why don't you make an educated guess?" asked
Hansen.

Moreau grinned crookedly. "All right, cowboy.
Fisher's here in Europe on a beer-tasting tour. How's
that?"

Hansen shook his head in disgust.

"So what are we waiting for?" asked Valentina.
"Let's get going."

* * *

HANSEN and Ames were en route to Bavigne, which is about sixty to seventy kilometers north-west of the city, deep in the countryside. The place is about as European small town as you can get, with only about 125 residents living within a community whose architecture seemed torn from the pages of a children's fairy tale. It was Old World Mayberry, and when Hansen tried to make that comparison to Ames, the guy didn't get it. He'd never seen any of the old reruns of the *Andy Griffith Show*. Ames was an uncultured swine.

While Moreau remained behind at the hotel, Gillespie, Valentina, and Noboru went off to check out several of the youth hostels. Fisher wouldn't play the credit card game now, unless he wanted to be caught, so he'd probably stay in one of the hostels, where he could pay cash, no questions asked. Then again, the people at those hostels tend to be very discreet and not at all forthcoming with information. The others would have to play their hand just right if they wanted to learn anything.

Hansen checked his watch. It was nearly 1:00 P.M. They were heading up E411, near another small town, Thibessart, when the Zafira's engine sputtered and stalled. Hansen glided to the side of the road, stopped, and for the next few minutes tried to get the engine to turn over. They had a full tank of gas.

Groaning through four-letter words, they got out, raised the hood, and attempted to diagnose the problem.

"You know anything about cars?" asked Hansen.

Ames rolled his eyes. "What do you think?"

BETWEEN the tow truck, and the drive out to deliver their replacement rental car, this one an upgraded Audi A8 like the one the others had rented, Hansen and Ames did not reach Bavigne until nearly three in the afternoon.

During the two hours they'd spent waiting, they'd coordinated with the rest of the team, who'd been scouring the hostels around Luxembourg and come up dry. There was another weapons cache in Birkenfeld, Germany, about eighty-seven kilometers away from the hotel, so Valentina said they would go check it out.

Hansen and Ames stopped at a restaurant, the Auberge du Lac, and ordered some sandwiches to go. The woman at the counter suggested they have some lobster soup, and Hansen agreed. Ames went off to use the restroom and returned in time to help carry the bags out to the car.

"So we're in the middle of a mission, and we're stopping for lunch," quipped Ames.

"Yeah, but we're eating in the car, if this one doesn't break down."

"Where's our sense of urgency?" asked Ames.

Hansen shrugged. "I left mine back at the hotel."

They ate quickly, though Hansen wished he'd had more time to savor the heavenly soup. They drove northeast, then turned south again, according to the map, weaving between farmers' fields and the banks of a narrow river. They passed through a covered bridge and into a clearing where rose a log cabin that might have been built a century before.

"This is it," said Ames, as they climbed out of the car.

Hansen nodded, started forward, then crouched down. "Footprints."

"And they look recent. He's sloppy, all right. He was here."

"You keep calling him sloppy. I find that hilarious. If he's sloppy, then what are you? Fisher didn't bother to clean up these tracks because he's confident we can't use them. He's deliberate. Always. Come on."

They mounted the porch, knocked, waited. No one was home. They crossed to the back of the house and found a locked door leading down into a basement. Ames picked the lock and they eased themselves into a damp, dark root cellar, the musty stench making Hansen crinkle his nose. Back in one corner lay some fruit boxes, and Hansen flicked on his penlight to reveal a small wooden hatch set into the dirt floor. The hatch had been recently uncovered. Hansen flipped open the lid and found the hole below empty.

If Fisher had not been there, Hansen and Ames would be staring at a DARPA-modified model 1650 Pelican case with an encrypted-keypad lock and a C-4 tampering system that went *boom!* Larger than a suitcase, the pack held a standard equipment loadout: SVT; OPSAT; Trident goggles equipped with night-vision, infrared, and electromagnetic settings; SC pistol; SC-20K modular assault rifle with all the accoutrements; Mark V tactical operations RhinoPlate suit; and six grenades, three flashbang, two fragmentation, and one White Smoke. Fisher, it seemed, had now gone from the old school of jury-rigged cell phones to the newer Splinter Cell school, though the equipment now in his possession was still from the previous generation. Delta Sly had the latest and greatest toys, and they sure as hell would need them against Fisher.

"All right, everyone, this is Hansen. We're at the cache, and Fisher's definitely been here. He's got the weapons, the suit, the Tridents, the whole nine."

Ames drew in a long breath. "I think I liked him better in that goofy red shirt."

WITH Fisher's projected path into Luxembourg and up to Bavigne clearly evident, the team was now able to narrow the search for him, focusing on a grid northwest of Luxembourg and reaching up past Bavigne. Moreau kept close tabs on all the rental-car agencies in the area via Third Echelon's help, though it now seemed probable that Fisher had clean cards and ID (having secured them from Emmanuel Chenevier). Fisher had rented a car with impunity. He would be found on his terms. The other weapons cache in Germany had not been touched, and the rest of the team returned to the hotel, worn-out from the long drive and frustrated by the continued string of unknowns.

Hansen met alone with Moreau and asked what they were supposed to do now. The trail had ended at the weapons cache.

"Not exactly," said Moreau. "Those tire tracks you photographed before leaving are SUV tires. So I checked the rentals, and there was a little mom-and-pop agency that rented out a dark green 2001 Range Rover to Fisher. I went down there myself, and there was an old lady who recognized his picture."

"So he's in a Range Rover."

"Yes, that's a start. I'll run the tag, and we'll have the locals track it down."

Hansen took a deep breath. "Can I call you Marty?"

"No."

He moaned. "Mr. Moreau, you're stalling us."

"There's a difference between stalling and being very thorough. When you get older, you'll better appreciate that. You'll better appreciate the artistry of your work."

"Whatever. So what now? Should I just order the team to go driving around in the hopes that we happen to spot a Range Rover somewhere between here and Bavigne? You're not going to alert the authorities. You're just going to tell us you have."

"Watch your tone, cowboy. There are some traffic cameras we can patch into as well. I've already put in that request."

"Waste of time! Fisher could already be in Germany . . . or back in France. We could do a much better job if we knew more. You want us to play your game? Give us a few more rules."

"Where's the love, cowboy? Where's the trust? Where's the patience? Go relax. Go have a nice dinner. You deserve it."

"I'm still full from lunch."

"I heard about that. Lobster soup? Where's mine?"

Hansen stiffened. "When I went to Russia—that was being a Splinter Cell. I don't know what this is, but I hope, in the end, you make me believe it was worth it."

Moreau smiled, and a twinkle came into his eye. "I can't do that for you, cowboy. That's all up to you."

28

HANSEN gathered the team in his room. "He's just putting us through the motions. He already knew the weapons cache in Bavigne would be empty. He sent you guys to Germany to keep you busy. Checking the hostels was a waste of time. He says Fisher's driving a rented Range Rover. He says he'll have the locals help find it. I don't believe him. He's just telling us what we need to hear."

"So what're you saying, cowboy?" asked Ames.

Hansen leveled an index finger on Ames. "Don't call me that. Ever."

"How 'bout Tex?"

Valentina cursed at Ames.

"We all want you to die, Ames," added Gillespie. "Doesn't that bother you? When the bullets fly, we'll use you as a human shield."

Ames opened his mouth, but Hansen shouted, "Enough! Now, we either sit here on our hands, or we try to figure out what the hell's going on."

"How do we do that without them knowing about it?" asked Valentina. "We can't use our network or our personnel. They'll want to know why we're querying."

"She's right," said Ames. "We'd need someone outside of 3E but maybe still inside the NSA."

"Or the CIA," said Hansen, lifting his brows. "I have a friend. I owe him a favor, but maybe he'll make it one more for me, and I'll pay him back triple."

"What do you have in mind?" asked Noboru.

"If Grim and Fisher are talking, it must be through a cutout, and there's a chance that my CIA contact can drop a few names. Some of these guys in Europe work for more than one three-letter agency. If we can get the name of this cutout, maybe we can pay him or her a visit. . . ."

"That's a long shot," said Valentina. "It'll be like going to talk to Chenevier. The cutout won't hand over Fisher."

Hansen snorted. "Maybe, maybe not. But apparently, we have nothing else to do—until Moreau calls with a sudden and miraculous update."

"I'm all for it," said Ames. "Best idea you've had in, like, forever."

"You don't want to complain?" asked Hansen, dumbfounded.

"Hell, no. Call your buddy right now. But you can't use any of our cell phones. We need to get you one without Uncle Marty finding out."

Valentina opened her purse and tossed a cell phone to Hansen. "Try this."

"Yours?"

She cocked a brow. "Don't ask too many questions. And by the way, our Tridents should be here in an hour or so."

"How'd you pull off that?" asked Hansen.

She hardened her tone. "Like I said, don't ask too many questions."

AMES was very enthusiastic about finding Fisher because earlier in the day, when they'd stopped to buy lunch, he'd gone into the restroom and contacted Stingray.

Word from Kovac was that Ames could not allow Fisher to get anywhere near Vianden, Luxembourg. Fisher must be stopped before he got there.

The *why* was none of Ames's business. Kovac somehow knew that was where Fisher was headed. But more important, these orders placed Ames in a ridiculously complicated situation.

He couldn't tell the team that he knew where Fisher was going because he'd be unable to explain how he knew, which, in turn, would threaten his cover and his security as a mole.

But this . . . this was unexpected and quite beautiful. He would fuel Hansen's frustration and goad him into learning the truth about Sam Fisher's real mission—and Ames felt certain that Fisher's mission directly involved Kovac, which raised the stakes to the highest level of their organization.

And when you played a game that important, you'd be a fool not to have an insurance policy. Ames had already made certain that if Mr. Kovac decided to make him the fall guy, then together they'd take an express train straight into hell. Now all Ames needed to do was find a way to reveal the Vianden link via Hansen's desire for the team to investigate on its own. Or maybe Hansen wasn't the key. . . . Maybe someone else was. . . .

HANSEN used Valentina's phone to call his buddy back at Langley to see if the good old CIA could bail out the good old NSA—not, ahem, that there was any rivalry between those organizations. Hansen had to leave a message. Valentina and Gillespie went to their room to change. They were going down to the restaurant for dinner.

Ames ordered a T-bone from room service, and he raided the liquor, finishing off a couple of small bottles of whiskey before he realized how drunk he was getting.

Moreau came down and rattled off a list of possible leads on Fisher's whereabouts, and he reported that there was nothing yet from local police on the Range Rover. Hansen, Noboru, and Ames barely paid any attention to him. Moreau asked why they weren't following up on the leads immediately, and Hansen answered him with two words: "Just chill."

Mr. Moreau's gaze grew harder. He nodded, then left the room. Ames checked his OPSAT simply for the time, but the screen was blurry. "What time is it?"

"Almost midnight," answered Noboru.

"Are we doing anything else tonight except waiting around for your buddy to call?" asked Ames.

Hansen shook his head.

"That's good. I want to rent some porn."

Noboru glanced to Hansen. "Do we have to?"

"No, we don't."

"Aw, come on. You guys are going to sit there and tell me you don't like porn?"

Hansen lifted a brow. "Not as much as you."

* * *

VALENTINA ordered the vegetable plate and Gillespie decided that sounded good and ordered the same. They sat there, drinking sparkling water, staring at their vegetables, and wondering what the hell they were doing.

"I'm thinking about going back to being an analyst," Gillespie said out of nowhere.

"Maybe I'll join you."

"I thought we'd be doing something . . . I don't know . . . more dangerous."

"Yeah, I know what you mean," answered Valentina.

"And I sure as hell didn't think I'd be working on a team. No way."

"I hate your guts," Valentina said abruptly, then flashed a grin.

Gillespie smiled. "I hate you, too—because you're smart and pretty."

"And you're not?"

"You think I'm a slut."

"You're not a slut. I can understand how you feel."

Gillespie frowned deeply. "Oh, really?"

"Yeah."

For a moment, Gillespie's thoughts raced, and then she finally built up the courage to ask, "You slept with Fisher, too?"

Valentina began chuckling. "No. *No!*"

"Then, what?"

"I'm just saying I know what it's like to have feelings for a teacher or a coworker."

Gillespie bit her lip. "I wish I could take it back. Had I known it would come to this . . ."

"Don't have regrets. Just move on."

Gillespie nodded. "You know, I don't hate you as much anymore."

"Yeah, but I'm sure the boys would love a good cat fight."

"At least Ames helped us out. We both hate him more than we hate each other," she said through a chuckle.

"That's right. So, let me ask you, if Ben decides to follow up on this without Moreau and Grim, are you going along?"

"You mean break off from them and go find Fisher ourselves?"

"Yeah."

"Sounds crazy, but, you know what? I'm in. I think we'll call Grim's bluff and she'll be forced to turn over what she knows."

"That could happen."

Valentina thought a moment, then said, "So did Ben ask how Fisher got away?"

She nodded. "I told him the truth."

"Which is?"

"That he got out of there before I had time to take a shot. And that *is* the truth."

"I believe you. Did Ben?"

"He says he did, but I'm pretty sure he's still wondering and hoping that I'm not the one who'll have to make that decision. If I were him, I'd feel the same way."

"But do you trust yourself to take the shot if it comes to that? If I were you, I don't think I could do it."

Gillespie eyed her plate. "I can say, yeah, I'd shoot him because, really, in the end, he was a bastard. But I really don't know."

THE phone rang sometime after 4:00 A.M., and Ames thought he was dreaming. He barely heard Hansen speaking on the phone, and it seemed the room was still spinning. . . . Finally, the fool shut his mouth, and the world seemed to balance itself on its axis. Ames settled back into the cool darkness. . . .

NOBORU was down in the hotel lobby lounge by 6:00 A.M., sipping a cup of coffee and thumbing through a local newspaper, which he could not read, but the pictures were interesting. He observed the comings and goings of a few early-morning risers, and then, through the lobby's glass doors, he thought he saw a familiar face seated in a car parked across the street.

Gothwhiler.

No.

He rose, crossed over to the doors, but even as he squinted, to get a better look, the car pulled away from the curb and was gone.

It was just his paranoia. Again.

He turned around—and nearly knocked over Ames, who had glided up behind him.

"What's the matter, buddy? You look sick."

"Nothing. What're you doing down here so early? I thought you'd be hungover."

"I am. I came down for coffee. And now that you're here, I want to talk to you."

"About what?"

"We need your help. Hansen's got a good plan. I come from a law-enforcement background, but you . . . you were special forces in Japan, and I know for a fact that your agency has cross-trained with international forces. Now, listen to me very carefully. If I had to bet on it, I'd say Fisher's here on a job—and he's either working for Grim or at the very least getting help from her. And I'm willing to bet you've got a contact or two within the special ops community that could help us find him. People talk. Favors are owed. Money is exchanged, and information leaks."

Noboru didn't like the short man's tone; it implied that he knew a whole lot more about Noboru's background, and that was deeply troubling—especially after Grim's promise.

"I'm sorry. I can't help you."

"Nathan, let me put it to you this way: If there's anyone you know that could help us, you owe it to the team. You owe it to us. Do you understand?"

Noboru studied the man for a long moment. "You could die in an accident, and no one would question it."

"Come on, Brucie, don't be like that."

"Don't call me that."

"Oh, I forgot, only the big boy upstairs is allowed."

"I can't help you."

"Don't you want to put an end to this? Don't you think we should get Moreau to talk?"

Noboru considered this. He knew that if Fisher had gone mercenary, there was one man who might know where the ex-operative was.

Karlheinz van der Putten, a.k.a. Spock, lived in a village called Chinchón, southeast of Madrid, and Noboru had memorized his cell phone number and e-mail address. Spock had become a kind of "agent" and "packager" within the mercenary world, an old wizard of information who was once a formidable warrior himself and a dedicated collector of human ears, which he preserved and kept in glass trophy cases that he displayed on his office walls. His extensive collection had earned him his nickname, though he was hardly as even-tempered as that alien character. In the sixties and seventies, he had participated in more than a thousand operations, working for more than a dozen governments, and during that time he had formed alliances that now spanned the globe, alliances he had nurtured for nearly four decades.

Now in his early seventies, the once-muscular Aryan, with a jaw that appeared to have been hewn into shape by a hatchet, had grown fat, stoop shouldered, and hunched over, but he maintained the snow-white crew cut and narrow-eyed gaze that hinted at the menace of his past.

Indeed, Spock, the ear collector, always had his ear to the tracks, and maybe it was time to give him a call.

"I will give you a man's name and his number. But you cannot tell him where you got it, and you cannot mention my name," said Noboru.

"And you think this guy will know where Fisher is?"

"He might. . . ."

Noboru shifted in closer to Ames. "If you mention my name, it will be bad for you."

"I understand, Bruce. You're a badass. You'll kill me and all that. Now, give me the damned number."

29

AMES had no intention of calling one Karlheinz "Spock" van der Putten, but he had every intention of telling Hansen, in confidence, that Noboru had given him Spock's name and that Noboru didn't want anyone else on the team to know about it.

Now Ames had his cover story.

He would tell Hansen that he had called Spock, who said he had heard about an American special-forces operator heading up to Vianden on some mercenary job, probably to take out some rich businessman. It'd all click. Vianden was a small city, with about fifteen hundred inhabitants, and one of Luxembourg's main tourist centers, with a restored castle converted into a museum rising up on the rocks above the city. Several lakefront areas included the mansions of some very wealthy people who might easily wind up on a merc's target list.

Nevertheless, Ames still did not have enough information about Fisher's exact target, and he would need to contact Stingray and demand more specifics before revealing anything to Hansen.

So for most of the day Ames volunteered to partner up with Noboru and check out the leads that Moreau had fed them, even as Hansen, Valentina, and Gillespie did the same but were simply going through the motions as Hansen waited for a callback from his CIA buddy, who'd said he would try to help out. Ames and Noboru inspected the other weapons caches (untouched) and followed up on Range Rover sightings that all turned up empty. "I'm shocked," Valentina had groaned.

But not all was bad. Valentina, quite surprisingly, had managed to secure five pairs of Trident goggles and have them delivered to her at the hotel. When pressed, she finally revealed that there were two geeks at the NSA, twin brothers, who had both tried to date her. She promised them a date if they did what she asked and did not notify anyone else within the agency. It was a matter of national security, she'd told them. While she openly loathed using her body to gain friends, power, and classified Splinter Cell equipment, there was no denying that her cleavage and smoky voice worked every time.

By sundown, Ames was still awaiting his second update from Stingray, whom he had contacted earlier in the day. Ames, of course, had asked to know exactly where in Vianden Fisher might be, and he needed that information soon—because if Fisher was going to strike, he would more than likely do it at night, and the team needed to be up there and in position. It was only about a forty-minute drive from the hotel to Vianden, but forty minutes could be an eternity if they missed Fisher. Ames had considered the fact that they might have already lost Fisher, but if Kovac was as plugged in to the situation as he had suggested through Stingray, then they still had time. Fisher was a meticulous planner and was no doubt mapping every inch of his target, which might be why Moreau and Grim were so keen on stalling the team.

Finally, at about 1:20 in the morning, while watching porn with the sound turned off, Ames saw three flashes of light strike the nearby window. Hansen and Noboru were fast asleep. Ames told Hansen that he was going down to the exercise room, that he couldn't sleep and thought some cardio might help him out. Hansen groaned, muttered something, and drifted back into his faint snoring.

Ames changed, went down to the exercise room,

used his key card to open the door, and found the cell phone planted under the first treadmill. There was a text message waiting on the screen:

Lat 49°56'36.27" N, long 6°10'39.10" E.
Target: Yannick Ernsdorff.
Occupation: investment banker.
Move now!

Ames scribbled the numbers onto the back of an old business card taken from his wallet; then he erased the text message and dumped the phone in the trash on his way out.

MOREAU was awakened from a sound sleep by a beeping from his OPSAT. He checked the screen and sighed heavily through a curse. "Where the hell are you boys and girls going?"

Uttering another string of epithets, he switched on a light and activated the Trinity System. Within two minutes he had Grim standing beside him, fresh and awake.

"How'd they find out about Vianden?" she asked.

"That's a very good question. And now it seems these youngsters have gone rogue."

"They're trying to force our hand."

"That might work."

She hesitated. "Sam can handle them."

"Don't be so certain. The cowboy is smarter than he looks."

HANSEN drove one of their two black Audis, and Ames took the lead with the other. They were hauling ass up to Vianden in the middle of the night, in the wind and rain, on information that may or may not be credible, but the way Hansen figured it, all they had to lose was a night's sleep—and he simply loved the idea of sticking it to Moreau. And speak of the dark-eyed devil himself:

"Cowboy, where the hell are you going?" asked the irritated voice in Hansen's subdermal.

"We got the munchies."

"I'm not playing games here."

Hansen burst into laughter. "Dude, you've turned into the puppet master, but we just cut the strings. You don't like that, do you?"

"Just tell us who tipped you off. That's all I need to know . . . and trust me . . . I need to know. . . . Your life could depend on it."

"Trust you? You're kidding me, old man. You tell me what's going on, and I'll tell you."

"All right, Fisher's in Vianden, but you cannot interfere with him right now."

"Maybe I'd like to talk to him myself. Maybe he's going to tell me that you and Grim are the bad guys."

"I'm warning you, Hansen."

"Marty, what are you going to do?"

Moreau raised his voice. "Who told you about Vianden?"

"Spock did. Beam me up, Scotty. Hansen out."

MOREAU turned to Grim as they floated over Vianden, watching the team's cars below. "I'm sorry. I guess they won't play nice anymore."

"He wasn't joking," Grim said.

"Excuse me?"

"I said Hansen wasn't joking. I've heard the name Spock before. It's the nickname of a mercenary with ties all over the world. He was linked to Gothos, meaning Noboru would know of him. Nathan must've given up the name, and Spock might've tipped them off."

"How come I've never heard of this guy?"

"I don't know. It seems like a rather gaping hole in your intelligence education."

Moreau flinched and sighed.

"If Spock knows where Fisher is, then one of our cutouts might've leaked it or be on Spock's payroll."

"You're probably right."

* * *

THE team got into the city, then ventured northwest toward the outskirts and a bean-shaped lake. Up ahead lay an intersection, with the shoreline road curving toward the northwest, a second road heading west, and a third swinging down east, back toward the city. The rain had tapered off, but Hansen felt the wind continue to buffet the car.

Ames began to pull farther ahead of him, and Gillespie, who was riding shotgun, urged Hansen to accelerate. Ames's car vanished over the next hill.

"Wow, he's really flying. He'd better slow down."

"He knows more than he's saying."

"At this point, I don't care. I'm just glad he came up with something. I'm just glad we're not being played for fools anymore."

"How do you know that?" she asked. "How do you know this hasn't been all planned by them?"

"Kim, please. Just don't go there!"

AMES saw the man coming out of the grass, the suit, the goggles. . . .

But just for an instant. Ames was driving too fast.

"I don't believe it!" he cried. "That's him!"

He jammed on the brakes and threw the Audi into reverse. "I got him! I got him!"

* * *

"HE'S on foot, running southeast." Ames's voice shot through Hansen's subdermal. "We need to get back!"

They'd donned their suits, and goggles, and were armed for hunting bear, a.k.a. Fisher, so Hansen immediately flipped down his visor and went to night vision as he swung the car around and found himself now in the lead, heading back down the road they'd just come up. The grainy green fields on either side of the car appeared much more distinct now, unrolling in long, lazy waves.

"SLOW down," hollered Valentina. She was sitting in the driver's-side rear seat of Ames's car and rolled down her window. She directed a flashlight into the ditch and let it pan up toward the tree line. "Wait . . . there!"

Fisher, wearing a tac-suit and Tridents, appeared in the light, but in the blink of an eye he was lost in the trees beyond. Valentina's map told her the trees were simply a narrow stretch bordering two fields.

"Just keep going," she told Ames. "The road will curve around and we can flush him the next field over, behind the trees."

"I hear that, baby. I'm on it!" cried Ames.

"Baby? Shut up and drive!"

* * *

ON Valentina's advice, Hansen had veered off and was now heading east toward a wooden bridge. His first instinct was to have Valentina and the others chase Fisher on foot, but there was a good chance Fisher would double back—he was an expert at that—so Hansen sent them to flush Fisher while he served as a blocking force. It was a classic pincer movement, and Fisher would no doubt recognize it, but it was better than a foot chase.

Hansen swung his head around and stole a look at the field, where he spotted Fisher running, but he wouldn't stop and would maintain observation for the flushing team. Trees abruptly cut off his view.

"I've lost him," said Ames.

"Me, too," answered Hansen, pulling up the map on his OPSAT. "All right, we'll search the ditches. You guys check out that wedge of trees. You see it on the map?"

"I see it," said Valentina.

They spent the next thirty minutes combing through the woods and the field and ditches, and the only conclusion they reached was that Fisher had reached the larger forest to the east, where there'd be thousands of acres to search.

Gillespie met up with Hansen back at their car. "Check the map. Anything in those woods?"

"Just a campground. And this little town, Sch-euerof, over here," he said, tapping his OPSAT's screen.

"What if he left his car at the campground?" she asked. "To get out, he'd follow this road here through Scheuerof."

"But what if he heads south?"

"I think he'll keep heading east toward the German border. More rural, more cover. But you never know."

Hansen nodded. "Let's take a shot. I say we get up there and see if we can cut him off."

Hansen told Ames the plan, and they met on the road heading east toward Scheuerof. As they passed through the little down, they spotted a police car, lights flashing, heading in the opposite direction, and then, a few minutes later, another one.

Gillespie patched herself directly into the local police channel and reported, "There was some kind of incident up at the campground."

Hansen grinned to himself. "Fisher. We're close now."

"Why don't we just call Moreau? If Fisher's in his car, Moreau can see him right now."

"And he can lie to us about that," Hansen shot back. "No way. We're doing this on our own."

30

HANSEN'S determination to work alone and stay the course paid off. They spotted the Range Rover heading east about a mile ahead of them. Gillespie zoomed in with her night-vision binoculars and confirmed that Fisher was behind the wheel. She even saw him consulting an OPSAT, either Ames's or one he'd procured from the weapons cache in Bavigne.

They were racing down a winding road with a series of dips and bends that challenged Hansen's driving skills. Each time Fisher reached the crest of a hill, Hansen was better able to gauge his lead. Audi versus Range Rover? There was no competition, unless

Fisher was actually driving Chitty Chitty Bang Bang and planned to fly over the treetops.

"I'm right behind you, Boss," said Ames through the subdermal.

Hansen had not asked the man for an update. "Uh, yeah, I can see you," he said sarcastically, stealing a look in his rearview mirror.

"Don't slow down."

"Ames, we'll catch up to him. Relax."

Fisher disappeared once again. The road grew dark. Hansen accelerated a bit more, rose up and over the next crest, and started down.

Lights appeared out of nowhere in the middle of the road.

Reverse lights.

Hansen's mouth fell open. Fisher had stopped dead, waited for them, and thrown the Rover into reverse. He was now barreling backward, directly toward them.

With the better part of three seconds to react, Hansen jammed on the brakes, and while the Audi's sophisticated antilock braking and traction-control systems immediately kicked in, he still found himself skidding across the road, past the Range Rover, and sliding up onto the right-side shoulder. And then, with a jerk, the car dropped, as though on the rails of a roller coaster, and began to plunge down the embankment.

Hansen corrected course, rolling the wheel and taking the car back up toward the pavement as Gillespie clutched a handle near the passenger's-side window and said, "The son of a bitch was never a good driver!"

As they neared the top of the embankment, Hansen hit the brakes hard, burning rubber to a stop, front tires now up on the pavement, back still on the dirt.

"Now what?" Hansen asked.

"Oh, no," said Gillespie. "This is bad."

AMES had to blink hard as his headlight picked out the two cars seemingly parked in the middle of the road. Without thinking, he just reacted, cutting the wheel hard, sending the Audi into a flat spin across the slick pavement and careening down into the ditch along the left side.

The car wasn't stopped for three seconds when suddenly Ames found his door being wrenched open. He looked up at Noboru, who reached across Ames, unfastened Ames's seat belt, then ripped him out of the driver's seat. "You idiot!" cried the Japanese man, and this was the first time Ames had ever heard the usually reserved operator raise his voice. "I drive!"

Noboru dumped Ames onto the ground and jumped into the driver's seat.

"Ames, get back in the car!" screamed Valentina.

* * *

HANSEN gaped at the oncoming vehicle, transfixed, as though watching it all in an IMAX theater.

Fisher had thrown his Range Rover into drive and was now racing toward them. Reflexively, Hansen leaned toward the passenger's side as Fisher's car struck Hansen's door, the safety glass shattering. The Range Rover then turned, now broadsiding them, tires screeching, engine roaring. They were slammed back down into the ditch. Hansen didn't dare hit the accelerator until he could turn the Audi around. The Range Rover glanced off them, climbed back out of the ditch, and continued up the road.

They were on a thirty-degree slope, and when Hansen finally hit the gas, the back tires spun freely in the mud and began to dig deeper.

"We're stuck down here, Ames! Stay on Fisher."

"This is Nathan! I'm driving now!"

"All right, Nathan, stay with him!" Hansen turned to Kim. "You drive."

Before exiting the car, Hansen hit the trunk button. He climbed up, raced back, and removed the large, carpeted trunk mat from the back and slid it in front of one of the back tires. Then he got the two rear seat mats and did likewise with the other tire. Gillespie eased on the gas, and the little trick worked, getting them up past the mud and onto the harder ground. Hansen hopped into the passenger side, crying, "Go!"

NOBORU followed Fisher onto a side road that was mostly dirt and gravel. The road grew so narrow that only one vehicle could barely pass through. Freshly torn branches lay in the path, and Valentina reported that the Range Rover was definitely ahead, with Fisher hacking his way forward. It was raining a bit harder now, and Noboru switched on the wipers to clear the drops and still-falling leaves and twigs.

The road began turning radically, zigging hard to the right at forty-five-degree angles, and Noboru hit the brakes and rolled the wheel again. And again.

"If you don't slow down, you'll hit a tree," hollered Ames.

"Like you're an excellent driver?" spat Valentina. "Shut up!"

"Yes, shut up!" added Noboru, feeling his cheeks warm as, far in front of them, Fisher's taillights flickered into view.

Fisher had shifted to avoid a big rock in the road and had plowed into a berm on their left, leaving a huge trench where his SUV had pushed through. The canopy above had lowered, and his truck had sheared off dozens of more branches, which littered the road. Through the stands of trees, Noboru thought he spotted Fisher's taillights. He hadn't bothered to switch them off and go to night vision, but Noboru assumed that momentarily he would—once he realized he was still being followed.

Noboru was still a bit in awe that the tip he had given Ames had actually paid off. Noboru had obviously underestimated Spock's influence in the mercenary world. Yes, he'd thought Spock would be the one man to know something about Fisher, but it'd also been a long shot. Still, according to Ames, Spock had been unable to confirm that it was Fisher, only an American. But that was enough, and here they were, pursuing the man.

There was something, though, that bothered Noboru. Spock, given his position, was not a very forthcoming individual. How had Ames gotten him to talk?

HANSEN should have let Gillespie drive in the first place. She was an ace behind the wheel, cutting corners tightly and catching up quickly to Noboru.

"Where the hell did you learn to drive like this?"

"I don't know. I've always liked fast cars. My first was a '98 'Vette. We added a supercharger and custom cam and really ramped up the rear-wheel horsepower and torque. The dyno numbers were great."

"Okay, that's Chinese. Just watch the road and keep turning like that."

She cut the wheel hard. "Hang on!"

* * *

AS Noboru came out of the second of two hairpin turns, he spotted the Range Rover straight ahead, and he took in the scene at once.

Fisher was rolling around a boulder at least as tall as his hood, and as Noboru accelerated even more, the berm to their left suddenly exploded in a shower of mud and shrapnel that blasted against the car.

Reflexively, Noboru cut the wheel. Fisher had cleverly tossed a grenade into the berm to force them into the rock. Noboru appreciated the beauty of that plan, even though he was on the receiving end of it. Thankfully, the tires held on the gravel, and they slipped past the boulder with just a slight, glancing blow and the crunch of fiberglass.

They raced forward, and within a minute, the road suddenly widened into some kind of a logging camp with piles of mulch along one side, piles of cut logs, and clearings made into the deeper stretches off to the north.

The road split into three, with the main one heading directly west and the two others north and east.

Noboru slammed on the brakes.

"Why are you stopping?" hollered Ames.

Noboru ignored him and turned to Valentina. "Which way?"

There were tire tracks all over the clearing, and it was nearly impossible to pick out Fisher's.

Valentina was already scanning with her goggles and told him to take the north road. He jammed down his foot, and they lurched forward as Hansen came thundering up behind them.

"You sure he's heading north?" Hansen asked in the subdermal.

"I'm sure," said Valentina. "Got his exhaust trail."

"Roger that."

Noboru drove farther on, the road growing muddier, as Ames informed them that they had crossed into Germany. They came up and over a rise, and there, ahead, lay a wooden bridge with a gaping hole in its center, a hole large enough to permit a vehicle, a Range Rover, perhaps.

"Aw, hell," said Valentina. "I think he broke through the bridge."

"Ya think?" cried Ames.

And then the incessant blaring of a car horn rose from somewhere down below the shattered planks.

Then the horn went silent.

HANSEN eased out onto the bridge and directed his flashlight through the gap, drizzle filtering through the thick yellow beam that found the Range Rover sitting upside down in a ravine about twenty feet below. The door was open. Fisher was gone. Hansen quickly shifted the light around, picking out the banks of the creek below, the water only a foot or so deep, the rocks piled up along the shoreline. To Hansen's left, beyond the bridge, the ravine trailed off into the night. He turned, aimed the light off to his right.

A concrete wall rose alongside the streambed, with more ornate concrete facades on either side of it. In the center lay a rusting steel door. Hansen squinted. On the door was an old white sign with red letters: VERBOTEN. SIEGFRIEDSTELLUNG WESTWALL.

Fisher didn't have time to get out of the ravine, Hansen thought. *He must have gone in there.*

"We need to get down there!" Hansen ordered.

"Over here!" called Noboru. "I think we can get down here!"

They rushed over to where Noboru picked out a rocky edge of the ravine that would allow them to descend—slowly and carefully—but at least they could get down without breaking out ropes or rappelling gear from the trunk.

Noboru took the lead, and they descended one by one, burning up valuable time.

"Hey, I called up this place on the OPSAT," said Ames. "They called it the Siegfried line. It's a whole bunch of bunkers built by the Germans after World War I. There are thousands of them and tunnels and

machine-gun emplacements all up and down it. Goes
for, like, four hundred miles."

"Great," Hansen said with a groan. "Another perfect place for him to lose us."

"Not if I have anything to say about it," corrected
Valentina, who reached the ground and took off running along the bank toward the door.

Noboru jogged behind her, as did Hansen, who
turned back to Ames and Gillespie and said, "Circle
around the other side and see if there's another
entrance up top."

They nodded and rushed off.

As they neared the door, Hansen motioned to
Noboru. "Sorry, buddy. I'm going to post you right
here."

Noboru made a face, but he drew his SC pistol and
nodded.

Hansen and Valentina reached the door, and Hansen gave it a solid shove with his shoulder. The door
seemed to give a little, then bounced back, as though
held by something elastic.

"Light," he ordered Valentina.

She moved in with a penlight, and in the gap between
the jamb and the door they saw weblike rows of paracord. Fisher had tied shut the door from the inside.

Hansen drew his combat dagger—the one that had
belonged to Fisher. He got to work on the cord.

31

HANSEN sawed through the first line of paracord and began working on the second.

"It's taking forever," said Valentina.

"Best I can do." The second one gave suddenly, and he began work on the third.

Something pinged hard just inside the door, near the concrete jamb, and Hansen realized with a start that he was taking fire. He pulled back the knife, shuddering as he did so.

"Shots," he said through a gasp.

Her eyes widened. "What did you expect? He's slowing us down even more. Come on."

Hansen took a deep breath—just as another round struck the wall inside.

"That came from a distance," he said, knowing that he would've heard a slight hand clap from inside but hadn't heard anything. "Warning shots."

"Just cut," Valentina urged him.

Hansen thrust his hand back into the gap and began sawing once more. "Kim, you find anything up there?"

"Not yet," she answered in his subdermal. "No other entrances or exits that we can see so far. . . . There could be some farther down the line. Or maybe we went the wrong way. Still, he's got to come out somewhere."

"Roger that."

Hansen cut hard into the last piece of paracord, which suddenly gave, and together he and Valentina shoved open the door.

They flipped down their goggles and switched to night vision. Water seeped down from a large crack in the ceiling, like a varicose vein bubbling with fluid, and, in fact, more water trickled inside from cracks all over the walls and floor, as though the place had become a sponge over time and was slowly being squeezed.

To their left and right lay a central passageway about thirty feet wide and seemingly miles long. Concrete stairwells intersected the passage, assumedly leading

up to the old pillboxes and machine-gun emplacements, a few leading downward to who knew where,
perhaps living quarters or storage facilities. Between
the dust and rank odor of mildew, it was difficult not
to cough.

"This place is a trap," whispered Valentina. "If he
doesn't get us, a slip or fall will."

"Go infrared," he told her. "I'm willing to bet he's
navigating this way. Check it out. You can see the cool
air rising up from the weaker parts of the floor . . .
those blue plumes..The greenish ones are warmer
air."

"I see it. You're pretty smart, cowboy."

"Thanks, cowgirl."

"Don't call me that."

"Ditto."

"Follow me," he said, staying close to the wall and
leading her down the main passage.

He picked up Fisher's footprints with the infrared
in no time, and they led toward a concrete stanchion
with a ladder built inside and leading up into a concrete shaft.

Something metallic pinged and clattered across the
floor, followed by a second metal object. Hansen gave
a hand signal to Valentina to get down. He zoomed
in with the goggles to spot a rusting old bolt on the
floor, accompanied by a second one. The bolts' heads
were rusty, but their shafts were darker, cleaner, as

though they'd been wrenched out of something, the wall probably. They belonged to the ladder and were loosened because Fisher was up there.

As that realization struck, so did something else, thumping into the floor. Hansen threw Valentina another hand signal: Don't move.

He zoomed in . . . and there it was, a Sticky Cam at the bottom of the shaft, panning toward them.

Hansen nodded to Valentina, and they advanced toward the shaft.

Another noise, this time from above, like a wheel turning hard against a rusty axle.

Now Hansen advanced himself, moving ahead of Valentina and ready to reach the shaft and mount the ladder rising up into the darkness.

But then, as he was about to steal a look up, something clanged hard on the floor, struck the upper edge of the shaft, and began rolling toward him.

The device was easily identifiable by its hexagonal end caps and perforated tube with brown and pastel green bands.

Of course the word "grenade" never made it out of Hansen's mouth. He turned away, about to dive out of its path, when the flashbang brought instant hell.

A piercing shrill, at 170 decibels, threatened to shatter his eardrums while eight million candela of stark white light entered the Tridents and forced him to slam shut his eyes as he landed hard on his stomach. At the same time, the concussion struck like a Rolls-Royce jet engine suddenly switched on. He was literally knocked over onto his back.

And then . . . nothing, save for the bang echoing in his ears and the light still flashing behind his closed his eyes.

"Ben, what the—" Her voice came tinny and distant, barely perceptible behind all the ringing.

"Are you all right?" he asked, unable to hear his own voice.

"What happened?"

"Flashbang. Don't try to move or do anything. Just wait a minute."

Hansen opened his eyes, flipped up his goggles. Nope. He couldn't see a damned thing, and his ears were now ringing even more loudly so that, despite the subdermal, he could barely hear Valentina say, "Okay."

GILLESPIE had led Ames along the top of a cliff where it seemed the bunker line continued onward. They had searched for openings or hatches leading inside but had found only patches of concrete covered over by thick clumps of weeds.

She had paused near what might be a crumpling machine-gunner's nest—it was hard to tell with all the erosion and overgrowth. In the distance she thought she saw something, a figure in silhouette. No, not one. Two.

And then they'd heard the muffled thump of something from deep inside the bunker. A gunshot? Grenade?

"Ben, where are you guys?"

No answer.

"Ben, you there?"

"Hey, check this out," called Ames. "I got a hatch right here. . . ."

NOBORU tensed as he listened to Gillespie trying to call Hansen. He'd heard the dull boom from behind those thick stone walls, too. He decided that if Hansen didn't answer within the next twenty seconds, he'd go into the bunker after them. It wasn't just Hansen he was worried about, of course.

He ticked off another ten seconds, then started toward the bunker door, when a voice came from above. "Nathan!"

Squinting up into the darkness, Noboru could not see the man at first—but he'd recognized that baritone voice.

Horatio.

Even as his heart sank and he lifted his pistol, Gothwhiler's unmistakable British accent came from behind him. "Good boy, Nathan. Don't move."

Noboru froze.

How had they managed to draw so close to him? Well, he'd been a fool, daydreaming about a life with Maya Valentina, about romantic, candlelit dinners and long days at the beach. She'd dulled his senses, softened him, left him vulnerable to much more than her perfume and charm.

And now his old "friends" had exploited his lack of focus and current position. They didn't want to face the rest of the team. They'd been waiting for the perfect opportunity to capture him alone.

And now they had him.

Or not.

After living with them on his back for so long, Noboru had come to the realization that, if push came to shove, he wouldn't be taken alive—and in a way death would be welcome and represent the end of the paranoia, the fear . . . finally . . . forever.

He judged Gothwhiler's distance behind him at three meters. Horatio was now coming down the rocks: distance nine meters and closing.

Gothwhiler no doubt had a gun pointed at Noboru's head, while Horatio kept his pistol up but was more concerned with judging his footing as he descended to the shoulder of the road, near the bridge.

Footfalls grew louder from behind. Closer. Noboru thought of making his move, but Horatio already had his pistol trained on him.

Abruptly, his Trident goggles were ripped off, and then the hard steel muzzle of a pistol made contact with that knobby bone covered by stubble on the back of his head.

"Just toss your weapon into the mud right there," said Gothwhiler, his voice squeaking like a mouse's. "Right there." He relieved Noboru of his rifle, sliding the V-TRAC sling easily off his shoulder.

"I did a job for you," Noboru said, his voice coming in a hiss. "I deserved to be paid. You ripped me off. I took back what was mine. There is nothing left between us. I told you that. I told you. . . ."

Horatio started forward. His pistol was a semiautomatic, to be sure, and he raised it to Noboru's belly.

"Nathan, it ends tonight. You've made a fool out of us. And now we'll send a message that no one can do that. Not ever. Now . . . hands behind your head! Kneel!"

Noboru tensed. "I've been your life's work, huh? What're you going to do without me? Who're you going to chase?"

"You haven't called your parents recently, have you?" said Gothwhiler.

Noboru began to lose his breath. "We had an agreement from the very beginning about them."

"You gave them the money. They spent it. They paid the price."

"You're lying."

"No, I'm not." Horatio raised his gun and pointed it at Noboru's forehead.

Noboru took a deep breath. He was going to spring up and attack Horatio, taking his chances—knowing full well he would probably be shot—but perhaps the round would not kill instantly the way a head shot would. He would not be executed. He would fight. And death would, as he'd promised himself, bring relief.

"Pathetic boy," Gothwhiler sang. "My grandfather was shooting you people out of trees during World War II."

Noboru was about to reach out when a short clap from nearby echoed down into the ravine.

An odd look came over Horatio's face. Then he just dropped to the ground.

Noboru craned his head in time to see Gothwhiler take a round two inches behind his temple. The gaunt man's head wrenched back as he toppled to the ground and lay there, immobile, blood pouring from his wound.

The two perfectly executed shots, from a remarkable sniper, left Noboru breathless. Absolutely breathless.

Yet even through the shock, he still recognized the sound of an SC-20 rifle and its 5.56mm ammo. There was no mistaking it. Someone on the team had just saved his life.

Or someone who just happened to have an SC-20 rifle.

Noboru stared off to his right, narrowing his eyes toward the shadows running along the cliff. He focused on a fallen log overlooking the lip of the ravine. That had to be the sniper's nest. Slowly, he lowered his hands from behind his head and pulled himself up into a crouch, still wary as he shifted right toward where he had tossed his pistol.

A round punched into the mud not six inches from his hand.

He lifted both palms and slowly stood.

It was Fisher. Had to be.

All Noboru could do was shrug. The man could easily kill him now.

Noboru just stood there, waiting for some sign or indication that it was okay for him to move. None came. Then he spotted movement near the bridge, just twenty feet from it, and turned his head for a better look.

A voice rang out. "No. Face the cars."

Definitely Fisher.

Noboru complied. "Was that you?"

"Was that me, what?"

Noboru jerked his head toward Horatio and Goth-whiler. "Them."

"I needed their car. Something told me they weren't cooperative types."

Noboru swallowed. Fisher had no idea what he had just done, no idea of the immeasurable burden that had just been lifted from Noboru's shoulders, and all he could manage at the moment was a simple "Thanks."

"Don't mention it," Fisher said curtly.

Noboru opened his mouth, about to ask a half dozen questions about Fisher's mission, about what the hell was really going on, when he felt the Cottonball make contact with his right shoulder, and the world went dark.

32

VALENTINA had been farther away from the flash-bang grenade when it went off, so she'd been able to recover more quickly than Hansen and now helped him back outside, through the main bunker door. He still couldn't see much, and she had a few sparklers winking in her peripheral vision.

Having heard a pair of gunshots from outside, Ames and Gillespie had taken up sniper positions and had reported frantically that they thought Noboru had been killed. He was on the ground and not answering their calls.

As her heart raced and eyes began to ache, Valentina

guided Hansen out the door and told him to sit down there, under cover. Noboru was up near the cars, and she'd be right back. He barely heard her, saying his ears were ringing loudly, and she understood, the explosion still echoing in her head.

With her mind screaming that this kind and gentle man might be dead, she climbed up to the road and knelt before him. Her trembling hand touched his neck, and she searched for a pulse. *Nothing . . . Wait, there it is.* She sighed and gasped, and for a moment a wave of dizziness passed through her, or, rather, a wave of relief so strong that she thought she might pass out. She checked him for a gunshot wound. Nothing visible.

The other two men, a heavyset bald guy with horrible burn scars and a scrawny man with hair dyed jet-black, lay on the ground in pools of blood. She reported her findings to the rest of the team, and Hansen told Ames and Gillespie to rally at his position and help him get up there.

Noboru began to stir, and Valentina ran fingers down his cheek. That felt a little too good. She shivered. "Nathan, it's Maya. Can you hear me?"

His eyes flickered open, and then he seemed to focus on her. Finally, he smiled weakly, and she allowed herself to breathe easier.

"Are you shot? I don't see any wounds," she said. "What happened?"

He took a moment to consider, then motioned for her to help him sit up. She did, and he rubbed the back of his head and said, "Just a Cottonball."

"Was it Fisher?"

He nodded.

"Who're these guys?"

Before he could answer, Ames, Gillespie, and Hansen came up and over the hill, onto the shoulder.

"Aw, hell, look at that," Ames cried, pointing at their cars. Only then did Valentina notice that the rear tires on both of their Audis were flat.

"Each car's got a spare," said Gillespie. So we'll still have a functional ride, once we swap out the tires."

"Time enough for Fisher to get a big lead on us."

"Hey, who're these guys?" asked Ames, staring at the two bodies.

"Maybe they were the guys tailing us back in France," said Valentina.

Hansen squinted at the men. "I'm seeing a little better now. Nathan, what the hell happened?"

NOBORU had to decide how he'd answer, and for a few breaths he sat there, letting Hansen's question hang as all eyes turned on him. Perhaps it was the rush of relief that overwhelmed him, he wasn't sure, but he decided right then and there to tell them everything. The truth. Now that they were dead, the pressure was gone, and he should also relieve himself of the burden of carrying around the secrets of his past.

So he let it all out: the job with Gothos, the mission, his claiming what they owed him, the night they chased him. . . .

And when he was finished, he added, "I spoke to Fisher. He saved my life. We can't kill him. We have to take him alive."

Ames crossed in front of Noboru and got in his face. "We'll take him any way we can—and if you can't handle that, then maybe we need to talk to Grim and get you sent back home, Brucie. Got it?"

Noboru grabbed Ames by the neck and held him. He pulled the short man down, toward him, actually forcing Ames to kneel. "I want you to stop talking. Forever . . ."

"Nathan, let him go," ordered Hansen.

Noboru shoved Ames back so hard that the short man fell onto his rump. He cursed at Noboru and rubbed his sore neck.

"All right. Everybody up. We've got some tires to change out," said Hansen, still blinking hard. "I'll give Moreau a call and see if we can get help with these bodies. And, Nathan. I respect the fact that you only took back what was yours, but at what price? You endangered the team to keep your secret."

Noboru took in a long breath and nodded. "I'm sorry."

BEST WESTERN HOTEL INTERNATIONAL
LUXEMBOURG

MOREAU ordered them back to the Best Western in Luxembourg, and Hansen reluctantly complied. There was no reason to go on a blind chase across Germany when the operations manager already knew Fisher's destination. Moreau was sending a couple of men to pick up the other Audi. Once the team returned to the hotel, the bodies of Gothwhiler and Horatio would be disposed of: bundled in the remaining Audi's trunk.

Hansen respected Noboru for coming clean regarding those men and his relationship to them. That had taken a lot of courage for the young operator to admit, and Hansen suspected that the others felt likewise. Noboru had been put in a terrible position, but he had also placed the team in danger, and for that Hansen was still upset. Nevertheless, the lines between good guy and bad guy grew less distinct the longer you remained a spy, and Sam Fisher would certainly attest to that.

Late the next morning Moreau asked Hansen to come up to his room and patch into the Trinity System for a conversation directly with Grim.

Masking his awe over the virtual-reality space, Hansen stared across the sky above the hotel until he saw a point of light that suddenly blossomed into the image of his boss.

"Hello, Ben."

"Can I say that this has been a cluster—"

"Let me stop you right there," she said, raising her palm. "I understand your frustration. But all I need from you right now is compliance. What's at stake here is . . . everything."

"I am prepared to be enlightened . . . about everything."

"How did you know Fisher would be in Vianden?"

He grinned. "I could tell you, but then I'd have to—"

"I'm too tired for that crap, Ben."

"All right, we played a hunch." He told her about Noboru's contact, Karlheinz van der Putten, a.k.a. Spock, and how Ames had made a few calls and had helped narrow down Fisher's location. The rest was police-scanner monitoring and a healthy dose of luck.

"Can you just sit tight for me now? I'll need to get you back on the road, but for now, just do as I ask."

"Grim, I can't promise that anymore. You're making it difficult. I really don't know who to trust. And we didn't come over here on vacation."

"If you can't trust me, then walk away now."

"You know I won't do that, but you need to throw me a bone. I need something more here."

"Ben, I can't. And if you insist upon moving without authorization, I'll pull you out of there. All of you."

"Really?"

"Believe it."

"That's your choice. Here's what I'm thinking: We're going to get Fisher. My plan is to take him alive. And if you won't, then he's going to tell us everything. And, you know what? I think he will, because I have a feeling you're using him the same way you're using us. I think this is all about you saving your ass, and we do the dirty work. I've already put a lot into this job. I'm not going to screw it up over one administrator."

"Ben, you'll drive yourself mad if you keep trying to read into all of this. Just do as I ask."

Hansen shrugged. "Yeah. Whatever."

THAT evening Ames stole an opportunity to contact Stingray. Ames had a request for Kovac: He wanted Karlheinz van der Putten terminated, just in case Hansen decided to follow up with the man, who would say, "No, I never spoke to anyone about a special-forces operator in Vianden."

No loose ends.

Ames told Stingray that he wanted van der Putten's murder to look like a revenge killing. He wanted Spock's ears chopped off. Stingray said he would take care of it. And then Stingray passed on another bit of news. It seemed Kovac had his own set of feelers reaching out for signs of Sam Fisher, and he'd just received an excellent lead.

Fisher would be in Hammerstein, Germany, and

would be having a meeting with Hans Hoffman, a major player in the Bundesnachrichtendienst (BND), Germany's Federal Intelligence Service. Fisher was supposed to meet Hoffman at 2:00 P.M. but the exact location of the meeting was still unknown. Kovac still wanted Fisher dead, and Ames still had his orders.

Ames returned to the hotel room and decided that he would take advantage of an already interesting situation.

Once the team had gathered in Hansen's room, Ames gauged his words very carefully. "I just got off the phone with Spock. He's got an update on Fisher's whereabouts." Ames filled them in on what he knew, but he left out the time and location of the meeting.

"Kim, pull up everything you can on Hans Hoffman," said Hansen.

"I can't, unless you want Grim to know about it."

"Use the hotel's Internet access, and I'll get you into the Gothos database," said Noboru. "I'll bet they've got plenty of info on this guy."

"Do it," said Hansen.

"But, Ames, how did you get Spock to talk?" asked Noboru. "He's a very private man."

"Not that private." Ames rubbed his fingers together: money.

"Where are you getting this money?" asked Hansen.

"I was just getting to that. I had some fun money left over from another account and another job, and I used that, figuring we'd stick it to 3E yet another way, but I'm down to fifty bucks. Spock will give us the time and location, but it'll cost us another $50K. And believe me, that's dirt cheap, given who we're talking about."

"Everybody kicks in ten grand," said Hansen.

"Are you kidding me?" asked Valentina. "I'm not using my own money to pay off some geek informant. That's insane. I say we tell Moreau what we got and get the money from them."

"Or we go pay Spock a visit and squeeze it out of him," said Gillespie.

"That would not be wise," said Noboru. "Spock is a very well-respected and extremely well-connected man who knows how to take care of himself."

"And there's no time for that," said Ames.

Hansen sighed. "All right, I've got some fun money myself. Tell you what, Ames. I'll give you the fifty—which, by the way, also happens to be 3E's—but I talk to Spock myself."

"He only trusts me at this point. And believe me when I say he knows exactly where Fisher will be tomorrow. I need to wire him the money right now."

Hansen thought it over. "You tell Spock if he's wrong, we'll be coming back to collect."

Ames chuckled. "He knows that. This guy's been playing this game longer than we've been alive."

"Grim will eventually find out about all these money transfers," said Gillespie.

"Yeah, but by then it'll be too late," said Ames.

Within an hour, Ames had $50K in his fun-money account, money that would not be delivered to Spock but would be, he hoped, spent on hookers and booze, and all the while he would be laughing his ass off at Hansen's naïveté.

WHILE Ames was on his computer, supposedly working out the deal with Spock, Hansen pulled Noboru aside. "You could have come to me with everything. I hope you know that."

"I know that now."

"Not sure if we'll work together after this, but if we do, the team comes first, before you or anyone else."

"You don't have to tell me that."

"Apparently, I do."

"Ben, it's your team. I didn't want to let you down. I didn't want to let any of us down."

"I get that. You're not the best agent, but you're the biggest ass kicker we've got—and I can't afford to lose you. And can I say I'm not thrilled that you confided in Ames." Hansen glanced across the room at the short man banging on his computer.

Noboru sighed deeply. "Neither am I."

"Do you think we can trust him?"

"The intel for Vianden was good. If Spock knows where Fisher's going to be, then, yeah, we can trust him."

"I was talking about Ames."

"I hate him."

"Me, too. But we don't have to like him to trust him."

Suddenly Ames slapped shut his laptop and cried, "Ladies and gentlemen, start packing. Fisher will be in Hammerstein tomorrow. He's got a meeting at 2:00 P.M."

"A meeting where?" asked Hansen.

Ames winced. "That's where it gets a little sketchy, but Spock's got a few ideas. . . ."

"What do we tell Moreau?" asked Valentina.

Hansen squinted into a thought. "Let me handle that."

33

THE team caught the first flight out of Luxembourg
to the Cologne-Bonn Airport, just an hour away from
Hammerstein. They arrived at 9:10 A.M., rented a pair
of Mercedes sedans (no more budget rentals for them,
Hansen swore), and drove out to the small town, taking in gorgeous views of the Rhine along the way.

The night before, Hansen had gone into Moreau's
room and put it to him bluntly: "We know Fisher's
meeting with Hoffman tomorrow. We're flying up to
Hammerstein. If you can just buy us a little time to see
if we can intercept, I'll let you come with us."

"Oh, you'll let me come with you, huh, cowboy? That the way it is?"

"You can't stop us. So you might as well come."

"And how did you obtain this information?"

"We intercepted a Klingon transmission."

"Don't you mean Vulcan?"

"Whatever."

"I'm warning you, Hansen—"

"What are you going to do? Assemble another team to take out the team that's supposed to get Fisher? I get confused just thinking about it."

"You know what?" Moreau let the question hang, then suddenly smiled. "You're a fool, but you remind me of myself back in the day. Arrogant, cocky, one badass mother—"

"Pack your bags, Boss."

Moreau finished his curse. "Grim will be pissed."

"Join the dark side."

Moreau frowned. "Now you're mixing up sci-fi universes."

THEY spent the better part of the morning and early afternoon driving around Hammerstein and considering probable meeting locations. There were a few outdoor cafés and three small wineries, should Fisher have chosen a public place for his meeting, and it wasn't as though Moreau would volunteer that information. In fact, he admitted that he and Grim did not know where the meeting would take place. That was between Hoffman and Fisher.

Ames got back on his laptop and said he'd received an update from Spock. The meeting was being held at a small, locally owned winery called J. P. Zwick Weinstube Weingut.

"And how the hell does Spock know that?" asked Moreau.

"Because this guy is as well connected as they get. It seems like 3E doesn't know jack compared to him," said Ames. "Maybe we should all go work for him and we'll have some decent intel for a change, instead of this garbage you've been feeding us, right?"

Moreau shook his head, not buying it.

Across the street from the winery was a boat launch's parking lot, and they arrived there at about one fifteen, approximately forty-five minutes before the meeting was scheduled to take place. Hansen ordered Ames, Valentina, Noboru, and Gillespie to comb the lot and read off the tag numbers of every car there so Moreau could immediately run them. They were looking for Hoffman's car and any rentals.

In the meantime, Hansen left the Mercedes, stepped over the guardrail, and headed onto the shoulder of the road. He waited for a break in traffic, then began to cross the street, aiming straight for the winery.

Gillespie called over the subdermal to say she'd just intercepted a police call. There was a report of a maniac in a BMW smashing into cars in the marina parking lot south of the winery, and the guy was now heading south down Highway 42.

"You think it's him?" she asked.

"I don't know. Stand by."

Hansen frowned, continued on, and appearing from between two bushes ahead was . . . Fisher himself!

The man started immediately toward a big BMW sedan parked nearby, drawing within ten feet.

"Don't, Sam." Chills shot up Hansen's spine. Had it all come down to something as anticlimactic as this—nabbing him in a parking lot?

Hansen raised his voice a bit more. "We've got you."

Fisher averted his gaze and kept moving. But Hansen was certain the man had heard him.

Even so, Hansen called even louder: "Fisher!"

Fisher was now five feet from his car, arm outstretched, thumb working a key fob. The Beamer chirped.

That noise sent Hansen's hand into the folds of his black leather jacket. He drew his SC pistol from the shoulder holster and ran toward the edge of the winery parking lot.

He raised the pistol.

Fisher opened the Beamer's door.

Hansen had the shot.

Fisher looked up, flashed the briefest of nods, then climbed inside.

"Damn!" muttered Hansen. *What just happened?* He had a Cottonball loaded.

Fisher started the car. The engine roared. He pulled out of his parking spot.

For a few seconds, Hansen wasn't sure what to do. He turned and sprinted back across the road, only then realizing that he should have switched to lethal fire and shot out Fisher's tires.

Another foolish move.

Admittedly, this was the first time he'd actually seen the legendary Sam Fisher in the flesh, and maybe he'd been starstruck, he didn't know, but he cursed himself as he activated the team channel and called out to the others over the SVT: "It's Fisher! In the BMW! He's taking off! Everyone back to the cars!"

Fisher's car wheeled around and raced off, heading south down Highway 42, along the river.

Moreau, who was sitting in the backseat of Hansen's sedan, arms folded over his chest, said, "He's getting away."

"How 'bout a little help?" Hansen asked.

Moreau pillowed his head in his hands. "You're on your own, cowboy. Grim doesn't even know I'm here."

Hansen swore and streaked out of the parking

lot. Fisher had a good lead on them already, a mile heading for two, Hansen estimated, leaving stunned drivers in his wake. A few drivers had become so nervous about the wild man in the BMW that they had pulled over to the side of the road, probably to catch their breath. Hansen began weaving through traffic himself, with Valentina, Ames, and Noboru now behind them. Noboru was at the wheel and driving even more aggressively.

They drove past the marina, about a quarter mile south of the winery, and saw people standing there, waving their arms and pointing to the damage their cars had sustained. And then Hansen saw a debris trail extending from the parking lot and back onto the road. *Fisher.* But what the hell?

Unless he'd done that to get the police involved. But the call had come in before he'd caused the damage. Strange. Or not so. Fisher had planned it all. But now what was he doing? Just fleeing? Or leading them somewhere?

"Where's he going, Marty?"

Moreau answered with a lopsided grin, then added, "Who's Marty?"

Hansen spoke through his teeth: "No more games. *I want an answer now!*"

Moreau threw up his hands. "Benjamin, I have no idea where he's going, except away."

Beginning to pant, Hansen drove on, cutting off

slower traffic and spotting a sign for the town of Neuwied.

"Uh, Ben, I don't want to say 'we've got company' because that's ridiculously cliché," said Valentina. "So how about this: The goddamned police are behind us!"

Hansen flicked a look into the rearview mirror and spotted the flashing blue lights. "Yep, we've got company. And you know who called them? Fisher."

"Why the hell would he do that?"

"Interference. Makes for a good show, too."

"Aw, here we go again!" she groaned.

Gillespie was up front with Hansen, now peering through the windshield with her long-range binoculars. "He's on the L258 now. Of course, a satellite feed would help. . . ."

That last part, uttered as snippily as she could, was meant for Moreau, who lifted his voice and said, "You're doing fine, boys and girls, you're doing fine!"

Hansen took the next turn a little too sharply and clipped the front end of a Toyota pickup truck. The driver leaned on the horn.

Fisher continued on, following L258 into a highway interchange where he took the Highway 256 exit, south and east toward Neuwied. Hansen tried to stay with the flow of traffic so as not to draw any more attention. He got well ahead of the pickup truck, whose driver pulled over to assess his damage. The police from Hammerstein had drifted farther back, out of sight for now, but he assumed they'd radioed ahead to their brothers in the next town for help. No sense waving a flag to them, so long as the team still had Fisher's BMW in sight.

"He just floored it," said Gillespie. "You'd better speed up or we'll lose him. And, whoa! He's fast and furious now, flashing his lights. . . . You'd better go!"

"I'm on it!"

Hansen kicked the gas pedal and the powerful Mercedes leapt forward, rolling up to 120 kph. They streaked past a sign that read RAIFFEISENBRÜCKE 3 KM.

That would be the Raiffeisen Bridge, spanning the Rhine.

Holding his breath, he rolled the wheel hard left, weaving around another slow-moving commuter car and passing the next sign: RAIFFEISENBRÜCKE 2 KM.

The bridge rose into view, a two-lane affair with a central A-shaped pylon shimmering like a white monolith with talons of support cables radiating from its sides. That pylon rose at least 150 feet, and Hansen took a few seconds to appreciate it before the lights in his rearview mirror stole his attention. Damned police were back again, coming up the Sandkauler on-ramp to drop in behind them.

"He'll cross the bridge," said Gillespie.

"Gotcha," Hansen replied. "I'm with him."

Even as he finished the sentence, they were immediately stuck behind a slow-moving lorry overloaded with crates. *Damn it!* Hansen slammed his fist on the steering wheel, then punched the horn. Traffic in the oncoming lane was too heavy to allow him to pass. The truck driver sped up, but only a little.

As they neared the bridge, an island that Gillespie said was Herbstliche Insel, or Autumn Island, appeared to their left and lay in the middle of the channel like a slightly opened mouth, tapering at the ends. Lush green trees stood in sharp contrast to the darker, muddier waters encompassing the narrow strip of land.

"What the hell?" Gillespie said through a gasp.

"What?" cried Hansen.

"He stopped! He stopped right in the middle of the goddamned bridge. He's straddling the center line."

Hansen could see Fisher's car now, seconds away from being T-boned by the oncoming traffic.

Across the center guardrail, traffic had slowed to a crawl as drivers hung their heads out their windows to gape at the car blocking traffic.

"What's he doing?" asked Moreau, leaning forward and clutching the back of Hansen's seat.

"Jesus . . ." Hansen could barely speak.

The oncoming traffic neared Fisher's car.

"Come on, Sam, get out of there," muttered Moreau.

"You want him to escape?" cried Hansen.

"You're damned right!"

Hansen snorted. "Unbelievable."

Abruptly, Fisher's car backed up toward the center guardrail, tires smoking as his rear bumper thudded hard against the heavy steel.

"What's he doing now?" Hansen asked.

"Oh, no," said Gillespie. "No. He can't. . . ."

It seemed as though every driver on the bridge, no matter the lane, was now tapping his or her car horn, and even through closed windows the racket was nothing short of remarkable, an atonal chorus carried on the wind.

Hansen braked hard as those ahead of him did likewise, and just a hundred yards beyond was Fisher, throwing it into drive now and leaving twin smoke trails behind him as the powerful BMW barreled directly toward the opposite guardrail. . . .

And into the murky depths of the Rhine River below.

"You got to be kidding me!" cried Moreau.

Gillespie leaned toward the windshield. "Oh, my God!"

Hansen held his breath.

The rail was scarcely taller than a meter, as was the

abutting suicide-prevention hurricane fencing, and neither was a match for the BMW's broad front bumper and its five-hundred-plus-horsepower engine.

The car horns faded, and for just a few seconds, all Hansen could hear was the drumming of his heart.

Then, abruptly, the screeching of metal on metal made him shudder.

With widening eyes, Hansen watched as Third Echelon's most lethal and effective Splinter Cell crashed his car through the rail—and in a moment as surreal as any, a moment in which time slowed and he seemed to watch it all from God's point of view—the car arced in the air, then pitched forward and began its fifty-foot descent toward the unforgiving water below.

34

HANSEN couldn't help himself and was out of the Mercedes, running between the lines of parked cars toward the section of bridge where Fisher had blasted through. He reached the edge, clutched a jagged piece of metal, and with a throng of other bystanders, stared down as the shattered rear bumper of Fisher's BMW vanished beneath the foam like a torpedoed ocean liner.

And then, as the gasps and murmurs continued around Hansen, the water grew still, and the waves began to settle. Hansen held his breath and waited for a head to pop up from the brown water.

Moreau was already calling him back on the sub-dermal and telling Noboru to turn around and get his car the hell out of there because the police were rushing toward the bridge.

Noboru hadn't yet entered the bridge ramp and was able to comply, but as Hansen reluctantly started back, a horde of cops came rushing forward. Several passed him, but one stopped and questioned him quickly in German, stating that they knew two Mercedes sedans were following the BMW.

Hansen told the man they'd seen the maniac in the BMW and had been chasing him, trying to keep him in sight until the police arrived. The guy had cut off Hansen and had caused front-end damage to Hansen's rental car. Hansen admitted to a little road rage, and the cop told him to return to his car and wait, that he'd be back to ask more questions. Hansen did so, but the cop never returned.

Gillespie buried her head in her hands, and neither Hansen nor Moreau said a word as they followed the long line of traffic over the bridge and around the crash scene.

After a few minutes, Hansen called Noboru and told him to meet up near the airport. They'd get a hotel and wait to find out more about Fisher, staying well clear of the bridge. Hansen couldn't wipe the frown off his face. What the hell had Fisher done?

Finally, Gillespie looked up and said, "He's still alive. I know it."

"He could have lost us on the other side of the bridge," said Hansen. "I don't know, Kim. I got a look at him before he got in that car, and—"

"And what? He looked suicidal?"

"I don't know. He looked *troubled*. But it doesn't make any sense."

"He got away," she insisted. "I'm telling you. He got away."

Hansen sighed, feeling helpless to console her. "I'm sorry. Maybe you're right. Or maybe he over-estimated his chances. I think we need to be realistic. He's a ballsy guy, but driving off a bridge? Man, that's insane."

Moreau took in a long breath. "If I had to bet on it, I'd say he drowned."

THEY booked a few rooms at the Holiday Inn just north of the airport and waited while Moreau and Gillespie monitored police communications and checked back with the NSA via the Trinity System.

The local news stations were all over the story, and Hansen sat on the sofa, watching and shaking his head. He wondered if maybe, just maybe, Fisher had had enough and had decided to go out with a bang, or a splash, as it were. Given their line of work, the stress, and what Fisher's life had become, it wasn't unreasonable to assume that he'd grown depressed, perhaps tired of running, of mercenary work, of everything. Hansen suddenly blurted out, "Maybe Fisher killed himself."

"I'm sure he did," Ames responded, quick to jump on the Fisher-bashing bandwagon. "That old man was a coward who murdered his boss. Then he becomes a two-bit merc, gets bummed out, and offs himself when he knows we're going to bust his ass. What a freaking loser. I wish he were here right now so I could tell him to his face."

It was a good thing Gillespie had left the room to get a drink and hadn't heard that, Hansen thought, otherwise Ames would by lying on the floor with a woman's nails sunk about an inch into his neck.

However, she wasn't the only one who'd take issue with Ames's assessment. Moreau rose slowly from his desk and loomed over Ames, who was seated in one of the reclining chairs, sipping a bottle of beer. "You have no idea who you're talking about. And if you ever become one-tenth of the man Sam Fisher was, then you might make a name for yourself in this community. Do you get that, Mr. Ames?"

Ames rose and had to look up into Moreau's eyes. "You don't intimidate me, old man. And I thought you liked me."

"I did. But then I spent more than five minutes around you."

"Hey, man, give me an hour, and you'll be suicidal yourself." Ames chuckled under his breath and returned to his seat.

"What do you think, Moreau?" Hansen asked. "You think he did it? You think Fisher killed himself?"

"Not intentionally. But if he survived that little Olympic swan dive into the Rhine, I'll buy the man a steak dinner."

"You all keep talking like he's a hero," said Ames. "He's a thug and a murderer for God's sake. How can you even get past that? All the missions he ran just wipe the slate clean? I don't think so. Lambert's dead."

"Ames, you're done," said Hansen, firing a hard look at the man. "You're done."

"Yep, we're all done here."

RESCUE teams were out searching the Rhine for most of the evening. The next morning Fisher's BMW was found nearly a mile away from the bridge, having been dragged along the bottom by the Rhine's current. There was no sign of the body, which had been separated from the car and assumedly drifted off on its own. Teams were searching the shoreline down river.

New orders came in. Hansen and the others would

be flying back home aboard a commercial airliner. Moreau had already booked the tickets. Hansen thought returning was odd and highly premature, since they still hadn't found Fisher's body. Moreau said the order had come in from Grim and that they were leaving, period, unless the team planned to go rogue again.

After returning their rental cars (and Moreau had a good time discussing the damage to the one Mercedes), they boarded a shuttle. Hansen bit his lip and glanced around at the others. They looked as exhausted as he felt. Maybe it *was* time to go home and reflect on everything, on a mission that left him more and more confused. He closed his eyes and spoke to Fisher in his head:

"*Why did you kill Lambert?*"

"*It's complicated.*"

"*I see. They want me to bring you in.*"

"*I can't let that happen.*"

"*Then I'm sorry.*"

This time, though, Hansen couldn't pull the trigger.

He saw Noboru telling him that Fisher had saved his life.

He watched as Fisher nodded at him before getting in the BMW.

That nod, one of mutual respect, now had a growing importance in Hansen's life. It was as though Sam Fisher had said, "*Yes, you are one of us now. You are worthy. You are a Splinter Cell. I'm passing you the baton.*" Hansen wanted to believe that so badly that he could taste it.

"*Sam, are you alive? What're you doing?*"

Fisher put a finger to his lips.

HANSEN had assumed that once they arrived in Maryland, Grim would need to debrief them. Nope. She told them to take a week off. Enjoy some R & R. She didn't even want to see them. They'd all been pushing it really hard. Hansen could hardly believe what he was hearing: the blow-off from his boss on a mission that she'd implied was more important than anything else that had ever come across her desk, a mission that implicated Kovac in criminal activity? No debriefing? And she wanted them to take a vacation? Had marijuana been legalized while they were in Europe?

Gillespie concluded that Grim's order for time off was proof positive that Fisher was alive. They were being pulled off the pursuit to buy Fisher time to do whatever he had to do. His assumed death might satisfy Kovac for a while.

AT the airport, as they each picked up their bags, they said their good-byes.

"Where are you going?" Valentina asked Hansen.

"This cowboy's heading back to Texas. You?"

She glanced over at Noboru. "Not sure yet."

Hansen nodded and wriggled his brows. "Be safe."

"Always."

Ames came over and slapped a palm on Hansen's shoulder. "You should come down to Florida with me. I'm going to watch the Yankees during spring training."

Hansen forced a smile. "Have a good time."

He shifted away and went over to Gillespie. "You all right?"

She nodded and said, "I don't want any time off. I'm going back to the situation room to go over the intel."

"That's a mistake. Grim won't let you in."

"How do you know?"

"I know."

"Then what am I supposed to do?"

He hoisted a brow. "You like Texas barbecue?"

THIRD ECHELON SITUATION ROOM

GRIM tensed as Kovac stormed into the room and raised his voice, his gray brows knitting in fury. "I just heard you pulled the team out of Germany! They're already back here in the States?"

"Fisher's trail had gone cold, which is to say, we believe he's dead."

Kovac took a deep breath, and his words came out in a growl: "I'll believe he's dead when his pale and bloated body is lying across my desk. . . ."

"Sir, please calm down."

"Oh, I'm calm."

"Look, my people have been running on overdrive for days. If we get a new lead, I'll have them back out there ASAP. You're the deputy director, sir, but this, I believe, is my call."

"Your predecessor wouldn't have been as careless . . . or as bold."

"I'm sorry you feel that way."

"Maybe you need to take a little vacation yourself."

Grim removed her glasses and rubbed the bridge of her nose. "I wouldn't go there, sir. I've already brought the director up to speed on this, and we've got his full support. And since he's your boss, you might want to talk to him directly about this. . . ."

He took a step toward her. "Let's cut to the chase."

She smiled, nodded, moved to the door, and opened it. "Sounds great. This is the part where you leave."

"Whatever you're up to, Grim, I urge you to remain cautious."

"Is that a threat?"

"I'm just concerned about your future here."

"Well, that makes two of us. Enjoy the rest of your day, sir."

He left. The door closed behind him.

And Grim nearly passed out.

FORT STOCKTON, TEXAS

HANSEN and his father—who resembled a bespectacled, gray-haired scarecrow—were out on the front porch of his parents' three-bedroom ranch house, about two miles down the road from the school where his dad taught. They'd just finished having dinner— barbecued ribs, along with Mom's homemade macaroni and cheese and some baked potatoes, and were now nursing some beers and staring up at the night sky while seated in their rocking chairs. Mom and Gillespie insisted upon doing the dishes, even though that was Dad's job: She cooked it; he cleaned it up. But since Hansen was visiting, the rules had changed, and Gillespie was having fun chatting with Mom, so she'd volunteered to help clean up. The conversation seemed to lift her spirits.

"This was such a great surprise, Ben," Buck Hansen said. "And it gets me out of KP duty."

"Like I said, Pop, sometimes they just throw us some time off. Good to be home. Just to smell it, you know?" He took a long breath through his nose and sighed. *Texas*. He could already hear the drawl returning to his voice.

The older Hansen laughed. "The ribs smelled great. But if you're talking about all the horse dung and Joey Reynolds's old pickup truck, the one that's still burning oil . . ."

"Yeah, I actually was."

"Well, then you're nuts."

"Just smells like home. So how's it going?"

"Same old, same old." His father squinted into the night sky, rubbing the gray stubble on his chin.

"I'm afraid to ask what you're looking for."

His dad turned suddenly and faced him. "Two nights ago I was out here, and I saw something again."

Hansen took a long pull on his beer. "I believe you, Dad."

"You know, I was thinking, what with you working for the government all this time, maybe you'd be willing to change your mind about this. I've got some pictures I can show you."

After tensing, Hansen sighed and said, "Dad, I'm just a low-level analyst. So is Kim. We can't be hacking into government computers looking for UFO encounters and cover-ups. If I have any close encounters with hacking the system, I'll be fired."

"I know that, Son, I know it. But you can't blame your old man for trying."

"Why is this so important to you?"

"Well, it's like Charlton Heston said in *Planet of the Apes*: I can't help thinking somewhere in the universe there has to be something better than man. Has to be."

"Why?"

"Because we're all doomed to destroy ourselves."

"I like your positive outlook on life."

He took a sip of his beer. "And I like your taste in women. I do love a redhead."

"She's just a friend from work."

"Good kisser?"

"Dad, come on."

"You're no fun."

Hansen thought for a moment, then said, "Can I ask you something? You ever know anyone who killed himself?"

"Yeah, I knew a fella once."

"Why'd he do it?"

"Wife left him. Took the kids. He got depressed. Starting messing up on the job. Got fired. Then one night we heard the gunshot, not that anyone was surprised. Why you asking me this?"

"I don't know."

"You're not depressed, are you?"

"Me?"

"Well, yeah."

"No, I've been busy with work, but we had a guy who might've done that."

"Why you say that? Could've been murder."

"No, he just kind of vanished. Might be dead or not. No body."

Dad leaned forward in his chair. "There are certain members of our government who are more suscep- tible to alien abduction, you know that, Son, right?"

Hansen repressed the desire to roll his eyes, sipped his beer, and said, "Good point, Dad. Good point."

"All I'm saying is that you cannot rule out the possibility."

"No, sir."

Gillespie came out onto the porch, beer in hand. "Mr. Hansen, I want to thank you for dinner. I really enjoyed it."

"You're welcome, sweetie. Anytime. Now, I'd better close my mouth because anything else I say is going to deeply embarrass my son."

Hansen smiled at his father. "Dad, after all these years, you're finally learning."

He winked. "Sometimes we teachers are the worst students."

35

THE call had come in at 3:00 A.M., and Hansen and the team were back in the air and racing toward Odessa, with a plane change in Frankfurt.

Unsurprisingly, Fisher had quite literarily returned from the depths of the Rhine and had resurfaced in the Ukraine. According to Grim, Fisher was seeking medical treatment from an old friend, Adrik Ivanov, a former medic in the Russian army. Ivanov was single, in his fifties, and a compulsive gambler who'd been hard-pressed to hold a steady job since being discharged.

It wasn't until they were on the ground in Odessa, at 9:40 P.M., that Grim came through with the

particulars: Ivanov lived in a duplex near the Tairov
cemetery but spent most of his free time at a bar
adjacent to the Chornoye More hotel. Hansen had
asked if the man was an alcoholic, and Grim had only
snickered. Of course he was. Moreover, something in
her tone told Hansen that Fisher wasn't really going
to see Ivanov for medical attention; in fact, all of it
sounded exactly like another ploy. Hansen already had
his guard up.

Moreau said that surveillance on Ivanov's duplex
apartment indicated no lights, assumedly no one
home, but Hansen sent Valentina and Gillespie up
for a look anyway. They picked the lock, searched the
place, and found no evidence of Fisher having been
there or any medical treatment performed.

Grim then told them that Ivanov worked as a
night watchman at a LUKOIL warehouse annex at
the city's northern industrial docks. LUKOIL was the
largest oil company in Russia and its largest producer
of oil, with obviously relaxed standards for its security guards. Grim followed up with the warehouse's
location, uploaded directly to their OPSATs. Hansen
found it interesting that she selectively released information, as though buying someone on the other end
a little more time. . . .

The team jammed into a single rental car and
drove from Ivanov's place to the warehouse, which
was set off the road and about a hundred yards from

the beach. Other warehouses were clustered around it, but most looked abandoned, with signs in Cyrillic indicating they were for lease.

They parked about two hundred yards away and skulked off into the complex, a refinery hub whose innards swept overhead, making Hansen feel as though they were in the bowels of a dying old beast. Some of the larger pipes snaked down through the lot and plunged into the sand at the beach line.

With a little help from Moreau, they pinpointed the LUKOIL annex, a redbrick building splotched with graffiti and long rust stains where broken gutters sent rainwater down the walls.

After a cursory scan of the building's blueprints, and realizing that the annex had only one main door, Hansen ordered the team to fall in behind him.

"You want us to get in there with goggles and scan for heat signatures?" asked Gillespie.

"I'm not worried about it. I think we'll find Ivanov, but I think Fisher's long gone," answered Hansen.

He worked his magic on the door's lock and eased it open, stepping through with his SC pistol leading the way. The place was dimly lit by weak overhead bulbs and smelled like a combination of mold and rusting metal.

Gillespie, Valentina, Noboru, and Ames moved in behind him, and he sent Ames and Valentina off toward an office area visible behind glass walls while hand signaling Gillespie and Noboru to work the perimeter and finish clearing the place.

The annex was relatively small, perhaps fifteen hundred square feet, and split on the right side by twenty-foot-tall rack shelves buckling under the weight of boxes and crates. A few rows of fifty-five-gallon drums labeled as cleaning solution were stacked three high, off to the left, creating a wall of curving metal.

"I think we have our boy," whispered Valentina into her subdermal. "Don't move, buddy," she added in Russian. "You're coming with us."

"All clear back here," said Noboru.

"Roger that," answered Hansen. "Clear. Okay, bring him out."

Hansen started over toward the office, where Ames ordered Ivanov forward, and the old man's arms splayed outward in a froglike manner. Apparently, the old man wasn't walking fast enough for Ames, who suddenly shoved him much too hard, and Ivanov hit the concrete, belly first, right in front of Hansen.

Ivanov tried to pull himself up, but Ames jabbed his heel into the man's butt and forced him back down.

Hansen glared at Ames. "Enough, Ames. Leave him be."

Ames mumbled something about trying to soften up the guy, but Hansen translated it into: *Bite me, boss man*.

Kneeling beside Ivanov, Hansen helped the man

to his knees and confirmed his identity. He looked leaner and more haggard and weatherworn than his file photo.

"Who are you? What do you want?" asked Ivanov, his English a bit broken but certainly acceptable.

"We're looking for a man," Hansen said. "An old friend of yours named Sam."

Ivanov's expression turned guilty. He denied knowing any Sam. Hansen insisted that Fisher had been there, and the old man went on about how he worked alone and had come in at six o'clock. Hansen cut him off: "You owe some people money."

Ivanov raised his voice, saying he'd paid them off.

Hansen explained about how computers were wonderful tools and could make people seem as if they still owed money. In fact, Hansen went on to say that they could make it appear that Ivanov owed a lot of money to some very dangerous people.

Ivanov protested.

"Tell us what he wanted," Hansen insisted.

The old watchman gave an exaggerated shrug, then spread his arms in confusion, but there was something—something in the glimmer of his eyes that told Hansen he was lying.

Hansen pointed at Valentina, told her to make the call and start out Ivanov at three hundred thousand rubles, about ten thousand dollars.

Valentina began working her phone, and Ivanov finally shouted, "Yes, okay, fine. He was here."

Ivanov said that Fisher had come about an hour ago. He was hurt—something wrong with his ribs—and he needed someplace to sleep. He said he gave Fisher the keys to his apartment.

Without tipping his hand and telling Ivanov that they had already been to the man's apartment, Hansen continued his line of questioning about Fisher: Was he armed? Did he have car? Was he alone? And so on. Hansen put on a good front but was getting the uneasy feeling that Fisher might be watching them at that very moment.

Hansen finally said, "You can forget about this visit."

Ivanov was no fool and agreed.

"If you cross us, I'll make the call. You'll have every Russian mobster in Odessa looking for you. Understand?"

He did.

Hansen regarded the others and tipped his head toward the door. All they could do now was set up surveillance of Ivanov, who might eventually lead them to Fisher—if one, the other, or both got sloppy.

Hansen then warned the man to stay off the phone, and Ivanov agreed but suddenly added, "Hey, you're Hansen, aren't you?"

Hansen stopped, gasped, and looked back at the man.

In fact, the others heard Ivanov as well, and they stood there, aghast.

"What?" Hansen finally asked. "What did you say?"

"He told me to give you a message."

Hansen asked who did, and Ivanov only said the message had to be delivered in private.

"That's crap!" cried Ames, raising his voice. "What the hell is this? Hansen—"

"Quiet!" cried Hansen, cutting Ames off. He faced Ivanov. "Tell me."

The old man shook his head, double chin wagging. "He told me, only you. Listen, I've known Sam a long time, and, to be honest, he scares me a lot more than you do."

Ames chuckled at that. "Well, dummy, in about fifteen minutes good old Sam is going to be dead or tied up in our trunk. If you've got an ounce of brains, you'll—"

"Everyone outside," cried Hansen.

"No way. I'm not going to let this . . ."

Ames trailed off as Hansen shot him a look that said he'd kill him if he didn't move out.

Ames lifted an ugly smile and filed out with the others, although he banged shut the door behind him.

"What's the message?" Hansen asked Ivanov.

The man opened his mouth.

And in the next breath there was an anesthetic dart jutting from the side of his neck. Ivanov's eyes creased in pain, his hand began to reach up to the dart, and then he fell backward onto the concrete.

Hansen glanced up in the direction of the shot, toward the overhead shelving, while slowly raising his hands. He lifted his voice, and although he had yet to see the man, he said somewhat resignedly, "Hey, Fisher."

Fisher moved out from behind one of the crates, having created an expert blind for himself from which to observe the action below. His eyes were a little bloodshot, his expression long and weary. There was more stubble on his cheeks than Hansen remembered from the last time they'd encountered each other.

"Hi, Ben."

"I guess this is what you'd call a rookie mistake."

"Mistakes are mistakes. They happen. How you handle them is what counts."

"I'll keep that in mind." Hansen then asked what they were doing, what was going on.

Fisher ignored the questions and ordered him to take his pistol and set it down on the floor. Hansen did, then decided to kick it toward Fisher, hoping the noise might attract one of the others outside. His subdermal was off and he couldn't activate it without reaching his OPSAT first. Fisher told him not to kick the weapon, just to leave it there. Then he added, "Interlace your fingers and place them on your head. Take ten steps forward."

Maybe it was Hansen's ego, but he just didn't want to feel so helpless and trapped. He remained where he stood.

"I won't ask again. I'll just dart you, and this will turn ugly before it's started."

With a deep sigh, Hansen did as he was told. Fisher instructed him to face the office, then drop to his knees with his ankles crossed.

Fisher next climbed down the rack ladder and maneuvered up behind Hansen, holding back about ten feet, Hansen estimated. Hansen stole a look back and said, "You've been a pain in my ass, you know."

"Sorry about that. It was necessary."

"Is that what you want to talk about? That there are extenuating circumstances? That you didn't really kill Lambert?"

"No, I killed Lambert. He asked me to."

"Bull. You've been jerking us around for weeks—you, Grimsdóttir, and Moreau—but as far as I'm concerned, you're a run-of-the-mill murderer."

"You sound angry, Ben."

"Damn right, I'm angry. You've run us ragged. Five of us, and we never even came close."

"You came close. More times than you know. You almost had me in Hammerstein."

"No, I didn't. You pushed me into a split-second, no-win scenario, and you knew I'd hesitate." Hansen laughed under his breath. "You know what gets me? I don't even know how you . . ."

All right, the plan had worked. He'd lured Fisher into the conversation to distract him, and he sensed the man had moved a couple of steps closer.

Fisher might have the experience, but Hansen had the agility and reflexes of a man half as old, and, in one smooth motion lifted a leg, brought down the boot, spun on his heel, and lurched forward, cutting the distance between them in half.

Although Fisher's pistol was raised, Hansen's lead arm was coming toward him in a backhanded arc.

Even Fisher's expression said he knew what would happen. His shot would go wide.

Now his glance flicked down to the dagger Hansen had simultaneously drawn from the sheath concealed by his coat. Hansen held the blade in a reverse grip, keeping it tucked against his inner forearm, and within the better part of a second, he would have that blade pressed firmly against Mr. Sam Fisher's throat.

36

"I'M going back inside," said Ames.

"No, you're not," Valentina said, crossing in front of him. She was a couple of breaths away from punching him squarely in the jaw. In her mind's eye, she watched him drop to the oily pavement, hand going to the blood trickling down from his mouth.

Ames cursed loudly and added, "Games, games, and more games! I'm over this! Aren't you all?"

"Look, whatever the message is, I'm sure Ben will share it with us," said Gillespie.

"But why was the message only for him?" asked Noboru.

"Yeah, you see what I'm talking about?" Ames cried. "Now Hansen is one of them, and the four of us are being used. You can't trust anyone here. I'm telling you. You can't trust anyone."

"Give him another minute and we'll find out," said Valentina. "But I'm sure Ben is not, quote, 'one of them. . . .'"

HANSEN expected Fisher to duck, but instead he took a sliding step forward, lifting his right hand to block Hansen's knife arm. Then, with his free hand balled into a fist, Fisher struck a solid jab into the nerves and soft tissue of Hansen's armpit. It was a strange and unpredictable counterattack, which sent pain shooting up and down Hansen's arm. He sensed his momentum faltering as Fisher clamped down on the wrist of his knife hand, then spun around his back, forcing him to shift likewise and lose his balance.

Fisher tightened his grip, and Hansen felt the twisting, stretching, and tearing in his hand a second before he could do no more than release the knife, which clattered to the concrete. He tried to repress a gasp but couldn't with the fire blazing in his hand.

Before Hansen knew what was happening, his feet were kicked out from under him and he was on his back, with Fisher's knee jammed into his chest and the air escaping from his lungs. Hansen's cheeks began to warm, and when he tried to breathe, no air would come.

The dagger swept down across Hansen's throat, and in one ego-shattering moment, Hansen knew he was defeated.

"This is my knife, Ben. Why do you have my knife?"

Hansen tried to answer, but he couldn't. Fisher released some of the pressure from his knee. Hansen stole a breath and eventually got out one word: "Grimsdóttir."

"Grim gave you this?"

"Thought it . . . thought it would bring . . . luck."

At that, Fisher's lips curled into a broad grin. "How's it working for you so far?"

Hansen sucked down air. "Keep it."

Fisher said he would and warned Hansen that he was climbing off and not to move. Hansen had no problem with that and asked Fisher what the hell he'd just done to him.

"I'll take that as a rhetorical question," Fisher answered, his grin turning crooked.

He then told Hansen to call Grim and ask about Karlheinz van der Putten.

"The guy that gave us the Vianden tip? Ames's contact?"

"That's him. Make the call."

Hansen did, and what Grim told him left his jaw

hanging open. Hansen finally looked up at Fisher and said, "She says you'll answer all my questions."

"As best I can."

Hansen added that Grim was sorry about the knife. Fisher laughed, then told him to contact the team and tell them he'd be finished shortly. That done, Fisher went on to confirm that he and Grim now believed that Ames was a mole.

"The Vianden ambush tip came from Ames, who claims he got it from van der Putten. You know that's bogus, correct?"

"I'm taking it on faith for the time being."

"Fair enough. I found van der Putten dead, his ears cut off. That was Ames covering his tracks."

"If not van der Putten, where'd he get the tip?"

"Kovac, we believe."

"Kovac? That's nuts. Ames is working for Kovac? No way. I mean the guy's a weasel, but—"

"Best-case scenario is that Kovac simply hates Grim, and he wants her out. What better way to undermine her than to catch me without her? Here's how it'd be played for the powers that be: Kovac, suspicious of Grim, puts his own man on the team dispatched to hunt me down. Grim's inept handling of the situation allows me to escape multiple times until finally Kovac's agent saves the day. Same scenario at Hammerstein. Kovac called in a favor from the BND."

Hansen was having trouble fitting all the pieces

together, not because they didn't fit but because he didn't want them to fit. "What's the worst-case scenario?"

"Kovac's a traitor and he's working for whoever hired Yannick Ernsdorff."

Hansen didn't know that name, but he figured Fisher would explain further. The man went on:

"Up until I went off the bridge into the Rhine, Kovac had been getting regular updates from Grim. The moment it became clear to him that I was heading to Vianden—to Yannick Ernsdorff—he got nervous and Ames's tip miraculously appeared. Think about it: After I lost you at the foundry in Esch-sur-Alzette, did you have any leads? Any trail to follow?"

"No."

"That's because I didn't leave one."

"Okay, some of what you're saying makes sense, but Kovac a traitor? Grim suggested that a while ago, but that's a big leap."

"Not too big a leap for Lambert. It's why he asked me to kill him. It's why I went underground. He was convinced the U.S. intelligence community, including the NSA, was infected to the highest levels. Have you ever heard of doppelgänger factories?"

"No."

Fisher explained that these secret Chinese manufacturing facilities were dedicated to cloning and improving on Western military technology, not unlike the way other Chinese manufacturers stole and produced knockoffs of other American and European patented products, but on a much grander and more sophisticated scale. Fisher said the Guoanbu, or China's Ministry of State Security, stole schematics, diagrams, material samples, basically anything it could acquire to feed to the doppelgänger factories' production.

"Sounds like an urban legend," said Hansen.

"Lambert didn't think so. He thought they were real, and the Guoanbu was getting help from the inside: politicians, the Pentagon, CIA, NSA. . . . No one's willing to admit it, but when it comes to industrial espionage, the Guoanbu has no peer. You don't get that lucky without help."

"So, Kovac—"

"That, we don't know yet."

Fisher said that Yannick Ernsdorff was playing banker for a black-market weapons auction starring the world's worst terrorist groups. He and Grim called the collection the Laboratory 738 Arsenal after the doppelgänger factory it was stolen from. Fisher said he'd found the crew that completed the job: They were former SAS boys led by Charles "Chucky Zee" Zahm, who had, in fact, become a famous novelist.

· "You can add professional thief to his résumé," Fisher said, then explained about Zahm and his Little Red Robbers. Zahm had proof of the job, including a complete inventory of the arsenal, Fisher added.

"What kind of stuff?"

Fisher said he'd show Hansen an inventory list later, but, more important, they couldn't let the 738 Arsenal get away from them. "Ben, you might have seen a piece from the arsenal."

"Come again?"

"The doppelgänger factory that Zahm hit was in eastern China, near the Russian border. The Jilin-Heilongjiang region, about a hundred miles north-west of Vladivostok, and about sixty miles from a Russian town called Korfovka."

Hansen frowned at the mention of that town, and suddenly his thoughts swept back to that mission, that very first mission as a Splinter Cell, and Rugar drawing back his fist. . . .

"I was there," Hansen finally said. "A while ago."

Fisher said Korfovka was the town where Zahm delivered the arsenal about five months before. Hansen explained that he was there much earlier than that.

"I got out because somebody helped me. Stepped in at just the right moment."

Fisher did not flinch. "Lucky break."

"Yeah . . . lucky." Hansen narrowed his gaze even more. Was Fisher just being coy? If he hadn't saved Hansen, how would he know about Hansen catching a glimpse of a piece of the arsenal? Had Grim told him? "This is a tall tale, Sam. Doppelgänger factories, Chinese replica weapons, this auction, Kovac . . ."

"Truth is stranger than fiction."

Hansen took a long breath and decided to con-firm with Fisher what he already knew: "This cat-and-mouse game we've been playing has been for Kovac's benefit."

Fisher noted that this was a statement, not a ques-tion. Hansen agreed that he and the others had already realized their strings were being pulled.

But now Hansen had confirmation of why Grim had been forced to put a team in the field to hunt down Fisher. If she refused, she'd be out, and all the work they'd done since Lambert's death would be lost. Fisher's mission was, indeed, more important than Hansen could have imagined, and while he still loathed being used, he understood, and that provided a small measure of reassurance.

Fisher explained that he'd hacked into Ernsdorff's server and learned more information about the planned auction, which was now only days away and at the point of no return. Hansen and the team would no longer be straight men in Fisher's comedy road show, which was, of course, fantastic news.

"Exactly. Yesterday I tagged one of the auction attendees. A Chechen named Aariz Qaderi."

"CMR, right?" Hansen asked, the name familiar to him. "Chechen Martyrs Regiment?"

"That's the guy. I tagged him. He's headed east into Russia—on his way to the auction, we hope."

"Hold on. All the attendees will be scrubbed before they reach the auction site. Any kind of beacon or tracker will be found."

"Not the kind we used."

Fisher said they didn't have time to go into an in-depth discussion of the nanobot trackers he'd used but that they needed to start moving east until the trackers phoned home.

"What about Ames?" Hansen asked.

"We'll deal with him later. For now, he's part of the team. We include him in everything."

"What about his cell phone? And his OPSAT? He'll try to contact Kovac."

"Let him. Grimsdóttir's made modifications to his phone and OPSAT. Every communication he makes beyond our tactical channels will go straight to her. She'll be playing Kovac and anyone else Ames has been talking to. He'll get voice mail, but Grim will respond to texts. Your phones aren't Internet capable, right?"

Hansen was already grinning. "Right. I like it. I like the plan."

"I thought you might. One thing, though: One of us has to stick to Ames like glue. If he slips away and gets a message out another way, we're done."

"Understood."

"How do you want to handle your people? I'd prefer to not get shot in the confusion."

Hansen beamed. "I'll see what I can do." Hansen then suggested that Fisher grab a seat along the back wall in the dark office. He wanted a moment to speak to the team before dropping the bomb on them, and he worried about Ames's reaction if Fisher were to suddenly appear.

Fisher did so, after putting another dart in Ivanov to be sure they would have their "privacy," as he'd put it.

Hansen called in the rest of the team members and, out in the main storage area, told them about Fisher's mission to locate the auction site and prevent the Laboratory 738 Arsenal from winding up in the hands of terrorists. When Hansen got to the part where Kovac might be involved, he turned his gaze to Ames, who was already shaking his head.

"If you're going to stand there and try to convince us that the deputy director of the goddamned NSA is involved in some ridiculous scam to sell Chinese weapons knockoffs to terrorists, then I'm going to turn around and walk out of here because it's pretty goddamned clear that you, boss man, have gone insane."

"This whole thing is linked to my first mission in Russia. Lambert, Grim, and Fisher were working on this well before we ever became Splinter Cells. Lambert sacrificed himself for this—and it's not some ridiculous scam. That's why Fisher's taking this to the limit. No one can stop him. And I don't blame him. The blood's been drawn. He will end this."

"How do you know, Ben?" asked Gillespie.

"Because I do."

"What about Kovac? If we were putting on a show for him—" began Valentina.

"He won't have time to do anything. The clock's already ticking. The auction will happen."

"So where's Ivanov?" asked Noboru.

Hansen ignored the question and quickly said, "One last thing. We're taking on a new member. He's going to be our team leader from this point on."

"Who the hell—" Valentina began.

"Why would Grimsdóttir make a change at this point?" asked Gillespie, who abruptly turned toward the office doorway, where stood Fisher.

As she reached for her gun, Hansen called, "Stand down, Kim. Everybody, hands at your sides."

"You gotta be kidding me. Look who it is," said Ames, wearing his blackest grin.

"Ben, what's going on?"

Hansen steeled his voice. "I think I'll let Mr. Fisher explain that. . . ."

37

"I don't buy it. Not a word of it," said Ames, wondering how the hell he was going to navigate around this unforeseen complication. Fisher linking up with the team was not part of the plan and would make terminating him all the more difficult. "This is just another circle jerk," he told the others.

Fisher tried to argue. Ames cut him off, told the others they were fools and that Fisher was probably setting them up to take his fall.

No one spoke for a moment; then Gillespie, that dumb-ass redhead, said she believed Fisher (of course she would; she'd screwed him); then she looked at him, all glassy eyed and puppy-dog-like, and said, "That night at the foundry . . . I almost shot you. You know that?"

He nodded.

Thankfully, Noboru went off on Fisher, saying that the team should have been notified up front of Grim's plan. Fisher said they couldn't have risked that, but the time had come now to drop the ruse, for two reasons:

"One, to stop this auction I'm going to need your help. There are too many variables, too many unknowns. We won't know until we get there, but my gut tells me this won't be a one-person job. And two, when I went off the bridge at Hammerstein I bought myself some time, but I knew they'd find the car. Kovac would get suspicious and accuse Grim of anything. Any excuse to get her out. If I resurface, you guys get deployed and Kovac has to back off for a while."

Gillespie, her voice cracking, questioned Fisher about how he'd survived the plunge into the Rhine, and he described his use of an OmegaO unit that had allowed him to breathe underwater. He'd waited until the car hit the bottom of the lake before getting out.

Noboru and Fisher spoke once more of their encounter at the Siegfried bunkers, and Noboru thanked Fisher for taking out Horatio and Gothwhiler, the mercs on his tail.

All this happy talk made Ames nauseous. He wanted to step outside and call Stingray, but then he remembered that Grim had issued them new phones and OPSATs before they'd flown out to Odessa. He stared down at the OPSAT on his wrist as though it were a piece of alien technology. Did they know about him? Had they given him a "special" phone and OPSAT so he could be traced? He'd been careful about that in the past. *Interesting* . . . At least now he'd be able to give Kovac more definitive information regarding Fisher. And he'd have to make contact himself, since his cutout Stingray couldn't get to the area in time. Ames could resort to texting, if he must. . . .

"Now that we're in on the con," Valentina said, "we'll need to be real careful about what gets back to Kovac. If he's involved with this auction stuff, he can't get a hint of what we're doing. If he's not involved but wants Grim out, we can't give him any reason."

"Agreed," said Fisher, glancing around. "Are we good?"

Everyone nodded, but perhaps Ames made his disdain a little too obvious.

"In or out, Ames?" asked Hansen. "Either you're with us or I'll kick your ass back to Fort Meade."

Ames stepped up to him and stiffened. "You'd like that, wouldn't you?"

Hansen cracked a grin.

Ames answered with a sarcastic smile of his own. "Yeah, okay. I'm on board. We don't have to hug or anything, right? I ain't doing that."

* * *

HANSEN and the others waited outside the annex for Fisher to square things away with Ivanov. A mere fifteen thousand rubles would keep him happy and silent. Once Fisher returned, they split up and checked into two hotels near the passenger port terminal. Fisher reported, via phone, that he'd spoken with Grim and that Qaderi, the auction attendee he'd tagged, was heading east toward Irkutsk. The nanobot tracking technology Fisher had employed, a technology code-named Ajax, was working flawlessly so far. Fisher was still hesitant to say much more about it, though he assured Hansen that one day he'd get a chance to read the full report. Fisher was also emphatic about not disclosing Qaderi's identity to Ames, and Hansen agreed. Qaderi would be known simply as "the target."

Fisher added, "Clarity is overrated—especially in our business."

Hansen grinned at that. "I'm sure Ames will have something to say about your unwillingness to fully disclose all details."

"He can say whatever he wants."

GRIM managed to book them on a Czech Airlines flight leaving at 4:00 A.M. They had connections in Prague and Moscow and would be touching down in Irkutsk about eight hours behind Qaderi. They would, unfortunately, have to abandon most of their gear, including weapons, in order to fly commercial and make it past customs. Fisher had a very special set of shaving cream cans that he guarded fiercely, each containing more of the Ajax tracking darts. He felt certain he'd make it past customs with them, as even X-rays wouldn't reveal anything suspicious to security. Their OPSATs could pass for PDAs, but pretty much everything else, including their subdermals, would have to be left behind, in a cache, to be picked up later by Third Echelon personnel.

In the wee hours prior to leaving, Hansen managed to "accidently" knock Ames's cell phone into the toilet, now limiting him to OPSAT communications. Oops.

Irkutsk, though situated in Siberia along the Angara River, and among rolling hills and thick taiga, was still a metro area of more than six hundred thousand citizens. While it hardly measured up to Western standards, the city was the largest in the region. What troubled Hansen, however, was the place's subarctic climate and extreme temperature variations. Recent reports of spring snowstorms didn't help matters.

Nevertheless, there was still something nostalgic about returning to Russia, the country of his first mission.

DURING the first plane ride of their journey, Ames found himself sitting across the row from Fisher, and after thirty minutes of simmering, Ames finally had to say something. "You tried to wash me out, didn't you?"

Fisher slowly woke up, looked up him, and said some unintelligible nonsense about training and evaluations and Ames lacking the temperament.

Ames told him to go to hell; then he tried to pry info from Fisher about the target they were after. Maybe Ames should have told Fisher to go to hell after his info-gathering attempt. As expected, Fisher wasn't talking.

"So let me get this straight: You won't tell us who we're after or how we're tracking him, and we don't have jack for a plan."

"That's about the size of it."

Ames muttered, "Great, just great," then folded his arms over his chest, closed his eyes, and rehearsed the eight silent ways he'd murder Fisher. He'd already imagined a dozen other methods that were markedly louder.

Gillespie leaned forward from the seat behind and whispered, "Don't worry, Ames. I'm sure Sam will take good care of you. . . ."

He turned back and met her sarcastic grin with a hard scowl, then flumped into his seat.

IRKUTSK, RUSSIAN FEDERATION

THREE planes and what felt like two weeks later, they finally began their descent into Irkutsk at about ten at night, local time, only to learn that, yes, indeed, a late-spring snowstorm had struck the area. After landing, they rented a pair of Lada Niva SUVs, a kind of stubby version of a Jeep Cherokee, then headed away from the airport and into the city. Fisher drove the lead SUV, with Hansen riding shotgun, and took them to a still-open diner, where they sat and discussed their course of action.

Fisher got right to the point: "We need weapons, equipment, and cold-weather gear."

The nearest Third Echelon cache was three hundred miles north, in Bratsk, and the nearest multiple cache farther still. Fisher explained that they had to get inventive.

"Noboru, you did some work in Bratsk once, right?"

Noboru was surprised that Fisher knew about that; then he remembered to whom he was speaking, and said he had. "Great town. A lot of gray cinder-block buildings. Very Soviet."

Fisher wanted him to make some calls, see if he could secure any weapons. Valentina and Gillespie would hit the hobby and electronics stores for communications devices. Hansen and Ames would be responsible for cold-weather and camouflage gear.

Grim interrupted the meeting with a call to Fisher to say the target was 210 miles northeast of their position and that there'd been no movement for three hours. Qaderi was, in fact, on the western shore of

Lake Baikal, a worm-shaped body of water and one of the largest freshwater lakes in the world.

"The guy is going up into no-man's-land," said Ames. "What the hell is he doing there?"

"That's what we're here to find out," Hansen answered impatiently.

Grim updated Fisher once more, saying that the road was blocked at Qaderi's location, which accounted for his stopping. "We're not going anywhere tonight," Fisher said. "We'll find a place to stay, settle in, and wait for daylight. If we can get on the road by noon, we'll only be four hours behind our target."

LIGHT blue upholstered furniture, peach carpet, and gold curtains gave the hotel's lobby that wonderful "I know I'm in Russia" feeling that accompanies its nightmarish interior design. The garish colors reminded Hansen of the interior of the ferry he'd taken to Vladivostok nearly two years before.

While everyone else was settling in, Hansen and Fisher sat at one of the settees and discussed the Ames issue. As they got closer to Qaderi, Fisher would release more info in the hopes that Ames would try to contact his master.

"Then do we get to string him up by his ankles?" Hansen asked.

Fisher cocked a brow. "Something like that."

* * *

THEY were all awake by 7:00 A.M. and gorged themselves at the hotel's breakfast buffet. Fisher reminded them that this would be their last decent meal for a long while. The Russian pastries were heavenly, though the eggs were watery and the bread slightly stale. Hansen pigged out to the point that he regretted it.

By 8:00 A.M. they had split up and gone on their separate hunting/gathering missions. Ames and Hansen found a military surplus store that specialized in selling old gear to hunters in the area. They loaded up on everything they'd need, though a lot of the gear had to be double-checked for age and damage. They tried to ignore the smell.

NOBORU called his old contact in Bratsk, who set up a meeting with his best friend, a bald, heavily tattooed man named Pavel, who lived on the outskirts of the city in what appeared to be an old farmhouse. Noboru was led into a basement unlike anything he'd ever seen: nearly two thousand square feet of nothing but ordnance, a veritable department store of destruction, with rows of heavy metal shelving stretching off into the shadows and lightbulbs strung loosely from the old wooden beams. He could almost hear the assistant manager on the intercom:

*"Attention, shoppers, we have a two-for-one sale
going on! By one fragmentation grenade, get the second
absolutely free! That's right, shoppers! And we also have
Semtex plastic explosives and detonators. Stock up now
for those weekends when you know you're going to blow
the hell out of the neighborhood!"*

"What do you need?" Pavel asked in a thick Russian accent. "I have . . . *everything.*"

Noboru beamed.

ONCE he'd arranged automatic payment to Pavel via
Third Echelon, Noboru stocked up, drove back to
the hotel, and met up with Fisher. He handed over
a list of what he'd procured, beginning with several
fun items:

4 Groza OTs-14-4A-03 assault rifles

2 SVU OC-AS-03 sniper rifles

6 × 600 PSS Silent Pistols with armor-piercing
   ammo

The Groza was a sweet little toy—a noise-suppressed
assault rifle with a short barrel for sweeping around
corners in urban combat; the SVU rifles were
improved versions of the classic Russian SVD Dragunov sniper rifle; and the PSS pistols were designed

for special-forces ops and featured a unique cartridge with an internal piston, making them some of the quietest handguns in the world.

Fisher glanced up at him, aghast. "These are Spetsnaz weapons, current issue."

"Yep." Noboru cracked a grin that said: *Don't ask.*

The rest of the list contained items like fragmentation, smoke, and stun grenades, along with some spotting scopes, night-vision headsets, binoculars, gas masks, and the requisite Semtex plastic explosives, along with pouching and web gear for packing all that firepower.

Noboru watched as Fisher's gaze fell on an item that Noboru knew would give the man pause.

Fisher looked up, an expression of awe washing over his face. "An ARWEN," he said with a slight gasp. "You got an ARWEN."

"My guy had one. Wanted twenty thousand for it. I talked him down to eight." Noboru had saved 3E a few bucks. Call him a frugal hero.

ARWEN stood for Anti-Riot Weapon, Enfield, and the ARWEN 37 was a five-shot SAS weapon developed in the sixties as a less-than-lethal alternative to anything they faced ahead. The launcher could fire Impact Baton, tear-gas, smoke, and Barricade Penetrating rounds, among others. It was perfect for creating diversions to expedite escape.

"Good work," Fisher said.

He went on to describe a special project he needed

accomplished: He wanted Noboru to convert a pair of paintball guns so they could launch the Ajax grenade darts Fisher had smuggled into Russia via the shaving cream cans.

"I'm going to need tools," Noboru said.

Fisher pointed to a shopping bag sitting before a chest of drawers. "Get started. Call if you need anything. I'm going to check on the others. We leave in an hour."

As the man headed out, Noboru rifled through the bag and saw that Fisher had purchased just the tools he needed. Now it was time to get creative. Noboru gathered all the materials on the bed, stared at them for a moment, then got to work.

38

QADERI had started moving again and was presently a hundred miles north of the Rytaya River estuary, about two hundred miles ahead of the team.

They loaded the SUVs with the gear Hansen and Ames had bought, as well as the electronic equipment Gillespie and Valentina had found in a few local shops. And they bolted off in the afternoon, the moment they got word, and were now working their way through blowing snow along the western bank of Lake Baikal—and the twelve hundred miles of shoreline that twists and turns along its four-hundred-mile length. The lake's massive proportions were dwarfed, however, by its depth: almost a mile, making it the deepest freshwater lake in the world. When Hansen gazed out across it, he could not see the opposite shoreline through all the wind and snow.

The road was narrow, snow-and-ice covered, and Fisher didn't dare push past fifty miles per hour, so it was generally slow going.

From the backseat, Ames announced that is was nearly 5:00 P.M. and the sun was beginning to set. "What's the plan?"

"Depends on our target," Fisher answered. "If he keeps going, so do we."

Hansen agreed and asked Ames if he had a problem with that.

"Not really," said the man, crossing his legs. "But can we take a bathroom break?"

Hansen snorted. "Hold it."

THEIR target finally paused at 7:00 P.M., about twelve miles from the lake's northern tip, in a town of twenty-seven thousand called Severobaikalsk. With nightfall came even heavier winds and snow, and Hansen, serving as navigator and sifting through satellite intel from Grim, led Fisher toward a shantytown of hunting huts on Cape Kotel'nikovskiy. The town was no more than a dozen or so thick-canvas yurt-style tents, circular structures with cone-shaped roofs.

Fisher explained to the pestering Ames that the roads were icing up and that most of the path for the next fifty miles was a single lane running along the cliffs above the lake. They could easily slide off the road, and that would be that. Moreover, their target had stopped for the same reason: weather. Ames argued that he could have reached the auction site. Fisher said that maybe he had, but others were coming and they, too, would be delayed, so they would make the best of it until the front passed. They hauled their gear into the most secure-looking hut, where they found eight wooden bunks with thin straw mattresses organized in a circle around a potbellied stove. After they'd fired up a pair of kerosene lanterns hanging from the cross-beam, Hansen spotted a sign, handwritten in Cyrillic, on one of the posts:

Honor system. If you stay here, leave something: money, supplies, etc. Together Siberia is home; separate, a hell.

Ames said he was going to leave them something, all right, and headed back outside toward the outhouse.

Fisher looked at Hansen and cocked a brow.

NOBORU got the high sign from Fisher and went outside to help him carry in some more gear. Fisher asked about their little project, and Noboru reassured him that he felt good about the modified paintball guns and estimated a 90 percent chance of their operating correctly. Noboru said he wasn't comfortable keeping their plan a secret from the rest of the team, as Fisher had instructed him to do, but Fisher assured him that all would be revealed in time.

Back inside the yurt, Gillespie was complaining about her sleeping bag: "It looks like it's from the Cold War!" She went on to moan about the bag's moldy stench.

Hansen said she'd have to live with the smell, but at least he'd bought them for a dollar a piece—a bargain!

Ames, of course, couldn't allow anyone to have any fun and immediately dampened the mood by asking Fisher why they couldn't just blow up the 738 Arsenal.

"Two reasons," Fisher replied. "One, I doubt whoever arranged this auction is stupid enough to keep it all in a big pile; we're talking about tons of equipment. We don't have enough Semtex for that. Two, they're going to be our Trojan horses. Once they leave here, we'll track them wherever they go. In the space of a week, we'll learn more about this group's logistics and transport routes than we've learned in the last five years. When they arrive at their destination, we mop them up, along with anyone else we find."

Ames tried to poke holes in the plan.

Fisher said he'd make a deal: "If this all goes to hell and we're both still around when it's over, you can say you told me so."

HANSEN glimpsed at the time on his OPSAT: 11:00 P.M. The others were fast asleep. He sat up and glanced over at Fisher's bunk. He was already awake and nodded to Hansen. They rose and slipped into their cold-weather gear, then moved to Ames's bunk. Fisher pricked Ames just below the ear with an anesthetic dart, while Hansen held his mouth. Ames nearly bit Hansen before he went limp.

Holding his breath, Hansen lifted the rat bastard in a fireman's carry and went outside, taking Ames to another yurt. Inside, he lay Ames spread-eagled on a bunk and used some old paracord to bind his wrists and ankles to the rickety wooden platform. They'd removed the mattress; that would come into play later.

After a moment to catch his breath, Hansen found and lit another kerosene lantern, though he kept it dim to conserve fuel. Fisher went off to fetch the others.

A few moments later, they all filed into the tent, shocked about what they were seeing. Fisher warned them about what was happening, while Hansen slipped outside to fetch the bottle of gasoline they had earlier prepared.

Within five minutes, Ames woke up, and after voicing his questions and demands, and being summarily dismissed, Fisher cut to the chase: "You're a traitor."

Ames whined like a little boy, denying everything, and even tried to emphasize that he was a Splinter Cell.

Hansen wanted to tell Ames what a rat he was, and then pummel the runt to within an inch of his life, but he held back. Fisher was asking the questions and went on to tell Ames that they knew he'd contacted Kovac's office when he'd gone off to use the outhouse. Fisher said he could prove it because he had a transcript, which he'd sent to all their OPSATs. He instructed the team to review the script, and there it was, in black and white, Ames's full text report. He'd given up everything: their location, make and model of their vehicles, weapons, and the details he had regarding the auction and planned attack on the Laboratory 738 Arsenal. It was all there. Hansen guessed the little bastard had been desperate enough to send the text because he no longer had access to a cutout.

"Ames has been working for Kovac for a while," said Fisher. "We're not sure how long, but we're about to find out." Fisher went on to explain how Ames used Karlheinz van der Putten as a scapegoat, since he couldn't reveal that he'd learned where Fisher would be through Kovac's office. Fisher said that van der Putten had not received any money for the information. Fisher had personally gained access to van der Putten's financials, and they reflected no payoff from Ames.

Fisher also explained that he'd been in Vianden to visit an Austrian named Yannick Ernsdorff, whom he'd already told Hansen about and who was, he now shared with the rest, the banker for the auction they were hoping to infiltrate. Kovac was nervous because he and Ernsdorff were working for the same man.

"And who is that?" Noboru asked.

Fisher sighed deeply. "We don't know."

"Does he?" asked Valentina, gesturing to Ames.

The little man began his whining again. Fisher cut him off, saying the best case was that Ames was working for Kovac simply to push Grim out. Worst case was that Kovac was, indeed, a traitor and was helping whoever was behind the auction. Either way, though, Ames had been a mole from the start.

And Hansen found it even more ironic that Ames had done nothing from the beginning to hide his disdain for the others. In fact, he'd actually made himself the most obvious person to be suspected as a mole. Maybe that was his plan? Be too obvious? No, Hansen figured that Ames just didn't care, that he hated them so much he figured he'd play it that way and just enjoy the ride. There was no deep-seated rationale behind his thinking. He was just a little runt bastard who needed to be taught a lesson.

"Ames thought he was talking to Kovac on the OPSAT. He probably knew Kovac was going to pass on the information. When we reached the auction site, we would've been walking into an ambush."

Gillespie made a face and said, "There are a lot of ifs in there, Sam."

"True. We can settle this pretty easily. We know Ames is working for Kovac. We have the proof. What we need to know is whether Kovac's just an ass, or a traitor, and whether Ames is in on it."

Hansen got his signal from Fisher. He shoved the straw mattress under Ames's bunk; then Fisher took up the bottle of gasoline and poured a little around the edge. The odor spread strong and fast, and Ames's expression tightened in horror.

KATY stood at the window, coughing, staring at Ames, reaching out to him as the flames danced at her shoulders. Ames's mother screamed something, her words turning into a shriek as his father cried out her name—suddenly an explosion rocked through the house.

And Ames stood there on the front lawn, immobile, knowing he should have run back inside but too scared to do anything, a coward in the face of the flames. A coward. A boy who didn't save his family. A boy who'd watched them die. A boy who should be punished. A man who took every risk he could in his life because he knew he deserved to be punished.

Fisher was looking at Ames now, saying something, but Ames was just shaking his head, not against Fisher's words but against the inevitable, the image of those three bodies being carried from the house, draped in white sheets.

Now Fisher was pouring gasoline all over Ames's body: the cold, foul liquid seeping through his clothes.

They were going to kill him, and it'd be too easy, out in Siberia, in the middle of nowhere.

But he deserved it. He should take his punishment like a man. He needed to burn like them. *Burn . . .*

But an unconscious need for self-preservation kicked in, and Ames began bucking against the cord, the bunk rising and falling from the floor.

Fisher told the others that Ames would know the name of the man they were tracking. If he did, then it was clear Kovac gave it to him and that Kovac was in up to his eyebrows.

"Ames!" Fisher screamed.

And with a gasp, Ames fell still.

Fisher spoke slowly, the foreboding in his tone making Ames swallow in fear. "Tell me the name of the man we're tracking, or I'm going to set you on fire."

The name, Aariz Qaderi, came out with no

hesitation. Ames wasn't telling Fisher a name; he was telling his father that he was sorry for not saving him, for not saving the family.

"Ben's going to ask you more questions. Answer him," said Fisher; then he gestured to the door for the others to leave.

Once they were alone, Hansen glanced down at Ames, then reached into the man's right front pocket, where Ames kept his Zippo lighter.

"Maybe Fisher wouldn't roast you alive," Hansen began. "But you can rest assured, I will. Let's start at the beginning. How long have you been working for Kovac?"

"Grim found me, but he recruited me only a week after that."

"How could you do this to us?"

"It's only business. And, by the way, your buddy Sergei? He worked for us, too."

Hansen's eyes grew wider. He bared his teeth, then flipped open the lighter.

"Careful with that!" cried Ames. "I'm telling you this because I'm willing to talk. I've got enough stuff on Kovac to put him away forever, and you guys will need that, so you don't want to hurt me. I'm your ticket to bringing him down. Do you understand me, cowboy?"

"I told you—"

"I can call you whatever I want—because I still hold all the cards here."

"You could've fooled me, tied up to a bed, about to be burned alive. What else do you know about the auction?"

"As much as you. He keeps me on a strict diet. But you have to believe that I can help you."

THE front passed, and the team was able to get an early start, putting in about ninety minutes of road time before sunrise. Fisher drove the lead SUV while Hansen followed behind. Hansen and Fisher had cleaned up Ames, tied him once more, and stuffed him in the cargo area of Fisher's SUV, where he remained, although Hansen was certain the guy still smelled like gasoline. Hansen hadn't been able to get anything else out of him.

After another few miles of travel, Hansen's OPSAT beeped with incoming intel from Grim. Qaderi was moving again. He was already outside Severobaikalsk and heading—and this was odd—heading *south* back toward them.

Fisher suddenly stopped his SUV, backed up, and followed a side road that splintered off the main one and wandered into walls of pine trees.

"Where's he going?" asked Gillespie.

Hansen shrugged. "I don't know."

39

THE mountains were haloed in pink and orange as the sun began to rise, and Hansen continued following Fisher up and into the woods and inland. It now seemed clear that Fisher was putting them on an intercept course with Qaderi, following the heavily rutted and snow-covered path through a series of tortuous runs. Fisher shut off his headlights, and Hansen did likewise. Visibility was limited but the sun was rising fast.

They swept around yet another curve, and then, off to their right, peeking out from below a carpet of trees that unfurled to the shoreline, lay the calm, cool waters of a small lake, perhaps a half mile wide.

"I know where we are," said Gillespie. "Sludjanka Lake."

"Maybe this is it. Maybe we're here," said Hansen.

"Ben, there's another SUV on the other side of the lake," said Valentina, staring through her binoculars. "That's the target."

Fisher pulled along the side of the road, their vehicles hidden behind the thick stands of pine trees. They met between the cars. Hansen asked Fisher if this was the auction site. Fisher wasn't sure and lifted his own binoculars. "I'm not sure if that's Qaderi."

With everyone hidden behind the trucks, they watched as the SUV stopped at the top of a gradually sloping hill overlooking the lake. Hansen zoomed in and watched as the front passenger door opened and a man came out. He turned around, leaned back into the car, and took out a briefcase. When he turned back, his face was illuminated in the rising sun.

Hansen had reviewed the file photo of Aariz Qaderi. This was not him. "What the hell is this?" he asked Fisher.

"I think Qaderi just got uninvited to the auction."

With his back to them, the man opened the briefcase, sifted through its contents, then rose and just stood there for about ten minutes.

Fisher made an affirmative grunt, as though he knew what was about to happen.

From the east came the whomping of a helicopter, and soon a blue and white Sikorsky S-76, a medium-sized single-rotor chopper, swooped down over the lake, hovered, then landed behind the SUV. The cabin door opened, and out rushed four men. They, along with the driver of the SUV, rolled the car over the edge of the hill and sent it plummeting toward the lake.

The SUV hit the icy water with a significant splash, then, amid the waves and foam, began to sink.

That the chopper had approached from the east and remained on that side of the lake was the only thing that saved the team from being spotted, Hansen thought with a shiver. Hopefully, they would not fly overhead. Otherwise, game over.

"They must've known Qaderi was tagged," said Valentina, her breath hanging on the air.

And Hansen bet that Kovac had tipped them off.

Fisher agreed and mentioned that Grim had briefed Kovac a few hours before but had left out any mention of Ajax, so Kovac had probably assumed standard Third Echelon–issue beacons.

Hansen checked his OPSAT. "The bots are heading due east at 150 miles per hour."

Fisher said they needed to hide. He'd explain why later.

* * *

HANSEN found an abandoned mica mine built into the cliffs a mile west of the lake. It took them an hour to reach it, and they backed the SUVs into the broad main tunnel to keep them invisible from the air.

Noboru asked Fisher to explain why they were hiding, and Fisher obliged:

"They killed Qaderi because Kovac reported the trackers. Grim told Kovac we were still in Irkutsk, and the weather was causing problems with the GPS. That's why the Sikorsky didn't look for anyone tailing Qaderi's car. My gut tells me they'll be back—about the time we would have arrived if we'd left Irkutsk when Kovac thinks we did."

Hansen said, "You and Grim put some thought into this, didn't you?"

Fisher nodded.

"How long do we wait?" asked Valentina.

"Depends on where the Ajax nanobots go and how long it takes the Sikorsky to leave."

TWO hours later the chopper resounded in the distance, confirming Fisher's suspicions, and after its search over the lake and foothills, the bird touched down 30 miles due east of their position, about

1.5 miles inland from Ayaya Bay. The location was about two-thirds of the way between the bay and a calmer, V-shaped lake called Frolikha.

"Middle of nowhere," said Fisher. "The perfect spot for a black-market auction."

Hansen said that location was on the other side of the lake. Gillespie added that there weren't any roads to get around the lake. Fisher agreed. "We're going to need a boat."

They would have to wait, though, because Fisher warned them that the chopper would no doubt return. And it did, shortly before noon, spending several more hours searching for them. During that time, they checked their gear and Gillespie discussed the operation of the hands-free headsets she and Valentina had found as well as a jury-rigged flexicam they'd constructed. Hansen showed them all the black uniforms and web gear he'd bought, along with full balaclavas. Noboru unveiled his paintball project, then mentioned that he'd forgotten something out in the SUV.

A moment later he called out, and Hansen rushed over to see what was wrong.

Ames was gone.

KEEPING a straight-edged razor blade hidden in your boot heel was one of the oldest tricks in the book, perhaps way too obvious for the team to have considered—but that was Ames's style: That would be way too obvious. And so he'd managed to contort himself into a position to gain access to the blade and use it to saw through the plastic flex-cuffs they'd used to bind him. He'd slipped right past them, abandoning the cuffs at a triple branch in the tunnel and laughing as he did so.

"Adios, assholes. A little gift for you."

HANSEN and the others took up their Groza assault rifles and began the search for Ames. Fisher found a pair of flex-cuffs, then returned and said that Ames had a big lead on them and the team couldn't be distracted with a search for him now. They had bigger fish to fry. Hansen vowed that after all this was over he'd make it his mission in life to find and punish the man. The others agreed wholeheartedly.

They waited until nightfall, then returned to the SUVs and headed up to the town of Severobaikalsk to find transport across the lake. They "borrowed" a pair of johnboats with electric trolling motors from the marina and set out in darkness for the long journey across the frigid waters. It took several hours to make a stealthy approach to the shoreline, switching the trolling motor on and off to glide as much as possible. Fisher and Hansen kept a close watch of the heavily wooded hillside as it came into view, their night-vision goggles peeling back the shadows. Once in the mouth of Ayaya Bay, they paddled ashore and, in a staggered single file, charged up toward the forest.

Hansen's OPSAT reflected the position of the Ajax bots: all tightly clustered around a position two miles inland, sitting smack-dab between them and Lake Frolikha. A sign higher up the beach indicated that they were on the Great Baikal Trail, which would make the hike inland so much easier. Perhaps the auction organizer had chosen this spot because the trail would allow the attendees greater access? Hansen wasn't sure. Situating an auction near a public trail was risky and odd.

The team covered about a half mile in twenty minutes, and by 3:00 A.M. they'd closed to within a quarter mile of the target site. They came into an oval-shaped meadow, and for the life of him, Hansen could not imagine anyone transporting a weapons cache to this site. He suddenly feared that they were on a wild-goose chase, the bots leading them to a diversionary location while the real auction went on elsewhere. He voiced his concern to Fisher, who told him, no, they were in the right place.

As they fanned out and searched more, they spotted a section of field where no doubt the helicopter had landed. The smaller shrubs were bent back and telltale track marks scarred the ground.

Over on the north side of the meadow rose a

cinder-block hut with a rusted sheet-metal roof. Vegetation, still brown from the long winter, had swept up the hut's walls. Through it Hansen could see that the structure was probably very old.

"Move back to the hut," Fisher told Hansen.

They converged on the small structure, where they found a sign in Cyrillic: METEOROLOGICAL STATION 29. The hut's single hefty steel door was heavily pitted with rust, but the padlock was brand new, and while Hansen wasn't entirely adept at remembering such things, Fisher knew exactly what they had before them: a Sargent & Greenleaf 833 military-grade padlock with a six-pin Medeco biaxial core, ceramic anticutting and antigrinding inserts, and the capability to withstand liquid nitrogen.

"This must be one special meteorological station," Hansen quipped in a whisper. "Can we pick the lock?"

Fisher said the job would take a while, hours probably, and that the station itself was hardly big enough to hold the arsenal. The only thing they might find inside was Qaderi's briefcase. Nevertheless, the bots' signals were strong. They were sitting right on top of it.

There had to be something more underground, and Fisher said they'd take an hour to look for another entrance.

FORTY minutes later, Valentina called over their makeshift comm system to say she'd found something about three-quarters of a mile away and directly north of the hut. She placed a marker on their OPSAT maps, and they converged on her location, a simple ravine about six feet deep and cordoned off by pine trees. About twenty yards ahead lay a near-perfect circle of melted snow. Fisher donned his night-vision goggles, crawled to the spot, then signaled for the others to come.

It was an air shaft, and warm air was being piped up from somewhere below. The shaft was protected by a steel grating, and they found no locking mechanism or alarm system. Fisher and Noboru double-teamed the grating, and with some considerable tugging, it finally pulled free from its rusted framework.

Gillespie moved in behind him with her rope coil already removed from her pack. She lowered the rope down to the bottom, rolled it back up, and said, "Thirty-five feet." Fisher gave her a nod. They set up a secure line, and one by one descended down to the bottom of the shaft courtesy of a Swiss seat rappelling harness that Gillespie had tied off for them. She was first to descend, and Hansen pulled up the rear.

Gillespie's LED flashlight revealed a roughly triangular room, about ten feet wide, with ceilings angling up and more vent grating overhead and in the middle of the floor. Warm air blew past them and rushed up through the shaft, and from somewhere above, Hansen detected the faint hum of machinery. Fisher moved ahead to a door, eased it open, vanished a moment, then returned with the news: He'd checked a circuit panel and some lights were on somewhere. They were in a utility room, and judging from the size of the panel the place was damned big.

Fisher also said a service tag on the panel read "March 1962."

Valentina guessed they were in a Cold War bunker or some kind of test facility.

"Either or both," Fisher said. He suggested they pair up and do a little recon. Hansen would branch off with Gillespie, while Valentina and Noboru would serve as a second team.

That left Fisher alone, and Hansen voiced his concern.

Fisher grinned. "I'll get by."

Hansen was almost embarrassed by the question. He'd grown so used to working with his teammates that it suddenly seemed unnatural for a Splinter Cell to be working alone. With a curt nod, Hansen turned back and headed off with Gillespie.

40

ONCE Hansen and Gillespie left the utility room, they came into a wide corridor with a low ceiling barely seven feet high. The floor was painted with faded red, yellow, and green lines that fanned out away from them, not unlike the lines Hansen had seen on some hospital floors. Three-letter Cyrillic acronyms were stenciled onto each line. They donned their night-vision goggles and took Fisher's order to head down the corridor to the left. Noboru and Valentina fell in behind.

They moved quickly down the hall, keeping tight to the wall, rifles at the ready, until Hansen spotted something and called for Fisher to come to their position.

They were staring at a map of the complex, protected by a sheet of dust-covered Plexiglas. Cobwebs extended up from the sign and rose to the ceiling. Hansen wiped a gloved hand across the glass. The complex was shaped like a cloverleaf with four concentric circles at its center. A label read RAMPS TO LEVELS 2, 3, 4. Each leaf was marked as a zone, and each zone was divided into four areas interconnected by more corridors.

"Medical, electronics, weapons, ballistics," said Gillespie, reading the labels for each zone. "It's a test facility." She hoisted her brows at Valentina, who'd made that guess earlier on. Valentina nodded curtly.

"I assume ballistics means missiles and rockets," Gillespie added.

Fisher nodded, and Hansen glanced over at Noboru, who said, "This place is massive. Take a look at the scale."

Hansen watched as Fisher used his thumb and finger to check the map's gradated line, then measure the complex from one end to the other. "Twelve hundred meters."

With his jaw falling open, Hansen said, "That can't be. That makes it a square mile."

Valentina shook her head. "Four levels. *Four* square miles."

Fisher squinted hard at the map, deep in thought. "Ballistics and electronics. If you were experimenting, you'd want access to water for cooling and fire suppression."

Hansen agreed.

"We'll clear it as it's laid out, by zone and level, starting here and moving down."

He assigned Hansen to the medical zone, Valentina to electronics, Gillespie to weapons, and Noboru to ballistics.

"I'll loiter at the ramp area and play free safety. Questions?"

They were good to go and started off, but not before discovering a freestanding elevator shaft that Hansen thought might lead up to the "meteorological" hut they'd found in the meadow. Fisher took up a position beside the ramp railing while everyone else split up.

HANSEN picked his way down to the medical zone, the corridor festooned by overhead piping that dripped here and there. He ventured about two hundred yards farther and came to a pair of doors marked with a laboratory number. He tried the handle: open.

Tightening his grip on his rifle, Hansen eased the door open, braced himself, and slipped inside, sweeping the rifle over what was, in fact, another, shorter corridor with doors on both sides. Hansen poked his head inside the first open door and saw a laboratory with workbenches, sink area, rolling stools, and complicated networks of Pyrex tubing, test tubes, and beakers. He shoved up his goggles and flicked on his small LED flashlight. Gray metal shelving lined the walls. On the shelves were large glass jars filled with a yellow liquid. Hansen drew closer, wiped the dust from one of the jars, and something inside it shifted and pressed against the glass.

Hansen blinked hard. Cursed.

Was that a tiny human head? A nose? He gasped and backed away from the jar. "Sam, meet me in medical zone one," he called over the headset.

Within a minute, Fisher arrived and they moved on into a hospital ward where the long rows of beds were equipped with shackles. They moved on to the next two areas, encountering more laboratories and hospital wings.

"There were a dozen or so gulags within a hundred miles of here," Fisher said. "There'd always been rumors of prisoners disappearing and either never coming back or coming back . . . different."

Hansen swore under his breath.

Fisher called for a status report, and the others checked in. They regrouped at the main ramp, where Gillespie said she had found an indoor target range. Valentina said she'd found a test area full of antique electronics, even some stuff equipped with old vacuum tubes. Noboru just shook his head: drafting tables and workbenches. No high-tech arsenal.

They started down the wide ramp toward level 2.

No more than a minute later, Fisher signaled a halt, advanced, leaned over the railing, then returned and filled them in.

"Two guards stationed at the entrance to the ramp below. They've got AKs. No night vision that I could see."

So they had two guys down on level 3, and Hansen told the others that where there were two, there were no doubt more. Fisher agreed. They opted to check level 2 before contending with those guys below.

NOBORU had been charged with clearing the ballistics area of level 2. The test facility was already sending chills up and down his spine. It seemed that back during the Cold War the Russians knew no bounds when it came to discovery and experimentation. He was almost afraid of what they'd find next.

And, in fact, what he found next left him standing there like a proverbial deer in the headlights.

Slowly he slid up his goggles, flipped on his flashlight, and gazed up into the massive, man-made cavern that had been carved into the rock and earth. The place was at least two football fields across and lined with engine-test scaffolding that looked like something from Cape Canaveral. Four massive steel bays still held rocket motors, their colossal nozzles sitting before giant, concrete, sewerlike pipes whose innards were blackened. The pipes were no doubt some kind of exhaust system to flush the motor fumes and gases out of the test zone.

Noboru doused his light, refit his goggles, then charged down the row of scaffolding to make a perimeter search. He reached the zone between the second and third nozzles, rushed past a wall lost in deep shadow, then did a double take. He froze, looked back, and started toward the wall, which in silhouette seemed to be part of a pyramid. He passed several thick posts that had partially blocked his view, and then he saw it.

VALENTINA slowly opened the first locker and found nothing but coveralls and a moth-eaten parka. She didn't bother opening any of the others. The entire locker area appeared as though it hadn't been touched for years.

She came back out into the corridor, and for a moment, she thought she saw someone at the far end of the hall. She dropped to her knees, and did, in fact, see a shadow shift slightly to the right.

But then it was gone. She blinked. Had she really seen it?

A call came in from Fisher. He wanted everyone down in ballistics.

HANSEN gasped at the twenty-eight Anvil cases ranging from the size of small footlockers to that of bedroom furniture. They looked exactly like the case he'd seen back in Korfovka and were secured by the same type of padlock they'd found on the hut above.

Gillespie remarked that this couldn't be the entire arsenal. Fisher estimated it to be about a third, so the rest was elsewhere inside the facility or, perhaps, not in Russia at all. Valentina was concerned about Fisher's Ajax nanobots being able to get inside the cases to tag the weapons. He assured her that they needed a gap that was only a fraction of a hair's width and was certain they'd penetrate.

Fisher ordered them back, then drew one of Noboru's modified paintball guns and fired at the ceiling. The dart bounced off the rock, hit one of the Anvil cases, then rolled to a stop.

Hansen wanted to say, *"That's it?"* but just stood there, watching. He expected something far more dramatic.

Noboru had already initiated an uplink to the bots and glanced up at Fisher. "Nothing yet."

"What if there's no power for them to gravitate to?" asked Hansen.

Fisher explained that just about every weapon or system on the inventory list was equipped with some form of EPROM, or erasable programmable read-only memory, a low-power battery for housekeeping functions like date, time, and user settings. If the item didn't have an EPROM, then it wasn't one of the higher-end items and losing it was no disaster.

Within five minutes, Noboru was reading multiple pings from inside the cases. He grinned. "I'd say our first live-fire exercise is a success."

Before they left the area, in search of more of the arsenal, Gillespie pointed out a section of extra venting between the blast funnels and the wall. To Hansen, the gap at his feet resembled a bottomless pit, and his light faded before it could pick out any floor below. The vent probably extended all the way down to level 4.

VALENTINA took no pleasure in killing the guard, and she sensed that Noboru felt the same. She did, however, take great pleasure in working with Nathan, and she knew once the mission was over she would succumb to her feelings and ask to see him again . . . on a personal level.

She thought about this, even as she held her blade in a reverse grip and approached the guard.

Her hand rose to the man's mouth at exactly the same time Noboru's did for his guard.

Holding her breath, she drove her blade down into the guard's neck to make a perfect kill shot to the spinal cord. The slash to the throat or knife thrust to the heart that instantly kills someone is the stuff of Hollywood inaccuracy. Most knife fighters would tell you, if you don't get a kill shot to the spinal cord, your victim is going to stay alive for a while, and things will get very, very sloppy. Slashing the jugular was one of the last things you wanted to do. Sever that spinal cord and he's dead, Jim. Instantly dead.

Valentina and Noboru dragged the bodies up to the top of the ramp, where Hansen and Gillespie would take over and stash them in the medical area.

NOBORU took point, leading the way down into level 3. He headed off into the ballistics zone once more and found yet another stack of Anvil cases set up on tables within an electronics repair room adjacent to another, though smaller, rotor motor testing facility.

Now, this was more like it. This resembled an auction site. While the items weren't fully prepared, they were being arranged for display. Noboru was glad he'd packed the second paintball gun. He fired a round, waited, and smiled once he got back the pings he needed. He rallied with the rest back at Fisher's location near the main ramp and reported his find.

"Two down, one to go," said Fisher.

* * *

LEVEL 3 of the medical section sent a shudder through Hansen. He was crouched near the main doorway, staring past the half-open door, into an operating area that had been converted into a barracks. He counted about twenty beds . . . all occupied. They were all men, mostly nondescript, a few European looking and a few markedly Middle Eastern.

He returned to Fisher, his cheeks warm, heart pounding, and reported what he'd seen.

Fisher agreed that those were probably some of, if not all, the attendees, at least those who'd been able to work around the weather conditions. More could be coming. Many more.

But they all agreed that the big fish was most certainly not among them. Who was the man behind the auction? That was the burning question Hansen hoped they could answer before leaving the facility.

"We've got one more level to check," said Fisher. With any luck, he added, they'd be back in Severobaikalsk for breakfast.

Suddenly a familiar voice rose behind them. "Not gonna happen."

Hansen cursed, turned, and realized that the man in the shadows to their rear—the rat bastard known as Mr. Allen Ames—was privy to everything.

"He's got a grenade," Valentina muttered.

41

AMES stood about sixty feet behind Fisher and Hansen, and he knew they'd have no time to react before he tossed the grenade. It was glorious. Just glorious.

"Don't even think about it," he said in a slight rasp. "Don't even turn around. I go down, so does the grenade."

With that, Ames darted forward for the ramp railing, moving to within forty feet.

And then he emerged from the shadows and watched as the entire group turned to face him.

He'd told them not to move, but what did he

expect? Compliance from a group of misfits? "Not another step," he warned.

Ames hung his arm over the railing, prepared to drop the grenade down to level 4, where it would explode and set off alarms throughout the facility. He was sure they wanted to know what he was doing there, how he'd arrived, and what he wanted, but it was quite nice just letting them hang for a few moments—after what they'd done to him.

"What do you want?" asked Fisher.

Ames snorted, told Fisher that, yes, he was a survivor, and that was all he really wanted—just to say that. Fisher probed him about how he'd escaped, and Ames gave him the condensed version, said he'd flagged down the helicopter that had been pursuing them and had convinced the boss man that he was working for a mutual friend.

That left Hansen puzzled. If Ames had spilled his guts, why wasn't the facility on high alert?

Fisher must've been thinking the same thing and asked, "Do they know we're here?"

Ames shook his head. "I told him you were still in Irkutsk."

"Him?" Fisher asked. "Who?"

This was the part where Ames laughed. "You've met him. In fact, he told me you had him in your hands and let him go."

Fisher's expression soured, and his mouth moved, almost forming the name.

"Yep, that's him," Ames confirmed.

"Who?" asked Hansen.

"Zahm," Fisher replied.

Hansen frowned. "You're kidding me."

Fisher shook his head and sighed.

Ames's smile broadened. Good old Sam Fisher couldn't see the forest for the trees. The damned bad guy had been right in front him. The same guy who'd pulled off the weapons heist in the first place was the guy orchestrating the auction. No brainer, Sammy boy. It was the introduction of the banker that made the plot seem larger, when, in fact, it was all quite simple. And Zahm was just the kind of maniac to push things over the top. He never knew when to quit, and never, ever, had enough . . . of anything.

"Where is he now?" Fisher asked.

Ames grinned and shrugged. "Around."

Hansen glanced at him emphatically. "You can still do the right thing."

"I could," Ames agreed, "but I won't."

He'd already pulled the pin on the grenade and let it slip from his hands. In the same instant, he sprinted back up the ramp, even as he knew they were swinging around, bringing their rifles to bear on him.

* * *

THE explosion echoed up from the level below, and Hansen, along with the others, was on his belly as the corridor reverberated and a sulfurlike stench wafted their way.

"We gotta tag the last of the cases," cried Fisher, which meant they were going down, not up, to escape.

"Gonna be trapped," Hansen told him.

Fisher answered in a deadpan: "Bad luck for us." Then he turned to Noboru. "You have the ARWEN?"

"Yeah."

Fisher spoke in a rapid fire. He told Noboru that the initial counterattack would come from the medical zone, where Hansen had spotted the attendees. Zahm had most assuredly placed some of his guards near and around them. As soon as Noboru heard them moving, he was to put two gas canisters downrange. Valentina and Hansen would back him; then they would leap-frog down to level 4, split up, and make a last sweep of the zones for the rest of the arsenal.

With wide eyes, Fisher wished them all good luck, then took off with Gillespie. They would hold the ramp intersection, while Hansen, Noboru, and Valentina made their sweep.

Once they reached the medical zone, Noboru set up about fifty feet from the twin main doors leading to the makeshift barracks. He clutched the ARWEN tightly and gave Hansen a quick nod: good to go.

One door shifted open and Noboru fired, the gun echoing with a *fwump*. The gas canister arced through the gap in the door and clattered on the floor inside. Shouts in Russian and a few other languages announced the attack as the hissing canister spewed a thick funnel of smoke.

Hansen, who had tucked himself tightly against the wall, steadied his rifle, ready to unleash his first salvo, while Noboru stood ready once more with the ARWEN. He had a five-shot capacity in the weapon's rotary drum.

The doors slammed open, and through the smoke, a pair of gunmen appeared, AK-47s held high. With a grunt and thump, Noboru express-mailed another gas canister.

At the same time, Hansen and Valentina sent their first wave of automatic fire punching through the veils of smoke. The two guys dropped like drunken frat brothers. He and Valentina couldn't see much after that, but they didn't need to because Fisher's plan was already working. They kept firing, and farther back, Hansen stole a second's glimpse of two more men hitting the floor. Four down.

Valentina abruptly charged toward those doors and took cover on the left side. Hansen gave her a look that said, *What the hell are you doing?* She ignored him and drew a fragmentation grenade from her web gear, pulled the pin, then extended her arm and pitched it inside.

With bug eyes, she came racing toward them, screaming, "Time to rock and roll!"

Hansen exchanged a look of surprise with Noboru as they dropped in behind her. Call that the Valentina Day Massacre. A heartbeat later, one of the doors blew off its hinges behind them. But what was worse, somewhere down below echoed the sound of more gunfire. As he ran, Hansen spoke into his headset, telling Fisher they were on their way.

They were out of the corridor in thirty seconds and reached the main ramp to head down. Below they spotted Fisher, who nodded to Hansen, then jammed his rifle around the corner and fired two shots.

Hansen led them down to Fisher's position, and there Noboru dropped to a knee and aimed the ARWEN back up the ramp.

There was a sudden change of plans. Fisher now wanted Hansen and Valentina to clear medical. Noboru would hold the ramp. Fisher and Gillespie went charging off to ballistics, where Gillespie thought she'd heard Ames shouting at someone.

* * *

GILLESPIE was about a hundred yards down the corridor, running just ahead of Fisher, when she heard Ames's voice again: "Shouldn't have left it sitting here alone, Chucky."

And then came another voice, presumably Zahm's, given the British accent: "Aw, bloody hell, you little weasel! Come down here so I can put a bullet in your brain!"

"Can't do that, Chucky!"

"Don't call me Chucky!"

They reached sight of the main door into ballistics, level 4, then peeked around the corner. Similar to the zones above, the level was cavernous, like a stadium with a stone roof, and lined with engine test stands and ancient-looking tractors and treads for moving the heavy motors. Fisher raised his binoculars and saw that Zahm was at the far end of the zone with two men. They were near the mouth of the center blast funnel, near the last collection of Anvil cases. He told Gillespie to keep her eyes sharp for Ames. He was in there somewhere, and, she figured, had probably been double-crossed by Zahm, which was why he was still around and possibly about to exact his revenge on the self-appointed auctioneer as well as his best buddies in Third Echelon.

She and Fisher moved past the door and crept over

to the nearest workbench. She took point and immediately found a covering position, while he eased in beside her. She got her first look at Zahm, a tall and stocky character with a thick shock of wavy hair. He was probably about Fisher's age, though his hair was suspiciously devoid of gray. He wore a dark green turtleneck with suede patches on the shoulders.

Zahm lifted his voice. "Give it up, Ames! You won't get 'em open!"

"Don't want to!" Ames answered, his voice emanating from somewhere above.

"What's he doing?" she whispered to Fisher.

"Don't know."

The others checked in over the headset. Noboru had heard the remaining guys moving around, trying to call the elevator. Fisher told him to hold position and that they had Zahm and what was left of the arsenal. This wasn't exactly the original plan, but they'd take it. Hansen would clear weapons and electronics, ensuring no surprise attacks for their escape; then he would rally back at Noboru's position. Valentina would do likewise.

With that, Fisher gestured to Gillespie, and they hustled off, working their way between the shelves and equipment, the vehicles and engine parts, keeping low and tight to the corners, advancing fluidly like two lethal components controlled by a single brain.

The strangest sensation washed over Gillespie, and

she found it hard, for a moment, to concentrate. There was something incredibly sexy, even erotic, about darting through the shadows with him, the threat of being caught reinforced by every footfall. When they paused at the next bench, she just looked at him, in awe, and he looked at her: What? She just shuddered and mouthed, "I'm okay."

No, Sam, I could never have shot you. Who was I kidding?

They came within a hundred yards of Zahm and his two men. He gave her the hand signal to take the man on the left. She nodded. Set up. Took aim. The Groza felt perfect in her hands. Groza means "thunder." Oh, yeah, she was about to deliver her thunder. . . .

They would do it just like training. She waited for his shot. The instant she heard it, she squeezed the trigger. Her target could not react in time.

Both of Zahm's men dropped. One, two. Textbook head shots.

The man himself spun away, but Fisher was already running toward him. "Hi, Chuck."

Gillespie dropped in beside Fisher.

Zahm whirled to face them, a 9mm semiautomatic clutched in his right hand. He looked at Fisher, then at Gillespie, and she could almost hear the ticking of his thoughts: *If I shoot Fisher, then the woman kills me.*

You can bet on it, Gillespie thought.

Fisher ordered Zahm to lose the gun.

Zahm set down his weapon. "Fisher," he cried, as though to a long-lost friend.

Fisher shot Gillespie a look, then motioned her to the exhaust vents ahead to search for Ames. She rushed forward, past Zahm, and began her search, while behind her, the conversation continued:

"You just couldn't sit still, could you?" Fisher asked. "Couldn't have stayed in Portugal, enjoyed your villa and your mojitos and your boat."

"Boring. Too damned boring."

"Then you're going to hate prison."

"You can put me in, but you can't keep me there."

From somewhere in the space above, Ames yelled, "You're both wrong!"

"He's not in here," Fisher called to her. "The echo's wrong. He's above us—ballistics, second level. He's yelling down the exhaust shaft."

Gillespie glanced up into the exhaust shaft, but she couldn't see a thing. She switched on her flashlight, aimed it up, and still nothing but piping covered in a thick layer of carbon.

Fisher was suddenly on the radio to Hansen: "Move now, back to the ramp. All of you get topside as fast as you can."

"What's going on?" Gillespie asked.

"Do it. Blast your way through whoever's up there, but don't slow down."

"Roger."

Gillespie was about to question Fisher when Ames shouted again: "Okay, Chucky, here it comes. . . ."

Fisher screamed to her, "We're leaving. Move!"

She was still confused but wouldn't argue and began jogging back to him.

From the far end of the space came a crash. She turned back to see an Anvil case about the size of a footlocker bounce off the middle exhaust funnel and slam into the wall behind it.

Zahm craned his neck and stared at the case. "Son of a bitch! Ames!"

A second case dropped, this one so big that Ames must've used all his might to push it over the side. It was as large as a gun safe, Gillespie guessed. It struck the floor so hard that it broke open. Dozens of cylindrical objects spilled out and rolled across the concrete. And yet another case dropped. Then another, while Zahm continued shouting at the top of his lungs. He even screamed for Fisher to go up there and shoot the bastard.

Ames shouted, "Missed one. Here it comes!"

Gillespie stole a look over her shoulder at the exhaust vent, just as a white object about the size of a brick plummeted out of sight to the bottom of the tube.

"Aw, bloody hell," cried Zahm.

Gillespie shouted to Fisher, "What?"

He had two words for her. "Semtex! Run!"

42

GILLESPIE'S legs were burning as she and Fisher retreated at full tilt toward the door at the far end of the zone. They were, Gillespie estimated, about sixty or seventy feet from the exit when the Semtex detonated.

A slightly muffled boom came first, followed by a single echo; then through that hollow ringing came several more explosions, grenades perhaps, and, finally, a deafening explosion that stole the air from her lungs and threatened to burst her eardrums.

Not two seconds later, the shock wave swept her into the air and sent her hurtling, end over end, like a

Barbie doll flung by an angry four-year-old. The floor and ceiling spun, and there was utter disorientation until she thought she whacked against the door and suddenly dropped, as though someone had thrown the GRAVITY ON switch. She hit the floor, facedown. Felt her shoulder pop. Her arms and legs continued to burn.

She tried to look up, but a wave of nausea took hold, the room still spinning. Was that Fisher calling her name? Her shoulder throbbed now. She thought she could move her legs despite the fire.

What was that sound? Like Niagara Falls . . .

Finally, she glanced at the far end of the zone. The entire back wall was gone, and the concrete blast funnels now lay in mountains of rubble. In their place was a massive hole like the business end of a huge, fully opened fire hose. Car-sized pieces of rock were already being swept aside by the jetting water and unstoppable current.

Fisher crawled toward her, and, remarkably, her headset was still clipped tightly to her head. "What the hell was that?" called Hansen.

"Level four is blasted open," Fisher answered. "The lake's coming in." He looked at her. "Can you walk?"

"The hell with that," she said, glancing back at the oncoming water. "I can run!"

She rolled over, pulled herself painfully to her feet, felt some sharp pains in the shoulder, but otherwise she could indeed run. They sprinted together toward the ramp, around the railing, and started up the incline. She paused a second as the world seemed to tilt slightly on its axis. *Whoa!*

The first wave of water surged through the inter-section, sweeping so quickly down the corridor that she thought it'd be only a minute before the entire level was flooded. The hissing and crashing of water against doors and blasting into the various zones was entirely surreal. She got the chilling feeling they were aboard a sinking ship, and the ice-cold water did noth-ing to dispel that sensation.

A second wave crashed into their legs, shoving them back and into the side railing.

She looked over at Fisher.

He was gone.

"Sam!"

She looked back the ramp, now fully engulfed, the water like boiling oil in the flickering light.

And then a head appeared. Fisher was there, but his face was covered in blood. He must've bashed his nose, blood was streaming from his nostrils. She started back toward him, clutching the railing, but the current was beginning to carry him back and away. She reached out just as Valentina came up behind her, grabbed her arm.

"No, I'm okay," Fisher cried. "Keep going!" Then his gaze turned to Valentina. "Take her!"

Gillespie tried to pull away, but Valentina was far stronger and dragged her back up the ramp.

Meanwhile, Noboru, who'd come down right after Valentina, positioned himself over the railing and was leaning over, trying to reach Fisher, while Hansen darted behind and grabbed onto his legs. Fisher shouted something about them taking off, but they kept trying to reach him. Finally, Noboru caught a hand, and they brought Fisher back onto the ramp.

"He's okay," said Valentina. "We're going now!"

Gillespie nodded.

HANSEN didn't believe Fisher when he said he was okay, but there wasn't time to discuss it. He and Noboru hurried back up the ramp. When he looked back, Fisher was limping, barely able to keep up.

"Your foot," cried Hansen.

"Fell asleep."

The water suddenly lapped over Fisher's ankles. Hansen started back to him. "I can help you, Sam."

"Get everybody topside. I'm right behind you."

This was an argument Hansen would not win. He nodded and double-timed back up the ramp.

At the top, with the water rising rapidly, he turned back for Fisher, who was gone. Hansen cursed and tried to call him on the radio. Nothing.

*Stubborn bastard. What're you up to now? You die,
and you'll really piss me off. . . .*

AFTER checking on the elevator, Hansen and Noboru
linked up with Valentina and Gillespie on the first level.
The entire facility seemed to tremble under the weight
of the flooding lake. Pipes screeched as they were bent
like taffy in all directions, and most of the lower ramp
had been swept away to crash into the walls.

They came rushing into the utility room, where
their rope still hung down through the air shaft. Hansen could already hear the water rushing up toward
them. He tried to call Fisher again. Nothing. Noboru
went up the rope first, followed by Valentina. Together
they would help pull Gillespie up. Hansen remained
there, pacing like a fool, calling Fisher over and over
until finally . . .

"Ben, where are you?"

"First level. Bad guys are either gone or dead. Elevator's out of commission. We're getting out the way
we came in."

"Good." Fisher said something else, but the transmission was garbled. Hansen waited, then:

"Leave the rope for me."

"Roger."

From the sound of it, Fisher had no intention of
coming up to meet them, and the 'leave the rope' line

was just BS. He either had his own plan of escape or had already realized that it was too late for him.

Hansen glanced up the shaft, saw that Gillespie was almost at the top. In a minute they'd drop the rope to him. He took a deep breath and heard the footfalls a moment before the man appeared, brandishing his AK-47.

He was one of Zahm's guards, a heavily tattooed Brit clever enough to escape, and he trained his rifle on Hansen even as Hansen did likewise. *Standoff*.

"We can both get out, mate," he said, his face covered in stubble, his teeth yellow. "No need for a shooting contest."

"Here comes the rope!" cried Noboru.

"Hold up!" shouted Hansen.

"What're you doing?" asked the guard, his glance flicking up toward the shaft.

There were moments, Hansen knew, where muscle memory and reflex took over, where all the calculations in the world wouldn't help you. You just reacted, barely conscious of the effort, based on the instinct to survive.

Hansen shot the guard.

Three rounds punched into his chest. Just like that. No forethought. No afterthought. Just noise. And death.

The guy fell back before he could get off a shot, and as he hit the floor, a wall of water came blasting through the corridor, sweeping him away and sending Hansen crashing into the wall behind him.

"Throw down the rope!" he screamed. "Throw down the—"

Another wave took him under, and the water was so cold that for a moment he swore his heart skipped a beat. Frantically he kicked up, tried to find the surface, but his head banged hard into something metal, and there was only white foam before his eyes, nothing to focus on. He reached out, trying to find the rope, groping frantically like a man with an anchor tied to his waist.

He was beginning to lose his breath.

And a bitter resignation took hold. After everything, he would now drown in an air shaft because some asshole guard had decided not to play nice and die when he should have. Where were Dad's aliens now? Hansen could sure use an alien abduction at the moment. *Beam me up, Scotty.*

He reached out one last time, and something brushed against his outer forearm. The rope. He rolled, kicked hard, and took hold, now advancing hand over hand, pulling himself against the current until his hand felt dry, and then, in the next instant his head popped above the bubbling water.

The gush of water resounded. He was in the air shaft, being carried up. He sucked in a huge breath as, above, Valentina and Noboru screamed, asking if he was all right.

Sure, he was fine. Couldn't be better. And how are you?

He took one more breath and cried, "Pull me up!" And the water once more rose over his head before he could climb any higher. The rope began moving through his hands. He tightened his grip as they hoisted him up.

NOT two minutes after Hansen cleared the air shaft, he watched as Gillespie rushed back to it. "He's not coming, is he?" she said, watching as the water streamed out of the air vent.

"Tell you what. You stay here and wait," said Hansen, still shivering and blinking hard. He looked at Noboru and Valentina. "Perimeter search. Maybe he found another way out."

Valentina looked grim, Noboru grimmer.

"Let's get this done quickly. This entire area is growing unstable."

Hansen thought about his rise up the air shaft and decided to hit the meadow hut first. And when he did, he almost laughed. There was Fisher, lying on his side, soaked to the bone, having dug his way out of the hut by exploiting the weakened grout between the cinder blocks.

"You should've come with us," Hansen said, dumbfounded and grinning.

Fisher rubbed his sore eyes and shuddered. "Didn't want to slow you down."

Hansen looked at the hut, the water still pouring from the hole in the cinder blocks. "Nice exit."

"I'm usually a little more discreet."

Hansen grinned. "Gotta move now. Sinkholes opening up all over the place. . . ."

THIRD ECHELON SITUATION ROOM

KOVAC burst through the door and marched up to Grim, who was seated behind one of the computer terminals. She didn't look back at him. Not yet. He panted in anger.

"What the hell's going on here?"

Slowly, she turned around, then glanced past him to Moreau, who was standing in the shadows with a security team.

"It's the end of the world," she said. "Your world."

He snorted. "You're done, Grim. Done. Do you hear me?"

"I don't think so."

"Mr. Kovac," called Moreau. "If you'll come with us . . ."

"What's this?"

Grim narrowed her gaze on him. "This is you going bye-bye. Say bye-bye. . . ."

He began to hyperventilate. "You have no idea what you're doing."

"I'm curious. Why'd you do it? Not just for the money . . ."

"I don't owe you anything but a pink slip."

She dismissed him with a wave. "Marty, get this scumbag out of my sight."

"Yes, ma'am."

Kovac cursed at Moreau, who looked at Grim. She nodded.

And Moreau took Kovac by the back of the neck and led him out of the room, saying, "Mr. Kovac, are you familiar with our Lord and Savior Jesus Christ? Are you familiar with the stories of torture in the Bible? Are you familiar with the barbaric means men once used to extract information from each other?"

"You can't torture me! That's illegal!"

Moreau cackled like a hyena. The door closed after them. Grim took a deep breath. It was over. Or just beginning.

PORTINHO DA ARRÁBIDA, PORTUGAL

FISHER looked much better than the last time Hansen had seen him, three months before. He was refreshed, well groomed, and deeply tanned. The veteran Splinter Cell had stayed in Washington only long enough to have surgery on his ankle and attend three days of intense debriefing. Then he'd vanished off the face of the earth. Or at least that was how Hansen's dad would have put it. Apparently, Fisher had gotten a one-year lease on Zahm's old place and was taking time off to relax and enjoy the villa, the mojitos, life. . . . Would his name ever be cleared? No one knew. Not yet, anyway . . .

Fisher, Grim, and Hansen were now sitting under an umbrella overlooking the pristine waters, and Hansen was sipping his own mojito. Fisher asked about Kovac.

Grim explained that two hours after his arrest for treason, he'd tried to hang himself in his cell. A guard saved him. Too bad. Ames's insurance cache had provided ample evidence to incriminate the deputy director. Unofficially, he was being kept in an FBI safe house, answering questions and naming names. No one was torturing him, of course—wink, wink.

Hansen told Fisher that Lambert had been right about the size of this doppelgänger-factory operation. At least the Laboratory 738 Arsenal had been taken out of circulation. It turned out that Zahm had leased the Russian test facility from Mikhail Bratus, the GRU agent Hansen had been tracking in Korfovka. Only six of the auction guests had made it out alive, and they were arrested. Ernsdorff, the money man, was found in a hotel room, gutted like a fish.

"What about our old friend Ames?" Fisher asked.

BURNING MAN EVENT
BLACK ROCK DESERT, NEVADA

MERE words are not capable of describing exactly what the Burning Man event is or even why it takes place. To state that it is an annual event at which more than fifty thousand artists gather and celebrate the creative process is to lose sight of the intricacies, complexities, and possibilities associated with the gathering. Allen Ames was there for a very different reason, though. He wanted to see the wooden effigy burn, and the compulsion was so strong that he didn't care how many days he had to wait or how many hippies would not sleep with him, despite employing some of the best pickup lines he knew. He would remain until the giant man lit up the barren desert with flames shooting from his appendages. In fact, Ames had already been lying awake in his sleeping bag, imagining that moment and rolling his Zippo between his fingers—the new Zippo he had purchased because that bastard Hansen had never returned his.

On the third day of the event the Russians finally arrived, and Ames told them what he knew and what he could offer them. They said they'd have to talk to their friends in China but that the offer sounded profitable for all parties concerned. Then they asked why they'd had to meet him in such a strange place. Ames dismissed them without explanation.

And then, finally, it came. Saturday night. The flames swept up the man's body, and Ames shuddered and thrust his arms into the sky, dancing with the others, chanting like a madman, howling at the moon, and swigging whiskey straight from the bottle. It was all here: earth, air, *fire*, and water.

— EPILOGUE —

THE sixty-five-hundred-square-foot home had been built two years before, in a cul-de-sac overlooking the C-15 canal. The house boasted a clay-colored tile roof, four-car garage, private tennis court, and Olympic-sized swimming pool entirely screened in along the back of the place. The landscape surrounding said pool must have cost a fortune, and Moreau knew as much because he had installed similar plants at his own Florida estate up in Bay Hill.

Moreau had been watching the place for two days now. He sat in his rental car, parked across the street, sipping a mocha latte. He consulted his watch.

In the driveway sat the man's pride and joy: a white 1971 Corvette Stingray, fully stock with no aftermarket modifications to any part of the engine, interior, or exterior. The car had won multiple awards at car shows and was, Moreau had learned, rare because it had not been modified and had some kind of gold certification from Bloomingdale's or something.

Too bad.

"Finally," Moreau muttered, watching as the old white-haired man emerged from his front door.

The old man paused, yawned, looked toward the newspaper at the end of the driveway, then started toward it and the Corvette.

Moreau sighed and pressed the remote.

After a one-second pause, the Corvette heaved from the ground and exploded in a fireball that knocked the old man onto the ground. Even before the shattered hood and rest of the debris reached the lawn, Moreau was screeching his tires and racing up the driveway. He leapt out of his car, charged up to the old man, and grabbed him by the shirt collar. "Stingray! You son of a bitch! You sent a man to kill me. You think I forgot about that? My God is a God of justice! And you will know his wrath! You will feel his fire!"

"My goddamned car," cried Stingray. "Why'd you have to blow my goddamned car?"

"Because you love that car more than life itself. Hallelujah!"

"You've been waiting a long time to get me."

"Building my case. You're good at cleaning up after yourself."

"Look, Moreau, I'm too old for this. Just do me. Right here, right now. Let your God have his way. I can't do time. I'm too old."

Moreau released the old man, reached up to his shoulder holster, and drew his pistol with attached suppressor.

"Take me out like a man," added Stingray.

A gunshot ripped into the brick driveway not a foot from Moreau's boot. He shot a look across the street, where a figure rose from behind a palm tree on the opposite house's lawn.

He did a double take. It was Hansen, dressed in a tac-suit. He cupped a hand around his mouth and yelled, "Can't let you do that, Marty!"

"What the . . ."

And then Hansen came jogging across the street, still gripping his sniper's rifle. "Lower the weapon," he said.

"Cowboy! Go home!"

"Grim sent me."

"She what?"

"Let's go." Hansen pointed his rifle at Moreau's chest.

From the corner of his eye, Moreau saw Stingray's arm reach to his back.

Moreau whirled, but not in time.

Stingray came around with a pistol and fired at Hansen, who staggered back, one hand clutching his abdomen as he fired an errant round into the garage door behind them.

Moreau fired at Stingray, hitting him directly in the chest, but at the same time the old man got off a round that caught Moreau in the shoulder, near his collarbone, wrenching him sideways.

Screaming through a curse, Moreau fired three more rounds into Stingray's chest, and the man fell back across the pavers, blood pooling immediately around his back.

Moreau stumbled, lost his balance, and fell onto his rump as the flames from the still-burning Corvette began bending his way. He coughed and waved acrid smoke from his eyes.

Hansen was lying flat on his back, and Moreau crawled over. "Cowboy? You stupid bastard. Cowboy?"

He reached Hansen and unzipped the tac-suit, revealing a Kevlar vest.

Moreau swore and said, "Wake up, pretty boy."

Hansen slowly opened his eyes. "Why'd you let him shoot me?"

"I didn't, you dumb ass."

Moreau winced and helped Hansen sit up. "You shouldn't have come."

Hansen grimaced, looked down at the slug

embedded in his vest. "Just following orders. She wanted me to stop you before you killed him."

"So she sent you, and you forced me to kill him. How do you like them apples?"

Some of the neighbors from the surrounding homes were approaching, gasping, covering their mouths, and Moreau turned to them and said, "Take it easy, ladies and gentlemen. We're just filming a movie here. Hidden cameras! It's all make-believe! Sorry for the noise! So sorry for the noise!"

"That looks like real blood," said one obese woman, covering her mouth as she stared at Stingray.

"Yeah, they do a pretty good job with special effects these days. Now, please, off the set. Off the set! We need to do this all over again."

"They don't believe you," muttered Hansen.

"I can see that."

"Then why don't we get in your car and get the hell out of here?"

"Yeah. I think I need a hospital."

"What about him?" Hansen asked, lifting his chin at Stingray.

"He doesn't need a hospital."

Hansen made a face. "The body?"

"Forget him. I got ballistics covered. And so do you. Get in the car."

Moreau smiled at the throng of onlookers, then rose with Hansen.

"This ain't no movie," said a portly black man wearing a polo shirt two sizes too small. "You guys just killed our neighbor, and you're not going anywhere."

"You're probably glad he's dead, aren't you?" said Moreau in a steely voice. "You wrote that letter complaining to the HOA about him. That gives you motive."

"I didn't write any letter."

"Oh, no? Better call the HOA. . . ."

The guy recoiled and stepped out of the way. Moreau and Hansen got in the car and hauled ass out of the neighborhood, leaving the smoldering Corvette, the shocked neighbors, and the dead spy/car enthusiast behind.

Hansen frowned at Moreau. "I just want to say, that was a brilliant piece of fieldwork. No witnesses, no footprints, just beautiful."

Moreau sighed. "Cowboy, I'm not proud of what I did back there. But let me ask you something. . . . Did you know Ames was tailing you back in Korfovka? Setting you up to die? If you had a chance to take him out, would you?"

"Hell, yeah."

Moreau cocked a brow. "All right, then. You and I have a lot to talk about."

"Don't you mean you, me, and Grim?"

Moreau drew in a deep breath. "No, Son, I don't."